THE JOURNEY

THE *Carrero*
HEART

The Carrero
Series

L.T.Marshall

The Carrero Series

Jake & Emma
The Carrero Effect ~ The Promotion
The Carrero Influence ~ Redefining Rules
The Carrero Solution ~ Starting Over

Arrick & Sophie
The Carrero Heart ~ Beginning
The Carrero Heart ~ The Journey
The Carrero Heart ~ Happy Ever Afters

Bonus Books
Jake's View
Arrick's View

Other books by L.T. Marshall

Just Rose

For Team Carrero.
You kept me going when I wanted to give up. xx

Chapter 1

"Here." I pass Jenny the sketches we have been working on across the table, and the pretty brunette leans in to pour over them with curious soft brown eyes. Tall and slender and a little shy in her mannerisms, Jenny is my classmate and fast becoming one of my closest friends. Next to Christian, both of whom I met on day one of orientation. Something just clicked with the three of us straight off. I have something real with these two, and despite myself, they have both wormed their way under my self-defense system over the last few weeks until I needed them around me to function.

Christian is standing five feet away and draping some wild bohemian fabric on a tailor's dummy to no avail. All tall and immaculately groomed in his "preppy boy" outfit today. Blonde floppy hair and gray-eyed, a grin aimed at his two best girls. We are tucked in the corner of the busy sewing room while the hustle and bustle of the other students around us float this way and the commanding voice of today's lecturer. They have split everyone into groups of three this week to work on designs. Our first assessment of simple tailoring skills is fast approaching.

"I think if we go with this one, it's pretty much a circle skirt and easy bodice, simple enough for us to draft ourselves, and we could make it edgier if we are clever with it." Jenny slides back one of the drawings, tapping a pink floral idea I have been mulling over, based loosely on a trending dress I have seen everywhere for a new season release.

We've been in class for a few weeks, and it's been almost three months since I walked out on Arrick and booked myself into a hotel. Two weeks later, Jake found me a cute two-bed apartment within walking distance, and school started days later. Everything was swift in his capable hands, as I assumed it would be. I've concentrated on my studies, getting my apartment how I like it, and going home every four weeks to see my family. It's been hard, far worse than even I could envision a life without him, but I'm doing it; day by day, I'm still breathing, fighting, and not falling to a watery end like I thought I would.

I can live an Arry-free life.

For the most part, I can push down the empty ache that I know is him, focus on work and blank the need to bring his name up in my cell every day. I deleted all our pictures on my phone, so I don't have the memories of his smile, those hazel eyes, or that gorgeous face. He made me hate him for a moment ... then I shut down the parts of my soul that he's entwined with and blocked him out. It's better this way.

Arrick has been a missing chasm in my life, but it seems both of us concluded that we shouldn't contact one another. A real wall of silence at last, and even Jake avoids mentioning him when I see him at our fortnightly lunch date. He knows how I feel, how much I don't want to know how he's getting on and how angry I still am that he could throw me away like I never meant a thing to him. I never really knew him if this was how he could treat me after everything I was supposed to mean to him. He told me I was a part of him, yet he let me go as if I meant nothing.

It hurts a lot more than I thought it would, considering he told me that life sucked without me, and yet here we are, three months of no Arry ... no calls, no texts, and no chance encounters, despite living close to one another. I guess I haven't tried to reach out to him either, but then why would I? He made it clear that night that she was his future. There was no way around that I couldn't be, and I'm learning how to live with a broken heart that will eventually disappear.

He seems to plan his trips home when he knows I won't be in the Hamptons, so I guess he relies on Jake for that, seeing as I fly home with him once a month. To date, I haven't run into him in passing in the city either. Not that it's a surprise. I've kept my head down and left the party animal in me behind, and apart from the occasional party, Arrick never used to travel in the same circles as me. His fight career and Carrero Corp means he will never randomly roam the city or any women's fashion stores. I'm just focusing on the future I want for myself and finally feel more in control of some aspects of my life.

I'm doing it ... growing up all by myself.

I go home at the end of the day and spend time with my new-found two best friends, watching movies or working in my custom-made sewing room, where I find so much joy nowadays. Eating, breathing, and living the life of a fashion student and compiling an impressive array of mock-up designs hanging on clothes rails, despite the early days of my student life.

I'm excelling and seem to have a natural talent for this. The opportunities to attend catwalk shows, new releases, and sneak peek of next season's designs completely overtake my life. Enough to cope with the constant black hole of ache that happens when Arrick is a missing part. I won't let this affect me.

"Lemme see," Christian moves over the table to nosey at our group project. We've been challenged to come up with a summer item of clothing to fit the current trend of loose, floaty, feminine, and floral. With me being the one who loves to sketch designs all day long, I'm the appointed designer on this one.

Christian leans in close, smelling a little too sandalwood good, as he always does, and surrounds us in a fog of scent. I squint at his comical expression as he regards the papers.

"Lift the hem by a few inches, and we have a winner." He smirks cheekily; despite his aversion to sex with the fairer species, he has a thing for female legs on show. I'm borderline sure it's a fetish and does not fit at all with his love for men's abs and what's between their thighs.

3

"We're going with classy and fifties-inspired." Jenny nudges him in the ribs as he leans over her, making it awkward for her to sit straight. Jenny is the quiet one of our trio, shy and softly spoken, while Christian is the flamboyant drama queen. The one who eye rolls and huffs, much like he does now.

"Whatev's. Far too conservative if you ask me!" He goes back to trying to wrap his fabric around the dummy, and we leave him to sulk, giggling at his grumpy stamping and glares cast our way. He likes to think he knows best, but his strengths are edgy, bold design, nitty-gritty, and daring. Jenny is classier and more stylish, while I seem to have a bit of a mix and a keen eye for trends.

"You guys still coming for lunch today, my treat?" I glance at Jenny across the table, reminding them of the celebratory plan. I finally finished my apartment and felt like it was worth celebrating over. My first steps toward real adulthood. No more boxes or half-furnished rooms and mess, no more bare walls and feeling like it's a temporary home. It's finished, decorated, and adorned with all my little touches. And it only took me two and a half months of abusing my two besties to help me get it that way.

We have come so far in such a brief time. My parents visited a week ago and made me feel like I've finally found my place in life. Now I've regained their trust, love, and things are looking up. Leila hates that I have moved here permanently, but she is warming to it, and my frequent trips home mean she can forgive me for it. She refuses to come to the city to see me though. Apparently, leaving this life behind to marry Daniel means she has an aversion to ever leaving home.

"Oh, shit, Sophs, is that today? I can't, it's Mark's birthday, and I promised him I would meet him at lunch." Jenny's big eyes and wobbling lip dismiss any urge to be mad at her. Her boyfriend works crazy shifts, and she barely sees him. I know they have been having a rough time together lately. Well, truth be told, she never seems happy when it comes to him. I can't be mad for her wanting to see him on his birthday, over my nothing lunch.

"It's okay, as long as Chris doesn't bail too." I lift my brow at him as he wiggles his very muscular pert butt our way, laughing at his weirdness.

"I wouldn't bail on my queen." Christian blows me a kiss, and I can't help but think, not for the first time, how unfair it is that a guy as perfectly formed and handsome as him is gay. When he isn't being overly camp and emphasizing it, then he pulls off a straight guy all day long, and he is always immaculately dressed. I sigh at the unfairness of life, having found a man I get on with almost as much as "him, whom I will no longer name," only it's typical that he is out of bounds.

"Well, I fancy somewhere more upmarket; on me." I smile his way, and he shrugs in return. I want to throw on the dress I brought with me, flick out my hair now that I'm back to rocking blonde, and have a sophisticated lunch with my new favorite beau. So not in the mood for fast food or our usual deli today.

Second favorite beau, even if the first one no longer deserves the title.

"I think I know the perfect place. It only opened a month ago, and no reservation is required." Christian beams at me with that dazzling, all too white, cosmetically enhanced grin, looking a little Calvin Klein model with the way he's leaning in.

"Sure. I trust you as long as it's not sushi! I do not like raw fish." I frown and mock throw up with fingers down my throat in his general direction. Jenny giggles at me with an adoring expression that makes her seem cutely juvenile.

"Ewww, no ... I prefer meat to fish! I can swallow that all day long, bitches." Christian sasses with a dirty wink, and Jenny and I eye roll and grimace at his filthy joke. Sometimes Christian is shameless and likes to shock.

My kind of friend.

* * *

I'm trawling my phone messages after we finish eating, my sister reminding me of her anniversary party this coming month. Leila has been married only three years, but this is an annual event that no one misses if they want to remain physically unharmed. Sort of the highlight of everyone's year and a chance to glam up and get the party groove on. I reply, informing her I'll be coming with two guests, Jenny and Christian, as they have promised to be my strength at a party I know *he* will be at. Even the Carreros never miss Leila's parties, what with the two families being almost family in themselves, and the last thing I need is to rock up alone and come face to face with the dream couple acting like they never knew me at all.

Yeah, that won't be awkward at all. Or painful in the slightest!

"You done, kitten?" Christian's smiling my way, throwing down his napkin after settling the bill, despite all my pre-warning that this was on me. He's a sneaky boy, always diving in with that damn chivalry that I used to love so much about someone else. It irks me right now.

"Hey, I said I was paying!" I protest as I spy the receipt on the plate, but he only grins back devilishly. Christian's family is much like mine in that I never want for anything. Well off and generous to a fault; we both come from wealthy homes and have more than comfortable allowances to live on.

"I pay for my girls." He smiles again, but I only eye roll, as Christian constantly implies that Jenny and I are his "women." However, we all know he has been secretly dating a senior fashion student a couple of years above us, who has not yet come out of the closet. James is his blue-eyed boy with a severe fear of being "outed."

Christian holds his hand out to me as he slides from the table, impeccably dressed in jeans and a button-down that only emphasizes his toned body. He's not overly tall for a guy, around five feet ten, but he's perfectly proportioned and muscular. I take it graciously and let him pull me to his side, keeping our fingers entwined. Christian is a very affectionate soul. He loves nothing more than manhandling Jenny and me constantly and likes to walk everywhere arm in arm, or hand in hand, usually with one of us on each side. He reminds me of Arrick that way, and I'm forever trying to stop making that connection.

"Is my princess ready to go?" He glances down at my chair, checking I have everything as I nod with a huge smile. Christian always makes me feel like smiling. He's one of those friends who put sunshine in your day just by being there. Always a gentleman and a lot of lovely. When he's not being an overly dramatic nightmare of a queen, of course.

"I am." I giggle at him as he tugs me against him to settle my arm in his like an old biddy and links fingers loosely, ready to walk out of the restaurant. He moves the chair aside and guides me towards the door, away from our table and onto the wide walkway that clears up the center.

"Sophie?" A male voice halts me from behind, my body bristling at the familiarity of it. The undeniable tone and hoarse sexiness send my stomach into an instant nosedive, and my nerves immediately tingle. I can barely conceal my reaction, tensing on Christian's arm as I wince in something similar to pain. I turn towards the source impulsively, my heart thudding heavily, even though every part of me tells me to walk away.

My heart is pounding like it's gone into shock as I turn slowly, tense and scared at what I know will hurt worse to see. Months of nothing at all, and the one day he's been plaguing my head mercilessly, more than any other day, he physically appears.

Arrick Carrero is standing straight as a rod a few feet away, obviously just arriving with two men behind him, all casually dressed, and I recognize one of them as someone he regularly hangs out with. The familiar face casts a friendly smile, a nod of recognition that I return with a half-smile before bringing my focus back to Arry. I don't know how to react, so I grip Christian's fingers harder, begging him to help me. He squeezes them back silently. His little show of support.

"Hi." I breathe weakly, unable to hold the gaze of those perfect hazel eyes in that flawless, clean-shaven face. Not a thing about his appearance has changed, and he's still as devastating to my soul. He looks like the guy I miss in every little tiny way, and it only hurts me irreversibly that he seems so normal and unaffected by finally seeing me again. There is definite weirdness and uncertainty in how I should act, and I feel like I don't know him anymore. My heart is playing the rhumba, and my legs go weak as blood courses to my heart in a stupendous fashion. Physically I'm dying. Outwardly I am still and cool like he always was.

Christian lets go of my arm, unhooks his fingers, and slings a supportive arm around my shoulders. He knows who Arrick Carrero is; any hot-blooded admirer of gorgeous men in New York knows who he is, and he knows the backstory between Arrick and me only too well. A night of wine and movies ended up with my sobbing my heart out and confessing the whole sorry story to the two of them at stupid o'clock one Saturday night. They know every detail and decided he should earn the crown of "idiot of the century" for letting me go.

Arrick narrows his eyes a fraction, a slight tension to his jaw as he tries not to run his eyes over the way Christian is draped around me. I see the subtle tells. Not sure how to take it at all. Not sure I should even care if he doesn't like it. I owe him nothing anymore.

He hurt you, remember. Discarded you like you meant nothing.

"How have you been?" He clears his throat as his two companions wander off further in the direction of their table, leaving him alone with us. It's wholly awkward, and I resist the urge to fidget, aware of how my heart and soul quiver at his mere presence and alert me to the fact that three months have not changed a lot between us. I still fall to pieces at the sight of him, my heart aching, and the sudden sadness of realizing I still love him hits me in the gut. No matter how often I've told myself I'd never need him again, never want to... Here we are.

He looks like him. Flawlessly pulled together, emotionally cool, and stunning as he always was. Hair spiked on top, lighter in color, freshly cut, clean-shaven, while those brown eyes are a lot greener today. Then I guess seeing me would stress him out, especially if he swore to Natasha that he would never have anything to do with me again. He doesn't go back on his word, ever.

Well, unless it comes to me. I guess promises made to me don't mean anything when it comes to her.

"I'm good, just getting on, and you know? ... I have school." I answer unsurely, lost for words, my voice noticeably young. Christian seems to sense my unease and leans past, extending a hand. I almost forgot he was draped around me, only seeing Arrick in this place, as though everyone and everything else faded into non-existence.

"Hi, I'm Christian, Sophie's told me about you being childhood besties, and I have to say I'm an admirer of your fighting skills, Arrick. I see you had another knockout victory two weeks back against Tiger Marse." Christian lays on the straight guy act super thickly, and I cringe inwardly. I hate when he plays the macho guy, it doesn't suit him.

Arrick regards his outstretched hand a moment, and I think he might ignore it. He seems strangely torn before shaking it firmly, and a little too firmly, judging by Christian's tensing body. I note that both have gone into guy mode, voices a tad huskier and mannerisms a little more rugged, like an alpha male tug of war or some nonsense. I don't get it, but Christian seems to be in the zone with his pretend play and pulls his hand back to his side.

"Thanks. Nice to meet you, Christian." Arrick goes to say more, but one of his friends calls on him, making him look back with a frown. He turns around with an unreadable expression, and there's another awkward pause between us as his eyes take me in quickly. His gaze travels over me as though his hands skimmed me instead, and every part of me warms crazily. Standing in my floral dress and dainty flats, completely vulnerable to him. I know I must look different from the last time he saw me. I've found a new girly style again, with floaty short dresses and sweet shrugs that are not so severe as the glamour chic that Camilla inspired. My hair is longer and softer in its grown out, stripped back to blonde, light bob style, and my makeup is natural.

"You look good, Sophs. You always were more beautiful as a blonde. I like this on you, the sweet girl look ... It's more you." His eyes come to rest on my hair, a steady look that translates so much, yet so little, and it only deepens the heavy feeling in my heart to an almost unbearable level.

"Thanks. You too. I mean ... you look good." I blush shyly, looking down at my hands as the emotion in my throat builds up to choke me. The man nearby, the unfamiliar one, calls on Arrick again, and this time Arry signals at him to wait another two minutes with a hand gesture. He turns back to me, all but ignoring Christian's presence. Christian is being strangely silent for a guy who normally never shuts up.

"I need to go, Sophs; are you going to Leila's party?" Arrick seems rooted to the spot as if he has no intention of moving, but Christian is quick off the mark, sensing my growing inability to function the longer we stand here. I'm getting quieter and more nervous, unsure how to talk to him as my throat closes on me. My body is starting to tremble subtly, and I'm pretty sure I'm losing the use of my legs. This extreme physical reaction only happens with him, and I hate that he still has this effect on me.

"We sure will be, won't we, sweetheart? Can't wait to meet Daniel and, of course, Leila. Her parents have told me she's the family fireball." Christian squeezes my shoulders, and I throw him a mild frown. I know what he's doing, and I'm not sure I like it. Arrick looks away, again his cool unreadable facade back in place, that tiny muscle in his jaw making the slightest of movements. A little Arrick tell that he's not as unaffected as he likes to pretend. The master of indifference is back and even feeling this estranged from him. I can still sense some of his moods.

"Guess I'll see you both there then." Arrick smiles my way tightly, eyes locking briefly, and it's like a thunderbolt to my heart. That devastating half-smile that can crush souls with a tiny flash, dimples hinting, but it doesn't reach his eyes. He looks somehow deflated. I wonder if life with Natasha is back to what it once was, seeing as this is how he always used to seem with her. I guess the lack of my problematic self means he has everything back under control and boringly normal.

Just how he wanted it, right?

"Guess you will." I smile quickly. My face tenses because it's completely unnatural, and I look down, away from that gaze with a heavy sigh. It's beyond me how one person can affect every tiny part of you with the smallest of efforts.

"I better go before they kick off and eat the tablecloths." He motions casually toward his two friends at a nearby table, and I nod, my stomach twisting in two. Hating that he still makes me feel this way and wishing I hadn't seen him again, but at the same time, wishing I was alone, wishing he hadn't thought Christian was my boyfriend and he would have given me an old Arrick hug, like the old days to wipe the slate clean. I can't deny that seeing him has only emphasized how much I miss him and how much I would have him back, even as friends, because this distance is worse than hell. Seeing him only reminds me of how much I still need him, and it hurts more than any pain I ever knew I could feel. I'm torn, knowing we should leave, but my feet don't want to move. It's like my brain desperately wants to cling to him in any way it can, even if he did rip my heart out.

God, I am so pathetic.

"I suppose, bye, then," I answer softly, close to tears. I let Christian tug me away, obviously realizing that I can't do it myself, throwing a casual wave and smile and acting as he owns me as Arrick watches me go. Throwing me one last look as our eyes connect, and for a mere second, I swear I catch a hint of raw unguarded regret and a subtle sigh. Arrick looks hurt, maybe. His eyes lose focus on me, his brows dip for a moment as he frowns and seems to lose that façade momentarily, a slight sag in his posture, but then it's gone, and I'm being ushered out of the restaurant by Christian, and into the afternoon sun and fresh zingy air.

"He's far sexier in person. Damn, I would tap that ass if he played for my field." Christian cuts into my thoughts of imprinting Arrick's voice and face to memory, whether I want to or not, placing a hand over his heart dramatically.

"You better cut that out if you're still trying to convince him I'm your bitch, Chris. You're looking decidedly camp right now." I throw him an eyebrow lift, and he smiles cheekily. I don't know whether I'm scolding him or light-heartedly telling him off. I'm so confused about how I should feel over Arry thinking Christian is my beau. I'm still reeling from the shock of seeing him and not sure how I should feel in general. I need to get away from the restaurant so that I can think.

"You mad at me, princess?" He hauls me into his chest and

wraps his arms around my head before planting a kiss on top of it. I struggle free, borderline suffocating and having my face squished into oblivion, aware that we are still in front of the huge windows of the eatery and Arrick can most likely still see us from wherever he is. I try not to make it obvious that I'm untangling myself and pushing him off. Heaving breaths in and rubbing my poor face in the process.

"Why let him think that you and I are together?" I pout, obviously irritated, rubbing the bridge of my nose as he leans in and pins an apologetic kiss on the tip with a wink.

"Because, my love, if that guy has any sense at all, then the green-eyed goddess we call jealousy will be poking his gorgeous pride. I could smell the regret swarming off him in droves when he caught sight of my sexy girl." Christian catches my hand and twirls me under his arm, almost colliding with people on the sidewalk who are innocently strolling by and setting me off balance. I giggle and shove him playfully in the chest, caught in his arms as he rights me again.

"You are a bad boy!" I chide with a genuine smile, losing my doubts and falling into Christian's constant good mood. He's eternally playful, sinfully naughty, and somehow always seems to get away with it.

"Oooh, say it again. I like it when you get all sexy and pretend to be mad. If I were into girls, I would totally do you when you call me that." Christian leans in and plants a kiss on my cheek, ruffling my hair and smacking my ass as he pushes me ahead to head back to school. It's only two blocks away, and the mild weather means it's a pleasant walk. No cab is required when it's a perfectly calm day like this afternoon. Christian takes my arm in his, his expression dropping to become serious, and he eyes me reflectively.

"How was it, though? Seeing him again after so long?" He squeezes my arm reassuringly.

"Hard. Awful." I swallow down the weird lump that started with the sound of his voice and grew when I laid eyes on him, heating my belly to insane levels. "Much harder than I thought it would be ... I still love him." I sigh sadly, pushing it back down behind that wall of indifference as hard as I can and almost succeeding. Christian frowns at me, dropping my arm and pulling me close with a consoling squeeze around my back, hugging me in like the best friend he is.

"I know, baby girl. It's his loss. He should have seen what was right in front of him and grabbed on with both hands because you are worth grabbing onto, Sophie. You will find someone who adores the ground you walk on, and I promise you'll get over him one day." Christian nudges my shoulder with his and gives me a sympathetic half-smile. He knows this story well enough to know that I do not like talking about this and that I want to appear always in control and emotionally undamaged.

My mask of strength.

"I'll hold you to that." I sigh dejectedly and carry on walking, looking ahead so I don't have to see him studying my expression. My heart calmed to its previous steady beat, although I can't dislodge how good he looked from my mind's eye or how he sounded and smelled. Nothing about him has changed, and there isn't anything about him that doesn't get to me on every level, even now.

"So, do I continue to be your sexy man at this thing?" Christian eyes me seriously, but I sigh and shake my head at him in defeat.

"My parents would only be confused; they already met you and know we are incompatible. You told my mom about your man troubles, and I have never lied to him, even if we no longer see each other. I don't want dishonesty between us." I turn away from his knowing eyebrow wiggle and that cheeky grin plastered across that handsome face.

"You still have it so bad. You could have had fun with this and tortured him a little." Christian giggles, but I sigh sadly.

"He chose Natasha; she may even be there, so I don't see how your acting like my boyfriend will make a difference." I tuck my chin down to hide that my eyes are misting up with this topic, hating that even after three months, he still gets me upset. That her name still hurts me, like being stabbed in the chest with a dull knife.

"Well, maybe you should ask Joey to go with us, that guy has been mooning over you for weeks, and you won't even go out for a coffee with him." Christian stops to face me on the sidewalk abruptly, hauling me to him with a devilish air to his tone. Joey is the guy who lives two doors along my hall, he's asked me out a dozen times, but I only ever find excuses to turn him down. He seems nice enough, tall and dark-haired with grey-blue eyes. I would have seen no problem dating him months back, but he isn't Arrick, and my heart is struggling to get past that fact.

"I'm not ready." I sigh, looking at my feet and admiring my pink flats with cute sequin details to distract my aching heart and wandering mind from tall, handsome Carrero men.

"I don't think you will ever be ready; you need to give him a chance. Grab a coffee, and keep it casual. You have nothing to lose." Christian is in bossy mode, eyeing me up with his no-nonsense attitude. He has an idea in his head, and like a dog with a bone, he isn't about to let it go.

"I don't know, Chris." I pull him forward as a group of rowdy boys try to slide by on the sidewalk. One of them eyes Christian up with a double glance and blushes as he moves on.

"Nothing to lose, except maybe your heart." He winks happily, oblivious to the passing "hotty," and I eye roll, knowing it's unlikely anytime soon.

To lose your heart, you need to have gotten it back first so that it can let someone else have it, and mine is still most definitely in the tightly gripped hands of one sandy-haired, hazel-eyed heartbreaker of   a   Carrero.

Chapter 2

"No, Christian." I haul out the sexy dress from my case for the third time and throw it back on the bed. He borrowed it from a senior after a runway show they put on days ago, and I am not impressed with his choice of dress for me at my sister's party.

"He will have his eyes pop out of his head if you wear this." He smirks, holding up a scrap of cloth and sashaying around my bedroom like a movie star, molding it against him.

"I think most of me will be popping out in this. He's seen me in various forms of skimpy clothing, and trust me, it does nothing for him. I know him, Chris; this will just make him think I've gone back to slumming it with sleazy men and backstreet nightclubs. I don't even care about making an impression on him, so it's unnecessary." I swipe the dress from him and throw it away, over the bed this time. Glaring sternly, trying to make him stop interfering.

Ever since he met him, he has not stop tried to goad me into playground tactics and far-flung ideas about Arrick being jealous or heartbroken without me. If any of that were true, he would have contacted me in the last few days, and he hasn't.

Or in the last three months!

"Of course, you don't. That's why you have spent the last two days obsessively trying on dresses and makeup for a seemingly innocent family gathering." He smirks at me with a knowing brow lift and a sassy twinkle in his eye, and my temper bites.

"Fuck off." I wave him away as he starts snooping in my case again, infuriatingly. "Don't you have a boyfriend you should be kissing goodbye right now? Jake has the car picking us up in an hour for the flight home." I shove him away by the face as he starts messing with my lace lingerie in the open bag. Christian sighs and throws himself on the bed dramatically, adopting the Hollywood pose of a distraught heroine with a palm on his forehead while making loud, weird noises that I'm sure are meant to represent misery.

"I already gave him the customary kiss and fuck. He's off playing straight tonight while he meets his father in the city." His boyfriend's double life is a huge sore point in Christian's and James's relationship. Christian figures that all parents are as easy as his when announcing one's sexuality and cannot empathize with anything different.

"Well, go pick up Jenny. She should have been here by now, so we can all have a little chill-out drink before I need to get on a plane with you know who." Jake sprung it on me less than an hour ago that Arrick and Nathan will join us on the flight home to the Hamptons. Something Arrick rarely did was fly, and I don't know how to feel about this. Jake's been at the office sorting issues out, despite taking a break to help Emma with their new baby and is adamant we all go back together tonight as one big happy family.

He is clearly deluded and can't see past his brother's ass.

The party is tomorrow night, but that means my family gets to spend some time with me beforehand, and I can properly introduce my two best friends to everyone. Christian met my parents when they came to the city for dinner with me; my mother loved him. Pretty sure she missed all his gay hints until he confessed his boyfriend problems to her and broke her heart for any wedding plans she had brewing in her head.

"The shift dress." He points out the neatly folded item on my vanity, the dress I haven't worn since Natasha got red wine stains out of it. It reminds me too much of them both, and it's sat there for weeks, unsure what to do with it. You don't just toss Louis Vuitton away, even if ever wearing it again makes me want to cut my heart out with a spoon.

"For the flight." He winks at me with that irritating-as-shit, know-it-all look that is now becoming the thing I hate most about him.

"You always look super sexy in an understated way, in classic shift dresses, especially with those heels with the ankle straps." I gaze down at the skinny jeans and tank I was thinking of keeping on for comfort but realize he is on to something. I'll have to endure Arrick for an hour minimum, and maybe it won't hurt to look good while flying home and pretending to be over him. He sure as hell didn't seem that broken up over losing me when we saw him that day in the restaurant.

I chew on my lip thoughtfully, pushing the memories of him away, like I've done tens of thousands of times since that day, and ignore the brewing storm inside of me.

Do not let him get to you. He doesn't deserve your pain.

"You know I'm right. Go get your face on and fluff out your hair while I chase up our girly. Won't be long, sexy." Christian slaps my ass as he walks by and leaves in a cloud of designer aftershave that's too sexy for words. I need to ask him what he wears, as it's seriously alluring, like a little trail of oomph wherever he goes. It reminds me of Arrick's scent, but I don't want to make that connection, shaking the thoughts away again.

I regard the dress on the vanity and frown, knowing I don't owe it to Arrick to dress up and look pretty, but a part of me wants to. To show him that I've gone on with my life without him. I kept my shit together and am doing okay for myself without him.

I don't need him.

Dressed in jeans and a tee, I look relaxed but also way too casual, and I want to show him that I am more than I was when he rejected me from his life. That I am worth more than what he chose over me. I need to feel like I had a lucky escape, not focus on everything he used to be, everything he was to me.

My apartment around me is my pride and joy and the homeliest comforting space I have ever known. I have real friends around me who care and don't use me as a means to an end for my money. My family and I are mending bridges, and there is a new-found trust in me because they seem to know this is different and giving me gentle breathing space to find my way. Sticking with school and doing well for myself, excelling at the top of my class. I have everything to be proud of.

These past few weeks, I've learned enough of the basics of sewing and designing to kit out my own sewing room and spend all my spare time sewing beautiful simple things and binge-watching tutorials. I enjoy every second of being creative and fashioning things for myself, designing my own wardrobe. An eclectic collection of styles and eras as I have been fully opened to the fashion world and the vast number of talents around me. I have purpose and meaning in my life that was lacking before, and I feel like I am finally on a path to something happier. I have nothing to hide from him.

I move to my wardrobe and decide on a compromise to what Christian thinks I should wear. A floaty summer dress that is modest yet cute and a little short and flirty, paired with sandals and a cardigan. I won't look overdressed, but feminine and young like I used to. Hair loose in its longer bob and my now trademark natural makeup. I need to show Arrick how much better I am alone and that I don't need him anymore. How much more settled in my old skin I am.

Half an hour later, I am ready as my duo of sidekicks walk back in. Christian whistles, handsome in chinos, a white shirt, and loafers. Jenny is in a long jersey dress with short sleeves and leggings and looking curvy for once, equally cute with her delicate features and gentle smile.

I love these two to death, and they complete a part of me that would be struggling so much worse if I didn't have them. They are the only reason I've been able to stay strong and not cave, keeping me occupied and being my strength when I waiver. Without them, I would have called him a million times in the past weeks. Within the first month.

"You look really pretty, Sophie." Jenny beams at me, dragging her weekend case behind her and propping it against the two cases we already put by the door. All ready for the dreaded two days home with *him*.

"Some Dutch courage for the road?" Christian lifts a bottle of Prosecco from his shoulder bag, smiling as we nod in unison. Loving his forward-thinking and knowing what I need.

I think I should just marry Christian!

* * *

I'm seated comfortably in Jake's jet, Jenny beside me, while Christian is sprawled in a seat across the aisle, looking completely at home. Jake is talking to him across a table while we wait on Arrick and Nate, and my nerves are on edge, tapping my foot restlessly while trying so hard not to keep looking at the open door at the far end of the plane. It has only been minutes, but already I'm restless and antsy, barely able to keep myself in check. Having Jenny slap my hands every time I start chewing my nails.

Jake looks my way a couple of times with fatherly smiles, and I smile emptily back. He was a little cagey when we arrived. I think he expected me to pull him up on Arrick's appearance, and my lack of mentioning it confuses him. I feel sick with nerves and want this to be over with.

Jake has to know everything; Arrick always confides in him, and I tell Emma everything, which pretty much translates to Jake knowing my side of events. I've avoided any alone time to chat with him, other than our lunch dates every two weeks, but he tends to ask me about school and my apartment and generally helps me with my bills and stuff I should be doing alone.

He asked me about three weeks after Arrick asked me to leave if I wanted to talk about it or wanted to know what Arrick was doing or saying about all of it. I told him I didn't, and he has left it alone ever since. Right now, he is entertaining Christian and talking about fast cars, boxing, and even more fast cars. Something they both have a love of, it seems.

I can tell that Chris feels relaxed around him; his flamboyant camp side is clearly on display, and I keep getting weird glances from Jake as though he is trying to assess if I know. He asked me once if Christian and I were close, and I told him I loved him to bits. It never dawned on me that he would read anything into that. It's one topic I never thought of broaching with him because, well, why would I? Until now.

He is most definitely doing the "I wonder if she knows her boyfriend is gay?" look at me. I smirk, realizing that despite talking about Chris and Jenny, I have never made it clear I wasn't dating him, and I guess he figured I was. I guess that means Arry thinks I am too, as Jake would probably have mentioned it. However, the restaurant would have been enough to tell him so.

Not that I care.

My head almost snaps up when I hear the tell-tale noise of people boarding the plane. Holding my breath, blood draining from my face as I stare at my exposed knees and wish I could sink into oblivion. My heart lurches, and my stomach knots. I start inhaling slowly to calm all outward reactions to him boarding. Jenny reaches out, taking my hand in hers, and squeezes gently. Reassuringly sweet as always and giving me just what I need. I take another deep breath to calm my outward persona and try to stay unflustered.

"Hey, all." Nathan is first in one of Arrick's most regular companions at all Carrero family functions. He has been to many a Huntsberger party too. He grins at everyone, eyes lingering on Jenny a little longer than appropriate, and that little Casanova twinkle tells me he thinks he found his new plaything for the weekend.

I think not! She is far too sweet for the animal in him. He would snap her.

"Hey, asshole." I scowl my warning and get nothing but that infuriating wink from him, saying, "game on." I will beat him if he messes with my new female best friend. Jenny has a boyfriend. Okay, maybe she doesn't seem happy with him, but still. The girl doesn't need Arrick's lothario sidekick making moves on her innocent self and messing with her head. Nathan would crush her in so many ways.

He decides he wants to sit opposite us with that and moves to slide in directly in front, moving over towards her side, so he leaves Arry a seat facing me. I freeze. The urge to kick Nate so hard is undeniable, and I panic inwardly. The asshole will be more than aware of what happened with us, and I could honestly choke him. I scowl at him, catching that infuriating smile as he slides into the seat in one fluid movement while throwing Jenny his "Hi, beautiful" smile, which signals he's in predator mode.

Nate is handsome, I have to hand it to him, and he's also tall, muscular, and pretty solid. But I also know he's a commitment-phobe with a constant hard-on, and his bed count is even higher than Jake's back in his heyday as a man whore! Arrick, at least, used to bed the same bimbo for a couple of weeks before moving on, while Nate is more like a couple of hours. He never backtracks, and he never keeps them around to remember their names.

"Hey." Says Jenny, blushing furiously as she tries not to react to the overly male hormones sweeping her way and gets a wink from him in return. Jake and Christian nod his way with guy smiles, oblivious to Nate's schmoozing, and everyone goes back to silently awaiting the last passenger. There's definite uneasiness in the air, and I'm not sure if it's just me or if everyone seems to be holding their breath while we await the man of the moment. I guess maybe it's true, everyone in here knows the story between us, and they probably think it's going to be awkward or seriously explosive. I'm counting on neither. I aim to be mature, act like I don't give a shit, and ignore him to the best of my capabilities.

Arrick hesitates when he boards a minute later, eyes immediately meeting mine. Almost as soon as he ducks in the door, it's like some mysterious force that makes us both look at one another and then away as quickly. I'm a completely weak idiot, incapable of not looking when I should have kept my head down. My chest almost explodes with the effort of keeping my heart in place, and my hands start to tremble involuntarily. My face tingles with the creep of heat, and breathing that is instantly a little difficult.

He moves down the aisle towards us as I keep my eyes on the book in my lap that I brought for this exact reason, pick it up, and start to thumb the pages in a bid to appear nonchalant about his arrival. I feel like the whole plane is suddenly buzzing with tension, and my sixth sense tells me all eyes are on me.

Arrick stops between the two sets of seats, his body heat and heavenly scent too close to be comfortable. We're on his left, Jake and Christian on his right, giving him limited seating options. Leaning in to give Jake a man half-hug, shake thing, seeing it as an excuse, he slides in beside his brother across the aisle, facing Christian instead of opposite me.

Thank God.

He sits diagonally across from me instead of directly facing me. My heart flutters a little, although my nerves are in chaos like I've run a marathon with how lightheaded I am. I keep concentrating on outward calm, nonchalant expression, and if needs must, the odd impassive gaze if he speaks to me. I let out a tiny sigh of relief, letting out the breath I wasn't aware I had started holding. Knowing it will be less traumatic if I don't have to dodge those sexy hazel eyes or stop myself from starting at that flawless square jawline every time I look up. Or occasionally brush one another under the table, seeing as he has long legs, and this is not an overly huge space.

"Hey everyone, I'm Arrick ... Arry." He nods towards Jenny; I catch it from the corner of my eye, feel her move as she leans out, and I guess he's offered her a handshake, the gentleman he always is. He greets Christian too, but I keep my eyes glued to the book to ignore him.

"Hey, Sophs." His voice hits me in the gut. I know his eyes are on me this time, and the familiar way he says my name hurts me more than I expected. I glance up quickly so as not to draw attention to us and give him a quick half-smile. That soft look and eyes trained on mine make me lose all resolve to be cold and distant, fumbling with my book in my lap.

"Hey." It comes out a little too breathily, completely shaken as heat creeps up my face even further, looking away fast so as not to let him know how much I fucking suck at hating him.

I want to keep hating him so badly, keep being so crazy mad at him.

Almost gasping at how awful it is on my heart when his eyes

meet dead on like that. Today they are greener than brown, and he's looking at me like he wants to say something. Despite myself, I glance up at him again, catching his eyes locked on me once more before they flicker to Chris across from him and then look away. I scold myself, shake myself internally and tell myself I need to get a grip on this and stop being so pathetic when it comes to him. I pick up my book, open the pages and stuff my nose inside, trying to get engrossed and read this trip away.

Breathe, count to ten ... Read and ignore. Repeat.

"Seatbelt, Sophs." Arrick's soft tone cuts straight through my guise, and I look up to see everyone belting up. His eyes are on me as he does the same, hurting with the force of a tidal wave and reminding me how many times he would lean over and put mine on. Like a weird habit or impulse from years of doing them for me when I was younger. I always had trouble getting them to latch, so he always did it and never stopped. I guess he's feeling it too, being in the same space and not doing it for me for the first time since I met him. I guess this will be the first flight, road trip, or whatever we haven't sat side by side while occupying the same space.

I pull on my lap belt, with a tight half-smile his way, and try not to let the tingles creeping up from inside hit my face and show him that he still gets to me on every level. I struggle with the stupid thing, trying to get it to clip before Jenny leans over and does it instead. I avoid his eyes, knowing fine well he's watching, and feel like a dumb kid all over again. This is his fault. If he had ever left me to do this alone, I might have learned by now.

So much for being so mature and having my shit together. Who can't latch goddamn safety belts?

Me, that's fucking who!

As soon as the plane starts up for take-off and maneuvering on the runway, I go back to my book in a bid to zone them all out and act like I really couldn't give a rat's ass if the entire reason for three months of sheer hell is sitting three feet away from me, looking like my dreams. I don't want to be here anymore. I'm suffocating because he's here. I'll never do this again. I would rather get a four-hour sweaty coach trip than this hell.

Nathan's already pulled Jenny into a conversation about some movie they both watched recently, and I can hear Jake and Christian talking across the aisle about something mundane. Chris has gone back into "man" mode and seems to be trying to act like he isn't probably drooling over the two hot Carrero brothers and making like a straight boyfriend. I feel Arrick's eyes on me every so often. Even without looking, I know it's him. No one else has ever made my skin prickle the way he does, and I want him to stop. I don't even know why. Maybe it's the hair, reverting to clothes I used to wear long ago. Either way, he needs to leave me alone and look elsewhere. I flick the page and absorb myself in the words on the page before me in a bid to get into the story and zone out the audience.

* * *

"You never told me that, baby girl?" Christian's voice floats my way as Jenny nudges me gently and nods across the aisle. After all, I had finally gotten into my book and blanked them all out as I was pulled into a magical world of Vampires and Werewolves fighting over human girls. I look up bewildered, catching Arrick glancing my way with that infuriating unreadable expression and yet softness to his face that I haven't seen in a long time. He almost looks a little bit happy, making me feel shittier.

"What?" I look at Christian, leaning with elbows on his table casually and pondering me with an open expression. Everyone seems to be looking at me. Which only makes me feel more antsy and confused.

What did I miss?

"That you were some sort of adrenaline junkie adventurer who used to do things like base jump and snowboard with Arry here. He says he even taught you some self-defense moves when he was training. You're like a little stealth ninja. Now I can only picture some sort of blonde wonder woman in very tight ski suits. Woof, Woof." He winks suggestively, and I tense, hoping to God he realizes the Carrero brothers are not people you can make any sexual or lewd remarks in front of when it comes to me. I know what he's like, and they will tear his head off if he says anything a little less safe. I throw him a wary look to warn him to be careful with what he says.

"We just used to hang out; if he did something, I wanted to try it too, that's all." I answer flatly, eyes on Christian in my serious "leave it alone" look. I turn back to the novel I'm reading, hoping to become more oblivious. My hair is used as a veil to hide behind, especially as I'm pale and nervous, and thoughts of Jake ripping Christian's spine out flit through my mind.

"Sophs was always fearless. She saw everything I did as a challenge and always kept up with me." Arrick sits back in his seat, adjusting his jeans as he does so, inadvertently drawing my eyes to his crotch. I blush wildly and glance away, turning a page quickly, gulping down the stupid reaction I'm still having to him. Chastising myself that I even did that. I looked there and saw that he packs something worth looking at. Luckily, he doesn't seem to notice.

Stupid girl!

"Pretty amazing for a girl as dainty as her to not only try but handle everything I threw at her." He finishes, sounding somewhat proud, and I glance up, catching the half-smile at me, eyes more hazel again. He seems lost in memory. A little moment of reminiscence between us that yanks harder at the pain in my chest, and I can't stay locked his way. I don't even know what to say to that. It's like he's trying to make things okay between us, probably trying to make the atmosphere less tense. He has no clue how far down the road to no longer liking him I am, and nothing can ever come of trying to be friends again. He ruined all of it, and I have no desire to forgive him.

"My little hellcat! Could I love you more?" Christian sighs with big, adoring eyes that only makes me genuinely smile back at him, lifting my mood slightly. He has a way of making me feel lighter, even without meaning to, and right now, I need it.

I catch Arrick out of the corner of my eye, shifting in his seat, slightly frowning with that infamous Carrero glare that almost mirrors Jake's normal frown. It's in Christian's direction. Then he looks away out of the window and seems to be trying to bring back his usual unreadable expression. It's obvious he doesn't like Christian's affection for me, playing it "straight" and implying I am his girl. It gives me a little tug of power inside. A sense of justice that he knows a tiny ounce of what it feels like to be on the jealous side, watching someone you have feelings for choose someone else and be happy with them.

Christian is maybe onto something with this game of illusion. Fuck you, Arry!

"Sophie is easy to love when she's not being a class-A brat." Jake cuts in, sits back in his seat casually and looks very much like a guy that is comfy in his own skin. He's been unusually quiet for the last part of the conversation and seems to be observing. I wonder what that quick brain is summarizing, knowing he is definitely in paternal mode and not cheeky brother. Normally he and Arrick are like twins in a laid-back, casual way, but sitting beside one another, only highlights how unrelaxed and stiff Arrick is on this flight. He's tense, sitting straighter than he normally does, and a lot more reserved in his brother's company than normal.

"Thanks, "Uncle" Jake," I smirk, knowing how much he hates when I call him that, almost as much as he hates me calling him dad. I get a perverse pleasure in always winding him up, as much as he does to me.

"I am way too sexy and young to be your uncle, Sophabelle. I can still throw you off my plane, you know? Even while being in mid-air." Jake winks my way, and I roll my eyes with a sigh while Jenny giggles beside me. Nate is also unusually quiet. Now the lull in the conversation has happened on the long flight; he is watching my girl unusually intensely and probably planning his seduction if I know him.

Since meeting the Carrero men, Jenny has been giggling and blushing a lot, although a heck of a lot more since Nate sat down. She isn't immune to them the way I am and has fallen victim to that old Carrero charm and good genes like every other female in New York. Sadly, also to that wolf-like skill, Nate has of entrapping innocent souls. I try not to glare at him.

"Pretty sure that constitutes as child abuse." Arrick cuts in and looks pointedly at me with an icier tone to his voice, clearly still sulking over Christian's adoration of me. He's trying to be his normal jokey self, but I can see through it, although subtle. I can see his jaw tense as his eyes grow greener and lack warmth. The tone alone is devoid of his usual humor, and despite the urge to bite and tell him to go fuck himself, I sigh sweetly. He's taken on the cool and distant Arrick look, lost in his thoughts and effortlessly locked away emotionally. Reminding me that he will forever only see a kid.

"Thanks, asshole." I grit back at him, trying to act normal and not let him get to me on any level, with the skills of a trained actress and the completely controlled mannerisms of a girl who feels nothing anymore. It wasn't unknown for him to goad me into a Carrero brother argument and them torturing me as teammates in the past. I know the drill. I play along for the sake of appearances. I know he is just trying to lash back because he's one dumbass who sulks over my ability to move on, and I will not let it piss me off.

"To us, Sophs, you will always be that big-eyed kid who needs big brothers to take care of her." Jake winks at me now, all of his irresistible charms wrapped up in a Hollywood-perfect smile, effortlessly at ease with knowing he is hot. That devilish air of Jake, a man with a plan, and I wonder what he is up to. He seems oblivious to his brother's mood and not at all interested in appeasing or scolding him.

My eyes lift and meet Arrick's first, my brain concluding that this would always be the problem where he is concerned. His head was torn between protector and brother, who planted me firmly behind platonic boundaries long ago and vowed to keep me safe. He will always struggle to separate that damaged little kid who cried into his chest many times over the dark memories and nightmares with the woman I have become. He couldn't cross boundaries and let me grow up, so instead, he abandoned me.

Arrick regards me for a moment with a thoughtful expression before turning to look out of the window, almost oblivious to those around us. I wonder if he is pondering the same thing I am, thinking about why it was such a dick move to leave me heartbroken and alone.

I wonder why his girlfriend isn't here on this flight. She's been to every other party in the past two years, and it isn't like him not to have her clinging to his side at family functions.

Not that I care.

"Sophie *is* still a big-eyed kid. That's what we love about her, though. She's a woman child, all vulnerable and innocent, yet fiery and passionate. The perfect girl!" Christian is dramatically eyeing me up, all wide-eyed adoration and sultry looks that only make him seem hopelessly in love with me, and I curb the urge to roll my eyes at him. He's laying it on a little thick, and even Jenny's looking at him like he has something wrong with him. I sigh and throw her the "Christian is at it again" face, she raises a brow, and we exhale slowly, in perfect unison.

"I don't know. I think she's pretty independent. I see a strong woman with youthful charm but more than capable. She is definitely a grown-up." Jenny cuts in. Ever loyal to me, her new-found best friend, and patting my hand maternally with a soft smile. Sometimes she is the only sanity between these two, especially when Christian is off on this new tangent of "let's make Arry jealous!"

"I think you should all find a new topic and leave Sophie alone!" I cut in with a sigh, eyeing Christian warily with my best "drop it" look. Jake smiles my way with an infuriatingly knowing expression and lounges back casually in his seat. Arrick is slumped down beside him in the same pose, yet he isn't giving off the same casual vibe as Jake, and I want to go back to reading until we land and get away from him. This right here is a unique type of uneasy torture.

I'm uptight, antsy and anxious, and overly aware of him, like my senses are on high alert, and the last thing I need is a juvenile anxiety attack that he would no doubt swoop in to try and calm because he is the one of the few who knows how to.

Knowing him as I do, I can tell he's agitated, despite his calm demeanor and poker face. Arrick has always been the master of coolness and indifference to even the most observant eye, and it took a long time to pick up on his tiny tells. The subtle jaw tense, the slight flex of a muscle, or the deadpan calm of his face, given away by the increase of green in his eyes. The little flicker of that muscle in his cheekbone or the slight dip to his brow. A million almost unnoticeable quirks that all show different emotions.

Arrick, unlike Jake, is always so hard to read and never seems to erupt in the way his brother does or wear his inner thoughts on his face in a readable way, but I know him better. Jake has his equal share of a poker face when he wants or needs it. God knows he uses it in business, but with close loved ones, he wears his heart on his sleeve for all to see. Arrick does not. Arrick is pissed, sulking, and I do not care one iota.

You made your bed. Now lie in it.

"Well, as we are heading for landing, maybe we should all get ourselves together?" Jake is back in bossy mode, nodding at the magazines strewn on the tables, and the open laptop in front of Nathan, who has been engrossed in something he is doing. The array of cups and discarded junk wrappers littered among us. Evidently, Dad is telling the kids to tidy up his prized plane. We all make a move to do as we are told before buckling up for the descent.

Chapter 3

I unload my clothes from my bag into my wardrobe, alone in my bedroom, while Jenny and Christian are shown to guest rooms downstairs after a less stressful drive from the airport. Jake had two cars waiting for us upon landing. Thankfully, Arrick went with his brother and Nate in the other vehicle and left us three to head to my parents" home in peace. My head and heart are still reeling with the after-effects of being so near him for that journey. I feel drained, uptight, and antsy, like I am all out of whack and can't get my act together. I need some cooling-off time to breathe and accept the fact that, YES, that asshole still fucks me up whether I like it or not.

Whether he deserves it to or not!

After being welcomed home by my mom and dad, I'm taking some time out, getting my head together after seeing him again. I must admit, I need this more than I thought I would. Being around him still hurts more than it should. Part of me aches for how we used to be and hates the distance between us now, despite everything.

I hate how much I still miss him, even after months of not seeing him. Time has not eased the severity of my pain or longing. It's not getting any easier. If anything, the depth of how much I miss him has only worsened the longer it's been. I hoped this would eventually get better, not worse, and seeing him was torture.

I hate that I am this pathetic, despite the pep talks, the late-night tears until I fall asleep, and the willingness to hate him. I can't. He did too much for me in my past that lingers too close to my heart.

He took me under his wing and introduced me to his friends and lifestyle. He sheltered me from everyone and let me use him as a human shield whenever I needed one. He lifted my mood when I couldn't get out of bed and brought me movies and hugs when I was sick. Even when he left for trips or college, he never broke contact. He always came home, and I was always the first person he came to see. Always with some gift from his absence, a trinket, a keepsake, or one of the ten million stuffed unicorns I own.

Then in one fell swoop, he became someone I didn't know, who threw all that in my face and turned his back on me. I don't get how he could have turned out to be the best thing in my life, to the absolute worst, in one change of feelings. I never thought he would be the one to deliver the blow to my heart that could completely ruin me. I should have learned a long time ago that, in the end, everyone you let in ultimately hurts you. The only person you can rely on is yourself.

I finish hanging up my clothes and wander to my en-suite to run a bath. I need to unwind before dinner with my family, Jenny and Christian. Leila wants to meet my besties before her party, and I don't want to face anyone until I can carry on this ruse that Arry and I are how we have always been, with all of them. No one knows or suspects anything, and I hope it won't be obvious that we no longer talk at the party.

It will break my parents" hearts to know I have lost the one person in my life who held me together for years. I don't want to tell them, don't want them to hate him or feel sorry for me. I want everyone to assume that life is normal, fine, and rosy, and it's so much easier never to bring him up when they come to the city. They all assume we are still hanging out.

I want to pamper and beautify myself for my grand entrance at my sister's party tomorrow, show everyone how far I have come in such a brief time, and act like everything is alright.

* * *

"So, you're not dating either of them, then?" Leila looks pointedly at Christian across the table, waving her fork with that crazy, narrowed gaze. Christian smiles sassily, perched between Jenny and me at my parent's dinner table, and shrugs. As dinner begins with the first bout of sisterly interrogation, everyone looks his way. We have barely had time to get our starter down our necks, and she is on his ass. Completely predictable Leila.

"I know. I am a total demon, right? Two beautiful and classy women on my arm, and neither one floats my boat. Wrong sex, sweetie." Christian raises an eyebrow and then dives into his soup, smiling like the cat that got the cream, and Leila turns her attention to Jenny, looking a little unimpressed. Until she met him face to face, I think she harbored hopes he was husband material for her problematic kid sister.

"Okay ... so then, your boyfriend is ... ?" Leila is trying to suss out from our conversations how everyone fits together and being blatantly rude about it. Looking at Jenny as though she better answer or the offensive fork she's waving around may be jammed in her eye.

"Mark. We have been dating for almost two years. He doesn't go to school with us. He is a chef and works in a hotel kitchen." Jenny blushes, hating that all eyes are on her now and getting increasingly uncomfortable. She squirms in her seat, drops her chin to hide behind her bangs, and concentrates on pushing her soup around with her spoon. I throw her a supportive smile, squeeze her shoulder and rub it a little as if to say, "ignore my psycho sister."

This is just Leila being Leila.

"And you?" Leila is back on me, unsurprisingly. I knew she was only working her way to me as mom told her to stop singling me out when she arrived. She has been wheedling her way towards me again from that moment.

"Yes, Leelou?" I throw her that "what now" look that she adores ... *Not.*

I am in no way intimated by Miss. Bossy Pants and her need to demand Intel at the slightest drop of a hat. I only saw her two weeks ago. Nothing much has happened in such a short space of time to be interested in.

"I'll beat you if you use that name again. Still no man? Still not dating? What about that cute guy that Mom said lives down the hall?" She blinks at me seriously, thinking she is somehow commanding an action just by bringing it up. I don't even know why they are so obsessed with me settling down with a guy. From what I have seen, they are a lot more hassle than they are worth.

"Mom, really? You told Leila there was a cute guy? What are you? Twelve?" I throw my gaze at her accusingly, and she giggles innocently. My mom, who may be old as the hills now, can sometimes be incredibly girlish and juvenile. Joey is young enough to be her son, yet that didn't stop her from checking him out.

Ewww.

"He was very cute for a young man, and he held the door for us when we arrived. Lovely boy said he was your neighbor." My mom smiles sweetly, and I catch my dad rolling his eyes in a teen girl way. Luckily for her, he knows my mom is a shameless man admirer and would never do anything other than ogle. Faultlessly loyal, and she does adore my father to death.

"Pretty sure you probably interrogated him, much like she's doing now. It was probably Joey and, no, not dating him and don't want to." I pout, going back to dunking my bread roll in my starter and stuffing my face with all the ladylike manners of an ape. Ignoring the inquisitive sisterly eyes is my best plan.

"Sadly!" Christian sighs and gives me that "you are a completely hopeless child" look he has perfected from watching the little mermaid one too many times. I know he thinks it's cute, and Sebastian the crab is currently his obsession, but it's plain weird.

"Get your panda eyes off me. You date him if you like him so much." I throw my napkin at him, and my father gives me the "behave" look. Christian throws it back with a challenging grin. Not phased at all by my dad's attempts at being the head of the table.

"So, Sophie, how's school?" Daniel cuts in, being the man of the

33

moment and saving our family from ourselves, like he always does. He puts a hand on Leila's shoulder and squeezes her, which I know is Daniel talk for "lay easy on her for tonight." He's the only human in existence who can sometimes control that rabid beast.

Leila has been circling aggressively since I got here. I don't know what's with her. I hope to God she's not pregnant again, but all the signs are there. Irrational moods, weird sporadic tears, aggressive behavior, and questioning, like she belongs in the Gestapo. If I see her eat anything with cream, I will buy her the damn test myself. She hates cream, milk, dairy, and anything like that, yet she lives on it pregnant. Biggest neon sign ever, and I eye up her plate with serious doubt. Nothing creamy on show.

If there is a God above, please do not let her fall pregnant while I am nearby.

It's not that I wouldn't like my sister to have more kids. It's just Leila is awful when pregnant, and to be fair, as a mother, she is kind of terrifying. Unlike Emma, with her earth momma vibe and gentle nature, Leila is a hot mess who runs her twins to school in her pajamas and hair rollers. She drinks way too much wine when her kids drive her insane, and as both boys have ADHD and are the most hyper kids known to man, I can hardly blame her.

She loves the convenience of microwaves and had to hire a cook to ensure they had a decent diet, yet she loves to fuel them on anything that shuts them up. Even if that's daily soda and chips when Daniel isn't looking. Pregnant, she hates everyone, and everything, breathes fire and makes everyone suffer along with her. I don't get how Daniel survives at all.

"Good. I love it and feel like I have found my calling in life." I smile gently at him. I love Daniel. For a guy who used to be one lady-killing party boy with serious sex addiction, he was the best thing that ever happened to my sister, and he adores her. He is the calm to her wild, the serene to her crazy, and he knows how to handle her.

"She's amazing. You should see the portfolio she is building. I think we have the next big thing on our hands." Jenny beams: far more comfortable talking about others than herself, and she smiles with pride at me. She reminds me of that girl next door stereotype in movies, who always turn out to be the cute girl who gets the hot man at the end.

"I think both of you are equally talented. We work well, the three of us. Different strengths, different characters, and we merge to make one amazing team." I laugh when Christian fans himself a little dramatically. Jenny laughing along with me and nudging him playfully.

"But I, of course, bring all the pizazz." He beams at us, fluttering those annoyingly dark long lashes and looking all coquettish.

"True!" Both Jenny and I say in unison and then giggle. I catch Daniel eyeing me warily; I can almost sense that little mind working away behind brown eyes. I give him an intense, narrowed look and get that Daniel Hunter special smile. The "I know what's going on" cheeky glint that Leila usually hates him for.

"I would love it more if you had a nice fella to come home to every night. Is Arry still keeping an eye on you? The city isn't safe for single girls anymore, Sophs." Leila carries on, digging into another round of bread with relish, and I seriously revisit the pregnancy thing. She isn't normally a big eater. I catch Daniel frowning her way too and wonder if he thinks the same thing as she demolishes her third bread roll.

"I don't need Arrick to take care of me anymore. Pretty sure he has enough women to be taking care of nowadays." I snap a little too hastily, the interrogating eyes on me, and curse myself at my lack of control. I need to learn not to react whenever he is the subject.

"Meaning?" Leila is full boar staring at me now. Most of the quiet chit-chat around us falls away as everyone listens in with interest. The sudden silence is the moment of bated breath where they all sit, astonished that I am no longer the puppy dog trailing Arrick Carrero.

"He has a life and a woman. We don't see each other much now. We're both so busy." I lie expertly. Deflecting flawlessly with a raised brow and an air of nonchalance.

"But she has us. I live nearby, and Jenny is three blocks further out, and we're never away from her side." Christian cuts in. Savior that I adore and knowing how to sidetrack the interrogator faultlessly.

"It's not like him not to be around as much? Have you two fought?" Leila has her eyes on me, homed in, and scrutinizing me. Almost like that little bloodhound side to her paranoid personality is suddenly sniffing something out, I steady my breath to appear unaffected.

"No. Can we stop talking about him, please? I'm sure I can have a life that doesn't revolve around him, and it had to happen one day ... you know, growing up, moving on. I can't live in his shadow forever." I keep my voice deadpan, and my nerves steady and concentrate on carefully funneling soup into my mouth. Precision perfect.

"Arrick's a busy man, babes. I'm sure he is still looking out for her in every way like he always did." Daniel cuts in, throwing me an unreadable look. He clearly knows full well that Arrick is no longer in my life. Jake is his best friend, and that makes Arry one too. His choice not to tell my sister, however, baffles me. But then I guess he is just looking out for me, knowing fine well she would demand I return home without my eternal guardian. Like little Sophie is incapable of surviving without his ever-looming presence to ensure I don't mess it all up.

Figures!

"We just saw him last week. Complete, sweetheart." Christian smiles softly, deviously vague and curbing more suspicion.

"Right. And he has that girlfriend, Natasha, to be caring for too. It's not down to him to be solely responsible for our girl. She's got to learn to do it solo." My dad cuts in, and I tense, anger bubbling at the mention of her while Leila is riling my nerves. Suddenly ultra-touchy with this subject when I know the source of my heartache is less than a hundred feet away at his parent's house tonight. This is why I have avoided family dinners, where everyone gets to come together to focus on me.

"Nice girl ... never really seen the connection, though. She's a bit ... I don't know ... bland. A bit quiet and tame for our Arry." My mom is frowning my way as if she expects me to have some input, and I frown hard back at her.

"Lame more like," Leila mutters, and for once, I find myself smiling at her impulsively. I always knew she was lukewarm to the other girl, but she has never openly insulted her before.

"Leila!" My mother scolds, giving her a stern maternal look of displeasure.

"She's a very sweet young lady and seems like a genuine homely person. She is always very polite and well-mannered." She adds with a gentler tone that doesn't seem all that genuine, and I wonder how long I have been oblivious to my family's distinct lack of affection for the girl Arrick has been bringing home for two years.

When did this happen?

"Again, lame. I can understand someone like Rylanne hooking up with Natasha. I mean, he is all for a 1950"s housewife who wants to stay home barefoot and pregnant. That's why he is dating Brie but never a Carrero. Definitely not Arrick!" Leila's stuffing her face with more bread and throws me an odd look that gets a flat response. I won't be goaded into a reaction that betrays anything. My friends have fallen silent and eating to deflect attention, and my face is flaming. Hoping they all drop this topic soon. As interested as I am to hear they don't all adore her, I am not relishing his name being passed around or his relationship analyzed when all I want to do is forget him.

"Arrick likes her, so I guess it's none of our business!" I point out steadily. I catch Daniel frowning at me for a moment before he clears his throat and looks away, it's an odd moment, but I let it slide. Not sure what to make of it.

"True. Everyone gets to make their own choices in life. Even if they are the wrong ones." Daniel cuts in, sighing heavily and sitting back casually. He rubs his flat stomach, stretches, seemingly bored with how this conversation is going and finishes with his starter. He has always been completely comfortable at my family table. Leila throws him a sarcastic look, reminding him of all his wrong choices in their past, and he hits her with an award-winning smile and swoops in to kiss her on the mouth. A quick, chaste peck that makes her soften visually.

Still weak for him then. Kinda cute, yet also gross.

"Talking of which, where are the rest of them? Surely everyone is coming to the party tomorrow?" I look at my mom and then Leila, wondering why my brothers get to escape this unbearable dinner tonight. Family tradition dictates we all have to be here on the eve of Leila's smash-up, and I could have used the numbers to avoid this strained topic.

"They are all arriving at different points throughout the day tomorrow. Life Sophs, kids, jobs ... everyone will be here for the party." My dad frowns, motioning for the housekeeper to remove plates for the next course. I watch Leila almost wrestle the bread plate from her angrily.

"Except the kids ... I told you, Mom. No kids this year. I plan to get completely bladdered, dance up a storm, and have a kid-free night, and no children will be ruining our buzz." Leila growls at the housekeeper, who puts the bread plate back on the table like a feral beast protecting her babies.

"My sweet maternal little wife." Daniel rolls his eyes, but my mom smiles patiently, used to the diva in her and her not-so-maternal demands.

"Yes, Leila, we all know. I made sure to inform all guests that this is a child-free affair. We have a kid's get-together for everyone on Sunday afternoon." My mom tries to smooth her ruffled feathers with a warm tone and gentle smile.

"Should have made that Monday, Mom. Hangovers can be an all-day thing when you're an alcoholic like Leelou." I smirk her way and catch the evil glare.

"Shut up, or I'll impale you with my breadknife." She sounds deadly serious and holds up a rather long and sharp implement that she has swiped from the bread plate in the center. Daniel leans in smoothly and removes it from her fingers, handing it off to the passing housekeeper with a grateful smile. Leila glares at him coldly.

"I agree, though. Hangovers and family fun days do not mix. Leila is like a beast the day after a party." Daniel concedes, giving my sister an eyebrow wiggle that breaks that icy look to a softer, almost grudged smile, and my mom sighs heavily.

"Sunday is the only day they will all be staying until. People have lives, for goodness" sake, and I want to see all my babies and grandbabies in one place before you all leave again." She seems close to tears, deflated at her ruined plans.

"I don't have kids, and I will be on a flight home Sunday afternoon, Mom." I shrug unapologetically. I do not want to be around for that little get-together with a hangover. Screaming kids and arguing family is my idea of a hangover nightmare, and I could never subject Christian and Jenny to that mess.

"I don't know why I bother sometimes. I really don't." My mom huffs and sighs as my dad pats her hand sympathetically. Giving her a tender smile that seems to perk her up.

"I plan on staying in bed till Monday." Leila ruins it with that little exclamation, in diva mode, with a spoiled brat tone.

"I'll bring the kids. Don't worry about it. We have Christmas coming in a few months, and you know that's a week-long family get-together." Daniel is trying to be the savior again, my poor momma gripping on with her fingertips to her dream reunion.

"Because that's something to look forward to." I roll my eyes sarcastically and then laugh when Leila throws her bread at me and sends my mom into scolding overdrive.

Chapter 4

The Huntsberger house is transformed, and the huge adjoining dining room and family room have been emptied through the day and are now styled. With floral arrangements and seating, which pours out into the gardens from the wall of veranda doors. It looks like a huge function room in any classy hotel.

Leila has always insisted on using "home" for her parties. I think it's a little sentimentality and that this place signifies safety and happy memories for her. It also means strictly no paparazzi for any of the more well-known guests, and we can monitor who gets to come in and let everyone relax to have an enjoyable time.

Food is being laid out in the adjoining TV room, music is blaring from the sound system outside, and a huge marquee housing a bar and extended lounging area is set up. I can see a wooden floor for dancing inside and here. They have gone big and bold for this one, the place is bursting with friends and family galore, and even though it's early in the evening, the house is crowded.

I work my way out through the room from the hall. Christian and Jenny are mingling, welcomed with open arms into the Huntsberger family last night over dinner and drinks, and feeling at home already. Jenny is in intimate conversation with Nathan in one corner, looking decidedly cozy together and uninterested in milling guests. Christian is in an adoring group of Carrero women, nieces, and cousins galore, all fanning for his attention, so I leave them both to it. They both seem happy with their current situations, and I am still trying to find myself a level of sanity to get through tonight.

I make a beeline for the outside area, pushing among friendly faces that stop me to hug and smile, commenting on how much I have grown and changed of late. The same old repeated affections, and I smile and persevere. Pushing between two burly Carrero men with trademark dark hair, wide shoulders, and those green eyes. I manage to squeeze out the other side, only just, with effort, looking back apologetically and walking straight into the hard-muscular back of another male in a tux with an "ooft."

"Sorry, I wasn't looking where I was ..." I trail off as Arrick turns my way with his hazel frown and devastating smile, temporarily catching my breath in my throat. I immediately hit that zombie-like state of "I do not know how to behave" and do that awkward little eye avoidance flustered thing. Jake leans in past him and grins at me. My heart decides now is a great time to flutter crazily while my stomach churns into knots, and my palms are instantly sweaty.

"Still as graceful as ever, Sophs." Jake winks, and Arrick hands me a glass of champagne with a half-smile as though everything is completely normal and not at all weird. I accept it carefully so as not to touch his fingers and try to appear relaxed, despite the conga of nerves running through me. Arrick seems more chilled tonight, and a slight haziness to the green in his eyes suggests these two have already been drinking the bar dry before the party got into full swing. I turn the glass, raise it with a quick smile and sip it gratefully, suddenly overcome with awkwardness and unable to stand his eyes on me.

"Just looking for Leila." I raise a brow and look around, straining on tiptoes to see over the hordes of super-tall people and avoid looking directly at him. His presence has me all edgy and light-headed, and even though I have the urge to run away, I stand my ground to prove I am over this. Arrick raises his chin and looks around too.

"She's over there, wrapped around Daniel, and already looks

pretty smashed." He raises his glass, pointing with it into the crowd of tuxedoes and sparkly dresses. One thing my family knows how to do is party in grand fashion. I try to follow his direction, turning my head, but I am not tall enough to get any real view of her, even in strappy heels. I'm aware that if I stretch too much, my sparkly silver short dress will hitch a little too high. It's not fitted, more of a floaty style, so it will be risky. I sink back onto my shoes, defeated, and turn back to them with a sigh.

"What's new for Leeloo?" Jake smirks, looking up and over the people around them, tall enough to view her from his standing point and see what I cannot. I try to stretch some more in a second attempt to see and fail miserably, cursing my height for the first time in my life.

"Guess I will wait till she finds me then." I smile their way and catch that tiny eyebrow flicker and a slight frown from Arrick, almost fleeting as his eyes meet mine and then disconnect. I turn back and catch Jake hauling at his bow tie around his neck as though it's strangling the life out of him and pause, glass midway to my mouth, waiting to see if he dares to pull it off.

"Leave it alone." I reach out and slap his elbow, throwing him a scolding look, knowing fine and well what he's doing. You can almost set your watch by how long it takes Jake to discard any form of a tie at an event.

"I hate these things; I feel like Emma has tied a rope around my neck." Jake squirms some more, pulling it so much it comes loose, and then looks like a wicked schoolboy who just broke a vase. That pleased twinkle in his eye at his mischief, pretty sure he has an excuse now. "Oh well, guess it comes off now then." He smirks, pulling it a little more, but I only shake my head at him, ready to remind him how bat-shit crazy Leila will go if her party photographs are less than perfect.

"If yours is off, then mine is too." Arrick doesn't wait. He yanks it at one corner, so it not only unties but slides cleanly off and hangs like a dead animal from one hand, and I honestly think he might dump it on the passing tray of drinks. The two brothers grin at each other, and I sigh out loud.

"Nope ... Nope ... Nope. You both know that if she kicks off because men are starting to take these off, you two will get it. Leila is crazy. She will hurt you. Please wait until the photographer has done the rounds before doing that. At least she will be too drunk to care." I impulsively grab Arrick's bow tie from his hand, knowing he can only tie them in front of a mirror, and throw Jake a no-nonsense glare. I point the finger at his face, and he folds in less than a millisecond.

"Fuck sake, woman!" Jake growls at me but starts redoing his bow tie once more, a little look of defiance in that green gaze as he mumbles under his breath and can't shake my glare. I turn my attention back to Arry, watching me a little too closely for comfort, and try not to react to how much it catches me off guard.

"Scoot down. You're too tall." I implore him, trying to avoid the way he doesn't hesitate to lean into me, so his face practically touches mine, eyes locked to mine intensely. He takes my glass to hold for me. I hesitate a moment before sliding his tie around his neck. I put my arms behind him carefully to avoid touching him much, bring it around, and start tying it the way my mother showed me many times. I focus on his tie, not the suffocating closeness and the way he's looking at me. Fiddling with clumsy fingers because he is too damn close like this, and his expression is so soft it's killing me. I can smell everything that is him, feel his gentle breathing on my face, and close enough to graze my nose across his. My breathing is deteriorating, as are my nerves. Arrick is staring right at my face, his hazels practically boring a hole into my eyes and making it nearly impossible to think straight. I re-tie it twice as I make such a mess while under scrutiny and hope he doesn't notice.

"You look beautiful tonight ... you always do." He says it so quietly it's almost inaudible. His voice tingle on my lips, a slight sensation of vibration that makes me ache to kiss him and struggle to keep myself in check. My legs are turning to Jell-O, and my insides are a washing machine on spin. Tying it neatly, I give it one last tug and impulsively smooth my hands across his shirt and lapels without thinking, hands burning with the feel of him.

I have tied these for him a million times, and it's almost like breathing to me, the way I instantly reverted to Sophie of old. Arrick seems to take a moment, leans into my palms, before he moves back to straighten up and coolly passes me back my drink. I can barely catch my breath. The sudden lurch in my center makes me instantly emotional and unable to keep this act of indifference up.

"Thanks." I blush wildly, feeling the heat rise from my feet, and look away to break the penetrative gaze he has going on with me. Small shallow inhales to cool the torrent of agony crashing through me at speed. I won't let him see me break. I won't show him how close to tears he has me.

I won't ever let you see that you can affect me again.

"Your boy ... Christian. He seems like a good guy." Jake interjects, his eyes trained on his brother's profile and adopting that infuriating Carrero unreadable mask. A brotherly trait, obviously. Jake looks a little smug, and I wonder what his game is. At least he distracts me, draws my attention to him, and gives my head some much-needed focus.

"He is ... a really lovely guy who does his best to care for Jenny and me." I smile with real affection in my tone, a topic that instantly relaxes me, and glad of not only a change but a reason to move back and look at Jake instead. To give myself room to breathe. Noticing his tie is crooked, I gesture him over and click my fingers for him to scoot down to my height too. Jake dutifully obeys, and I straighten his tie before patting him on the cheek with a cheeky wink and a mock air kiss. He eye rolls at me.

Arrick downs his glass of champagne in one go, surprisingly for him, and immediately lifts another from a nearby passing waitress holding a tray, as though he has decided he's getting hammered tonight. He instantly seems disengaged from the conversation, finally looking anywhere but at me. I can almost sense the change in the atmosphere and wonder if he dislikes Christian or if it's the thought of me with Christian.

Stop caring.

"As long as he makes you happy, Sophs?" Jake is now the one analyzing my face, looking a little too closely, which only makes my heart race as though I have something to hide. I wonder now, really, what he is doing. He has that knowing look in his eye, smug yet cool with a hint of "all-seeing" about him. I wonder if he has told Arrick that he thinks Chris is gay but judging by his mood, I guess maybe not.

I have no clue what he is doing or why he would still carry on the ruse for no purpose when it affects his brother, who is his best friend. I also start questioning Natasha's lack of appearance. I was sure she would have shown up by now, yet he is here solo, except for Nathan. Who is also AWOL and more intent on trying to seduce Jenny.

"Umm, yeah, I guess. You know ... you make your own happiness, right? I evade the question as best I can, smiling widely and hoping to make it look like my usual cheeky-faced self. Avoiding any eye-on-eye contact for more than seconds while I find my acting hat and push it firmly back on.

Arrick turns his head a little my way and regards me with a sideways glance, an unreadable look in response to my answer. I look away, scanning the room while downing my champagne, overly aware of how stupid this whole thing has become. How juvenile it is, and right now, I could kick Christian up the ass for making me keep this up.

The lies we tell to keep face. Dumb, so very dumb.

My parents know Christian is gay, my whole family for that matter, after meeting his camp side last night and hearing all about his boyfriend. I doubt Jake's "Gaydar" is that broken. He was chatting to Christian long enough before Arrick boarded the jet to see enough to figure it out. Before the macho mask came into play, Christian implemented his "let's make Arry jealous" plan.

"Right!" Jake lifts an eyebrow my way, sarcastic-toned, and that hint of smile immediately hits home that he knows; he is fully aware.

Jake is being Jake. Smug and Mr. know it all. With an "I know what you're doing" look that makes me narrow my eyes at him. I wonder why he still allows his brother to think that Christian and I are a couple. Giving him a questioning look, he shrugs behind his brother's back, throwing me a little head shake with a smile as if to say, "I have my reasons!".

I don't get it at all.

"I can see my sexy wife looking like someone's making a move on her! I have to go beat some guy into submission and stake my claim." Jake growls, his whole manner swiftly changing, dodging his head to the side aggressively. I follow his line of vision, making out a man in his thirties talking rather animatedly to Emma and Sylvana Carrero in a corner through a clearing in the crowd. Jake is fast moving towards them before I have time to say a word, like a hawk with prey in its sights.

"He never changes, does he?" I giggle as I watch him swoop in on the women with deathly speed. He tilts his wife back dramatically in his arms and throws a passionate kiss on her mouth that most definitely involves tongues and a lot of ass groping. Sylvana slaps him on the back, telling him off for the rather sexual display on his wife, as the man gets wholly uncomfortable and doesn't seem to know where to look. He moves towards Sylvana, says something, and then wanders off awkwardly. Jake, as usual, does not give a rat's ass about any displays like this, only wrapping Emma around him more snugly and letting his hands roam her possessively, giving his mother a devilish smile of satisfaction in response. I giggle louder.

"He was never the jealous type before Emma. I guess that's what "the one" does to your mental state." Arrick replies flatly, looking over my head at his brother and seemingly avoiding looking at me. His party mood has deflated in the last few minutes, and I can almost sense the tension sweeping from him. I wonder if it's because he knows he shouldn't be near me, that his girlfriend probably won't like it, or if he is having some manly time of the month that has nothing to do with me. I wonder if they are fighting, and that's maybe why she isn't here, why he's in a strange mood.

"Do you get jealous?" It comes out before I connect my brain to mouth gear and curse myself inwardly. The last thing I want to know is how he gets jealous over her, whom I assume he is still with, despite her lack of presence. It's been three months of silence, and he hadn't mentioned her once on the plane, not once, and Jake didn't ask either. The way he is acting now tells me there is still "a her" around though. Otherwise, what issue would he have with being near me anymore?

Arrick looks at me for a moment. Those soft eyes homed in rather intensely on me before he breaks the contact and looks away. It gives me the same internal tingles and flips, my body unsure how to react or feel, and I inhale slowly to push it all away.

"I never used to. Not in all the years I fucked around dating loads of women. But I guess things change when it's someone who matters to you. Really matters." He downs another full glass of champagne and discards the glass before stopping the waitress and asking her for something much stronger. She turns and leaves with a nod as he watches her trail off with a faraway look in his eyes. I realize I am staring at him and turn my attention to the people milling around.

"Natasha is pretty. I guess she must attract a lot of male attention." I try for a soft smile, faking the best I can, the urge inside to stay and talk to him, even if I hate the topic. Because for a moment, this is better than not talking and walking away to be strangers again. As hard as seeing and being around him is, it is a lot worse afterward, and I don't want to taint my night just yet. I catch that tense muscle movement in his jaw, the dip of brows, and he seems to sigh quietly. All tell-tale signs that he is not a happy camper either, and I curb the urge to ask him if he is okay.

Stop being weak, Sophie.

"Sooopppheeeeee." Leila bursts in and swamps me with her little naked arms around my shoulders and head against mine, kissing me messily on the face and ignoring my attempts to bat her away. She is already drunk, and I am starting to feel like the only sober person at this do, which is bizarre considering where I was six months ago. I have no clue why I am deliberately this sober still. It hasn't been intentional.

"Leila ... can you please stop." I untangle her lithe body from mine and stand her away from me with a cringe-worthy expression, still not one for overly affectionate touchy feelings from people. Even family. I prop my glass on a nearby table in case she makes me drop it with her over amorous advances.

"The videographer is doing the rounds! I want to see all my

favorites on the floor in ten seconds, dancing to my wedding song. You two get your butts in there and start dancing. Get it going!" Leila pouts at us both, grabs Arrick's sleeve and my arm, and yanks us toward the direction of the polished floor in the tent. Ignoring my attempts to get her off me and pulls us onwards mercilessly with that defiant, sassy little walk of hers. Arrick doesn't seem to object and is casually being led on with no argument.

It's lit with fairy lights, and the sounds of Ed Sheeran are already playing over us in a melodic wave that hits you inside the space. All are romantically set up with floral displays and flickering ambient lighting. She and Daniel have a thing for using his songs at their parties. We have all heard how he wooed her to a Sheeran song when she dumped his ass in a moment of insecurity. I have spent years listening to the uber-romantic tales of my family, my mom being a complete wuss at heart who likes to know every single detail.

I make to protest but fall silent as she lets me go, and Arry's hand finds mine without hesitation. It makes me stop my silent refusal and go almost limp at the unexpected touch. He pulls me with him silently and makes the last few steps toward the empty floor, giving me no choice but to have my hand encased in his. It's like being scolded at the same time as being stroked. The pain, the longing for that touch that sends my insides into a bizarre spin and renders me hopeless.

Looking around to see we are the first and Leila is going to get bitch-slapped from here to kingdom come, I spy the cameraman setting up in one corner, fully focused on us, and know I have no way out of this without causing a scene. I don't want to draw attention to the fact that we no longer know each other.

The now arriving others, as Leila does the rounds forcing couples this way, are soon starting to surround us, and I try my hardest to relax, tell myself this will not be that bad, that I can endure this. I turn towards him when he draws me to the middle and hesitate, swallowing hard, breathing harder when faced with his body edging against mine. I don't know how else to play this except look completely out of my depth.

"Relax. It's just a dance. Sure Christian won't mind." Arrick says flatly, looking over my head as though watching people come onto the floor behind us. I guess he can see or sense my tension. My expression must be one of shell shock. We stand awkwardly before he slides his hand to my waist and tugs me into him softly and slowly. Lifting his free hand and offering it to me, so I get the choice if I want to touch him again or not. I take it without thinking, then stare dumbly at how my hand fits so delicately in his like it always did. It hurts me in many ways, and I bite my lip to curb the urge to cry. To feel so right and so familiar this way, yet we are now worlds apart.

I assume the pose of waltzing, placing a hand in his and the other on his shoulder, turning my face away as I lean into him, so I can at least not look at him. His cheek comes down beside mine, gently against my temple, sending another wave of butterflies through me as he starts swaying me in time to the music. It's not the first time he's danced this way with me. At almost every party we ever went to, we danced like this more than a fair share of times. Just none of them felt as awful as this does. It's agony!

Held against him, feeling his body so perfectly slotted against mine, surrounded by his smell, the way he makes me feel when submissive to his movements. I have to bite down to hold it all in, remind myself how angry at him I should be. Find that inner fire of self-worth to keep my shit together because, at the end of the day... he let me go; the last thing he will ever deserve is my heartache. My heart constricts, but that inner defiant me slaps it down, shaking myself back to the reality that he does not deserve my tears.

As much as I love him, he no longer deserves any part of me. He fucked this up, not me.

"How's school? How's life?" Arrick says softly, right into my ear, huskily close and crazily sexy. I close my eyes, trying not to feel the devastation that deep tone gives me or how my skin tingles in response to hearing it right against me.

I missed his voice.

"Good ... I am doing really well. My tutors seem to love me, and I'm making friends ... real ones." I try to focus on the swaying motions and small steps we're taking in time to the music, not his expanse of chest or submersion into his familiar hold, aware of the crowd of dancers around us now and the cameraman flitting around in a bid to capture everyone. His touch destroys me.

I catch sight of Jake and Emma nearby, nose to nose, as Jake says something to her. His eyes are glued to hers, and she's smiling. Every bit infatuated by him as she has always been, her face glowing with sheer adoration. To me, they are the perfect example of when love goes right, and it just makes me feel even lonelier at this moment. She looks tiny compared to him, but he effortlessly seems wrapped around her, protectively caring for the love of his life and oblivious to anything else when she is in his arms.

Daniel and Leila are further back, swaying. Leila's arms around his neck, gazing at one another cutely as his hands slide around her waist before being firmly planted on her butt as he pulls her pelvis in against him a little more snugly. He leans in and kisses her softly. Despite the sexual pose, it's clear they are as blatantly smitten as Emma and Jake in their own way, and I realize I am surrounded by couples who all found their other halves so easily. The only pairing on this floor with no romantic connection is Arry and me, and it hits me in the stomach like a blow.

I turn back to Arrick, aching with the number of real couples around me. Spying Giovanni with Sylvana and even my mom and dad off to the side. Everyone seems so happy and look so right together. It's like being stabbed in the chest repeatedly while looking up at the one guy I stupidly pinned those hopes on. His cheek is still against my temple, so all I see is a perfect male throat and that up-close smooth skin of a clean-shaven man. My insides wrench themselves into a knot as a wave of pain hits me hard in the chest, and I have to combat my reaction with every ounce of willpower I can muster.

Why did you have to hurt me?

"I'm happy for you, *Mimmo*, really. All I ever wanted was for you to be happy. No matter how you got there." Arrick pulls back to look me in the eye, but I feel it coming and look away, so torn emotionally with that statement and the fact he is still calling me that. Fragile and devastated on so many levels.

A part of me wants to forgive him, return to how we were, like none of it ever happened, and have him back in my life. Yet that broken part of me who is still hopelessly in love with him holds onto anger and pain, and right now, he makes me want to throat-punch him for being this dumb. Always my most volatile when in pain, and right here, held in his arms, is the same as being tortured slowly.

"I am." I bite back flatly. Deadpan in my tone and expression. Not wanting him to see how much he broke me and telling myself I will never let him close enough to do it again, even if it kills me never to be close to him again. He sighs and goes back to leaning his jaw against my temple, adjusts his hold on me, and continues dancing in time to the soft music. We seem to fall into silence. Both are lost in thought for a long while as the music continues with other couples around us. I go back to watching the people around us and try to block out his touch, ignoring his presence while the lyrics to possibly the most agonizing song play around us.

Listening to the words is the only thing I can seem to do to take my mind off the way he is expertly moving me around, lost in his control and unable to do anything about it. Trying hard not to find anything in them to relate in any way and sway in time to the slow beat.

"There's so much I want to say to you ..." Arrick says quietly, so unexpectedly, as the song nears the end. My stomach turns over, glancing up instinctively and catching the sad look he is giving me, the way his embrace gets subtly tighter. For once, a genuinely unguarded glimpse of real emotion from him. With furrowed brows, his gaze locked on me with a look of sheer regret that physically wounds my heart. My already frayed emotions can barely handle it, and I have to breathe heavily to push down the torrent of tears in my chest. I clear my throat to cover it and fumble at any response.

Then the moment is broken as couples begin clapping as the song ends, and we break apart to join in awkwardly, aware that the moment is gone. I look around, anywhere but at him, trying to control myself and my emotions. Head crazily whirring at what I should feel or even say, I know his eyes are on me, I can feel them burning into my profile, but I cannot look back at him. I'm too afraid to show him any hint of weakening resolve. So close to tears, so very close to sobbing and throwing myself at him to make it all better. He opens up every vulnerable part of me and pulls the rug from under my feet. I can't let him, though, and there is nothing he can ever say to make anything about this right again.

Where he's concerned, the wall is up, and he never gets to hurt me again; I am battling my own will to build it faster. He doesn't get to see how he affects me, and he doesn't get to know that I still even care. I will die before I let him know that I still love him.

Once burned. Twice doesn't get to happen.

Christian bursts in before Arrick can say anything else, despite looking like he's trying to find the words. Throwing his arms around my shoulders from behind and kissing me on the cheek by the ear in a rather sloppy way. I try to shrug off the wet, slobbery kisses as I catch Arrick frowning and turning away, that Carrero death glare making a real play on his face. He looks out across the room behind him, catching Nathan's eye, and walks off toward him without another word. I watch him go, knowing this is out of character for him, being so rude as to walk off without even a goodbye or a hello to my friend. It goes against all his normal good grace and manners that he is famed for. I grit my teeth to push everything down and throw on my winning smile as I turn to Chris. Acting like this hasn't bothered me in the slightest, hoping he didn't notice how rude Arry was. Jenny strolls up towards us, from the direction of Nathan, with a beaming smile and rosy glow on her cheeks.

"You both look sexy." I smile, taking in the boy in the black James Bond tuxedo, crisp shirt, and bow tie and the girl in the clingy red dress who looks a million dollars and most worthy of some Hollywood red carpet. No wonder Nathan was keeping her all to himself tonight. She looks very sassy and sexual with minimal effort.

"You did say dress to impress as this was a glam do." Jenny smiles, fingering the detailing on my silver dress. It's knee-length and flapper style with lots of layered sequin and fringing, a high bodice with thin straps, and a scoop back. I've gone for sexy, sparkly, and yet modest. School has taught me a lot about fashion in such a brief time, and less is sometimes, most definitely more. Except where sequins are involved, then you can never have enough.

"We three look like we could take the town by storm!" Christian announces, hands on hips and a little wiggling to make his point. He's had a few to drink, and he is losing his macho guy act, thankfully. I prefer him like this; this is who he is, who I adore, and I don't like the pretend cuddling up with him either. I don't care if Arrick knows anymore. I am getting so tired of the whole charade and how awkward it makes me feel. I want everyone to relax and be who they are, stop watching over our shoulders, and get on with a good night.

"I hope to get through a family party without drama or major drunken antics. Thank you very much. I am still living in repentance for two years of making my parents crazy, and my sister will undoubtedly make an ass of herself tonight." I dismiss the offer of another glass of champagne as a waitress comes by with a tray. Not really in the party and get hammered mood right now. Christian frowns and picks up a glass on my behalf, shoving it into my hands.

"Hell no, we three are letting our hair down and having a blowout night. We have been good as gold in the last ten weeks of school, and I have never been trashed with either of you! That is my aim tonight! Drink up bitches. We are going to partyyy!" Christian raises his glass and downs it in one go. Looking at me with a serious look of challenge in those naughty eyes.

"Christian, I really ..." I object, but Jenny throws her Bambi expression my way with a sudden injection of serious frown and wet eyes on show.

"Please, Sophie. I need this. Mark and I broke up before I left, and I want to forget everything for one night." Jenny's eyes fill with more moisture as Christian, and I snap our eyes on her. Completely gobsmacked.

"What? Since when?" We gasp in unison, equally shocked by this sudden revelation. She has not said a single thing or even appeared even slightly upset in the last two days of being with us. I am shocked that she didn't tell her two best friends before now.

I guess this is how she is; she can be infuriatingly like someone I don't dare mention in that she plays a lot close to her chest and downplays everything as though she appears unaffected.

"It's been on the cards for a long while, we are never really together, and it's taking its toll. He doesn't seem to care. Please ... I don't want to talk about this; can we have a good night and leave all man talk right here on the floor?" She looks at us both with pleading eyes and a hint of desperation. Knowing her as I do, I know she will be happier if we let her talk about this in her own time and do as she asks. I lean in and hug her, feeling like she really should have told me, though, as Christian pats her shoulder as though she were a puppy.

"Three musketeers, babes. We shall drop all man chat, although we can ogle all these sexy butts. I mean, how many good-looking men can you get in two families? Woof woof!" He's almost breaking his neck to watch the progression of two Carrero relatives walking by in all their tall, dark-haired glory, with sexy square shoulders and that hint of Jake and Arrick about them. He has a point.

I notice Alexi Carrero, one of the more mysterious cousins, strolling by with a glass in each hand as he heads towards Arry and Nathan in the corner and catch a smile directed my way. I have always liked him, even if he's more of a formal and distant personality type who rarely comes home. He was always nice to me growing up and has a dependable and capable vibe. I smile back and give him a girly wave. Like most of the cousins, I know them all. They are all equally as swoon some.

The Carreros are gorgeous as a family, and the Huntsbergers are equally blessed. I look over, catching my brother Ben's eye and gaining a loving smile; Rylanne is behind him in all his blonde gorgeousness. I smile back affectionately and give them a little finger wave of affection. I only see them as brothers, but to someone like Christian, they are major eye candy and, I suppose, drool-worthy.

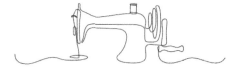

Chapter 5

"Sophieeee, you know I lurve you a million times over, babes."
Leila slurs over the top of me, alcohol breath almost flooring me
with its sheer toxicity, captured in her crazily strong embrace as we
both sway. I'm a little worse for wear too, having drunk one too
many champagne cocktails. The party is wearing down, but Leila is
beyond wrecked and slobbering a gush of emotion all over me as I
try to say my goodbyes to her.

"Baby, come on. Sophs is being suffocated by the fumes coming
off you." Daniel is trying to extract his wife's arms from me and
guide her towards the door, "trying" being the word, as he fights with
octopus limbs to coax her away. Many guests have departed already,
and Leila is being taken home to pass out or get up to whatever they
get up to when drunk and childless in an empty house for the night.
I do not even want to know what my sister and her husband are
into. If I am being honest, the thought terrifies me.

Daniel moves in a little closer, pulling her into his embrace, and
brings her face gently to his.

"Come on, beautiful. We have some drunken sex to be getting
on with, to celebrate another year of marriage without killing each
other." He smiles down at her before planting a kiss on her
smudged red lipstick. Not caring if he is now sporting a matching

shade and gazing at her as though she is still the most beautiful girl in the world. Despite all me seeing is a makeup-smudged hot mess who can barely see straight.

"I know! God, I love you ..." She pauses to kiss him back a little harder, groping him openly in full view, and I turn away, rolling my eyes, used to the naughty behavior of my overly sexed sister and Daniel over the years. Yet it still is not something I want to witness when I am practically attached to clingy limbs. Leila breaks free with a giggle, and another sway my way.

"I just need to make sure my baby sister is okay, you know, cos I love her more than life, and the world, and the earth, and the ..." She breaks off as something catches her eye, swinging under Daniel's arm, she grabs a passing dark suit and hauls them towards us backward.

"Arree!" She chants and startles him half to death with her ninja-style maneuver. Arrick stumbles a little with the sudden backward force, righted by Daniel with a quick reaction. He turns to face us all, completely confused by the sudden assault. It isn't hard to tell he is probably *as* drunk as Leila, unusual for him, well, at least it was three months ago, and the swaying he has going on matches the completely out-of-whack look in his eyes as he clears his throat. His eyes immediately come to me and scan me in one obvious swoop before looking back at my sister. I try to ignore the goosebumps or fluffy internal sensations it triggers and keep my eyes locked on Leila.

"What, Leeloo?" He sways in, bopping her on the head adoringly, and almost bangs noses with her. Pretty much falling into Daniel, who shakes his head in my direction as if to say "drunks." He pushes them apart and keeps hold of Arrick's arm too, to keep him steady on unsteady legs.

"Take Sophie home and look after her. She needs a real man to care for her, not that gay guy she hangs about with, making moon eyes at my husband." Leila is slurring so much worse now, barely coherent, but Arrick frowns, leaning in with a severe "what?" look on his face. My face gets hot, and I try not to react, hoping he assumes my sister is crazily under the influence.

"What gay guy?" He's slurring too, and genuinely confused. Daniel pulls Leila toward the door once more to control her wandering body and throws me a deep frown.

"Christian! He's lovely and all, but Sophie needs a real boyfriend, Arrick. Why don't you love my sister? She's awesome and beautiful, and she adores you. You would make such cute babies and look; we would be like a real brother and sister." Leila grabs his face clumsily and plants a kiss on his nose in a mortifyingly cute, gruesome way. Daniel has had enough and a wary glance my way, which reminds me that he is Jake's best mate for the past twenty-odd years and probably aware that Arry has no clue that I am not dating Christian. I suddenly realize what Leila has said in letting the cat out of the bag, and the tell-tale blush hits my cheeks as it dawns on me that he might get pissed about this little facade. I was never good at maintaining this kind of deviousness and care that he just caught me out, even if I shouldn't.

Shit!

"Come on you." Lifting her and scooping her legs, Daniel is drunk too, but as a seasoned ex-party animal, he handles it much better than she is. I am grateful that he takes care of my fireball sibling, even though she claims she doesn't need him to. Despite a rough start, they ended up being another fairy-tale couple who truly make each other happy, even if it is in weird ways. I am so glad of him at this moment.

"Leila, I'm staying here. I don't need anyone to look after me, and I don't need a boyfriend. I'm fine." My face is burning, aware of the way Arrick is staring at me as if I have two horns, and his gaze has not left my face since she said it. I cannot look at him as heat courses through me, and my heart plays the rhumba, knowing fine well he will probably be wondering why I even carried on with this charade. I feel strangely guilty, ashamed, and a lot mad at him that he will even judge me for this. I hate that I sort of lied, but he did so much worse to me.

I move to help Daniel maneuver my sister to the door, pushing through milling party stragglers and handing him her shoe as it slides off. Staying close to catch her discarding items, like her bag and bracelet, and more than aware that Arrick is right behind me. He seems unwilling to be parted, and I have no idea why he is even following us. I am trying so hard to ignore him.

When we get to the door, Leila hugs me around the head, slobbering a few more kisses my way, unwilling to let me go without a shower of love and garbled sentiments. Daniel expertly disentangles limbs, so I can get free before carrying her off toward home, which is only fifty yards away.

I wave her off with a relieved sigh at finally being free, turning back inside when Arrick grabs my hand, blocking my route with his body and a crazily serious expression on his face that stuns me. He yanks me back outside, giving me no option but to obey, and I'm not sure how I should react. He does not say one word, just hauls me, as though he has a right, into the darkness so that I start tripping with shoes on soft ground. He tugs me towards the side of the garden, out of sight, towards the Carrero house. He moves too fast for a drunk male, and I am hauled with him without resistance. I am too damned drunk myself to fight in any way and have to focus fully on not falling.

"We need to talk," he slurs, a vice-like grip of hot smoothness holding my hand in his, and I try to wriggle it free. The cool air hitting me suddenly makes me realize how much more drunk I am than I thought. My legs instantly turn to Jell-O, and my head gets fuzzier by the second. I try to tug my hand out of his again, but his hold is relentless, and I start to trip over my own feet with every step as he speeds us up.

Damn heels!

"Arrick, slow down, wait!" I'm falling, struggling to keep pace with him in stupidly high shoes not meant for this terrain. He pulls me diagonally across the street from the corner of my front garden towards the house he grew up in. I try to look back and see if either of my friends is milling around near the entrance, but I know it's futile. The last time I saw them, they were both engrossed with other people, in the marquees out back with every other straggling guest. No one else is here.

"Why did you let me think you and he were together?" He spins on me angrily, creating a human wall as soon as he's hauled me down the side of his own home. We're far away from the eyes of anyone leaving the party, concealed by bushes and much quieter. We are in the weird narrow side area of his house, a narrow grassy lane closed in on both sides, partially by tall bushes and completely by a high fence on the other side.

I stumble against him with a sudden halt, going over my ankle and yelping, grabbing onto him to stop myself from going fully down as his arms wrap around me securely to hold me. Arrick pulls me up, straightening me against him, and automatically scoops down to slide my shoes off swiftly, so I stand barefoot on the crisp, dry grass, giving my poor ankles relief. He drops them beside us and straightens up to look me in the eye, still with the same accusatory glare, and my temper snaps.

I shove him off as soon as I regain my balance and glare hatefully at him. So many emotions hit me, rage being at the forefront.

"I didn't tell you I was with him in that way, not once! Don't you dare hit me with this shit!" I spit angrily, annoyed that he has the nerve to even yell accusations at me after everything. That he felt he had a right to drag me here for this, away from my family and friends, so he could have some moral high ground of a go at me.

Who the hell does he think he is?

Fuck him!

Has he forgotten what he did to me?

"Then why would Jake think that? Why would you not want to see me again? Tell me straight, Sophie ... is there someone? Are you seeing anyone? Have you moved on?" Arrick catches my jaw in a firm hold, his angry tone dissipating fast, rambling incoherently as he verbalizes his internal brain mess. His fingers are cupping me along the side of my face and pulling me towards him, bridging the gap to my height as he leans into me, and for a moment, I think he might kiss me.

The past months' hurt, anger, and sadness well up like a dragon inside me. Enraged and seeing red at how much he pisses me off when he thinks he has a right to touch me in any way he likes. I shove his hands off me, pushing him to arm's length so I can breathe, and only let go when he stands away from me, his hands dropping to his sides in mild surprise.

"It has nothing to do with you." I snap, furious at the way he's making me feel. Hemmed in, heart racing and blood pumping fast. Just his touch alone is causing all sorts of an unwelcome internal meltdown, which is trying to slice through the anger and confusion. I am completely out of my depth and doing what I do best. I lash out and fight back at those who try to wound me.

"It does when I can't stop thinking about you, can't stop missing you. I need to know, Sophie, if I blew it ... if I'm too late?" Arrick is focusing on me, intensely gazing into my eyes, but I only see an asshole who thinks he can turn everything around. From angry to whatever this is, sorry, pleading. I don't want to give a shit about him anymore. His words don't heal, they only slice deeper, and I stare at him in open-mouthed disbelief.

You don't deserve anything from me!

"Don't you fucking dare! You don't have a right to do this to me again ... To say this to me!" Tears sting my eyes, and I slap his hand away as he reaches out to me impulsively, shoving him away harder so he steps back again with the force. Arrick's eyes stay on mine, an intense look of desperation on his face, and he comes at me again, hands up as though he can't control the urge to be nearer me. It's not what I need or want from him anymore; it's not fair on me or my heart for him to do this to me again.

"Sophie, I just want to talk, to explain." He starts, his tone ravaged, but I cannot hear this. I don't want to do this. I hate that he's making me do this. I won't go backward and let him fuck with my head and my heart all over again. My insides are close to splitting open and bursting all over the lawn, my lungs feel like an elephant is sitting on them, and my brain is as close to self-combustion as humanly possible.

"I'm not a toy you can pick up and drop anytime you feel like it, Arrick. You hurt me. You chose someone else. You don't get to come back and try again. You don't get back in." I grab my shoes, scooping to bend without caring if my dress flashes my ass to the bushes. Anger bubbling in full fury, heart, and soul ripping apart while alcohol lets all this stupid heartache loose to play like giddy kids in a cornfield.

He catches my wrist and hauls me back to him, but I fight back impulsively, shoving him away again and moving out of reach this time. Panting with effort as my heart erupts in my chest, and my lungs struggle to function. The pain in my gut has me clinging to my arms to relieve it, and I know I am losing control of the aching wave of tears rising in my throat.

"Don't touch me. Don't ever fucking touch me again." I yell at him vacuously, the tears breaking loose and pouring down my face in the final release. Reminiscent of a monsoon and hating that he has pushed me to this, showing him how deeply he wounded me. That inner part of me is trying so hard to fight back, to lift that wall of ice-cold indifference, but damn alcohol has made it near impossible, and his presence has ruined me. I was always useless when I was this drunk, and his suddenly hitting me with this has pushed me over the edge into no man's land, where my emotions run free, ungoverned by me, and my mind takes a long vacation from the "norm."

"Please, Sophie, hear me out. Give me a chance to explain and say what I have wanted to say to you for weeks." He lifts his hands defensively for a second time, as though trying to convince me he will behave and stop trying to touch me, pleadingly, but keeps his distance as I begin pacing around frantically. Anger spiking inside. Fear and heartache are pushing and shoving each other to dominate my heart. Like I am going to self-implode with the battle of emotions, thoughts, and feelings swirling like a cyclone. I feel like he's turning me into some crazy Leila version of myself, and I have no clue how to stop it. The months of forced self-composure and pain all come crashing in on me.

You don't get to fucking do this to me again!

"Why? So you can tell me how confused you are? How you don't want to hurt Natasha? How you love me, but you don't know how to feel? Go fuck yourself! I moved on ... I found a way to deal with things on my own, and the last thing I need is you fucking my head up all over again! Go away." I turn on my heel, in bare feet, tramping back in the direction we came from on unsteady legs, no longer caring about shoes, just the need to get away from him and this all-consuming thing he does to me. Terrified of how much more he could hurt me if I let him.

"Do you want me to beg? I will. I'll beg ... on my knees, Sophie. If that's what it takes for you to hear me out. That's all I want, just a chance to speak to you." His voice is torn, emotion making him sound different. And even though I am stomping away onto the rough ground and ripping my feet to shreds on harsh terrain and concrete on the road away from the house, I glance back and almost sob when I catch him on his knees in the middle of the street, like an instant punch to the gut.

It stops me, as does the fact that he has tears in his eyes and looks completely broken for the first time in his life. I have never seen him look this way the whole time I have known him. So desolate and ravaged. I don't know what else to do or say or how to react.

This isn't him; this isn't the version I have ever known, and I don't like it. It riles up some missing, broken piece of me that aggressively tries to make him stop.

"Stop it. Get up. Don't do that." I yell at him impulsively, hating seeing him like this, not wanting to see my Arry this way, waving my hands in agitation to make him get up. He doesn't get to be this way, on his knees like some sad, broken shell who has to beg. He was always my rock, my stability. The one who stayed emotionally cool when I needed him too. The one who kept me sane and calm. He isn't allowed to be useless and upset and look to me to hold him up. I hate it.

I storm back to him and tug at his jacket childishly, looking around because I don't want anyone else to see him this way. It's not who he is. I hate that he has left himself this publicly vulnerable when he is the last person in the world who likes people to see him as anything but in control. I tug, cry, and yank at him, but he doesn't budge.

He stays put, staring at me like he has lost all ounces of self-preservation and has no reason to get up anymore. It rips my soul apart in so many ways, and I start to whimper in defeat, pleading with him to stand up.

"I want you back, Sophs ... I need you. I can't keep going on like this without you. It just gets worse with every passing day. I can't do it .... I've tried and can't live a Sophieless life." He swallows hard, his voice breaking, his voice barely audible as a tear rolls down his cheek, shrugging dejectedly, and my floodgates open with a vengeance. I start sobbing too, in agony because I am unable to look at him or move away to give myself distance. Breaking because I broke him too. My rock isn't allowed to break. How can I be strong when he isn't anymore?

"I don't want to face a future that doesn't have you in it. I can't live that way. Nothing means anything anymore." He sounds exactly how I feel, and it's too painful to hear. I cover my ears, sobbing, and try hard not to crumble. Trying to block him out, moving to shield my face so I don't see him this way. Willing my ears to stop hearing him and my heart to stop caring about him. He completely ravages my soul.

I slide my palms over my eyes to gain control and calm the torrent of tears wracking my body when I'm suddenly enveloped by heat. His arms find their way about my shoulders. His hand slides under my chin and tilts my face towards him, my fingers sliding away obediently with the shock of his familiar touch. It's almost like he takes full control of my body in its weakened state, and I let him because I don't know how to feel, and I need him to help me. I need him to be strong, cool, and in control because I no longer am.

He steps in close, still as broken, and I can hardly look into his pained face. Unexpectedly, his mouth molds to mine, making me inwardly gasp, his lips crushing to mine in the same excruciatingly perfect way. The instant searing heat and passion consuming from the first moment of touch catch me in shock.

Weakened by a tiny second of hesitation, I let him kiss me. The joining of lips and slightly parted mouths before that good old self-defense system ingrained inside me react, shoves, and slaps out at him like a psycho. Enraged that he would do this to me all over again.

It's not the hardest of slaps I have ever delivered, but enough to snap his attention by connecting with his face and to the fact that he doesn't get to ever touch me like that again. Taking me by surprise that I would lift my hands to Arry, of all people, with a proper assault. He barely seems to register it at all, looks at me with that same wounded, broken expression that claws at my heart and adds another level of excruciating agony to this.

"You lost me. You don't get to do that anymore." I wail at him, pulling his hands off me and pushing him away again, finding his touch unbearable. Pain crushes me, my soul aching and guilt seeping in that I hit him.

I shouldn't care, I shouldn't feel anything but satisfaction, and I fight to stop the regret from washing through me. Arrick numbly stares at me for a long moment, breathing hard, seemingly unfazed by the fact I have left a small handprint on his cheek. It's staring at me like some horrible arrow in the face, telling me I am a violent bitch, as bad as Leila.

What's wrong with you?

"I deserve that and more, Sophie. My life is nothing without you. You have no idea how many times a day I think about you, how much it eats me up every second that I made you leave me. How much I want you back in my life, even if I only get to be friends." He's still sniffing back tears, making my heart ache harder, and I am trying so hard to hold myself together. Guilt added to the list of crazy feelings and emotions piling up in my head. I am close to hysteria and about as near the cliff of insanity as one can get before leaping off.

"You didn't make me leave you. You chose someone else and then told me to go. There is an enormous difference. You can't undo that." I throw back, my voice equally ravaged with raw pain and tears, so it hurts my throat. Losing all the resolve to stay aggressive and angry and becoming increasingly weak and childlike, reverting to the fragility I rarely show. Body in defensive mode and moving back anytime he tries to step nearer, knowing I am letting him see me more vulnerable than anyone has for months and hating myself for it. He looks like he desperately wants to grab me but is trying to keep his cool and give me my space. I know I can't let him touch me, or I will fall to pieces and give in.

"I didn't choose her ... I chose to do the right thing and try to fix all of it. My heart was always with you. It still is. I just didn't know until you were gone that I would never be able to fix anything. I never thought about what would happen if you never let me near again, Sophie. It's killing me. I can't function anymore, and I can't keep living every day hoping that I find a way to see you again." He rubs his hands through his hair, wipes his face, and takes deep breaths as though trying to control his emotion and failing. Every single bit of Arrick Carrero that he is famed for has slid away into oblivion. All the cool, calm-mannered, emotionally impassive, it's all gone, and I'm not sure I can handle him like this.

"What did you think would happen? That I would stick around and go back to how it was? That I would play happy families with you and her?" The manic laugh that bursts through my tears makes me realize how dumb this whole conversation is getting. We're not concealed in the middle of our street; everyone can see us if they want to. I storm past him back to the garden, not even sure why and he follows close on my heels. I don't owe him my time even to let him talk this out, yet I can't stop wanting to hear what he has to say without it being so public.

"I don't know ... I figured I would fix it, have both of you, and no one would get hurt. I wouldn't be the bad guy like my dad when he hurt my mom with an affair. I didn't think it through, Sophie. I thought you would still need me and would still be in my life. I thought our bond would save us. I reacted to what happened and thought you needed cooling off time. I never thought you would cut all ties with me and that we would just be over; I would actually lose you." He stops when I spin on him, complete sarcasm washing over my face, pure disbelief that he could be that dense.

"I did still need you, but what was there for me in that? Why would I stay? I told you I loved you and wasn't going to sit and watch you love someone else!" I shake my head at him, unable to fathom how his brain works, and step away when he reaches for me again. I lift my hands as if to warn him not to touch me. My head is so screwed up. He has me crazily upside down and all messed up that I don't know if I should be laughing, crying, raging, or leaving. I told myself I would never let him do this to me again. I am so fucking stupid.

"I know ... I know that now. It's all I have thought about for weeks. You are all I think about constantly, Sophs. I was stupid and crazy to ever let you go. The biggest jackass in the world. I miss you so much I'm going out of my mind. You have to believe that! When Jake told me you didn't want me to contact you anymore, it almost ended me. He told me there was maybe a guy, and I didn't know what else to do, so I stayed away as best I could. I know I fucked up, that I no longer had a right to be anything to you; I have lived with it every second, every day for months and hated myself for being so fucking dumb." His red-rimmed eyes are focused on mine, still full of tears and nothing but genuine regret. It hurts too much to see. I want to hate him so badly.

"Missed me so much that you just let me go, right?" I turn away, my soul still crushed and tears not subsiding. Hatred and anger are trying so hard to stay with me in a mind that is starting to fall apart.

"No! I came for you when I couldn't handle it anymore, and I saw you with Christian. I felt like my heart was being ripped out of my chest, and I left. I couldn't bear to see you happy with someone else, knowing that I let the best thing in my life go when you offered me everything. You have no idea how much I regret it... I have never stopped wanting you. You're ingrained in my soul. You're a part of me. I made a mistake that has been ruining my life ever since, and if there's even a glimmer of a chance, then I'm going to jump on it because there's no alternative for me. I fucked up everything that mattered when I let you go." His voice, like mine, is shaky and hoarse. Two souls in pain, and yet I can't stop the anger burning inside, even though a part of me is aching to forgive him.

Always torn when it comes to him and exhausted with the effort of keeping this all together. My head and heart are at war between sorrow and rage, and I'm on a precipice between needing him and hating him. I want to believe, to let his words heal and count, but I also can't. Because he tore me apart and left me alone when it mattered. I turn my back to him to give myself a little time to get control, to breathe slowly and calm my sobs, but his warm hands slide over my shoulders, making me flinch and freeze like a statue.

"What makes you think I will even care now? That any of this means anything to me anymore?" I shrug his hands off my shoulders and move further away, so his touch won't sway me or burn me. Wiping my face to dry the soggy mess, I jut my chin out defiantly. Trying hard to regain that fire.

"I have nothing else to lose. Without you, nothing means anything anymore. I won't let you go again without a fight. I know you, I know when you're hurt, you push people away, and that's what you're doing now, so I won't let you do it. I know it's what I deserve, but knowing there's no one else. You're meant for me. You were always meant for me, Sophie. I see that now." He pleads, his tone destroying me, and it only makes my tears fall faster and heavier, unable to dry them.

"Until you think you have me, and suddenly you don't know what you want anymore, right? Or you get a case of guilt again or cold feet. You're drunk. Go home. I don't need this." I sob quietly. My body is trembling with the wracking pain churning inside. My fight is dying because he has me emotionally drained and empty, and my hatred has walked off with a shrug. I'm so lost and broken.

"I love you! I'm in love with you! Every tiny little fiery, hellcat, difficult, yet beautiful part of you. And every part of me wants only you. It's not alcohol, Sophs, it's in me every second of every hour, every day, and it never stops. Anytime I see you, it only serves to remind me how badly I'm suffering. How stupid I am. I knew I loved you as soon as I lost you. That's never going to change. I'm not confused about this anymore. My heart left when you did; I don't want it back if it doesn't come with you attached." His voice breaks, and I look back to see fresh tears on his cheeks, which mirror mine and only strengthen the defiance inside me. I spin on him accusingly, so much sorrow killing me inside that all I have is my fury about what he did to us.

"You're an idiot ... you had me! You couldn't see what was in front of your face. Why would I listen now? Why would I let you have the power to cut me open again? To hurt me as you did, over and over. Just go away. You don't deserve me." I break again, hating everything about this, everything he's saying to me. That inner girl who feels like he will never be able to fix what he did to me because he does not understand how deep the wounds go.

The betrayal. That he made me feel worthless.

I turn away again, unable to keep looking at that distraught beautiful face, knowing I can only hate him when not faced with how much I still want him.

"I know. I have no excuses, only how sorry I am and how much I regret it. And I do, Sophie, I am... I'm so fucking sorry." He catches me and turns me back to him, ignoring me when I slap and shrug his hands off. He doesn't let up, holds on, and keeps pulling me gently, relentlessly, until I finally give in to his tugging and turn, trying not to look him in the eye. I lose all my fight and will as sheer fatigue consumes me.

"Just leave me alone." Tears pour silently down my face, my body giving up on me as everything saps the last ounces of my energy and empties me. There's nothing left. I'm losing my fight, losing the fire, and it's being replaced with a broken mess of emptiness.

"Tell me you don't love me anymore, and I will." Arrick breathes my way, his face crumbling to reveal a world of pain, eyes greener than I have ever seen them, his voice broken. I glance up at him, defeated, my tears continuously finding their way down my face, despite trying so hard to hate him. I have never seen him like this, and for a second, it calms my chaos to a softer hue.

It's not him. It's not who I have always relied on him to be. My strong, emotionally calm rock. I hate that I have made him cry. I hate seeing tears running down that flawless face. I don't want to see him cry.

"Stop it." I plead, trying to turn away from him, pushing his hands down as he keeps returning to hold me again. He's not giving up, clinging to me, and making it clear he won't back down or walk away. He has that stubborn Carrero air about him, and it's only tearing down my defenses. Reminding me of the boy who dragged me out of myself so many years ago when everyone else had given up trying to break through.

"Tell me that you no longer feel anything for me, and I'll walk away, Sophs. I'll leave you alone, knowing you no longer see me that way. That I really did lose you." He urges me. His heart on his sleeve and voice raw, and I want to tell him I don't give a shit anymore, that I don't love him, but I can't.

I don't want to say words that aren't true, no matter how much he deserves them or how much a part of me thinks it's what he deserves to hear. I want to hate him, hurt him, wound him for every second of pain I have endured at his carelessness with my heart. I can't because I'm not that way, and despite all he's done to me, I still love him. I never stopped needing or missing him, despite all of it.

I shake my head at him involuntarily, almost as though answering, even when I try to tell him to leave me alone.

"Why are you doing this?" I plead brokenly, willing him to stop torturing me and release me so I can go back home.

"Because I need to know, I need to hear you say you don't love me anymore, in any way. I can't risk missing even the tiniest hint of hope that I can get you back." His moisture-filled, almost green eyes penetrate mine with so much fear that it almost kills me.

"You're an asshole. You don't deserve my love." These are the only things I can say as the gulf of tears open up again, and I end up sobbing in front of him, crumbling inside at where we are and how we got here. So much pain I have been bottling up for months that I refused to let out for fear it would never stop, and it chooses now to come tumbling out. I close my eyes and cover my face with my palms. He comes around me and pulls me into an embrace, his arms tightening around my waist and shoulders, his face finding its way to burying into my neck. He almost squeezes the life out of me with a hug so strong I can't breathe.

"You're right. I am an asshole, Sophie, and so much more. I am so fucking sorry for what I did to you... to us. There are no words to tell you just how sorry I am. How much I regret every second of this. I love you, that's all I have, and I mean it. One hundred percent, hand on my heart, I will swear on the lives of everyone I care about that I love you, Sophie Huntsberger. In the way you once told me you loved me." Arrick grips me tighter when I try to push him away, crying hard, unable to stop it, and unable to fight the arms on me. He isn't letting me go, no matter how hard I push, and it exhausts me to try. The wetness from his face against my neck and his shallow breathing prove he is as emotional as I am. Crying against each other for the pain caused by each other. It's ridiculous in a really sad way.

Why did you have to tell me you loved me now? Why not months ago before you ruined me?

"Don't do this to me." I plead softly, unable to reign in my weeping, breaking apart in his arms, unable to control the fight of fire and sorrow and losing my war. Arrick lifts his face to mine, pressing his forehead to me, pulling me so I can't look anywhere but at him through a haze of blurry tears. Every ounce of battle armor slid away, weakening and exposing me.

"I need you ... I want you back. I'm a mess without you. I love you so much that I can't breathe anymore, and I want to be worthy of your heart again. If you let me in, I won't stop trying to put the pieces back together. Let me come home to you." He's equally fragile, begging me, and I do not know how to react. I'm torn to a million pieces, fighting an internal tug of war of fear, hurt, and confusion.

"You hurt me! You broke me, and then you left me alone." Is the only thing I can whisper, accusingly, crying not subsiding as his thumb comes to brush my face, and I impulsively push it away. He doesn't break his hold, brings his hand back, and tries again, patiently. This time I don't bite back and let him wipe some of the wetness away, closing my eyes at his familiar touch and hating that it still feels so right on my skin.

"I know, baby. I despise myself for every part of that and what I did. I'll never hurt you again. I'll never leave you alone again, I swear. Just give me a chance, please. Let me fix this. Let me try, Sophs. I'll do anything. I love you. I *really, really,* love you. An all-consuming 'lost to everything but you' kind of love, which I will never recover from, and I don't want to recover." He pleads softly, but I keep my eyes closed to block him out, trying so hard to control everything, letting loose. Unable to think straight when he is all around me, consuming me, and I don't have anything left inside of me. Emptiness and excruciating cramps are coursing through my stomach and churning me up inside.

"I hate you." The way it comes out sounds so juvenile and Sophie of old. I sob brokenly with no real conviction, as though I'm saying it to him after a stupid squabble or idiot thing he's done in the past.

"I know you do." He whispers softly, tilting my face to him with little resistance, and leans his forehead against mine. Testing to see if I will push him away again, but I know I'm weakening. He's always been the only one who got through my pain and helped me get past it, even though he's the cause now, and I want him to make it all stop. I want him to pull me from the dark and find the light once more, wipe away the agony like he has done so many times in the past.

His mouth finds mine softly, cautiously; his lips warm and soft as they meet tear-drenched skin. His nose comes to nestle beside mine as he presses us together, my body held tight in his embrace, and this time I do not react with rage. I let him kiss me softly, slowly, finding my mouth and lips opening to him despite every voice in my head telling me to push him away.

I am so confused as to what I want. He feels like my dreams. His kiss holds the possibility to push away so much pain, and I want to stop hurting. I'm lightheaded from the amount of emotional turmoil racking my body and still swaying from being too drunk, and nothing in this seems like a bad idea anymore, so I let myself go.

His hand finds its way to my throat, cupping gently, fingers sliding into my hair as he maneuvers his body around me, his height lower as he tries to get every single part of him in contact with my body. Holding me against his mouth so the kiss neither stops nor progresses. It's like he is breathing every part of me in, holding me here to imprint me to memory, and I give in completely.

So lost to how it feels to be back in his safe embrace, every familiar thing about him surrounding me and begging me to give him a chance. I have always been defenseless when it comes to him; yielding is like breathing when he asks for it.

I melt into him, my mind a whirring mass of confusion and fear and my own will telling me to push him away, but I can't. Arrick is my weakness, he has been since the day I met him, and all fight and anger dissipates as his hands slide around my face, cradling me in and teasing my lips open with his own. I surrender to the soft, warm sensation of the perfect kiss I could imagine. My hands slide around his neck as something inside me ignites, and I surely kiss him back.

Arrick seems to take my submission as a sign to let go, pushing my mouth open and caressing my tongue with his, the fire between us spiking and moving into an almost immediate fever from nowhere. We are fueled by everything we have brought to the surface and months of separation, loneliness, and heartbreak. We both cling to one another, kissing passionately, moving into something more satisfying than mouths moving in unison.

The arms around my waist tighten as he pulls me up against him and off my feet, as my arms and hands wrap around that strong neck and wide shoulders, tangling my fingers in his shirt collar and trailing nails up the short-cropped hair at the back of his neck. I lift my heels behind me in mid-air. Losing myself in him this way is the only thing I want to focus on, a break from my exhaustive and whirring emotions. Consumed by a hunger that obliterates everything else, and I don't want it to stop.

We're both panting, kissing hard when I flinch at the hard, stone surface against my back as he presses his body against me. Having backed me into the house wall, it seems to free the animal in me without warning. As though every thought and objection dissipates, all I have is a burning desire engulfing me. My fingers carelessly rip at his bow tie and push his buttons open at his neck, discarding it with no care about where it lands. Arrick moves from my mouth to my neck, trailing nibbles and kisses along my throat, sending my fever pitch sky-high as I angle to let him have full access, weakening physically to the burning touch of his mouth on my throat.

My legs find their way to slide around his waist of their own accord, and my dress rides high, so I am molded fully to him. Arrick's strong hands hold me up under my thighs as his body presses me flat against the wall, concealed by garden shrubs. His body feels so good, his mouth scorching me to insanity, and the aching burn between my legs pushes all my demon buttons as I claw at his shoulders to get his jacket off.

A car passing close by alerts us that we are still outside, very exposed, and shamelessly dry-humping in a place anyone could stroll. Snapping attention back to reality as he drops me back on my feet, headlights skim above our heads over the bushes as he stands in front of me to conceal me from anyone nearby. Arrick doesn't say anything. He's breathing hard and lingering close to my mouth, his pupils huge with sheer lust and mouth poised, ready to kiss me again. He slides my dress back down around my thighs, holding onto me, staring at one another for a long breathless moment as he puts me to rights. I gaze at the mouth I want back on mine, how he feels against me, and ignore the voices trying to break through this haze of horniness.

"I want you more than anything I have ever wanted, all of you, baby. Let me show you how much." Arrick's voice has some strength again, all thoughts of talking this out, fixing mistakes made, pushed aside in the face of this rampant hunger. We're both too fueled by champagne, burning with passion to think beyond the physical. I nod, completely unable to formulate words anymore as desire consumes me. Willing to follow him anywhere as long as his body is the reward.

Arrick moves into my mouth again, seemingly unable to stand the distance, kissing me as passionately as he can, hands ravaging my hair and throat to keep me close as humanly possible. I can't withstand his kiss. How it makes me feel, from inside out, an ache and yearning, burning to an almost unbearable fever pitch.

His tongue finds mine, pushing us further into kissing that leaves no misinterpretation of how much he wants to have sex with me. His hands move down to cup my breast as he pushes against me, my own work inside his shirt, unbuttoning as I go and revealing that expanse of hard naked torso and tattoos. He presses a knee between my thighs, the pressure making me writhe and grind back to him. We both know where this is heading, and I don't hesitate about whether I want it.

He slides his leg further between my legs and moves in against me, seductively teasing me sexually as his muscle rubs my softness. I let out a soft moan that seems to send him over the edge. I can feel his rock-hard arousal pressed into my pelvis, a real sign that Arrick is as sexually turned on by me as I am by him. Insanely so, and something inside me seems to take this as a sign to lead. Inhibitions dissipate between us. Sliding my hands down to his waistband and pulling the button and zipper open as he still kisses me into panting submission. I slide my hand into his trousers, seeking him out with no fear, no repulsion, just a dreamlike haze of drunkenness telling me how right this is and not to question it in the slightest.

I encircle him, shyness evaporating instantly because I know I now own this part of him, unsure if I am even doing this right but want to try. I gently caress his erection cautiously with inexperienced hands. Empowered by my hazy state, fueled by his instinctual responses, his tongue still in my mouth, and the subtle moans that start reverberating through him. The sense of power and sexiness it gives me fuels me with adrenalin, and I tighten my grip and slowly slide my hand up and down.

Arrick groans as I increase the pressure of my hand. He gently bites my bottom lip and sucks it into his mouth. His tongue traces my lip erotically before he captures me once more in a full-mouth kiss, teasing me relentlessly with the kind of passionate kiss I only dreamed I could enjoy. He slides my dress up from my thighs, one hand smoothing between them to seek me out, the way I sought him out, exploring between them until he skims the outer lace of my panties, grazing my heat and softness.

The touch sends a million tingles sweeping through me, so tantalizingly good that my legs almost give out as heat and an ache consume me. I push into him, urging his hand to explore more, but he pulls back instead. Bringing his forehead to mine and stilling my hand by grabbing my wrist. I don't want him to stop and give my emotions a chance to catch up; the consuming confused haze lingering nearby is only silenced by his kiss, which threatens to consume me again.

"Not here, not like this. You mean so much more to me than this." He pants, his voice husky and low, his voice not familiar this way, and it only makes my body vibrate with the sheer longing to have sex with him. Arrick slides his fingers into mine, pulling me with him towards the back of the Carrero house, and leads me at speed along the back wall under cover of bushes and overgrown roses. Glancing at me and stopping every few steps to kiss me again and run his hand under my dress and over my thigh.

Everything happens so fast. The fast-paced walk to find the back entrance and then high tailing it into the house in complete darkness while his hands and mouth are all over me, pulling me to him and walking backward within his tight embrace. We make out, fumbling, groping, teasing each other mercilessly while moving through the house swiftly. It's empty because his family is still in my parents" house. Eerily silent and illuminated only by moonlight.

He stops me at the foot of the marble stairway to kiss me seductively, his fingers trailing over my breasts and his tongue probing my mouth sensually, pushing me into complete surrender. I groan and cling to him, seeking out his manhood through his pants and tracing him, feeling bolder with every passing touch and kiss he lays on me, shocked at how much of him I can feel in his pants now that he is all mine.

Arrick picks me up, distracting me from my thoughts about his size and wrapping my legs around his waist as before, but this time he carries me upstairs. Fast scaling them while holding me close and keeping my mouth occupied with his so that I don't even realize when we reach the top in seconds.

He takes me to his bedroom amid bites and kisses along my jaw, neck, and mouth. Exploring how many ways he can kiss me and always gets an instant response, adjusting to him in every way. He doesn't seem to have an end to how many variations of kisses he has perfected, and I am completely lost to him and that sensual mouth.

All thoughts of anything but him on me have left my head. I never imagined it would be this way with him when he finally let up and kissed me without limitation. I realize how much he held back before, anytime he kissed me in the past.

We enter his room amid a flurry of passionate kissing, frantic groping, and the unbuttoning of clothes in a frenzy of horniness. He manages to maneuver me inside the door, pushing me up against the wall as he shoves it shut and continues making love to my mouth with his own. Both of us ripping off one another's clothes, drunkenness throwing all sense and caution away, and caught up in the sheer desire to quell the burning lust between us as the room spins and sweeps around me. Arrick puts me on my feet so he can drag my dress over my head, only breaking away long enough to pull it off and coming straight back, hand skimming my body and sending explosive tingles in every direction. He reaches around, unclips my strapless bra, and slides it away, expertly tossing it aside without a second glance as his eyes stay homed on what he has just uncovered. He devours me with a look before sweeping back to capture my mouth.

His mouth trails to my neck, my exposed shoulder, and my breasts as I arch against him. His hands smooth down to the edge of my panties and slide them down. He stops again as he gets them low, stooping to take them off, waiting as I lift one foot at a time, extracting them fully from my ankle, and the whole while, I find myself letting him do this with no sense of inhibition. It's as though I have completely become submissive to him, with no war raging inside or a sense of self-preservation. Stupidly trusting him because I want it more than anything, and I know he will guide me gently. There's no fear or repulsion, no trauma holding me back.

Soon we are both fully naked. He discards his clothes quickly, neither finding any shyness or awkwardness because neither is anywhere near sober enough even to care. I swear I am drunker than I was in the garden, and everything is starting to swim around me with a headiness that has me feeling a little unsteady and fragile.

I am having trouble processing the tidal waves of emotions coming at me from all angles over this. My body is yearning, burning up, and screaming for him, despite years of abhorring this kind of touch. My head is torn in two, only quietening when his mouth is on mine, screaming when it's not, that I shouldn't be letting him back in this easily. I should be fighting him. My mind's a mess, my heart's prickling and swaying one way to the other, and I cannot think beyond his touch.

I want nothing but the feel of him, the way he touches me and makes me moan as his hands and mouth move to my most intimate parts as he slides down my body to his knees. Still leaning against his bedroom wall, unsure how to behave or react, he lifts one of my legs behind the knee and bends it up to open me to him. I obey, watching the top of his head move in against me, unable to do anything but breathe heavily and watch in slow motion as his mouth connects between my thighs unexpectedly. I don't even know what I thought he would do, but I gasp in pleasure at a sensation I've never known and become completely engulfed in the need to be joined to him when it renders me useless.

I almost convulse as hot, warm wetness slides between my legs, a unique goodness that has my body erupting deliciously with prickles and flutters while his tongue probes and smooths within and around me. I gasp, tingling and writhing as I adjust to this alien sensation. He sucks me into his mouth and makes every part of me crumble. I groan loudly, grabbing his shoulder tightly with one hand to hold my weight as my legs start to give and use the top of his head, gripping my fingers in his hair with the other. Arrick's hands hold my legs stable to keep me up as his mouth does things that have me wriggling in complete ecstasy.

He makes me pant out, overwhelmed with a wash of sensation that rumbles up from my pelvis like a crashing wave. It starts as a tingle and has me cry out almost immediately as it comes upon me out of nowhere. A full body clenching of explosion.

So suddenly and so crazily responsive, clawing at his hair and shoulders as my body wracks and spasms with warm pleasure I can only identify as my first orgasm. I've heard enough from other girls to know that's what this is. I fall to pieces with the huge convulsion of fireworks that happen within me at super speed, turning me into incapable mush as I collapse on him involuntarily. I'm pretty sure making a girl cum in less than two minutes is some record for any guy, and whatever he did to me only makes me want so much more. It blew my mind, and my body is left tingling with the after-effects as it slowly dissipates, leaving me completely breathless. My weight held up by his strong arms.

I'm panting in the afterglow, my heart racing, my body sizzling, and unable to stay upright. Arrick remains between my legs until the spasms subside, and I realize his palm is flat on my abdomen, holding me to the wall as my body gave out on me. Keeping his mouth in motion throughout the convulsions before finally breaking free. t. When he lets my leg down, I almost fall over him, relieved when he scoops me up in his arms and carries me to the bed.

I'm suddenly less than useless after what he did to me and completely pliable under his expert hands as I slump out deliciously. He lays me down on my back on the cool sheets before carefully climbing on top of me, positioning himself over me and between my legs. His mouth is back on mine, so I can taste what I assume is me in his mouth, and I don't know whether I should like it or be disgusted. It causes a weird sensation in my stomach pit, yet no sense of dislike or fear.

Arrick lifts me under the thighs and slides me further up the bed, so he is fully on me. Pulling my knees up around his hips as he lowers on top of me to connect our bodies again. He still kisses me, moving to my neck and breasts and back up again as he captures my mouth. The room is spinning wildly, my chest aching as the walls start to close in on me so suddenly, and I grip his shoulders and try to focus on his face.

With him on top of me, his larger body is pushing against me. The darkness is hiding his face from view now that we are no longer near the window and the light. I begin to feel unsure. Like some deep terror that used to happen whenever men got near me, it starts to uncurl deep down, despite me begging it not to.

The anxiety that always circles around me seems to notch a gear higher as drunkenness and the realization that I am about to have real sex hit me.

I don't know if I am ready for this, I haven't had time to prepare, and so many emotions about him are making my head ache with confusion. Everything is swirling around us, even though I am still kissing him back. Still sliding my arms around his neck to find his face and bring it to mine in the darkness. I need to see him properly to help me relax once more.

His hand moves between my thighs, and I arch to him in hopeless response to how good it feels. My brain releases so many conflicting thoughts and feelings as he slides his fingers inside me slowly. I experience the pleasure of his touch, how strange and yet satisfying it feels, while at the same time, the crushing weight on my chest increases and fights against my head. Sending me into instant panic mode that I may have a real anxiety attack.

I try to look at him, but he ducks his head to kiss my throat, sucking, nibbling, lost in his lust-fueled haze of drunkenness and only thinking of sex now that we have gotten to this point. I start to breathe in rapidly, trying to push the weight away and release the pressure in my lungs, trying to claw back some of the control back to my brain and tell myself that he wants more than this.

That he won't disregard my feelings to satisfy an urge.

This isn't just sex. This is more. This is Arry.

Arrick pulls his hand from between us, kissing me on the mouth, and I manage to lock eyes for a mere second before he slides into me. No warning, not that I expected he would give me any. And I gasp and cringe as he penetrates me, slowly and surely.

The sensation is alien, nothing like my memories of burning pain, revulsion, shame, and devastation, and I inhale sharply at how new this feels. It feels completely different and in no way connected to the vile memories of my destruction as a child. This is good, body achingly good, yet the weight in my chest increases and knocks the wind out of my sails. My head spins with many flashes and memories as Arrick fills my body with a part of him.

I close my eyes tight, breathing hard, clinging to him as he moves into me, sliding in fully like I'm being filled up to my stomach and suddenly unable to stop this. I'm impaled, joined, and no longer in control as he thrusts surely between my legs. It doesn't hurt. It's causing the same pleasure and tingles, only with more intensity than his oral attention. I can't stop my mind from starting to unravel.

I start to panic, realizing how unable to move from under him I am. My body his to do with as he pleases because I let him get full control of me so effortlessly. Trying so hard to focus on the fact it's him, how good it feels, despite the chaos, that despite the heartache of the past months, I should trust him. But I don't - not anymore, which makes me afraid.

I lost a piece of my heart when he crushed me, and in turn, he took that trust from me and left me all alone. I may be willing to let him devour my body physically, but my heart is backtracking in terror that I don't trust him enough to do this to me. Not anymore.

My body moves with his, in and then out slowly. Finding a rhythm between us that heightens every sense and makes me pant, moaning in unison as pleasure overtakes me because him making love to me does feel physically good. Yet, my mind is starting to wildly claw me away from the feel of it and into a mental agony. His face is buried in my neck, so I can't see him, only feel him, and I try so hard to stay tuned to how he smells, how his skin feels against mine, and not fall into that pit of fear hovering beneath me. I'm losing to myself and retracting into my dark, lonely mental space. That cell where I used to hide.

The motion makes me claw at his shoulders and back, waves of pleasure pulsing to desperate levels, but I can't let go and relax. All I can hear is the heavy breathing, feel his weight on top of me, my head jumping back and forth to other dark rooms and places, and a man who held me down and made me endure this, and I am suddenly suffocating. Losing my tiny grasp on my reality, the alcohol making this much worse.

I turn my head to try to block it out and find some inner peace, but I can't. The goodness is dying as I lose a grip on the reality of my surroundings, and instead, fear and panic are gripping my insides so that I am no longer pulling him to me but pushing instead. Arrick's face is buried in my neck, oblivious to the torment going through my skull as he pushes faster and harder into me, groaning as he does so, and I can't take it anymore.

It feels like he has disconnected from me, that he's inside me, but all he wants is the end goal, to fuck me and leave me here like the broken mess I was when I met him. Like he's using me for a vile and dirty release.

I know none of that makes sense, but I can't help it, I'm losing control of all of it, and I am left open and vulnerable with another man who only wants to get inside of me, to use my body as a vessel for his perverted end. My sanity scatters in the wind as my past collides and pushes reason out the door. He is as good as holding me down this way, and I let him. I stupidly let him have me, to control me in every way to do with and use as he pleases until nothing is left.

He hurt me, he left me, and now he won't even look at me as he uses my body like I'm a dirty whore.

"I can't ... breathe ... No ... No!" I gasp out in panic, fingers clawing his shoulder and pushing him up, tears finding my cheeks and losing all sense of reality as my head gets lost between memories, and I no longer know where I am. Darkness overtakes me with one last weep of chaotic fear, and I lash out at the evil trying to break me.

My father pressing down on me, covering my mouth to gag my tears to silence as he rapes me brutally once again.

* * *

"Sophie ... Sophie? Look at me. Come back to me." His soft voice brings me back to my senses, and I realize my legs are closed. My tense body held rigidly and curled up in the fetal position. He's not inside me anymore, and somehow, I'm being cradled in his arms, my face turned away from him, gasping for breath. His arms are around my upper body as he cradles me tight against him and strokes the hair back from my tear-stained face.

"Just breathe, slow and steady. You're safe. It's me. It's Arry. You're safe with me." I zone back in, realizing I am gripping his arm with deadly intent, my nails digging in, yet he doesn't seem to care.

My face is soaked, and I am so dizzy I can barely get my head together. I don't know where I went or for how long I went there, but the taste of blood in my mouth shocks me, and I'm confused and scared. My whole body is shivering with waves of cold rushing through me, and I'm aware of the full vibrating shakes, both inside and out, which are consuming me. I am wound tight like a coil but feel exhausted, as though I have just run a marathon. Every limb is aching painfully. I'm covered in sweat.

"Where? What? I ... I ..." I don't even know what I am trying to say, breathing hard and coming to. I'm still in his bed, surrounded by him with a sheet over us. Not in a dirty room far away with a mattress on the floor. Not held down or hurt or restrained and gagged. His nose against my cheek as he soothes me, trailing fingers down my face, still trying to hold me, so I calm down in his embrace.

"Shh, now, it's okay. I'm not going to do anything to you, baby. Just calm down and relax. Breathe, Sophie. I stopped. I'm not going to do anything to you, I promise." Arrick's voice calms me a little, his arms around me, holding me steady and bringing back so many warm and calm feelings from his familiarity.

How often has he gotten me through my attacks, fears, and nightmare memories?

That's what this must have been. A horrifying flashback where I was caught in a past reality and fighting for my life.

I turn on my side away from him further and curl up smaller to feel safer. The pose of my childhood after many a time my body had been used and discarded. Arrick cradles me close, his breath against the back of my head, his heat surrounding me like a balm to everything.

"I'm so dizzy." I cry quietly, unsure how to explain what just happened or why I am crying. Not knowing why I even have blood in my mouth. I suck in my lip and realize I have cut it. The little lumps along the inner edge feel like a bite mark, and I realize this is what I used to do to myself back then when I was trying to close off my brain to what was being done to me. Inflicting pain to make myself divert from what I was enduring.

"Just close your eyes and sleep. I'm right here. No one's going to hurt you ever again. I will always protect you, Sophie. I'll only hold you and stay close, nothing else. I swear." Arrick softly soothes me again, his head leaning against the back of my skull and pulling me back to how many times I used his arms as my haven. I close my eyes and take a deep breath, calming myself as fatigue hits me hard, still vibrating all over yet finding comfort quickly in his security. He holds me tight to still my body.

"I thought you were him. I couldn't see you. Where did you go?" I inhale hazily, whispering, my head coming around in a circle as a flash of memory reminds me of where I was a moment ago. Arrick's arms tighten around me; his mouth brushes over my temple as he kisses me softly. Smoothing the hair from my face again, like he always did.

"I was right here, always right here. I'm sorry, baby. I never knew you hadn't done this. I always assumed with the men you dated ..." Arrick trails off, his voice ravaged with emotion, and I can only shake my head as sleepiness overtakes my brain.

"Never let any ... because I'm broken. No one wants a broken girl." I cry softly, sleep taking over despite emotion trying its hardest to consume me, mentally and physically done for, and I am lost in a dreamlike state. My body is shutting down to relieve me of the trauma I just experienced. His body around me is all I know as I begin to slip away into the darkness again, only this time, it's peaceful darkness. Not invading monsters, and I want it to take me. To soothe how I feel.

"I do. I always have, Sophie." Arrick's voice is the last thing I hear before nothingness relieves me from everything.

Chapter 6

A loud buzzing noise rouses me from the hazy darkness when I realize I am in a bed that's not mine. A familiar arm tossed casually across my waist, and sheets pulled up over me to my chin. Confused and disorientated, I blink my eyes open, blurriness clouding my instinct to be concerned, and begin looking for the god-awful noise with a groan.

Arrick groans next to me, reaching out to smack a nearby alarm clock and sending it crashing to the ground. Only the noise perseveres, and the next thing to meet the hard floor is his cell as he swipes it off into the room, bringing silence once more.

I sigh, a moment of relief, followed by the sudden realization that I am in bed with him. His bed, in his old room at his parents" house, and completely naked. Filtering through snippets of being kissed, lifted up, undressed, and "oh, my God," he had his tongue on my ...

I woosh awake fully, in utter shock. My eyes snap open properly as I turn my head to get a complete eyeful of toned and tattooed shoulder concealing half of his face, which is very still. His eyes still closed, despite killing the clock and his cell. He sighs heavily, shifts his head, so he faces away, and tenses his arm across my waist after a moment, as though suddenly realizing he has someone in bed with him.

Touché.

I pause, holding my breath as last night filters through my sleep-addled and still-drunk brain. That immediate pang of anxiety at the memories I conjure up and knowing this will be awkward. It seems he, too, has suddenly been reminded as his hand tenses again across me. He suddenly lifts his head, turning my way and blinking as he gets his bearings, looking half asleep and still drunk. His hazy eyes focus on me, looking very brown this morning, and his face crumbles to a frown.

"Fuck!" He mutters in alarm, drops his face back into his pillow, pulls in his arms to cradle his face, and lets out a frustrated moan. He scoots across the bed and starts fishing down the side for what I guess is the cell he launched a moment ago. It's like being sucker-punched in the heart, and I react as though he has done just that.

"Gee, thanks for that." I snap. Despite the room spinning, I throw back the sheets and jump out of bed angrily. Slamming around to find my discarded dress and underwear, which were thrown around the room in last night's crazy entrance. A combination of rage, hurt, and complete fucking disappointment in myself for ever believing in him again, has me stamping my feet and acting like a psycho fueled with rage.

"Sophie, I didn't mean it like that." He croaks, pulling himself up to turn. Seeing me naked and storming around the room, he looks away again with another moan.

"Jesus, Sophie, cover up, for God's sake. I can barely function as it is, and that isn't going to help me in the slightest." He groans louder, dropping his face back down on the pillow and grappling with the sheets to try and wrap around his nakedness, using his face as a lever while he lifts his torso to pull it around himself.

"Fuck you! Weren't complaining when you got me naked last night!" I snap again, a flicker of memory coming back at me, but still elusive. This time tears sting the back of my eyes, and emotion threatens to choke me. Consumed with an agony that feels like glass shards tearing through my soul. I feel so fucking dumb. I should have known that last night was too good to be true, and here we are, back to square one, and I'm waiting on him to tell me it was all just another mistake.

I search for my panties but cannot locate them, giving up and continuing with my dress, sliding it over my head hastily, concealing my body. Arrick manages to haul himself up, wrapping the sheets fully like a toga around his waist before turning my way once more, a look of relief that this time I am dressed as I still search for my bag and shoes.

Where the hell are my fucking shoes?

"I didn't mean it like that. This is ..." He is cut off by the shrill tone of his phone ringing again, and he curses under his breath. His face is a picture of complete bewilderment, looking around until he finds his cell on the floor under the edge of the bed. He reject buttons whoever is calling as I locate my bag by the door and see my bra under his side unit, stuffing it in my bag roughly. Glaring at him angrily, feeling stupid that I even woke up here with him after telling myself I would never let him close to me again.

I feel like such a fucking idiot.

He moves as if to say something, but his phone bursts into life once more. Whoever is calling is persistent and desperate to get hold of him. He sighs, looking down at the screen in his hand and then back at me with an imploring look. He hesitates, does a double-take from cell to me, and then looks like he may cry while I keep glaring at him as though I detest every single tiny part of him.

"I need to answer this. Please, wait, gimme a second ... it's Natasha." His voice drops dramatically, and I almost bawl, right there, in that second, as it confirms my worst fear. Natasha is still a factor, and nothing has changed except disastrous drunken sex, which he clearly regrets. If we can even call what happened that.

I dreamt last night of fighting and lashing out at an attacker in the dark and found myself encased in arms and legs as he tried to calm me more than once. I don't know how much was a dream and how much was what happened in my moment of zoning out or if I had slept fitfully and he had kept consoling me.

"Go to hell." I spit, emotion catching in my throat, so my voice sounds strangled. I turn on my heel and storm for the door, turning to say something scathing in departing, and pause as he holds out a palm, miming for me to wait and be quiet, and I realize he is already on the phone. It only angers me more, as if I am a dirty little secret he is trying to hush up and boss around like he has any goddamn right.

He can go fuck himself.

"Tasha, hey." He says softly, still motioning at me to wait frantically, but I only shake my head at him in utter disgust. I look him up and down as though I am seeing him for the first time and don't like what stands before me. Rage and broken aches tear through me at speed, making me feel dirty and worthless in one fell swoop.

He just cheated on that girl, and here he is, soothing down the phone as if nothing has happened.

Fucking dog!

Like most men.

I turn and haul the door open, not waiting to hear it close before stomping towards the stairs barefoot. I don't care that I have lost my shoes and probably look a fright. I have to get away from him before I stab him with something in the face. If I could find my shoes, then both would be firmly implanted in his skull about now anyway. I descend the stairs at furious speed, not caring who may see me at this early hour anymore. I am done being a secret.

As I reach the front door, I flinch at him calling my name, impulsively looking up despite myself and cursing about it as he comes after me hauling on jeans, concealing his nakedness. Making a bad attempt at trying to button them up while rushing my way. He is still barefoot and topless as I reach for the front door handle and pull it toward me, angrily scowling at him with a serious "fuck off" glare. I hate the ground he walks on and drag the heaviest pit of pain with me as I go. There is nothing he can say anymore; I fell for it once but never again. He turned out to be a lying scumbag, just like the rest of them, and I learned a valuable lesson about men.

None of them are worth it.

"Don't open the door!" Arrick yells to me as he gets to within two steps of me, panic all over his face. I frown at him and ignore anything he asks of me anymore. I turn as the sunshine hits my eyes with the sweep of the opening door and make to walk out, stopping dead in my tracks. I come face to face with one very shell-shocked and morning-fresh Natasha on the other side. Almost like being instantly punched in as I reel back slightly with a gasp and a heart lurch. The last person I expected to see while fleeing my sordid cheating asshole of a one-night stand.

A great start to my day, coupled with what happened upstairs. Everything sinks to my toes, and that big slap of "he did it again" overcomes me.

It is as though time stops for a moment, Arrick coming to a skidding halt beside me while looking from me to her with utter silence. The wide-eyed devastation on Natasha's face as she looks from me to Arrick in obvious stages of undress and parting ways the morning after. I'm numb, unable to formulate words, and stand dumbstruck. A serious sense of déjà vu and yet no longer guilt at seeing her. I'm too empty to feel anything except that hard, thumping ache that started in my core and is spreading out to consume me, like a heavy pounding heartbeat that hurts. I will not wait for another Arrick speech on how he is cutting me out of his life for her to salvage the seriously broken shit that they call a relationship.

Good riddance to both.

"Really?" Natasha squeaks his way, tears forming fast and falling down her face as she rounds on him with heartbroken accusations. I roll my eyes, realizing she deserves it if she keeps taking him back like a weak woman who would rather keep a cheating man whore than be without him.

That's not me in any way.

"Tash ... I ..." Arrick seems at a loss for words, looking at me and then Natasha, repeatedly with an expression and pallor that suggests all blood has dropped to his toes. I push him back with a flat palm on his hard muscular chest. Slide between the two of them at the open door and make to leave with barely a care anymore about what this does to her.

"This is between you two. I'm out. Go fuck yourself, Arrick." I snap, jumping onto the first cold concrete step as a warm hand latches onto my upper arm and halts me mid-motion. I stumble back, only to be met with another hand grasping my other arm to steady me, and I instantly start struggling in a fury to get free, using my clutch bag to slap at him over my shoulder.

"Natasha, go to the kitchen so we can talk. I'll only be a minute." Arrick seems to have regained some strength in his voice and sounds more commandeering than remorseful as he pushes me further outside to the next step effortlessly. He follows me out as the other girl walks in, avoiding my face and crying silently to herself like a pitiful puppy.

Still, there's anger at how pathetic she is, and I glare furiously as she passes. Hating her with all the venom I used to possess for her. He waits until she has stepped inside, turning to watch her as she gazes back with a tear-flooded face. I stand my ground, defiantly crossing my arms and tapping my foot while trying to control the demon in me from flipping out and smashing his skull with my clutch bag. Whatever he has to say will be lame, meaningless bullshit, and I have no clue why I am still standing here.

"I just need to talk to her first ... Go!" He nods towards the kitchen door behind her, watching as she turns to look that way and pulls the door shut to conceal her inside. I'm surprised that she would allow her boyfriend to have a cozy chat with his one-night stand, to be honest, and be so accommodating about it.

There is really something wrong with that girl.

He's still grasping one of my arms tightly even though I have stopped doing anything except icily hating on him from my frigid pose as he turns me towards him. My impulsive self is defensively poised like a stealth ninja. My arms are across my chest, and I lift my chin defiantly to meet his gaze.

"We will talk. We need to talk. First, I need to deal with her, then us. Sophie, this isn't what you think. Just give me a chance to get my head straight. I am still so fucking drunk, and this is like a punch in the face to wake up to." He's trying to pull me close to him, to bring my face to his with gentle fingers cupping it, but I shove him off, his hands dropping when faced with an angry fireball version of me. Even Arrick knows when to leave alone, and I'm guessing the blood-curdling look of rage on my face is more than a threat. I glare at him, my heart breaking, my head a mess with confusion, and tears brimming that he could do this to me again.

"Go run after your girlfriend, like you always do, and let me go." I turn on my heel before he can reach for me again, knowing how close to breaking down I am, but his voice halts me.

"She's not! She hasn't been for over two months, Sophs. Please. Give me half an hour to deal with her, and then I'll come to find you. I meant everything I said last night." I stand rigidly. My body paused as his words filter through, unable to formulate a reply as every emotion under the sun courses through me. I won't fall apart; I won't let him keep torturing me this way. "Please, *Mimmo* ... We need to talk about last night. Where we go from here." He sounds so genuine that the stab in my chest feels like death.

"Don't call me that, don't ever call me that again! Do what you always fucking do ... put her above everything and leave me the hell alone, just like you did before. It's what I expect. I can take it this time. I'm a big fucking girl who knows better than to ever trust you." I snap, turning on him aggressively, not caring if I have stupid tears running down my face. I don't wait for a response as he looks stupefied. I turn and storm off in the direction of home, hearing his front door open.

I guess I got an answer without asking a fucking question!

As much as I hate it, my heart responds to him, and it near kills me with pain. It makes me storm harder and faster across the street, not caring if everyone and their dog can see me doing the walk of shame. I want to go home and strip him from my skin, never to let him near again.

I don't know if my friends even made it home last night. The last I had seen of them was on the dancefloor before Leila dragged me off for sister hugs. I am still drunk, feeling rough as hell, and the tears begin flowing freely again despite myself. My body is aching and tingling all over because I cannot get the feel of him from all over me. I hate him so much that it hurts everywhere. Even my toes and fingers are aching with some new method of internal torture. I may even die from this pain or have heart failure.

Something catches me from behind unexpectedly, making me gasp in fright, too stunned to react, and I am spun to face Arrick right behind me as I hit my parent's drive. Lashing out to take down my attacker, but he catches my hand mid-slap and pulls me tight to his body. I realize he has a T-shirt and sneakers on now and looks like he ran here, panting, wild-eyed, and a little messy around the edges, like he didn't even look in a mirror.

"I choose you ... I always will choose you. I have always chosen you, Sophie. It wasn't a case of not wanting you. It was a case of trying to do the right thing for everyone involved. I will always run after you, no matter what. I won't ever make that mistake again." He looks devastated, a little out of breath, and seriously afraid, but I let my anger explode at him. So sure he can win me around with fast words and a shitty half reason for her being here like I am as pathetic as she is.

"I hate that you make me feel this way and hurt me every time I stupidly let you. I don't want to talk to you. I want to stop feeling anything anymore. I need you to leave me alone. You fuck me up every time I let you in." I start sobbing, words coming out hysterically as I wave my hands around, pushing myself away from him. Arrick catches my wrist and pulls it into him, grabbing the other wrist too, bringing them both together between us so he can hold me still.

"I'm not going to keep hurting you, Sophie. I love you. I meant that. Please, come upstairs so we can talk. I'm here. I'm yours for as long as you need. I'm not going anywhere. She can wait. She doesn't matter." He pleads, panicking, his eyes trained on mine and his body bending down to me, his voice gentle and trying hard to bring me back to him. He lets go of my wrist, so he can run a thumb over my cheek to remove some of the falling tears, but I slap it away. My hand stings with the collision, and I glare at him more defiantly.

"I told you. I'm done. You don't get to keep doing this to me." I sniff back tears, yank my other hand free and turn on my heel, turning my back on him to walk away. Confusion is crashing through me again, and I want to get out of this emotional rollercoaster he always throws me on.

"I'm not going to let you go this time; you can fight, run, and push me away. I'm not going to back down and leave you again. I'm never going to leave you again. Life has no meaning without you, Sophie... I regret every second of every minute that I let you leave me, and I've spent weeks trying to figure out how to breathe without you. You're stuck with me whether you want me or not, and nothing you say will change that... Last night proved that you still love me; that is all I am betting on right now. That's my tiny glimmer of hope, and I'm going to cling onto you like a dying man, Sophie." Arrick's voice breaks, and I freeze, tears pouring down my face as my heart thuds through my chest at his rush of words. I stay still, like a marooned stone when the tide has gone out, staring at the house looming above me as he moves closer. Unable to think straight and am caught as my heart chooses to stop my feet from moving while my brain tells me to run fast and far away.

"I know I have a lot to answer for and make up to you. All I need is a chance to talk to you sober. Time to tell you everything. Please?" His breath tickles my cheek, my resolve weakens, and I get angry at how pathetic and weak I am. That I am even considering letting him win me around and listening to him to cure the pain he causes me. Natasha appears in my mind's eye to serve as a reminder and a taunt.

I'm as pathetic as her.

"What about her? Sat in your mom's house like a good little puppy?" I bite, anger and agony colliding, and that age-old feeling of guilt where Natasha is concerned, finally winding a path to my conscience. I guess it was delayed with shock at the house, and now it's sunk in that she is here. I am starting to get the inklings of shittyness where she is concerned again.

Sometimes I hate my own head so much.

"She came because she needs a friend, nothing else. She doesn't matter in this. You're all that matters to me right now ... I'll explain everything. Let me come inside, or we can go somewhere else." Arrick tries to turn my face to him, but I pull away. So much mistrust for him and an inability to think rationally when he gets too close.

"So, talk. Right here." I pout, pulling my arms across my chest defensively, chin up and glaring across the gardens to keep my eyes away from his. He wanders into my eye view, coming to the front of me a little more confidently, and I hesitate.

"You can yell at me for this, but needs must. I'm not doing this in the street, Sophs." Arrick steps in front of me, confusing me as to what he means, then shocks me by bending down and throwing me over his shoulder. I start protesting right away, wriggling and fighting him, trying to haul myself off and slapping at his shoulder and back, but he just ups and starts carrying me towards my parents" house. Steadily sure he has a right and marches me to the door in easy strides. Not stopping to knock, he opens the door and immediately starts heading for my room via the sweeping stair to our left. So used to this house that he has no fucking shame about barging in.

"Put me down, you asshole. I hate you so much!! You have no right to even do this to me. Put me fucking down!" I yell at him, okay, scream more like. Catching sight of my mom walking across the hall in her bathrobe and looking our way. She seems as confused as I am, takes in that I am wearing last night's dress and no shoes, then turns, hums a song to herself, and walks off. Like Arry hauling me around during a seething, screaming match is not a big deal. I almost shout after her in an utter angry rage.

Thanks, Mom ... Real fucking help.

"I'll put you down in your room, you can go crazy at me there, but we are talking privately. Not out there." Arrick doesn't sound anything except normal, even with me wriggling and fighting to get put down, and his stubborn stronghold keeps me captive.

"FUCK YOU!" I scream so loudly it rasps my throat painfully as we get up the stairs and closer to my bedroom. He doesn't respond, carries me in, turns and shuts the door, and locks it before sliding me to my feet and moving to get out of my way fast. He darts sideways because he knows the explosion that's about to erupt. Obviously expects a retaliation, and for once, he isn't as dumb as he seems.

I lash out like a hellcat who has just been released from a cage, flying for him in full fury as he dodges me, darting backward on infuriating fast feet. He keeps dancing around out of my way, holding a hand on my head to keep me at a distance and dodging every swing and kick I aim at him. I would make Leila the crazy tornado proud with my fierce, violent attack as I chase after him.

"I hate you!" I scream in rage. Tears dried up and fury in place, getting frustrated at him that I can't maim him in any way. Aiming slaps, midair kick swipes, and flying hands at him getting psychotic. I pull his hand off my head and storm to the nearest set of shelves. I pick up the first object, a small trinket of a fairy on a tree stump, and throw it at his head in sheer rage. Arrick ducks, with it whizzing past his head at speed, smashing on the wall behind in an anti-climactic end. He stops to smile at me, a wicked glint in his eye and maybe a little amusement.

"I knew you were going to be mad, but Jesus, Sophie ..." He ducks again as another figurine flies his way. Looking less smug as he realizes I am standing beside more than three dozen potential missiles. Each is getting bigger, and I intend to use every one. His smirk fades.

This time he dashes forward, grabbing me, trying to hold my arms behind my back as I aim for him with bites instead. My legs move to kick at him, lost in the rage he's caused. Crazily explosive and looking to hurt him an ounce of what he's done to me in the past months and not caring if I feel guilty about this later, it will be worth it. Months of pent-up hell come out in one mental turn, unleashed. Arrick blocks my legs with his knee, quick with defensive maneuvers given his training, bends down, and stops me with a kiss.

Pushing his mouth to mine, kissing me with intention and cooling my jets completely as he tugs my arms across my back snugly. It's not a passionate, tongue-caressing kiss, but it hits the mark and renders me mute in the blink of an eye. Calming the tidal wave of insanity and making me surrender to him on every level with minimal effort. I hate that he suckered me this way and exposed a severe Achilles heel. Finally, he pulls free and regards me for a long moment.

"I'll let your arms go if you promise to calm down, take a breath and hear me out." He gazes at me imploringly, swallowing nervously, and despite myself, I stick up my chin in defiance. I nod. My heart is hammering from exertion, and my brain is trying to take control, but I am so spent. Breathing heavily and panting. The exhaustive outburst has taken what little energy I had left, and another bout of attack won't be effective in any way.

"Fine."

He waits for a second to see if I mean it before releasing me, and I pull my arms across my chest again as he does so. I turn away, taking on a stubborn and angry pose when really, I am scared that he's just going to deliver another blow to my wounded soul. Arrick moves back to give me space, moving to my bed and sitting down. Breathing a little excessively too and looking completely shattered. He pats the space beside him, gazing my way, but I only scowl at him and meet a resigned frown.

"I love you ... I am in love with you. I fucked up and screwed everything up because I was scared and stupid as shit. I made many wrong choices concerning you because of how much I thought I would lose, and I have spent every second since regretting it, Sophie. I lost the only thing which ever mattered to me in all of it. You have to believe that. I meant all of it." Arrick stands up again, obviously hating that I am still standing here like a statue. Anger brims inside as he gets closer to me. I turn on him aggressively before he can lay another hand on me.

"Why should I believe you? Where were you? Three fucking months since you asked me to leave your apartment. Where the fuck were you?" I yell at him, tears finding a fresh wave and rolling down my face. Even when I thought I had no more tears left to fall. He reaches for me impulsively, but I step back away from him and pull myself into a tight huddle, wrapping my arms around myself. He pauses and waits, realizing I am severely defensive and touch will only make me worse. He appraises my body language and expression, so fully focused on my eyes, with so many emotions on his face it's weird to see. The cool and calm poker face is gone, and instead, a guy who is seriously struggling to stay in control.

"I came for you. I did ... I swear. Three weeks after you left, I realized how badly I had ruined our lives, Sophs, like I told you. When I couldn't function anymore with not seeing you. I came to try and do this then." He reaches for me again and clenches his fist, pulling it back in frustration at not being able to touch me, but I stay glaring at him coldly. My heart is torn with the many things he still has to answer for, there is so much my heart and head want to hear before I can even contemplate forgiving him.

Like why is she even here if she is nothing to him?

"And?" I snap, not understanding why he's saying he came when he didn't. I had not seen or heard from him at all in all that time. I would have seen him, spoken to him, and maybe even been able to forgive him if he had.

"I saw you with Christian outside your apartment. I didn't know he was gay, and to me, it looked like you had found someone else. You looked happy. I knew I didn't have a right to fuck any of that up for you, even if I was there to try and get you back. Jake already told me that you didn't want me near you anymore. I didn't know how to react." Arrick turns away and back again like he has too much energy inside of him buzzing about and needs to release it. I stay still, scowling at him, so unwilling to let him past my wall and hurt me again, afraid to take anything he is saying at face value while I know she is sitting in his parents" house across the street.

"So, Natasha left you, and you came after your second choice? Yet because I wasn't alone, you gave up so easily." I turn my back on him and go off looking for a box of tissues, trying so hard to keep the tears at bay and failing. I am bristling with so much that I cannot even dissect how I feel about anything he says.

"No. She would still be trying right now to claw back what we had if I let her. She wanted to keep trying. She wanted to fix it and go back to how we were. I couldn't do it. I couldn't stay with her. You were never the second choice. You have always been the one for me, even when I couldn't see it. I felt like I had severed half of my soul and had nothing left to be happy about ... I never gave up on you. I saw you happy with him and knew you deserved that more than I deserved you. I screwed it up. I wasn't about to mess up your life again; I only wanted you to be happy, even if it wasn't with me."

His answer makes me stop, holding my breath, a strange calmness overtaking me at last, and I wonder if my seriously broken wall of defensiveness has finally come into play.

"Go on." I turn back to him and frown, watching his eyes on me wherever I go. Impulsively wiping away my tears, not that they have stopped flowing, and watch him warily. Strangely surreal and empty inside.

"I couldn't exactly make her forgive me for something I didn't even regret. And there was no way in hell I could stay with her when you were all I wanted. I was pining for you every second I was around her. All I thought about was you. This constant weight in my chest has been a reminder every second that I'm nothing without you, Sophs." Arrick swallows hard, his eyes glazing over and subtly clutching his t-shirt at his heart for dramatic effect.

"You are my biggest mistake, Sophie ... Letting you go was the single stupidest thing I have ever done, failing to see what you are to me. How much I need you." Arrick bites on his bottom lip and swallows hard, curbing his fragile emotions and sighing heavily. Watching me like a hawk as though looking away will sever his chance with me.

Suffocation hits me hard again, tears prickling my eyes as my heart constricts, and I lose that relieving sense of nothing that was all too fleeting. I can't look at him, turning away as more make their way down my face and curse this stupidity. I know I am still drunk, and half of this reaction is because of that and my emotional exhaustion. Trying so hard to stay strong, but he is saying everything I ever wanted to hear, breaking me apart in so many ways that I can" stay strong. I turn back to stare at him, unable to say anything while my head is this much of a wreck. Arrick sees my silence as a reason to keep talking, closing the gap between us.

"I don't deserve you ... but I will fight for you in every way I can. Do anything to be the guy who deserves you again." I turn from him when I can't control my tears anymore, not wanting him to see how badly this is ripping me apart as he gets closer, afraid to let him in. He comes behind me, unable to stop my sadness even when I feel his hands on my shoulders, and my traitorous body sags back against him.

"She's only here because she needs a friend. After I broke up with her, her dad was diagnosed with cancer ... he's dying, Sophie, and she's a mess. I couldn't just cut her off. I'm not that guy, I have never been, and I can't be cruel to someone who never deserved any of this. She knows we're over. She knows it's because I'm in love with you. She knows we're not getting back together, even if I never get you back. I asked her to come here and see my family this weekend, to get her away from the city and her problems. I never thought anything would happen with you, and waking up to the realization that she was arriving while we were together in bed ... I didn't know how to handle it... That's what the "fuck" was all about, not that you were beside me. That was pretty much the happiest moment in my life." Arrick sounds tired. Hell, I'm tired. I don't know what to think or feel, and I can't seem to get a handle on my feelings or this dumb crying. He turns me to him and cups my shoulders gently, bringing my face to his so we're mere millimeters apart and looking equally lost in this moment. Two people so afraid of each other - him in case I reject him, and me in case letting him in again kills me.

"I don't know what to say." I finally sniff, sighing as he slowly slides them down my arms, sending a million goosebumps in their wake, and sighs at me with unconcealed adoration. Now I am calm again and no longer staring at him with unconcealed hatred.

"That you want to try with me. Just give me a chance. That's all I am asking for. A chance to be with you ... It's what I want more than anything in the world." Arrick's eyes come to mine, so uncertain, and I see real fear in him for the first time. Something I never thought I would see in him, ever. That I could hold the power to wound him the way he hurt me, and for a moment, I am not sure I want that responsibility while my head is still so messy.

His phone rings in his back pocket, breaking the moment between us. He pulls it out, frowns at the screen, and slides it back with a heavy sigh that signals, "please, not right now." Before it goes, I catch sight of her name on the screen. Guilt and decency hit me in the gut, knowing I should be the better person for once. I may be sobbing in his arms about what he's done, but she's sat alone in his family's home, breaking her heart over more than him. I hate that despite my fury in life, I am this soft sometimes.

"Answer it. You can't leave her sitting over there indefinitely." I move away to give him room, but he only follows me when I make my way to the bathroom door.

"You matter more. I'm not leaving you ... not when I've only just got you back with me." His eyes rest on mine, a look of complete honesty, his hand coming to stroke my cheek with his fingertips. He seems to devour every inch of me with his eyes. I swallow down the uncertainty and cup his hand in mine reassuringly, pulling it away gently with a need to have some headspace. I need a little alone time to let all this filter in.

"Answer the phone. At least tell her you will come over soon or something." I glance away from him, hating that she's there, but hating knowing she is probably alone with her pain. Knowing why he is here with me if she knows how he feels. That can of weird worms concerning her and how I feel about her, rising once again to confuse the shit out of my brain.

Arrick hesitates, looks at me for reassurance that it's really okay, and kisses me on the forehead lightly. An old affection that knocks me off-kilter, another sweep of threatening tears that only reinforces the fact I need space from him to think. He ponders me a little nervously, then answers the phone when it starts to ring again, all the while staring right at me with apprehension.

"Hey... Yeah, I am." He frowns at me, then turns and walks towards my window and looks outside, obviously feeling hugely uncomfortable now that he has answered it in front of me and giving us space. "I'm sorry, Tash. I never thought this would happen. You know I haven't seen her." He sounds agitated yet remorseful. That cool tone is coming through now, and I watch him for a second, letting all my feelings bubble together for a moment.

There's a long pause as he sighs again. Part of me is grateful that he isn't hiding the call or what he's saying from me. He could have left my room for privacy but chose this.

"That will probably be for the best ... I'm sorry it happened this way ... Don't ask me that. I won't tell you either way ... Yes, I'm still with her now." He leans against the window, sighing, so he casts a breath down the glass and then draws in the cloudy space while listening. Absent-minded to what he's doing.

I smile softly, stupidly, when he writes an "S" and draws a heart around it like some love-struck teen, then lets it fade away, oblivious to the fact that I can see him doing it. It warms my insides a little because I know he isn't trying to be cheesy, it was impulsive while he was distracted, and for a moment, I believe that he means everything he keeps saying. Maybe, they are more than fast words to win me around.

I watch and listen, my head all over the place concerning him, and I realize I am still standing in my crushed dress and last night's makeup and have probably looked much better. I need some space from him like I intended, some time to get my emotions in check, to let all of this sink in for a few minutes, and just be still.

I walk off towards my bathroom and catch him looking my way with a half-smile and a warm look that translates so much. He seems like a guy who's found his long-lost something and can't believe his luck. It makes me feel heavy inside, so much lying on my head. I turn and point toward the shower and get a nod in return. I need the space to get my head together and leave him to do whatever he is going to do while I figure out if I can let him back in.

Chapter 7

Wrapped in a fluffy robe after a hot shower, I stare at my clean face in the bathroom mirror; it's tear-stained and pale. I downed painkillers before I got in here to combat the beginning of a hangover and feel completely wiped out. I don't even know if he is still in my room or has gone to see Natasha, and I am not sure how I feel either way. I'm crazily disconnected inside, that none of this is real and no closer to a decision.

I still love him; I can't deny that. Last night was incredibly stupid and most likely alcohol-fueled. The during was not exactly how I thought it would be, but part of me knows it's because I no longer trust him like I once did. He hurt me in ways that screwed my head up and last night proved I no longer felt secure to let him have access to every part of me.

A combination of emotional turmoil, anger, drunkenness, and the first time I attempted sex with anyone. It's no wonder my head went into a meltdown, and my lip is sore this morning from how I bit it. I still can't remember where I went or what I did, but I guess I probably freaked out. Like I used to do years ago, and he calmed me down the way he always did. I don't even know how to broach what we did last night. He's probably wondering what the point is in chasing a girl who can't even have sex with him.

Not that I would blame him.

Pulling myself together, I head out into my room, pulling my robe tight and preparing myself for the empty space that will probably await me. Even I know he wouldn't leave her sitting over the street indefinitely, especially while I spent thirty minutes in the bathroom avoiding him to get my head out of my ass. He's too considerate at times, too caring about her, even though they are no longer together.

I'm so confused about what I want. I want him, yet I don't. I'm terrified of letting him back in to hurt me, especially with her still hanging around, but I miss him like crazy, and I know I still need him.

With him gone, there's the hope of one day never feeling anything again, but I know I will probably never find anyone else who gets me the way he always did, the way he does. This isn't how it was supposed to be, and I am not sure he even really means any of it. I've lost faith in him, and it's bumped my self-esteem into submission, leaving me feeling insecure and torn. I'm not sure why I don't believe him, but maybe I am scared, and all of this will fall around my head as it did before. I'm afraid to hope.

I wander out, looking down at my robe as I tie it, sighing at the silence of my room and realizing he's no longer at the window or even anywhere in the space in front of me. I turn to face my wardrobe and jump with fright at him lying on my bed, watching me.

"I'm sorry. I didn't mean to scare you." He rises to a sitting position, looking exhausted and not the usual pulled-together Arrick I know. He's still in the same clothes, rumpled and unshaven, so it's clear he never left the room while I took an age in there. For him to show these many signs of tiredness, it must be bad, and I feel guilty for a second.

"I thought you would have gone?" I try to keep the pain out of my voice, but my words came out hoarse and shaky. Walking away from him towards the unit across my room where I keep underwear to get away from him and hide the fact that a shower hasn't helped me figure anything out.

"Everything I want is here." He says quietly. I pause, ears

picking up yet still afraid to tell him that maybe I want him too. That perhaps I want to see if this can work. Somehow admitting any of it is opening myself up to him fucking me over again, and I am so not ready to do that.

"Natasha must be pretty lonesome by now?" I carry on emptily, unsure if I am trying to start a fight or push him away instead of answering. He sighs and slides off the bed to his feet to walk towards me, my body stiffening as I anticipate his getting closer. Tensing before his touch gets to me, as I know it will only weaken me more.

"She is going back to the city. I'll talk to her when we go home. There's not much I could say." Arrick sounds pained, clearly hating that he is hurting her still, but certain about where he needs or wants to be. That tug in my stomach aches a little more, and my confusion only deepens.

"So, what now?" I blink up at him over my shoulder as he closes the gap between us, brushing tendrils of damp hair from my cheek and gazing at me with such tired eyes.

"That's up to you, baby. I told you what I wanted. I just need to know if you want to try." Arrick swallows noticeably, fingers tracing my cheek, eyes glued to mine for any hint of an answer in my face. Clearly nervous. I can almost feel his heart rate through his chest, his slightly labored breathing. He mirrors me in every way. The fear the uncertainty that this person who holds your heart also holds the key to destroying it.

"Don't think you can just win me over with fast words and kisses after everything. Don't think last night is not an issue either." I turn away stubbornly, catching the smile forming on his face as I do so. My response tells him he has more chance than he thought he did.

"Drunk fucking you was not exactly my shining moment, Sophie. You should have told me that you had never ... We didn't even think about a condom." Arrick frowns at me, concern etched on his face, but all I can focus on is the fact that he doesn't seem to care that sex was a complete failure. He's still trying to get me back despite it.

What's wrong with him?

"I'm on the contraceptive injection for my period pain, so you can strike that off your list of worries," I respond numbly, brain a mass of jumbled words, tetchy and bristling with agitation.

"I guess that's a relief. And I'm pretty sure neither of us has anything else to pass over. I've never had unprotected sex with anyone else, and if you haven't been near anyone..." He brushes my hair from my face again and frowns harder as he catches my expression.

"Why are you acting like last night wasn't a failure?" I bite suddenly, frustrated and upset, head reverting to chaos, pushing his hands off me as that itchy, don't touch me feeling takes over my skin. I'm irritated so suddenly because I'm mad at myself and my inability to be normal.

"Because it wasn't. You think I don't realize that you don't trust me anymore? That it plays a huge part in what happened. I never intended to get you naked and in bed, but it happened, and it's obvious that you aren't ready for that. I have a whole lot of groveling to do before I get back your trust ... to touch you that way. I don't care if it takes ten years, Sophie. It's not why I'm here. I'm here because I love you, and life without you beside me is pretty fucking desolate. I want you any way I can get you, even if that means we never have sex again." Arrick's voice breaks a little, his eyes misting as he pulls me back to him, stroking my face and turning me to plant a kiss on my forehead softly. Staying against me for a long moment, somehow cooling my wounded pride.

"Why do you want someone that's broken?" I look away from him as tears fill my eyes, unable to feel comfortable showing him my vulnerability, but I can't stop it. Exhaustion is making me overly sensitive, and I could use sleep. I don't feel the same way around him that he used to make me feel, and I know it will take time to get that sort of comfiness and dependency back.

"You're not broken ... you just require a different kind of handling and understanding. You're like a specially shaped puzzle piece that needs the right slot to fit into." Arrick reaches down and takes my hand, pulling my fingers to his chest, and presses my palm over his heart with concentration, etching that cutely furrowed brow. His eyes are a soft hazel, and he looks content for once. "This slot

... A perfect fit." He smiles, sounding strained, struggling to keep his voice steady, equally emotional, and trying hard to reassure me that I am what he wants. I watch him steadily as another stray tear rolls down my face at his comparison to something I once called myself, falling to pieces inside, a tiny crumbling of that wall, yet nothing but fear grips me.

"Give me a shot. A chance to undo what I did, to make this right. I know I can make you happy. No one knows you the way I do. Pretty sure no other guy in the world is as crazily in love with you as I am or ever will be. You're the other part of me, two halves of a whole. Pieces of a puzzle that belong together." Arrick slides his arms around my waist and pulls me to him, meeting no resistance and butting me right up, so every part of our bodies mold as one, and I have no option but to look him in the eye.

"Maybe Christian?" I smirk through my tears sarcastically, looking at his chest to avoid the way he's gazing at me with utter infatuation. It's what I wanted, and yet now it's unnerving me because I should feel surer than I do if this is the road to happily ever after, but all there is doubt and apprehension.

"He was so close to getting a beating about fifty times. I swear if he didn't turn out to be gay, I probably would have broken bones to feel better." Arrick smiles too, pulls my face to his, and leans in cautiously. Seeing no resistance, he bridges the gap, touches me softly, lips meeting gently, and slowly kisses me. I kiss him back, arms finding a way around his neck of their own accord, and open myself to him, lips parting and responding to the sweetest caress. Letting my instincts take control to find my way since my head isn't doing that great a job.

I finally break away and push him away gently, aware that I am no longer ready to give all in anymore; a part of me is guarded and unwilling to give him too much. He has much to prove to get back into my heart and my head fully. I'm too bruised.

"I need to get dressed. Give me a few minutes." I smile softly at him, pulling away to create space and bringing my robe tighter around me like a protective shield. Arry watches me with a serious expression and a hint of understanding before he sighs and waves me away.

"Take your time. I need to lay down and stop this room spinning for five minutes, or I'll be no good to anyone." He moves back to my bed and slumps ungracefully on top of my unused white comforter, pushing fluffy pink cushions aside as he wriggles in to get comfy. Making it clear he has no intention of leaving me. I frown but also find myself smiling unintentionally. The man who has been absent for months now seems incapable of leaving me be for even minutes, and I guess, in a way, it's what I need. I want this from him. Being left alone will only give me time to convince myself to tell him to walk away, and maybe my pride shouldn't be so fast to dismiss this.

I turn to my walk-in closet and head towards it to get dressed quickly. Pulling on a short jersey dress and leggings, I stand to stare at my shoulder-length blonde hair and big bright blue eyes, no longer seeing a child gazing back from my makeup-free face. In the last few months, I seem to have aged a little, maybe it's fatigue and my hangover, but I do not look as childish as I did. Perhaps it's my hair, the slight weight I lost from not eating properly when I was living in heartbreak, or maybe real turmoil adds years to a girl. Or maybe it was from last night and taking steps onto the path to sex, but something in me has changed.

Emerging, I realize his breathing has become deeper and slower, as though he is asleep, and I hesitate about disturbing him. Not sure if I should leave him be and eat downstairs because my stomach is practically assaulting me from hunger pangs. Walking around the side of the bed to where his face is exposed, I catch him looking at me, fully awake and seemingly lost in thought.

"Hey." Arrick sits up before pulling himself up, sliding down to stand beside me and towering above me while I'm still barefoot. He leans in and kisses me delicately on the forehead. Coming so close without physically touching me, still aware that he doesn't have the right just yet. An unspoken rule that he knows that touching is a privilege and not a given.

"Hey." I smile shyly. Trying to look at those deep soft eyes and not let my head run a hundred miles an hour again with all the craziness still mashed up in there.

"I was thinking about you, about us." He reaches out and softly strokes back a single strand of hair from my eyebrow. He tenderly lets his fingers trail down my cheek when he moves it, then leans in to rest his forehead against mine.

"And?" I frown up at him. Trying not to go weak at the knees with his touch, my resolve weakening with every moment I am around him, despite myself.

"I think we should go get breakfast and maybe find your friends and Nate and let this lie for now. I can only start proving that I mean everything I say with my actions. You don't owe me an answer, baby. Not until I prove things to you. I'm not going to pressure you, just be around if you want me to be." He gives me that cute boy half-smile with full dimples, and I can't stop myself from doing it back; it's infectious when he looks this way. Like he is lifting all pressure from me in one swift move, I suddenly feel more able to take a breath and relax.

"Sounds like a good plan to me. I need time, Arry ... and I am pretty hungry." I can't seem to look at him for long, shyness crippling me, an awkwardness that I can't understand, and I hope it's down to being overly emotionally tired. Maybe it's the months of separation, as surely, I can't be this shy with a guy who had his mouth between my legs last night and very clearly made me climax. I still cannot get that memory out of my head when I glance at that sensual mouth and wonder how he could be so gifted and so completely hot. My mind causing my inner body to heat up a little, surprisingly, and I cough to clear the sudden urges that hit me low down, feeling inappropriate suddenly.

"Food was always the way into your heart, *Mimmo*. I'm in no fit state to drive, so we're walking. How about Nancie's? You used to be obsessed with her waffles. I'll call Nate, and you can track down your two." He moves back to give me space, less obviously awkward than me, but I can sense his apprehension about acting normal with me. It's like we are both pretending that we are okay and everything is fine, yet we're both walking on eggshells and being weirdly abnormal.

Nancie's is a nearby little restaurant we frequented over the years. It started as an ice cream and sundaes parlor and moved into breakfasts and brunches in later years. Arry took me there on a whim whenever I craved their food, and he always knew it would cheer me up no matter what. I can't deny he's working his way back in without trying. Knowing me the way he does gives him an arsenal of advantages.

"I would kill for a banana and blueberry waffle, smothered in pecan syrup." my mouth's already watering, glad of the distraction, happy that I don't need to think about him or me right now or where this is going to go. Just focus on the food, getting fed, and maybe some sleep to let my head catch up on its own.

"How did I know you would order that? Whatever my girl wants. I need to grab my wallet from the house real quick and tell my mom we're going out for food. We better find the rest of them." He lets me go and hesitates before taking my hand in his gently. A small pause as he waits for me to pull away, but I don't. I let him interlace our fingers and throw him a soft look that I hope portrays the fact that I don't actually hate him.

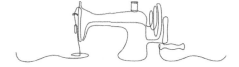

Chapter 8

Arrick reappears after fifteen minutes from his parent's house while I wait outside after texting Jenny and Christian, telling them to meet us here. Perched against the wall and picking petals from a daisy in my hand. Both responded and are apparently on their way to find me after explaining why I'm even with him without too many details.

"You were an age." I glance his way as he slides his hand in mine and pulls me close to kiss me softly on the cheek. I'm more aware that he's being cautious about throwing kisses at me, although he seems sure his handholding won't be rejected now. Sensing that he shouldn't kiss me on the mouth whenever he feels like it. Even though I'm here with him, there is an unspoken uneasiness, we're not okay yet, and I know it too. It will take time. I don't even know if I want this yet, it feels surreal and different, and I need a short adjustment period to feel like this is happening.

"My mom wanted words about Natasha's appearance and swift exit. She sort of loves the girl and wasn't too impressed with me." Arrick darts a look back at the house, almost warily checking if she is watching. He looks guilty of some heinous crime, and the flicker of regret in his eye makes me feel bad too. I gaze up at his house and sigh heavily. The weight of so much upon me today, and I want a moment of lightness for five seconds. "I didn't tell her about us just yet. She would go mad if she knew I dropped my girlfriend of two years to jump into another relationship. Especially when she's majorly protective over you, and I can't say I blame her. On paper, it's the asshole of all moves on my part. Besides, I know you haven't exactly agreed to anything, so there isn't much to tell her yet." He pulls me close to him and smooths a hand over my hair which has been flying around my face and irritating me. I frown at the little dip between his brows and throw him a sympathetic shrug that only emphasizes my inability to give him the answer he wants, feeling frustrated that I don't know.

"I know you. You're not the kind of asshole to dump someone on a whim and move on without caring. They will know it too." I smile softly, aware I bypassed the end of what he said, not ready to commit to anything. I like his plan of not focusing on it yet and getting through this day normally. Well, as normal as Arrick trying to kiss me and cuddle up every ten minutes can get.

"I feel guilty. Even more so learning about her dad just after I ended things. I know I should have made a clean break, but I couldn't. It would have made me feel even shittier about what I did to her."

We both regard each other quietly. A silent agreement that it is the shittiest of things to do to someone in any case.

"I never liked her, you know. It wasn't her. It was what she was to you, and now I feel sorry for her, I guess." I shrug and put some space between us again, still bristly where she is concerned and not feeling like I want his body heat touching mine when she is the topic. I have had that same pang of ache in my stomach for months from her name alone. Arrick watches me move around, his expression guarded and giving nothing away, but his eyes are calmly hazel, and he seems more relaxed in himself.

"That's because you're not an asshole either, and despite your stroppy-ass moods and impulsive attitude at times, you're a sweetheart with a lot of love inside of you, Sophs. Natasha will get over this. Maybe she'll even accept us eventually. I hope she finds her happily ever after with a guy who deserves her." He reaches out to me, lifts my hand, and kisses my fingers fleetingly, putting them back down so they hang between us in the distance I created, but he doesn't let me go. His focus on me steadily, and I can't deny how he looks at me, send my insides into a crazy swirl of tingles and butterflies. In one look alone, he translates that he loves me, and I don't know how to react. It's what I wanted.

I watch him for a second, a little enamored with the face I have known and trusted forever but somehow seeing him differently. Fresh eyes: maybe because we severed years of friendship in our parting, and we are finding a new ground between us that's different. Coming back to how we were, yet not the same. I feel different now, around him, inside my own skin, and it's not a terrible thing.

"Everything just feels unreal right now," I confess, catching his eyes studying my face still. Since he followed me this morning, all he has done is kept staring at me. Like he's worried I'm not actually here, or if he blinks, I'll disappear. I like it, but I don't. It makes me feel like he's intensely analyzing every part of me, and I'm less than confident in zero makeup, naturally dried hair, and casual clothes for a Sunday hangover. I don't feel stare-worthy, more like a plain child.

"This will be easier when we are back in the city and away from prying eyes. We need breathing space. We need some time to be around each other again." He scrunches his brows a little, throws me a boyish cutesy look, and, this time, gets a relaxed smile.

Worming his way back in with cute looks, huh?

"What do you think they will all say?" I flicker up at him with wide eyes, nodding towards his home. A niggling of fear in my mind as he moves my hand from his and into his arm so he can snuggle me closer without openly pulling me into an embrace. My body ends up beside his and is pulled in tight, so we touch. Being fly about his need to be together, but I don't resist. Nestling beside him and leaning into his body comfortably, glad of the resting place and liking his nearness a little more.

"I honestly have no idea. It could go either way; either a huge backlash of people thinking this will only end in heartbreak, or a lot of family rushing to buy wedding hats." He smiles, breaking the seriousness of the look on his face as he regards my expression closely.

"What do we do if they think we shouldn't be together." The sudden thought of Leila and my mom hit me hard, picturing them hating this and trying to get me to break things off with him. My lungs constrict badly as the sick feeling runs through my stomach, telling me I want this more than I'm letting myself admit. The gentle way he focuses on me hints that he's summarizing the same thing from my question. A twinge of a smile that he knows he already has a little bit of me, and maybe I've given too much away.

"Prove them all wrong even if they don't agree with this to start with. Once they see this is real, Sophs, that this isn't some impulsive thing, and I'm not going to leave you high and dry, it will blow over. You're younger than me, and it crossed my mind a dozen times that this might be too soon for you, too early in life, to have this kind of relationship. So I've no doubt that will be their first reaction." He's back to watching my face, but I turn away across the street to stare at the landscaped gardens and deserted peacefulness. Pulling my thoughts together to file them a little less messily.

"I'm not a kid anymore." instantly sulky, tired of people always referring to me that way, when inside, I've lived a thousand tears that no child should have known. Not as incapable and juvenile as they always think I am. I know I can act like a brat, and sometimes I'm selfish, but I can be self-reliant when I need to be, and I'm not a bad person inside.

"No, you're definitely not!" Arrick leans in, turning me back to him with a little chin coaxing from his fingers. He pauses a moment, so his mouth is mere millimeters from me, and waits. So inviting and gorgeous at this moment. When I lean the last distance and kiss him, he breaks into a huge smile, so we collide teeth before he catches my face with both hands and kisses me firmly. Closed lips but full-on squashing faces together with intention. He doesn't let it get out of hand. A kiss that's a little more than chaste and something only a lover or boyfriend would do.

Chapter 9

Gathering together in the street outside Arrick's house. Christian shows up first, followed by a timid-looking Jenny, who seems to appear rather closely to Nate. I notice Nate is rather attentive to my girl and tries to take her hand as he catches up with her; she looks away, pulling away from him, and slides an arm through mine in a coy move without catching his eye. I frown her way suspiciously and file it away to interrogate her as soon as I get her alone with Christian.

I'm now standing away from Arrick. As soon as I saw them appearing, I made him let go of me and moved two feet apart, needing a space to see my friends and let them know what had happened. My texts only outlined the briefest explanation, and I am so not ready to be identified as Arry's new love interest. I feel like they may judge me on my readiness to jump into a relationship when last night, I swore never to let him near me again.

"Well, hey, hey." Christian grins, swooning between us and looking far too wide awake and glamorous while the rest are rough. He winks at Arrick and gives him a coy-shoulder nudge.

"See, you finally manned up." He smiles at Arrick's frown and waves jazz hands in the air between them. So unmanly it's almost painful, but it makes me and Jenny giggle as Nathan also bursts into a grin. Seems he isn't surprised to see us together, and I catch the way he throws me a satisfied 'know it all' smirk.

"I'm still in two minds about whether I should beat you or hug you." Arrick tries for deadpan cool, but Christian only gushes at Arrick's sense of humor.

"Both. I am so into that." He giggles and winks, with a little twirl back to me and a butt wiggle. Arrick shakes his head and sighs before breaking into a huge smile. Obviously feeling dumb that he never once clicked that Christian is very unmistakably gay.

"I can't believe I ever thought this guy was straight." He laughs, and Nate throws him the 'you're a moron' look over everyone's heads. I catch it and giggle a little harder. Arrick must have been completely blind not to pick up on it before. I mean, Christian is currently sashaying around in a sparkly T-shirt with a huge rainbow heart on the front and wearing matching sneakers over ultra-skinny jeans. It's not exactly inconspicuous.

I turn away and give Jenny a little nudge, noticing how her eyes follow Nate as he moves in to give Arrick the familiar 'Bro' handshake and shoulder bump. The two of them lag behind as we start walking toward the exit of the street. Christian comes to my free side and loops my other arm, gaining distance on the two men behind us so he can cut in with a whisper. Like three witches from Hocus Pocus doing the crazy walk and huddling to gossip about men.

"Did you two do the bed boogie last night? Notice you disappeared, along with our shameless hussy over there and the rather sexy Nathan." He raises an alarming eyebrow at Jenny, whose face turns crimson. She recoils in mortification.

"Shh!" Jenny scalds him, glancing back between us to check they aren't listening, but the two of them are lost in conversation with equally serious expressions behind us and paying no attention to us. I glance back and catch Arrick smiling at something he is saying to Nate, and that heart-swelling warmth hits me as it used to when I looked at him. I push it down, turning back to my friends and the very serious subject in hand.

"Jenny, please tell me you didn't hook up with Nate?" I giggle at her in both shock and a little disbelief, not sure if I am happy for her or not. Nate is such a womanizer, and Jenny only just got dumped by her boyfriend of almost two years. I don't even know if I am impressed or seriously wowed.

"I got so drunk; I feel like such a slut. We somehow ended up making out in Arrick's mom's greenhouse. I don't even remember how we got there." Jenny's turning beetroot and unable to look us in the eye, trying to keep her voice on the low. Christian is grinning like a Cheshire cat, clearly proud of his 'hussy' girls and trying to coax the sordid details out of her.

"That's my girl! The only way to get over a man is to have a new one under you and fuck your brains out. So, did he?" Christian winks dirtily, and Jenny burns even redder, her face a picture of utter mortification, and she glares at him with an open mouth.

"Be quiet! ... There definitely has to be something said for men who have been around a lot of women." She smiles shyly. Glancing again quickly to see if they can hear us, and then at us. Blushing crazily and hitting the giggles, she looks so cute and girly right now, and I realize it's the first time I have ever seen her look this way.

"Jenny. I'm completely gobsmacked." I smile, squeezing her arm and figuring that maybe she needed to do something this out of the norm to feel better; she doesn't seem overly cut up about her ex, and there is no hint of guilt. I wonder if she had been ready to end things with him.

"He was sooo good. I thought I'd experienced orgasms before, but Oh, my God. I literally couldn't walk after. He took complete control of everything and did things I never imagined I would ever want. He makes me feel so crazily sexy." She whispers, then giggles at her revelation. I smile, but then my heart plummets as reality catches up with me and the fact Jenny isn't the type of girl to sleep around, especially not someone who gets into kinky aerobics in a greenhouse with a born womanizer. I don't want to crush the 'Christmas morning' expression she has on her face, but I know I can't let her go down this path to heartache.

"You know that's what he is, though, right? A guy who sleeps around a lot. Nothing will come from this except heartbreak if you want more." I point out honestly, watching her face as she bites on her bottom lip, curbing the smile and taking on a serious expression as she regards me with a nod.

"I know. In the first five minutes of meeting him, I figured out that he's a major man whore. I knew what I was getting, which is why I went for it. He made me forget about everything and feel really good for one night. Made me realize how much better than Mark I can do. Mark is a selfish prick who only thinks about himself and never even gave me one orgasm in two years." Jenny blurts out with a whoosh of relief, as though glad to finally get it off her chest. Christian's head almost snaps off in the way he turns to her with horrifying speed.

"WHAT? Oh, my God ... I would *die*! Pretty sure that borders on domestic abuse of some sort." Christian exclaims loudly, his face aghast, and laughs when we both Shh him with little slaps on his chest. Trying to muffle him down, glancing back quickly and very obviously at the men walking behind. We're both physically abusing Christian. There's no doubt in my mind that they probably know we are talking about them.

I glance back and catch Arry looking at me while Nate has his head tilted in, saying something to him with a serious expression and only half keeping his attention. Arrick catches my eye and smiles at me immediately. That half-smile, soft dimpled one he gives when he's feeling relaxed and happy. Despite myself, I smile back, all tingly and warm, my face heating slightly, before turning back to my friends.

"So, you two?" Jenny nudges me, my turn for the interrogation as she obviously caught that little moment between us and is now bringing the much quieter Christian's attention to my face too.

"He wants to try ... a relationship. I mean, like a dating relationship. We had sex, sort of. I was too drunk, and we ended up just sleeping together and kind of talked." I evade the details of what happened, I've never told them about my past abuse, and I never will. Explaining would be futile, and I still do not want anyone else to know. I watch the ground as we walk in case my expression gives anything away.

"He looks like a pretty smitten guy, to be fair. Even when we got on the plane, it wasn't hard to see." Jenny breaks in, looking thoughtful, slyly glancing back at the two men between our heads and locking eyes back on me.

"I got that vibe from the restaurant too ... See! Told you working the jealous angle would get to him." Christian's smug, and I shake my head at him. Not wanting to point out that if it weren't for Christian, Arry would have swept me off my feet two and a half months earlier and saved me a world of pain and anger for an extended period.

* * *

We walk on towards town, and the familiar sight of the little café turned restaurant with its outside tables already occupied. Morning walkers sit with pancakes and sundaes, despite the colder tinge in the air. Arrick catches me from behind and separates me from my entourage when we part ways to single file into the door. Taking my hand and pulls me against him from behind so he can put his other hand on my hip. Walking past the chrome tables and quaint umbrellas and inside the shop's shade. I notice Nate skirts by us and ends up directly behind Jenny, a hand on her lower back as he guides her towards tables behind Christian, and she doesn't remove it.

"What's the deal with him?" I nod towards his back with a questioning look, knowing fine well he is a 'love them and leave them' type and rarely gentlemanly with a girl after he has already banged her. By now, he's normally blanking them, forgetting their name and eyeing up a new conquest. He's acting completely out of character, and it's plain weird.

"Apparently, she blew his mind last night. Best sex he has ever had, and he is not ready to let that go." Arrick frowns, shaking his head at his mate's back with an air of disapproval. I guess, like me, he's finding the sudden change a bit weird.

"She's just come out of a relationship. The last thing she needs is this." I scowl at them as they find a table and start sitting down.

The three of them look completely at ease already, as though Nate has known them as long as I have.

"Maybe it's exactly what she needs. No strings attached sex with someone who will take her mind off it for a while. Sex can work miracles when both sides know that's all it is." Arrick shrugs my way, pulls me over with the speed of light, and deposits a kiss on my mouth, followed by a cheeky smile. He's getting bolder with throwing kisses my way, and I don't mind this time. I'm starting to like that he wants to kiss me anytime he sees fit.

"And here you told me that sex was not that big a deal!" I murmur it softly, mostly to myself, as my brain fades into last night, stupidly verbal. Swallowing that tiny hint of insecurity and a whole lot of self-doubt.

"It's not! Not when it comes to us, anyway. I told you ... What we have is worth a thousand times more than sex." Arrick squeezes me around the shoulders and kisses my temple gently, guiding me toward the booths.

I dart a look back at him for a moment, curbing the urge to say anything else, and let him push us to sit in the seats with our friends. Christian on one side of Jenny and Nate on the other as we slide in to face them, Arrick's arm immediately slides along the back of the seat behind me, so he's caging me in and leaning my way. Picking up the menu, he hands it to me first.

* * *

"Since when did you start eating banana and blueberry waffles with pecan sauce?" I laugh, staring at the identical plates placed in front of us after we all finally ordered food. We've all been chatting about the party, school, work, and nothing in particular. Oddly, we seem to all have gelled easily for a group of people who were separate the day before. Even Christian is looking decidedly at home with two very macho men. Sprawled in the seats and eyeing up everyone's food.

I guess he gets the vibe from both that being gay is fine. I knew it would be. Arrick has loads of friends who are gay, Nate's little brother is gay, and both are pretty accepting of most types of people overall. I can't stop myself from glancing at Arrick and realizing how quickly and easily I am falling back into being used to his company again. The initial confusion is draining away, and I'm more relaxed now that we are all sitting around with no pressure to be anything but sociable. He's being him, laying off the romantics and the touchy-feely and being who he has always been. Relaxed and chill in my company and yet still cutely attentive.

"You always seemed to love it, so I figured I would see what the fuss is about. Besides, I am so hungover right now, and this sounded better than a fry-up." He digs in, taking a mouthful and chewing it slowly as if to savor the taste before giving me an approving look and digging in for more. I shake my head and follow suit, trying not to moan with pleasure at the first bite of something I have craved since moving to New York. Literally, a taste sensation exploding in my mouth.

"You have to admit. This is sooo good." I gush between bites, slapping Christian's hand as his fork makes a dive at my food with a cheeky smile across the table.

"You are playing with fire there, buddy. She doesn't share, only steals." Arrick warns him with a smirk, winking my way and carrying on with his food while I scowl at Christian's hovering fork. I lean over my plate with a cat-like motion and give him my best 'I will maim you' growl. Arrick sighs and pushes his plate towards Chris.

"Here, try mine ... it will be less violent if you do." He sits patiently while Christian takes a forkful and throws me a triumphant eyebrow-raised 'ha ha' look. Smug that he got what he wanted after all and without physical harm.

"I will stab you with my fork," I warn him grouchily, meeting only smiles and winks before he blows me a kiss. I notice Jenny and Nate have gone into quiet conversation again. Heads ducked in as he says something that has her giggling. I frown across at him, wondering what his game is and mentally hoping to God she really does take this as a passing casual sex thing. She looks pretty this morning, carefree, and less stressed, and it's the first time I've noticed that she seems more relaxed than in the last few months. I wonder how much of that has been Mark.

"How do you put up with such a little brat like her?" Christian eye rolls at Arry, catching my frowny face as he meets my foot colliding with his shin under the table, giving off a womanly squeal as I scowl at him.

"Learning how to avoid her violent triggers helps." Arrick grins, lifting my hand from the table in his, bringing my fingers to his mouth softly, kissing them before letting me go. I have to admit the little stomach surge it gives me doesn't go unnoticed. Christian immediately goes pie-eyed and practically starts salivating at this show of cuteness. I, however, ignore it, push down the butterflies and carry on eating.

You don't get to see me go mushy yet.

"About that. Why is she such a demon at times? I have bruises in odd places from this stroppy little mare when she throws one on me." Christian sulks. I falter but shove more food in my mouth and try not to let my uneasiness about the topic show.

I know I have always been aggressive; I can't help it. My body reacts and lashes out before my mind does. The therapist helped me get better and less volatile, but I am aware that I have issues in that department, and it's not something I am proud of. It's PTSD at its finest. It also doesn't help that I grew up beside Leila, and half my violent outbursts are thanks to her.

"She's fiery, passionate, and a little hellcat at times; best things about her," Arrick replies huskily. Locking on me intensely as he brings his gaze to mine, complete adoration evident all around and no hint of knowing anything about why I am the way I am, even though he knows. I blush under his intense stare and go back to eating, loving him for always keeping my secrets for me, even when surrounded by friends who might know. The one thing he has never done, even with Natasha, was tell anyone the things I trusted him with. My past is not something I want people to know.

"Shut up and eat. You two are distracting me from the best waffles in the world." I frown at them both, picking up my milkshake to start washing away the food, trying to show how uncomfortable I am with two pairs of adoring eyes aimed my way as they bond over their love for me. I never thought this would be a scenario I would be in the middle of. Especially not when we were on the plane two days ago.

"I want yours." Christian sulks, looking down at his standard pancakes and maple and eyeing mine up woefully.

"I will hurt you," I warn with lowered brows, leaning over my plate with a poised fork in a stabbing motion. I catch Arrick smiling in the corner of my eye.

"She will. I won't help you either. I know what she can be like." He laughs as Christian's face drops more, his hand going to his brow dramatically.

"Look, if you wanted the same as me, then you should have ordered the same as me. No one touches my food, not even him." I thumb Arrick's way, which is only met with a smug smile from him as I am clearly pointing out that he's special to me.

Stop grinning, asshole. We all know it.

"True story, dude. I, on the other hand, have no choice but to let her eat my food, cos she's equally scary about that, and my life is worth more than pancakes." Arrick winks my way, giving Christian a mock look of sympathy.

"Some best friend you turned out to be. Even Jenny gives me hers." He sulks a little, still adopting his drama queen pose of unfairness and getting lower in his seat as he slumps.

"Ehh, I do not! A woman's food is a sacred thing. Men have died for less." Jenny leans forward, eyeing him up with a deadpan expression, scarily serious too. Having to stretch past Nate to see him as he leans back and slides an arm casually around her back.

"I agree. Never touch a girl's food. It's pretty much like fucking her mom." Nate shrugs, and all eyes dart to him.

"That's not even a comparison." I point out, my brows almost touching my nose with how his brain works and shaking my head at him. I catch Arry in the corner of my eye, stifling a laugh at his best mate's humor, and elbow him in the ribs.

"It kinda is." Arrick agrees, and both men do that whole nodding at one another facial expression and solidarity bullshit. This reminds me of why this is his best friend, even if sometimes I do not get it.

Arrick stretches his arms up and out before bringing them down, encircling my shoulder with one and squeezing me tight. Fly move for a player, and I sigh at his obviousness, yet leave his arm be. I'm starting to deflate, tired as hell, and my appetite has nosedived as the intense fatigue takes over. I push my plate at Christian with a defeated pout.

"Here, you can have them. I'm not hungry anymore." I sigh and rest my elbows on the table with a complete exhale of exhaustion, sad that I did turn down my favorite thing to eat. Christian is delighted and dives straight in, pushing his plate aside with relish like he just won the lottery.

"You okay?" Arrick's concerned tone in my ear has me turning to his worried expression, and I nod. He knows I rarely turn down food, especially not my favorite foods.

"Hungover, feeling like hell, and badly needing sleep. I think I will go home and leave you all to it for a while." I lift my shake and take one last mouthful before tapping his thigh gently to tell him to let me out of the booth, he slides out obediently, never taking his eyes from me, and I catch the utter disappointment on his face.

"You want me to call you in a bit?" He sounds wary and looks at me with an attempt at a smile, but it doesn't reach his eyes. I guess he hates the fact I'm leaving, and I hate the fact he hates it. Part of me wants the space, but a huge part wants him alone with me, but I don't want to stay here. I really need to lie down.

"You could always come too. You said you needed sleep." I mutter softly and coyly and push past him to get out of the booth. I turn as I get free and notice he still has half a plate of food left too. "It's okay. Maybe you could come when you're done eating." I add hastily, nodding at his plate and realizing how stupid I must look right now. How sad and clingy.

"I'm done ... I'm coming now." He doesn't hesitate, doesn't attempt to get back in the booth either, eyes fixed on me, and then he turns to the others. Mind made up and maybe needing to be alone with me too. I know he probably isn't done eating, but I guess I should accept the fact that he meant every word about being with me, and he is trying so hard to convince me.

"Right, guys ... breakfast is on me, and I guess we will see you all later." Arry raises brows at them with a smile, getting a round of grins in response from the best friends ever. He drops money on the table that covers the full breakfast and pushes Nate in the head, who seems to have his eyes on Jenny's cleavage.

"Make sure everyone gets back. Try not to lose them." He smirks, and Nate only grins right back.

"Pretty sure I can manage that."

Chapter 10

The walk back is odd. We're walking apart, my arms across my body as I feel like being by myself and not having contact. I'm tired and emotional and edgy. He's trying to make idle chit-chat, intent on keeping us talking about any topic he comes up with, and I am responding, but I am fully aware of his constant fixed gaze on my profile as we walk, and it's starting to make me nervy. I can't relax with how he seems honed into my every movement and mannerism.

"You can stop staring at me for, like, maybe five minutes." I point out and smile when his eyebrows dip in that cute way he has. He looks away for a minute and then back again.

"You noticed, huh?" He acts coyly and shrugs my way. Not him at all, he's always been super confident in every way, and this seems weird.

"Just a little, you know ... penetrating gaze latched onto my skull." I giggle at him, even more so with how sheepish he's become since I pointed it out, and let go of the tension a little.

"I can't help it. I spent months missing this view, dreaming about you, and I'm worried that if I look away, you might disappear again." His tone immediately turns serious and his eyes, although still facing my way, seem less zoned in on me, and I relax a little.

"I guess I know what you mean." I agree, knowing that I, too, am getting used to his sudden presence again, and it still feels unreal and dreamlike. That the last months are some sort of alternate dimension now. He was in my head so often in his absence that his real presence isn't quite normal to me yet.

"I missed you. I know it was my fault, but it doesn't take away how much it sucked. You're like a sunset or a pretty view of a shoreline. Some people like art, they like watching the sea. I've always liked looking at you. You have a unique beauty and the most breathtaking view on the planet." The seriousness of his statement makes my heart ache, and tears prick my eyes, knowing fine and well he means every word, and I don't know how to react. There's a silent moment as we both look away; he clears his throat, and I fiddle with my fingers awkwardly. Affected by how sweet he can be and so genuine, I am still afraid to let him see that he gets to me.

"You're so lame." I breathe through an intense emotional reaction, swallowing down tears, and his laugh breaks the tension.

"I missed that the most." He reaches out, pulls me to him by the upper arm, and finds no resistance. Bending in cautiously and slowly moving in towards my mouth. I see it coming a mile off, the way his eyes focus on mine as though seeking permission before he kisses me softly. His nose rubs mine, his lips part slightly, and I surrender to it, to him. Letting him feel me out as my eyes close of their own accord, Arry kisses me passionately.

My hands somehow end up cupping his sexy jaw, our bodies inching together, so we touch in every way, and his own hands get buried under the layers of my hair. Angling so he can kiss me properly. It reminds me of the night Emma had Ava, only so much more intense, and he doesn't pull away. He kisses me until a passing horn honk makes us break apart, giggling awkwardly when we realize we have probably been making out in full view for minutes. Oblivious to everything and the fact we are only a street away from our homes.

More than aware that the guy who never seemed to do any public displays of lovey-doveyness just made love to my mouth in broad daylight.

"You were made to kiss me. You know that, right?" He keeps

me close, nose to nose and tone low, still caught in the tender moment, even if we are no longer lip to lip. I nod, unable to reply, while he looks at me exactly this way. Heart bounding crazily in my chest and knowing this look right here is what I have been aching for all along. A look that says, 'I'm hopelessly yours.' A look I never imagined I would see on his face, given so freely and so honestly.

"I wish I could undo the past, but I can't. However, I do not plan on making the same mistake again and losing this. You're mine, Sophie. I finally know how it feels to kiss the girl you will only ever kiss again from here until eternity." He whispers breathily, and my insides fall apart. The last ounces of doubt that I don't want this with him fall around me, and my heart bleeds painfully.

"Don't hurt me," I respond shakily, parts of me on show that I've been too afraid to let him near again.

"Never again ... I swear. Hurting you hurts me too. I just want to make you happy."

* * *

"Better lock my door. Otherwise, my friends may come crashing in on top of us when they finally show face." I smile, stifling a yawn, very glad of the suggestion of some sleep. This morning's sudden awakening was bright and early, and my body is crashing as much as his; neither of us can stop yawning.

"On it." Arrick lets me go and turns, walking across the plush carpet as he kicks off his sneakers. Getting to the door, he locks it and heads back to my bed, taking a little run and jump so he lands in the middle, star-shaped. Looking like a child while doing so and beaming at me from his new position.

I giggle and walk a little more demurely. Sliding off my pumps, getting on my bed gently, and climbing onto my knees until I scoot closer to him. Arrick reaches out, catches my hand, and tugs me over, so I fall on top of him with a shocked yelp. Giggles follow it as he rolls over on top of me, flattening me to the bed, pinning me down so he comes nose to nose with me, nestled against my body in a perfect fit. His eyes scan my face, the hint of a smile at the corner of his mouth and one dimple shining through. I gaze right back into the depths of his eyes. Finally, feeling completely at ease, glimpses of mutual adoration shine through.

"I'm going home tonight on Jake's jet. I guess you three are too?" He rests his chin on my chest to gaze up at me, shuffling his body down the bed a little. I nod, slowly letting my fingers trail his manicured set of eyebrows down that chiseled face to the angular jawline, following my progress with his eyes focused on mine. "Come home with me, Sophs. Stay with me tonight at my apartment." He watches me, frowning a little as I smile, pushing him off so I can slide to my side to face him instead; his arms come around me, pulling me in so he can bring his nose back to mine.

Letting him make out with me has brought back the 'she's never off-limits to me' side of him again. I'm not complaining, I missed this as much as I missed him, and it feels as right as it always did.

"I'll think about it." I smile as he begins rubbing his nose against mine, the way I have seen Jake do to Emma a million times, and for a moment, it's weird to see what exactly is a Carrero trait rather than a Jake or an Arry trait. I wonder which parent it comes from.

"You're going to leave me hanging and work for it?" Arrick's expression turns serious, pushing his forehead against mine a little more. I shove him away playfully and give him that knowing nod. Giggling at his crushed expression.

"I don't want to leave your side. I spent months trying to imagine you beside me, and now you're here, I'm not ready to let you go home without me. I don't want to be parted just yet." He loosens his hold and starts fiddling with a strand of my hair, twirling it between his fingers while watching me intensely.

"Who are you, and what have you done with Arry?" I laugh, pushing him playfully, more than a little smug when he hauls me back to him and lassos his legs around mine, so I can't get away. Trapping me with sheer hunky muscle and that hard, carved body wrapping around mine.

"He died of a broken heart. Lack of Sophabelle." He pouts dramatically, with fake sad eyes and the cutest frown.

"Shut up, you weirdo." I poke him in the dimple

absentmindedly, aware that I'm falling back into old habits too easily, some of our rapport coming back slowly. Repairing some bridges that only yesterday felt un-mendable.

"See ... This is exactly what I missed more than anything, baby. Your sassy comebacks when you like to make out you don't even like me. It feeds my weird side and is becoming a borderline fetish." He leans into me closely and hits me with a chaste kiss on the corner of my mouth. A few more butterflies to add to my growing collection of them.

"I don't like you. I just feel sorry for you because you have no friends. I tolerate you because I'm nice." I burst into giggles when he hauls me under him in a flash and starts torturing me with tickles. Crawling on top of me to straddle me and pin my arms down beside my head as I try to fight him off. He renders me immobile and leans down to plant a kiss on my mouth, a little less safe and full-on this time.

"Come home with me, or I will typewriter you until you agree." He warns with a smug look, and I shake my head at him. The stubborn inner child is bursting out happily. All other thoughts and confusion are giving me a break while he's in a boyish mood and grinning crazily.

"You wouldn't dare. You are trying to make me like you again, remember?" I narrow my eyes at him, but he throws back a hint of mischief in a smirk with narrowed eyes. Sexily naughty while that square jaw and straightened brow make him look a little sinister so suddenly, tingles pulsing over me instantly. I swallow hard, knowing he means to do it.

"Yeah, but we already ascertained that I'm an asshole who does stupid shit sometimes." He grins wickedly, tucking my wrists under his knees as I fight back, a look in his eye that he intends to carry out his torture threat until I yield.

Chapter 11

I inhale deeply, savoring the memory as I wander into the middle of Arrick's apartment from the elevator while he follows with our bags. He dumps them by the end of the couch as I take in the open-plan space with joy.

I haven't been here in months, and its sheer familiarity makes me feel calm, like coming home. Instantly still inside, like breathing warm, soothing air after being out in the cold, I inhale slowly. The atmosphere washes over me. Welling up at how much I missed this place too. It smells like home-cooked food, men's aftershave, leather, books, and something familiar and clean. It's a weird combination, but it's how it always smells, bringing back so many mixed emotions.

Arrick's apartment has always been a place I love to be, as it's so very him; modern mixed with traditional. He has very male tastes but is also a little eclectic and sentimental. Open plan and industrial, with old battered armchairs and new comfy couches. Walls lined with abstract art and photographic prints in an array of wood, metal, and concrete frames. A mix of old bookcases and steel-framed shelves holding a collection of books, decorative pieces, and picture frames.

His kitchen is all steel and dark wood, minimal and usually

immaculate. Still, I notice a discarded box on the counter and what appears to be a broken picture frame on the surface next to it, with a mess of glass spread carelessly across it and the floor. I move towards it impulsively, but he stops me with a hand on my shoulder, frowning at the sight of it, and steps out in front of me to go towards it.

"I'll deal with it." He throws me a light smile and leaves me to get myself comfy. Left to look around and reacquaint myself with my home away from home.

I pull off my coat and glance to see him picking up the pieces until he pulls the picture free, looks it over, and then leans in to look over the box that is sitting open. He frowns harder and reaches inside, lifting a book and dropping it back in.

"Tasha... She was supposed to pick up what was left of her stuff and leave my key card back with Frank. Guess she was much more pissed than I gave her credit for." He drops the photo in the box and turns to open a cupboard to retrieve a brush and pan to clear up the mess. I wander over, eyeing the broken shards, and lean to catch a glimpse inside the box.

The picture is facing up. A love portrait picture of Arrick and Natasha at a wedding or party, leaning together to pose. I can't say it doesn't affect me because it does. A horrible sick feeling and a wave of chest pain that I try to push away.

Underneath is an assortment of things I recognize as Arrick's; a sweater he wears a lot when he trains, and I have even worn a book, some DVDs, a couple of his T-shirts, and some male toiletries. I move away, not wanting to keep coming back to the picture staring up at me. Looking at the broken frame instead.

"She broke this? Why?" I lift my hand to touch the picture frame and wipe away some scattered shards, but Arrick catches my hand in mid-air.

"You'll cut yourself, baby. Let me clear it up." He kisses my hand before moving it back and letting it go to sweep off the pieces quickly. I watch him quietly, keeping my hands out of the way, and try to let this go, let any talk of her go over my head.

"My guess is she came here when she landed, and this is her way of telling me to go fuck myself. It wasn't exactly pleasant this morning." He furrows his brow as he opens another cupboard and throws the pan contents in a concealed trash can. He is domestically capable and showcasing his pretty hot physique when doing anything manual, like bending and showing off an ogle-worthy tight ass.

"This was your picture?" I can tell by the frame's style that it matches those he has in his bedroom. The grey concrete frames are too masculine for Natasha's dainty pink and floral tastes. I hate that she came here and broke something that belonged to him, even if she was in it too.

"It was. It was still sitting in my study along with stuff I had for her to pick up." As though suddenly reminding himself, he turns and walks to the side of the room to check and comes back with a box. He places it next to Natasha's box and lifts the lid, looking inside and chewing on his lip. "She's taken what she wants, I guess." He closes it again and piles the two boxes together. Sliding them farther over to the corner of the counter to deal with later, eyeing me warily. Attention is returning to me now that he has dealt with her little tantrum, and I stare back at him with a heavy sigh.

"If you broke up over two months ago, why are you now only trading items?" I eye him suspiciously, watching the small shake of his head as he assesses me with an indulgent appraisal and a raised brow. Seeing hints of the green-eyed me coming out to play. My direction is clearly unsettling him, and he probably thinks a storm is brewing, considering the delicate nature of this particular subject.

"She was a little too emotional the past few weeks, what with her dad and us. So I didn't see it as majorly important. I guess this symbolizes that she finally realizes we are done and not going back." He seems a little mournful for a moment, that hint of guilt breaking through, but it disappears behind that cool façade quickly, and I wonder if he ever misses her at all, the way he missed me.

"She didn't accept it before?" I hate talking about this, but as usual, my curiosity is my biggest flaw. Overtaking my impulsive instinct to ban all conversation that concerns Natasha. I want to know more about what's been happening between them since I left here. A part of me wants to fill in the blank spaces, even if it hurts me. I want to trust him so badly.

"She was clinging to the hope that I still loved her enough to fix things. The only problem was that I would never have thrown away everything for you if I ever loved her. I guess I never loved her in the way I thought I did... It was hard for her to deal with that, and she is still struggling to come to terms with it. Not that I blame her ... I truly turned out to be a major shithead to both of you." Arrick turns and switches on his coffee machine, pulling out the drawer compartments to check if his housekeeper has refilled it, and then hits the front power button. Turning back to me with a sigh, eyes scanning me softly. I start fiddling with my nails, watching him while my brain runs through a hundred questions and niggles that I am not sure I even dare to put out there.

It's not that his confessions and adorations don't get to me. They do. Everything he ever says tells me that this is real. It makes my heart soar and my insides react. I am too wary of showing him anything just yet still feeling this out. Arrick's face seems to straighten suddenly, his expression taking on a serious tone, and he reaches for my hand, pulling it to his and wrapping it within his fingers protectively.

"Look, I need to be honest about this. I still answer her calls and talk to her if I run into her somewhere. I don't make a point of seeing her, but sometimes she shows up. I'm still her friend, and I want her to move on... If being in her life for a while longer helps her, then that's what I'm going to do. This stuff with her dad sealed the deal. She isn't in a good place right now... I don't want this to affect us, but I don't want to hide this from you either." Arrick leans his butt on the counter across from me so his head comes closer, catching my chin with his fingertips and tilting my face up to him tenderly. So much going on in his eyes, and I want to believe him and not feel like his words are slicing my soul.

"You have nothing to worry about. I'm yours. You're mine. No one will come between us if we don't let them, and I am sure as hell not about to go looking elsewhere. It may have taken losing you to realize how much I fall to pieces without you, but I'm not an idiot that makes the same mistake twice. I know where my heart is,

Sophs. It's always wherever you are." His focus on my face is mesmerizing. I bring my brows together and swallow hard to get my emotions to behave. Smiling softly, acknowledging that I love what he is telling me, trying to show a little more to him when he's so beautiful. His softening look tells me he sees it.

The spurt of the coffee machine makes him look around for a second. Straightening up before returning to the breakfast bar and sliding up behind me snugly, arms encircling my waist as he rests his body against me. My stomach is lurching, my heart aching as I take deep, slow breaths to keep it together. He always knows how to set me off so effortlessly, and I wonder if this is how Emma feels anytime Jake touches her.

I'm still holding my tongue, a thousand petty things poised childishly inside my mind, insecurely, waiting to pour out concerning his speech about her, but I know how immature and selfish that would make me. I know she is close to her parents, and her father's illness will ruin her. Being a nurse means she probably knows without any doubt that he is dying. I flinch at the wave of deep guilt concerning her, and it cements my inability to tell him how I wish he would just cut all ties with her for me.

Selfish girl.

He brushes my hair back, so he can nuzzle his face into the crook of my shoulder, letting me sag into him, and I let out a small sigh of satisfaction and contentment. He's learning fast in such a short space of time how to weaken my resolve and touch me for maximum impact. I always knew he was clever at certain things. I guess this is something he is very good at too.

"Sophie, you know me. I hope you still trust me enough to believe me. I've never been this way with anyone, even Natasha. That has to tell you how I feel about you." He pushes me gently with his knees behind my legs, so I collapse into his hold. I push my butt back into his groin naughtily in retaliation, the mood lifting at his playfulness. Pushing all other thoughts aside, for now, unable to ruin this moment.

"I do. I believe you." I respond softly, leaning my head back against his throat. He runs his fingers down my throat gently.

133

Closing my eyes at how it feels to be in his arms this way. So many times, I thought of how this could be, missed how this felt, missed him and his touch.

"I never got the whole mushy touchy-feely thing Jake is all about. The constant touching and smooching Emma, twenty-four seven. Never really someone who wanted to walk around pawing at my girlfriend or spend copious amounts of time only wanting to be alone to paw my girlfriend... Natasha used to joke that I was allergic to too much intimacy... Sophie, it's never been like that with you, ever. I want to be close to you. I have always touched, hugged, held your hand, and been comfortable being attached to you, even when it was innocent. I have always wanted you with me, no matter how often I saw you... You were my shadow for years, and it's only now I realize it's because I wanted to be with you all the time. That touching you was a necessity." He turns me in his arms, so I can rest my butt against the counter, his fingers trailing down my exposed arms, making them tingle. Eyes locked on one another steadily. "I know in myself how different this is. Because all I have wanted to do since we kissed again was to be wrapped around you, touching you, being connected to you somehow. Even if it's sitting beside you on a flight and holding hands." His fingers come to mine and connect, completely intertwined.

I chew my lip, my heart aching with everything he says, eyes glazed with emotion. There's a lump in my throat from how beautifully romantic Arrick can be underneath all the cool and aloof he shows the world. I never thought it would be like that with him.

The plane journey with our friends and Nathan was minus Jake, just a group of hungover people returning to the city. Nathan and Christian slept for the hour-long flight while Jenny gazed out the window, daydreaming sleepily. Leaving Arrick and me together. Side by side, with hands held under the cover of the table, I leaned my head against him. Listening to his heartbeat as he read a book, I napped in and out of consciousness. He hadn't let go until we got up to leave the plane, not once, and then didn't let go until we got out of the car at his apartment and carried our bags.

"I like that you're like this." I finally say, his hand trailing up to my jawline, tracing my lips with his thumb, eyes focused on my mouth and the obvious desire to kiss me. Starting to recognize the tell-tale signs. Of eyes dilated, brows slightly tensed to a tiny frown, the serious deadpan focus on my lips.

He is easy to read when you know how, and I love that he seems to want to kiss me endlessly. Even when he isn't kissing me, he's usually thinking about it.

"There is definitely a lot of fire and passion underneath that very sexy chest, waiting to get out, I think." I prod him in the pec with a smile. Loving the way it feels to be able to touch him without any boundaries or hesitation. I feel like exploring every part of him with inquisitive fingers and have to stop myself from lifting his shirt to go peeking.

"I guess it's been dormant for a long while. Or maybe I didn't have enough sexual chemistry with anyone to let it out until you." He grins cheesily, and I roll my eyes.

"Stop! Chat-up lines are lame, and I happen to know. Also bullshit. You were a Lothario before you settled down. I may not have been privy to your naughty antics, but I heard the rumors, and you stupidly told me things you shouldn't have." I slide out of his embrace and flit into the kitchen as the coffee jug fills up, reaching for mugs in the cupboard above. He moves to where I'd been standing and takes up the same leaning-down posture he had before. His arms are resting on the counter as he watches me ready our drinks.

"Reformed my ways ... just for you. Do you want to have a jacuzzi out on the roof and then come down for a movie before bed? Pretty sure there's a bikini you left here in my drawer from that party last year." He watches me with that infuriating poker face and smiles when I eye roll at his obvious lameness.

My mind flits back to that party and the fact he split up a drunken brawl between Natasha and me that night before forcing me to go to bed in his spare room. Shrugging it away, I glance at him slyly.

"Or, you know, we could skinny dip." I lift my chin with a naughty smile, completely serious. Not against seeing that perfectly sculpted body of tanned skin and black ink again since it is etched in my memory. I don't have any issue being naked with him again, either.

"We could ... but we're not." He stands up, stretching his arms over his head and joining fingers to ease his shoulder muscles. It's instantly erotic to me how his body elongates and moves fluidly, all muscle and beautiful masculine lines making me hot from within. I realize I am openly staring, and he catches my eye with a smile.

"Why not?" I pout as he returns to his casual pose. I think I will like playing with my eye candy of a man in a jacuzzi. From sex demon to sexy lounging model.

"Because seeing you naked again will seriously mess with my calm, especially when you are within arm's reach. I am struggling to function on the memory of you in all your glory as it is." He takes the mug I have now slid across to him gratefully, lifting it to take a sip while holding it around the base with fingers through the handle. He is such a guy in every way, and I find myself lifting my eyebrows with complete amusement at this fact. I never noticed until now how many completely 'guy' mannerisms he has.

"Hmm, I doubt that very much. I'm almost boy-shaped." I gaze down at my mug, then go snooping in the cupboard for creamer.

"Trust me. There's nothing boy shaped about you, Sophie, not anymore. Maybe when you were fourteen, but you have moved into a woman's shape a little too perfectly. You attract male eyes like flies to honey, baby. You're just oblivious to it."

I frown his way dubiously, regarding that genuine look and knowing he means it. Taking a look down almost impulsively in an almost childlike manner to see what he is seeing.

All I can see are slender legs, a flat stomach, and a modest bust. Everything is slim and in proportion, a little on the dainty side for my liking but nothing like the curvy bodies of some of the women I have seen him date.

"Maybe I'll fill out still, guess there's still time." I smile his way with a shrug, not body shy at all and not that insecure, despite a past that used to make me hate my body on all counts. Therapy has done so much for me, but I still fail to see myself as sexy and curvy and try to dress to make myself look more so.

"You don't need to fill out, trust me. You are already capable of making men horny as hell, *Mimmo*. The number of assholes I've had to intervene with on your behalf proves that. You can count me as one." He winks. A naughty hint of a smile as his eyes linger on me for a second as he works his way up over my body lazily. Definite interest peeking in that cheeky eyebrow wiggle he gives me. It's amazing how one loaded look can turn me to mush and sizzle simultaneously, and he isn't even touching me. I swallow nervously, trying to deflect from the topic I started, and realize this will be a whole new part of the relationship between us to explore at some point. It makes me unsure suddenly and antsy, and I look for another topic to focus on.

"I'm sorry I did that to all of you. I mean all the drinking, partying, and acting like an idiot for years." I chew my lip, looking away across the immaculate room with a sinking feeling in my gut. One thing I have done since starting school is pondered and regret the last couple of years all the time. Hating when I look back on it and all the pain it caused the people who love me. How childish I was in dealing with things and how I behaved toward everyone, including him.

"I'm beyond sorry I didn't figure out it was because of me, Sophs. I just thought you were going off the rails like Leila did, and nothing seemed to get through to you." We're both cradling our mugs, perched on either side of the counter, and looking at one another openly. The first time we talked with any space between us in the last few hours. I guess I need some distance for a few minutes.

"It wasn't your fault. I didn't even know why I felt that way." I shrug matter-of-factly, dismissing his blame for something he had no control over at the time. I hate that I can now look back and see the mess I was, yet he didn't give up on me all that time. It makes me warm inside, softer towards him at the memories.

"For the record ... I'm glad you feel that way; I'm glad things changed between us." He lays down his mug, standing up and laying his palms flat on the counter as though pondering whether he should stay there or come to me. I guess he can tell that I might need some breathing space, but I can also tell that he isn't liking the lack of touching going on. He's been insatiable for contact since this morning.

"You don't wish it was still how it was, and you were still ignorantly happy with Tasha?." I blurt out a little too painfully and raise a brow his way. I don't even know what that was, what I am trying to achieve.

Testing the boundaries, maybe?

He moves around the counter to me, obviously choosing to be closer, finding me with his arms and pulling me against him, so I have to put my mug down too. Drawing me in to face him and giving me no option but to obey as he slides my body against his faultlessly, perfectly molded as though we did break from the same mold once.

"Nope ... this feels right to me. Righter than anything I have ever known." He stoops a little, buries that cute boy face in my neck, and breathes me in before planting a kiss on my throat. I giggle unexpectedly when he hoists me up by the butt and legs onto the counter and slides me back to sit on it, nestling himself between my thighs, so we are nose to nose. Intimately joined, and I am his prisoner. This close to his face and that disarming smile feels much better than being across a kitchen, and the familiar tingling of my insides goes into overdrive.

"You make me want to wrap these around me every second of the day." He murmurs close to my mouth as he angles for a steamy kiss, pulling my legs around his waist so I can lock my ankles together behind his back. My arms are around his neck as he tilts me back and fits our bodies snugly. He is getting braver with how far he can push me with every single touch, it seems.

Casanova!

"Hmmm, what happened to the no sex yet, thing?" I nudge him warily, still not sure if I even want to contemplate trying anytime soon; we seem to have bypassed all the awkward getting to know each other again in half a day, and he is straight in with man-handling, a little too confidently. The heat is still there, but the memory of last night has dampened my desire to go there anytime soon. It didn't play out how I thought it would, and I would love to talk it through with Emma before I try again. Get her take on it. Understand why it made me react that way.

"Who's having sex?" He feigns innocence, catching my bottom lip in his teeth and sucking it in gently. I surrender to him and happily let him devour my mouth with a more passion-fueled kiss than any we have shared all day. I can feel his arousal between my thighs stirring quickly, and it's obvious he's hit the sudden horn. A little sense of achievement that I could do this to him, considering how many times before I left him I hoped I could. Forgetting my fears because I know I can trust him not to push me in this way, even if his body aches for it.

"Feels like someone wants to." I breathe heavily when he breaks the kiss, still nose to nose, grazing his mouth against mine seductively. Still holding my pelvis tight against him, I'm leaning back at an odd angle on the kitchen surface.

"Wanting to and doing are not the same thing, and I stand by my earlier oath of not going there until you're ready." He loosens me a little from his hold, bringing his forehead to mine, eyes locked and held captive.

"You make me crazy. I am not going to deny it, *Mimmo. B*ut you mean a hell of a lot more to me than sex." He's serious, the atmosphere between us charged, and I find it hard to resist him when he says things like this. He makes me want to throw all caution to the wind and let him have me in any way he wants.

"What if I want you to try again?" I regard him seriously, still clinging to him, aware of the build of heat and ache inside me with having him this close to my body. The fire in him set me off in ways I didn't expect.

Arrick kisses me chastely on the mouth and pulls back, letting me go so he can edge his pelvis away from mine. My arms hang loosely around his neck as he slides his hands down my thighs to rest on my knees instead. Putting very obvious cooling space between us and making it clear this isn't going anywhere. In a way, it makes me relax, even if there is a confusing hint of disappointment.

"Doesn't matter. I don't want to be the reason your head takes you back there; I hate that I made you already. I'm not saying we won't try at some point. I'm just saying there's no rush for it. It's not the most important thing, and I don't think it will be an issue in the future... I mean, I did get you to cum, quickly." He reaches for my mug and hands it to me with a satisfied grin, clearly patting himself on the back, forcing me to let him go and take it as he reaches for it.

"Big head." I roll my eyes, the heat in my face rising suddenly with how straight to the point he is about that. I have never talked about sex frankly with anyone, and it feels a little weird to be talking to him about it when he is acting like this is no more different than discussing ice cream flavors.

"I think I was too drunk, and it was ... I don't know." I falter, staring at him imploringly, unsure about what that head mess even is and still a little shyer about this topic than he is.

"Drunken sex. No romance and you didn't feel safe with me. Definitely don't trust me like you used to... I understand you more than you think, Sophie. I can read you like a book sometimes, and I can see part of your wall is very clearly up." Arrick sighs at me, a mix of regret and understanding, and strokes back my hair so he can tenderly kiss my cheek. A kiss that makes me want to close my eyes and savor him against me. He is starting to get a little addictive with his affections.

"I do trust you. It's just that ... I feel weird right now." I blink up at him with Bambi eyes, not wanting him to think I don't still care about him. Unsure as to what I feel in terms of trust after today. We slipped so easily into each other again, like we were never apart, and it has added to the washed-up cyclone of confusion inside of me.

"You aren't ready to forgive me yet, and I did a lot more damage than just choosing another girl ... I know that, Sophs. I know I fucked up royally. More than just this between us... I left you when I promised I wouldn't. I broke what we had. I let you go when I had always been someone you clung to, and it's more than your heart I broke... I know this is complicated, and things between us will take time to move on again. Don't think I don't know what I did. It's all I thought about for months. I know this goes so much deeper than breaking your heart over another girl." He brings my face back to his so we're close again, and that look of deep sorrow hits me right in the stomach; I don't doubt he is sorry. I can see it in every word he says to me and every expression on that handsome face.

"I want to forgive you. I do. I just might need a little time to come around." I respond softly, lowering my chin so I can look at my lap instead of the pain in the depths of his eyes.

"You have a lifetime to forgive me. I'm not going anywhere ever again. I know a promise won't mean much to you right now, *Mimmo*, but I promise you that you will never lose me again. I will never let you go." Arrick moves in and lifts me from the counter. Swinging my legs to one side and smiling at me before planting a kiss on my mouth, carrying me towards his room. "Maybe we should curl up in my bed, watch a movie marathon and call for some takeout tonight. I want you next to me for the next twelve hours minimum. Before I have to let you go to school and suffer your absence again." He lifts me higher, so he can plant a kiss on the corner of my mouth, and I slide my arms around his neck easily. Very happy with a suggestion that sounds to be exactly what I need.

"You're so lame sometimes. I think you may have it bad." I giggle at him as he carries me into his room and dumps me on the bed ungracefully, so I bounce and yelp.

"You know it, baby." He chuckles before diving on top of me amid squeals and screams as he aims for tickling and kissing combined.

Chapter 12

Arrick moves out of reach, wanders to the fridge, opens it to rummage through the contents, and pulls out some labeled tubs. His housekeeper is paid to keep it stocked and easy for him when he wants to eat; his strict diet when in training means he eats a lot of healthy foods and high protein, but he is rummaging for something else.

It's early morning. He woke me up with his alarm, and now he's showered and ready to go to the gym at stupid o'clock, even though I am half asleep and struggling to get ready for school.

Who even does that on purpose?

We were up so late, watching movies, fooling around, and even had a little steamy make-out session that could have gone a lot further if he wasn't such a gentleman. I am suffering now as I watch him, still in my clothes from last night, finding some breakfast before he takes me home to get ready properly. Normally I wouldn't be up for another hour at least, but I don't want to get a cab home this tired and dragging my weekend bags with me.

"I want to go back to bed," I whine petulantly, tiredness making me grumpy. I've never been a morning person and rub my eyes and head groggily. Arrick throws me back an indulgent smile and goes back to raiding the fridge, pulling out what looks like oatmeal and fruit.

Ughhhh, he's trying to poison me.

I join him at the fridge and poke around the huge pile of clear tubs with various titles. Spying a Chinese takeout box, I pull it forward and am disappointed to see it is being used to hold a variety of chopped peppers and salad.

"Do you never just want to grab a greasy dog and a chocolate bar?" I screw my nose up and dig deeper into the depths of organized eating; his fridge is a poster child for healthy living and organic goodness. Nothing in here even slightly calls to me to be eaten.

"Not at six a.m., Sophie, no. You do worry me sometimes about your eating habits. Please tell me you have not been fending for yourself with hot dogs and candy for the last three months." He runs an eye over my body as though to check if he might have missed any obvious signs of malnutrition, and I eye roll. I pull out a box without a label and sigh at diced chicken with some seasoning marinating for another meal.

"I want pancakes." I sniff a tub of dressing and stick a finger in to taste it, hoping it's some sort of syrup, and screw my face up at its chili taste. Wiping it off my tongue with my nail and catch him looking at me like I'm an alien creature he found in his kitchen.

"Baby, I haven't got time to make them right now. Just grab something quick so we can get ready and go. I have to get you home so that you can get ready. I need to meet Nate before five-thirty at the gym." Arrick throws two containers back in the fridge and pulls out a carton of fresh orange instead. Pouring two glasses beside the two bowls of oatmeal and fruit.

He must be insane if he thinks I am eating that crap.

"I don't like you anymore." I sigh. Pushing the fridge shut dejectedly and eyeing up the plates he is now carrying to the table.

"I know. Come on. I want to make sure you eat before I drop you off. I know how lazy you can be in the morning, and you're then starving by lunch." He's bossy this morning, a return to Arry of old and no longer pandering to my every whim while he's in paternal mode. I stick my tongue out at him behind his back.

"Let's go now and find a convenience store to stock up on junk food. I cannot come over here if you do not have a good supply for my womanly needs. Chocolate is a must, Cheetos ... we need some Pepsi for sure." I slump back against the counter once more as he turns and gives me that commandeering narrowed gaze frown, making me obey, and I follow him to what looks like granola with fruit, milk, or maybe yogurt.

Natasha comes to mind, and I screw up my face in disgusting memory. I follow him anyway and sit in my usual seat, sliding down as he pushes my bowl towards me and digs into his own. I hate that he is a sexy eater. It just draws attention to the muscles in his face and that crazily strong jaw, those perfectly soft, not overly full lips that were invented for kissing

"You eat like a kid; your diet is awful. I don't know how you are so thin and toned for someone who eats like a sugar-addicted five-year-old." Arrick scalds me, pushing my plate back at me as I push it away, with a raised brow that signals he's not in the mood. I move it sideways and lay my head on the table dramatically. Too tired to eat and hating that I have even met five a.m. on purpose. He has no idea how unhealthy for my disposition this is.

"I don't know how you got so beefy and muscular for someone who eats like a rabbit." I stick my tongue out at him from my flat posture and start running my finger in circles on the surface. Praying something falls out of the sky, which is both edible and energy-boosting.

"Well, if you're staying here a lot, then get used to it, as you will not live on Cheetos and Pepsi. I don't mind the occasional splurge when I'm on a training break, but I don't want you living on that crap, Sophs. I had to lose ten pounds after getting lazy with you. I am not doing that again." He frowns at me and then pushes my foot under the table with his to get me to sit up.

"Fine, we will stay at mine then. You can bring your rabbit food and leave me to my refrigerator of cold pizza, takeout, and junk food." I sigh and bury my face on top of my outstretched arms, ignoring his attempts to get me upright, closing my eyes in a bid to sleep on the table. I feel like hell, and now I wish I didn't spend copious hours playing tonsil tennis with one very practiced Carrero and slept more.

"You do realize this is me you're talking to? I will clean out your fridge and restock it. You're my girlfriend now, meaning I have more say." He sounds like he's smiling, and I look up to see him grinning at me while eating his gross food. Finding himself utterly amusing, and yet, weirdly, I do not.

"Oh, for a minute, I thought Jake was here ... You can only dream that you get to boss me around the way he does." I sit up and narrow my eyes at him, not about to take any crap from him at all, especially over food. I even might let the girlfriend comment slide, seeing as I have not agreed to any such thing yet.

"Maybe I need a list of things I do get to boss you around over." He narrows his gaze back at me. I guess testing the waters at my lack of picking him up on the girlfriend label.

"Setting ground rules or telling you which things are not your concern?" I raise my eyebrows cheekily at him, smirking and relaxing in the old atmosphere we always had. I feel better after sleep, even if I haven't had enough, and I am getting used to his presence again, falling into our roles from before. I like that we haven't lost the bickering banter and passive-aggressive affection from before. That was something I always loved about us.

"We need ground rules. The first one is I won't have my girl eating crap all the time. It may not affect you now, but it will eventually. Besides, the crabby ass moods you get in would probably improve with a better diet." He raises one dark brow, that slight smug hint of a smirk in the depths.

"I think you are probably the cause of those crabby ass moods, like ninety-nine percent of the time. I'll change my diet in small ways if you give me full-body massages once a week." I retort sassily, head thinking how good it will feel to let him strip me naked for that. I always did imagine what it would be like, and I can experience it now. Perks of Arry as my boyfriend, I think. I like that title. Maybe I should permanently let the girlfriend label slide.

"Deal. I'll give you more than one a week if you like. I'll give them daily." He winks, and I can see this conversation taking a different turn. I narrow my gaze at him, breaking when he chuckles and pokes me on the end of the nose with his thumb, returning to his crappy breakfast.

"Okay, with that sorted, let's talk sleepovers. After tonight I am back in training, overseeing a new merger in Carrero Corp, so it would be easier if you stayed with me some nights a week. That's if you want to stay with me?" He pauses mid-spoonful and flickers a glance down at me, looking incredibly young and boyish at that moment.

"We're not doing sex, but we're doing sleepovers?" I frown at him, confused why he would want that if he knows we are not going to do anything that requires a bed.

"Why not? I still want you beside me some nights, even if it makes me take a dozen cold showers." He smiles again and goes on crunching on his food, completely dismissive of any weirdness in that sentence. My stomach rumbles involuntarily, and I eye up the bowl a little defeatedly. I wonder whether I can eat it or not and know if I don't, I will starve. I don't do well on lack of food.

"I need to be home sometimes, to work, to study. I don't know what nights." I answer childishly, pouting over my lack of pancakes and staring out past the ceramic bowl to the New York skyline from his wide windows. It's raining today, and the sky is overcast, not that it's important, but I realize how nice the view is here at this time of the day.

"I'm not trying to pressure you to stay. If you want to, I want you to know it's an open offer, Sophs. I would have you with me every night." He draws my attention back to him with a little worried look, and I smile at him to ease his tension.

"Okay," I answer, not sure what else to say.

Yes, I want to be here with him too, but no, I am not ready to throw all in and give him everything while I still feel like I need time. A part of me still thinks he needs to work for this a little. Stubborn Sophie who won't back down.

"I'm sorry if I'm being pushy. I know I'm getting ahead of myself. I really want you here. I want this to work." Again, he looks so young and wary, making me feel crappy. I sigh and tilt my head up, moving to sit up properly.

"I want that too. I know you're not being pushy. I just need a little breathing space to get my head around this." I shrug, unable to look him in the eye for a moment because I know it's not the answer he wants.

"I understand, baby. Please eat, Sophs. I can't take you home unless you do. I hate seeing you living on pancakes and sundaes." He cuts in, changing the topic because he realizes it's not the time to go into this. I need time, and he promised me I could have it.

"Ughhh, for God's sake. I think I'm going to rename you Jake!" I snap. Never a morning person, and I hate how nagging he can sometimes be. He's worse than my mom.

"Jake would get fewer arguments from you. You do what he tells you." He points out with a frown, a hint of attitude because it's true. But then Jake is my godfather, and he can be one scary dude when he wants to be.

"Jake's less of an ass than you are." I retort, leaning out and picking up the spoon in my bowl to mix the mixture of food childishly.

"Thanks, I love you too, Sophs.... Okay, back to this ... I train every weekday morning and twice in the evenings; I can never schedule my work rota at Carrero Corp as lately it's been hectic, so we will have to take each day as it comes in terms of dating. I also fight in three weeks. I need to fly to Miami a week before. I guess I'll have to plan everything around all that." He pushes my bowl back towards me when he sees me playing with it, and I give him a look that equates to 'I am still not eating it,' which is met with a frown.

"Check us being all proper grown-up and organized. Do I need a calendar to write this all down?" I smirk at him, slapping his hand off when he tries to pick up my spoon to push at me.

"A spank, maybe. How about you text me daily and tell me when to pick you up? I'll tell you when I can't. I meant what I said. I would see you every second of every day if you let me." He sighs heavily, eyes homed in on my lack of eating, and I refrain from sticking my tongue out at Mr. Frustrating. over there.

"Why does this feel the same?" I sigh, eyeing him up with scrutiny suddenly, wondering if it's normal that we have reverted to us of old. Suddenly wondering what that even means.

"What do you mean? Same as what?" He stops and glances up at me from his bowl, looking at me like he has no clue what I mean. A teeny hint of concern in the depths.

"All of this seems just like when we used to make plans to go off skiing or to hang out. It doesn't feel different. We're being so ... normal." I wave my hands to emphasize my point and then flop onto my elbows, caging my bowl. Arrick straightens and shrugs at me, eyes on the food that I am once again stirring absentmindedly.

"Because it is normal. Relationships are like this, Sophie. Best mates who also fuck and kiss a lot. No other dates or people are in the way, but like we were, with much more intimacy and touching." He shrugs with one shoulder, looks relieved, and goes back to what he was doing, reaching out to stop me from sending the contents of my bowl over the edge with the way I am messing with it. He stills my hand and pushes the darn thing back at me more forcefully this time.

"What did you think it would be like?" He adds in afterthought.

"I don't know. Awkward maybe. That it would be, or feel different, and not feel so normal and non-scary. I thought it would be something new and kinda weird." I watch that perfectly calm face, the spasm of a neat eyebrow as he takes in what I am saying, and the little smile that breaks the corner of his mouth. I also pick up my spoon and go straight back to drawing patterns in my granola so that some sploshes on the table most satisfyingly. He looks at me like he maybe is rethinking the spanking comment and eats. Arry hates mess.

"When we get to sex, it will change the dynamics a little, but generally, we already had a close relationship. That's why we're doing this slowly. So nothing is scary or overwhelming for you, baby. Just us like this, and we will work up to more later if you want to. This is how it is. We already had something that worked." He seems confident in the fact, while I feel confused.

"Guess I'm used to guys who constantly try to hump my leg.

Fuck me about, leave me hanging, and screw my so-called mates when they don't get what they want." I shrug this time and go back to torturing my food with my spoon. Complacent about my dating past and not feeling anything about any of the scumbags who never deserved me anyway.

"None of that is ever going to happen with me. We have always been honest with each other. I might occasionally hump you, though, when I get majorly horny from you doing things like this." Raising a brow, he leans under the table and catches my foot which has crept up his warm limb under his pant leg of its own accord. Wiggling toes up his shin, not thinking of what that had been doing to him. With a hand around my heel, he lets my foot drop back to the floor with a furrowed, cute look.

"Oops." I blush and sit my feet together on the floor. Feeling a little cold on the wooden surface seeing as I am barefoot. Arrick adjusts his sweatpants and carries on eating, shaking his head at me with the half-smile that sets his dimples off. Sighing heavily that his girl about gave him a boner without intending too, with her foot because it was cold.

"Don't ever be afraid to talk to me, tell me what you're thinking, and call me out on bullshit. We are no different from how we were, only closer. I want us to be so much closer than we were." He picks up his glass of orange and takes a long drink, watching me carefully. Every mannerism controlled in his very Arrick way. I stare at him in fascination as he drinks his squash, at his Adam's apple moving sexily in that strong neck.

"That sounds ... nice," I answer, aware that he is a little too focused on me. His eyes go straight to my bowl with a brow flicker as he puts his glass down.

For goodness' sake, stop obsessing, Arry!

"Eat, Sophie, for the love of God, or I will literally spoon-feed you." Arrick looks at his watch and pushes my bowl back at me in agitation after I eased it further out again; getting up, he has finished and gives me that Carrero glare. He is trying to exert a little command and failing. I shake my head at him and meet a sigh of resignation.

"Okay, so we have all that agreed on ... Anything else?" I pout, pulling over the bowl, and taking a spoonful anyway. Because now, his sighing has me feeling shitty when all he wants is to take care of me, and his irritation is becoming evident. I am pleasantly surprised that it tastes good and start digging in while he takes his bowl to the sink and rinses it. He looks up, sees me chewing, and smiles impulsively. Happy that he thinks he has some sway over me when really, I didn't think I could handle any more of his womanly whining.

"You tell me. Is there anything you want to talk about or set in stone?" He asks pointedly. I have to admit it's odd to see him standing washing dishes at five a.m. while dressed in gym clothes and looking weirdly ... domestic. And that brings a certain 1950s aspiring housewife to mind.

I ponder telling him to cut Natasha off once and for all but hold my tongue, knowing that it is selfish and pathetically insecure, and he already explained to me why he won't. He won't be impressed if I say screw her father's cancer and kick her to the sidewalk. The little brat voice in my head says I should demand it with bells on, and yet Miss. Mature. who's trying to be a better person, tells me to keep it to myself if I want this relationship to go anywhere.

"I want to go out on proper dates." I blurt out instead, unsure which part of my brain formulated that one when looking for an alternative to burning Natasha in hellfire. I guess I want to experience that with him.

"Tell me where and we will. Or do you want me to surprise you?" Arrick doesn't even blink at my request, mind on planning our life, I guess, and it's strangely reassuring to see him back like this. Back to the guy who would drop a trip on me, jump at an idea, and plan everything I said on a whim. He stopped being this guy when he was with her like she sapped all the spontaneity out of him and forced him into the quiet lane of life.

"The aquarium and the zoo ... I miss skiing with you, and maybe we could do that rock climbing thing again in the sports place you used to go to." I lift my spoon and watch the contents pour back down into the bowl, mesmerized by the way it sploshes in the milk before trying another spoonful and again being surprised that it still tastes edible. I'm hungry enough to eat it now and decide I may not die if I allow him to feed me one healthy breakfast. My parents make me eat this kind of crap from time to time, so I might as well face it.

"So, you want me to take you everywhere we used to go and do the things we did before I moved out here?" He laughs, eyeing the mess I am making, and says nothing. I wonder if that little OCD part of his brain is thinking about putting a bib on me and maybe feeding me himself next time. Mess and chaos give him major anxiety. He can be really bad when stressed, but for the most part, it's been controlled for years.

"U-huh, except you know ... you could throw in a lot of romance too. Maybe a candlelit picnic at the zoo or matching ski suits with 'I love Sophie forever' written on your hat!" I shrug and stuff a huge mouthful in this time, crunching noisily even though some of it has gone soggy.

Still tastes edible!

"You don't want much, do you, baby?" He chuckles, tossing the dishcloth he is using to the side, and rolls his sleeves back down. It's oddly sexy seeing him being a house husband. "Sure, we could do all that and more." He returns to stand at his chair casually and watches me continue eating ungracefully. I wonder if eating like an untrained ape is sexy to him, and judging by the frown on his face right now, I guess not.

"I want Cheetos, Pepsi, and a corn dog for dinner when I come home from school tonight," I add, knowing fine well that after enduring this for my start to the day, I deserve a decent meal later.

"You can have pizza and a milkshake." Arrick adopts his no-nonsense fatherly tone. I have heard this a million times in the past and know I have zero energy for it. I can always argue the point later.

"Fine, but I want a chocolate sundae for dessert," I add, suddenly picturing ice cream in my mind's eye. Preferably a very big mountain with a million toppings.

"Okay, for tonight, but you will be eating better if you're staying here, and there's no arguing about it." He pushes his chair in, moves his mat from the table, and tosses it on the counter behind him.

"We'll see." I raise an eyebrow at him wickedly, and he only sighs heavily. Still watching me eat as though he has never witnessed feeding time at the zoo, and I wonder if he wants to video it. Maybe it's the fact he has never seen me put something moderately healthy in my mouth on purpose and is making sure it's not an illusion.

"I know that look, Sophs. I'm not going to fold so easily anymore. I already know what you're like to handle, and this is not how it will stay!" He challenges me, eye to eye.

"You know what you're letting yourself in for then. Therefore, don't expect any drastic changes to my eating habits." I shrug stubbornly and pout a little in his direction. Waving my spoon his way and splashing watery yogurt all over the place.

There's a long silence for a moment as we stare each other out with lowered brows, a non-serious face-off before he sighs again. I can almost smell his defeat in the air and feel strangely smug.

"You're going to make life hell for me, aren't you?" He seems resigned to the fact and has just realized how bad a life with me as a girlfriend might be. I wonder if he has had his first bout of second thoughts.

"Maybe. You chose this life, cowboy, so you better man up. You did say you would do anything for me!" I smile wider when he only sighs and shakes his head in defeat.

Chapter 13

I yawn as I wander from the elevator into Arrick's apartment, covering my mouth and dropping my oversized school bag on the floor by his coat rack in the entrance dumping ground for shoes. His jacket and sneakers are already there, and I can hear the soft strumming of a guitar as I wander around the little wall that conceals the elevator from his lounge area.

He is sitting on the couch strumming his acoustic guitar, oblivious to my arrival, and I stop and watch him for a moment with a huge smile across my face. It's been eons since he played his guitar, and I reminisce warmly over how many times he has played for me. A little shiver of joy that the boy I loved is making a slow comeback. He looks amazingly sexy with it on his lap, strumming it while concentrating so hard on what he's doing. He seems so at peace, not a single expression on that calm, beautiful face.

It has been over three weeks of dating him, and we are getting into a routine slowly. Going out together, having fun, and spending more nights together than apart. I left my friends from our Friday dinner and caught a cab here to wait for him as planned, but he has beaten me home after drinks with his friends at a nearby bar.

Sometimes we still do things apart. I still feel like I should be holding something back a little, not quite ready to throw myself at his mercy again fully, and he doesn't complain when I ask for a night to do my own thing. He still understands where I am at.

I slide off my flat pumps and discard my cardigan with my jacket, moving across to come upon him from behind so he won't see me until I run my fingers over those large shoulders that scream to be touched. These past weeks I've been braver about exploring that body when I cuddle up to him and discovered he has no boundaries where he lets my hands roam. Of course, as long as it's not down into his pants, which he is making sure is off-limits and things stay unheated.

Arrick pauses, looking up and seeing me smiling down at him, catches my face as I lean over and gives me an upside-down kiss. Crazily molding our mouths and managing a very erotic bit of lip-sucking that makes me giggle. I run my fingers over his face as I pull away and push my hair back behind my ears.

"Hey, beautiful." He returns to his guitar, pulling it back onto his lap as I come around and sit beside him. Curling my legs under me in my dress so I can get comfortable listening. I loved watching him play in my teens and cannot express the happiness of seeing him back to this after two years of putting it away because of Tasha. I get a little mental high-five at the fact he is back to playing again. A sign that he is happier and more relaxed in his own skin like he used to be.

"Sing for me." I urge him, smiling softly when he glances my way. All awkwardness I felt at the beginning of this relationship has fully dispersed in the last few weeks. I feel more like I used to, able to be myself around him for the most part, even with the silly quarrels and disagreements that mean nothing. We still have those, yet they are never about anything serious or important.

"What do you want me to sing for you?" He strums a few notes as he tunes his guitar again while I think back to all the songs he used to play well and suited his husky voice.

"The Creep, by Radiohead." I sigh at him, memories of that song one night two years ago when we were snowed in at a skiing lodge with no power and only warm beer and friends to get through the night. Arrick played this song for me when most were almost asleep or chilling by the log fire. I was haunted by the memory of how perfect that moment was for a long time after. Arrick smiles down at his guitar as though reliving the same memory, looking my way for a moment.

"I almost kissed you that night. I remember looking at you after this song and thinking how much I wanted to kiss you. Moving in close without even thinking about it and telling myself I was drunk and being an idiot." He frowns as he strums another couple of notes, eyes still on me and looking at me like he wants to kiss me now. All his subtle little tells are showing, and his eyes are all hazy.

"You never told me that before." I tilt my head to one side and regard him as he plays softly on his guitar, moving into that familiar pose. Hunched over and tapping his foot in time as he gently strums Radiohead's "Creep" tune.

"Guess I put it down to a moment of stupidity. I tried to play it off as being alcohol-driven." He shrugs nonchalantly and carries on regardless. Smiling as he looks down at the strings and then back at me.

"I remember you moving in close and moving hair from my face, I didn't think you would ever kiss me again, so I never thought that's what you were doing." I replay the moment, seeing it differently now I know what he had meant to do, and it makes me all warm and fuzzy inside.

"I don't remember kissing you before that; I know you told me I did. I guess it's true what they say about being drunk. Your real feelings come through when you let your guard down, and it seems I have a habit of kissing you when under the influence, or at least thinking about it." Arrick slides his guitar off over his head, much to my disappointment, but only moves it slightly to one side so he can lean into me and kiss me fully.

Softly at first, then moving in against my face and deepening it to an open-mouthed kiss. His tongue finds mine as passion spikes. Clearly, he is reliving his memory but finishing it with a new ending, and I'm not complaining. His kisses are always divine and have my toes curling no matter how often he does it. I've lost count over the past three weeks. Sometimes, it's a haze of being kissed by him endlessly, and this one is another five-star butterfly maker. His hand traces my jawline and down my throat tenderly, erupting a million tiny sensations across my skin.

Arrick has avoided letting our make-out sessions get beyond this level of passion for the last couple of weeks, always aware of taking things too far, and it is starting to get to me. Not sure if I am ready to get more physical, but his lack of pushing any boundaries is making certain that I will never know unless we try. He is being tender, cautious even, and infuriatingly gentlemanly.

When I've tried to heat things up, he breaks off and separates us, cooling it back down immediately. A part of me loves that he is this considerate, and this is just his way of respecting me and taking care of me. But on the other hand, I want to feel whole and capable of having a normal relationship. Part of me is afraid he'll get used to this weird something, stuck between platonic and not, and we will never move further. I want the whole package. I want to feel like I did in the first moments of that night when he brought my body to new heights of pleasure.

Like every other time, he breaks free when blood starts to warm up, and kisses become breathless and frenzied. Lets me loose and pulls his guitar back between us, back to strumming softly and calming himself down with a little space. I flop back on the couch and stare at the ceiling while listening to him, knowing it's pointless getting upset about it, even if it irks me. He's only being the guy I love. He's only thinking about what taking it further can do to me, and I can't be mad at him for that. His protectiveness is one of his most endearing traits.

He hasn't settled on a song and is still tuning his guitar. The alcohol I consumed at dinner with Christian and Jenny makes me sleepy and emotional, and when his phone starts ringing, I tense.

I'm not sure who it is. He always takes calls and texts from his family and friends, but my gut says it's Natasha. The woman has texted and called sporadically over the last couple of weeks. Tearful long drawn out sobbing conversations and hour-long texts begging him to see her. He hasn't, but he tries to appease her, soothe her tears, and generally tries to get her off his phone without being cruel.

It drives me crazy and is the one thing I am not honest and open about to him. I sulk, pout, and push him away when she calls, and we have had minor squabbles about it in which I always say I am fine and, no, it's not upsetting me. That I'm being an ass for the sake of it. He seems to think it irritates me a little, rather than the fact it shreds my insides to fucking pieces when I know he is still connected to her in some way.

At first, I understood. I mean, her dad is only getting worse, and they don't think he has much time left, but now weeks in, and more than a dozen of these episodes, I am losing my temper. I catch a glimpse of him pulling his phone towards him and sighing. I see that moment of self-doubt, where he is trying to choose whether to answer, and I can already tell he will. To me, it says it all. Saying nothing, I quickly get up from the couch and storm over to the kitchen to look for food. If I am out of direct sight, he might not see me hating on him and making death motions with kitchen utensils behind his back.

Opening the refrigerator, I pull out the chocolate and Pepsi he keeps for me, despite claiming he never would. I go rummaging for the box of snacks he dutifully keeps in the cupboard. I put some popcorn in the microwave and try to zone out as I hear his voice on the one-sided telephone call.

"Tasha, please, you can't keep doing this. Are you drunk?" He sounds tired and strained, but the fact he is still willing to put up with this shit only angers me. I'm tired and irrational, and I don't care if he sees me pissed at this tonight. I am so sick of acting like it doesn't get to me as much as it does. Tired of the little charade of the understanding girlfriend I have had to play for this long. Even when she showed up that one time to the movies when we were there, he ended up sitting with her for twenty minutes across the aisle and 'consoled' her. I thought of walking out on him that night and never coming back. He didn't see how pissed I was at all, and it's only been growing stronger.

Gathering up all my snacks onto a tray and leaving the popcorn in the microwave, I walk past him without a backward glance. Chin in the air and the walk of a woman who has had enough.

"I'm going to bed," I announce loudly, knowing fine and well Natasha will hear me and not giving a single shit about it. I have kept quiet long enough. Acting like I am oblivious and never make a peep when she calls, in case it upsets her that I am here, but I am in no mood anymore. This has been eating at me the longer it goes on.

Arrick is probably frowning at me for being unnecessarily cruel, but I am not about to turn back and look. Nudging the bedroom door open with my hip as he carries on with his obviously uber-important call.

"Yes, that was her. You know I'm with her, Tash." He sighs again as I try to angle my hip under the handle to open the door. The tray is too full, and I am also balancing a can of open Pepsi, so I can't let go with one hand. Arrick suddenly appears behind me, opening the handle and pushing the door open for me without removing his cell from his ear. I mutter some thanks under my breath and press ahead without turning his way.

I wonder if he is going to follow me. It wouldn't be unlike him when I announce I am going to bed, but instead, he seems to go back to the couch and continue consoling his ex fucking girlfriend.

"I know you do. I get that you miss me and miss that I was the one you always talked to." He lowers his voice. I resist the urge to kick the door shut on him and block it out, but I can hear the microwave reminding me of the popcorn, and I curse myself. I want to stay in here, rage, and not have to walk past him again and face that disapproving look he gives me when I am being difficult. I hate that even now, he can still make me feel like a childish, spoiled brat at times and isn't shy at making it obvious.

He has no concept of what a dickhead he is sometimes.

I lift my chin and pace the room for a moment, putting my food on the nightstand and killing time by turning on the tv and finding a movie to turn on low. It isn't overly late, and we have no plans tonight except to stay here and vegetate, as we have plans to meet his friends for bowling tomorrow night. Christian and Jenny are coming, and Nathan is too. We have been doing a lot of stuff like this with all of them, and even Christian's boyfriend has been on the scene, James and I like him.

I'm called by the ping of the microwave and try to remove any traces of severely pissed off from my face. I move to the door and walking out, I see him taking it out for me and bursting open the bag into a bowl. He has his phone tucked under his chin and propped on his shoulder, so evidently still talking to her, and I want to throw something at the back of his head from over here.

Marching over towards him, I avoid eye contact when he turns and realizes I'm there. Pretending to be absorbed in finding something in the drawer instead. Locating napkins and a straw and taking the bowl from him without any contact while looking down at what I'm holding. Arrick catches me by the upper arm as I head back to the bedroom and holds me steady.

"Natasha, I need to go. I'm sorry, but this is a bad time. Go to bed and sleep it off." He lets his phone slide, catching it with his free hand and hitting the red button before pushing it into his back pocket. He leans in to try and angle his face to mine, but I gaze off at the bedroom door instead.

"You're pissed." He states flatly. Still not letting me loose. I shrug and pop popcorn in my mouth, and act like I really don't give a shit. Simmering like a volcano inside but coolly calm on the surface. Still avoiding his gaze and trying not to erupt, even though everything inside of me wants to.

This is the only difference between us since coming back together. I don't tell him how I feel when it comes to Natasha, sometimes in general, and I know I should be. There is still that part of me that isn't ready to let him in yet fully. An insecure and scared portion of my heart is terrified he will hurt me again.

I know Natasha is a topic I deliberately don't broach because I am too scared to just come out with it and tell him to choose. My brain keeps reminding me that he picked her over me, and part of me is insecure that if I lay down an ultimatum, he will again. Even though I know it's dumb as hell even to believe it. Insecurity is a messy, shitty thing and logic has no place where it is concerned.

"Why?" He nudges me, urging me to look at him. I roll my eyes at him and shrug his hands off me. Making a move towards the bedroom impassively with no desire to even talk about this. I'm glad he hung up on her, and now I want him to leave me alone so I can hate on him in peace.

"Don't give me the silent treatment. You're pissed because she called, right? I have no control over that!" He sounds irritated too, and I remember he's also been drinking tonight. When drunk or even tipsy, Arrick is less patient and less understanding. He takes on a much colder and easily agitated version of himself that I can see was probably how he got through being such an asshole in his teens and using and abusing girls. I probably wouldn't have liked him much back then, but thankfully when I met him, he seemed to calm almost instantly. I guess I met him at the right stage of his life.

"Yes, you do!" I snap, all anger bursting forth. Despite telling myself to hold all this in, it has somehow wormed its way out. "You can stop being so goddamn nice and pandering to her! You broke up months ago!" I slam the popcorn down on the coffee table, spilling a huge chunk of it with my napkins and straw, turning on him in sheer frustration. "Tell her to leave us alone." It comes out like a spoiled childish stamp my foot moment, and I curse the cocktails I had with dinner for making me like this. Equally shit when I drink, in totally different ways to him. I get irrational, impulsive, and emotionally unstable and start tantrumming like a two-year-old.

Arrick stands stiffly and watches me silently, that flat calm demeanor coming into play instantly, which only sparks my fury more. I hate when he takes on this stance of no emotion because I know a lecture or argument is coming, and he is about to make me feel about twelve years old.

I hate when he does that.

"It takes more than a few weeks to get over two years. You have no clue how hard this is for her. What she lost and is losing... It was a full-on relationship. I was *her* best friend, we talked about everything, and she confided in me about everything, Sophie. I walked away and left her alone at a time when she needed someone to be there for her." He is a little too deadpan for that statement, and I want to throat-punch him for not realizing how much of an idiot he is. He cannot see the irony in what he is saying, that he left me alone, despite all that. He is stupidly dense not to see that right now.

"It's called life! I know about being alone and having no one, and I survived. She will get over it, but not if you keep letting her infiltrate our lives." Tears begin to sting my eyes, and I bite them down, not wanting this, but now we are here. I am not about to fall to pieces over it in front of him. Fueled by anger at this, her, his stupidity sometimes. I honestly feel like throwing my hands at his face and beating some sense into that thick Carrero skull.

"You're being insecure and jealous, nothing more. Natasha isn't a threat. She doesn't have anything to get between us with. She just needs a friend... You know I can't stand jealous women, Sophie." He walks off towards his study at the left of us and seems to dismiss me with a look. I erupt in good old-fashioned fiery hell hath no fury. The part of me that has been dormant since Leila's party. He has no clue how much of an asshole that sentence just made him.

"Fuck you. Stop talking down to me like I'm a fucking child! I hate it when you do that." I scream at him; seeing him stop and tense, he turns harshly, shocked by my sudden outburst and acting like a typical man. I can already tell the response will not be full of sweet nothings. That little tight muscle tense on his jaw, brows lowering and angry green glare.

"Stop behaving like a fucking child, then. She is in pain, and you've already got me. There is no need for any of this bullshit!" He yells back, eyes burning with rage and seething so instantly it makes me lose all courage. My lip wobbles as the tears break free and run down my face because of my one of two responses to him ever yelling at me. Cry or fight! And this time, it chooses to be the pitiful reaction. So severely disappointed in myself, but I have no control over what path my emotions choose.

Arrick grits his teeth, sighing and frowning hard but walks towards me anyway. His body is bristling with temper, but that part of him that cares about me is reigning supreme. He hates seeing me cry, even if pissed off, and it's that nice guy side to him that is caving right now.

"Don't cry. I'm sorry I yelled at you." He reaches for me,

despite the anger between us, and pulls me in as his arms envelop me. There is no gentle affection in the embrace, only a need to make me stop crying. He's still majorly pissed and consoling me out of duty. His arms around me are not comforting and snug. They hang loosely about me as he half-heartedly pats my back.

"I'm going to bed." I break free of his arms, hating how false it feels, pushing him away. My insides are twisting up in agony, and so close to bawling hysterically. He doesn't fight me on it, just lets me go and watches me gather up the stuff from the table and walk away. I can still feel his penetrating gaze on my back as I walk in the door and kick it closed behind me in a little hostile flag of 'I still hate you.'

* * *

I roll over in bed, aware he has followed me after twenty minutes in the dark, my tray dumped, and lights and TV off due to my low mood. I do not want to eat or watch any shitty romances anymore.

The bed dips as Arrick's body slides in beside me. We have gotten into a routine of sharing a bed, with me staying here or him staying with me almost every night and cuddling up. This is the first time I have been in bed before he has come in since the first few days. He slides his arms around my still body, oblivious to the fact I am awake, and buries his face in my hair behind me. I stay frozen, my heart still bruised, and even though the tears have dried externally, I am still crying inside. So much anger and sadness mixed up together.

"Sophie?" He whispers softly, voice hoarse and tender with no hint of anger anymore. Wrapping himself around me snugly so that every part of him fits me. I try to stay immobile and not react. Still upset and unwilling to let him know I am even listening, not sure what I even want him to say anymore. "I know you're awake. I can tell." He nudges me softly with his knee, a gentle Arry mannerism that makes the pain in my chest soften a little. Aching to be normal with him again and not lie here feeling this miserable. I sigh and turn a little to acknowledge him. Wrapped up tight in his embrace yet still feeling closed off and alone.

"What is it?" I whisper back icily, trying to keep the fact I was crying from my voice. I don't like letting him see when he hurts me. A part of me that has changed since we got back together. I know it's stupid to hide when he wounds me, but it's like a knee-jerk defensive reaction. Not letting him see my vulnerability is all connected somehow to how crazily messed up I still am and cannot even decipher it.

"I'm sorry. I hate fighting with you, baby. I'm trying to distance myself from her, Sophs. It's not that easy. I don't want to be cruel. I need you to understand and not give me a tough time on this." He sounds hurt, anger gone, and just my soft, gentle Arry lying in the dark with me. Winning me back around like he always does, smoothing over bruised feathers, and reminding me how grateful I should be that I even have him.

I turn in his arms and push my face into his neck, feeling him adjust so he can hold me this way and try so hard to let this go so I can feel better. He pulls me in close and runs his fingers down my shoulder and back up my spine through my tank top. Nestling close to me and finding a comfy position to sleep with entangled bodies is how he likes us to be.

"I love you, *Mimmo*. So much." He murmurs sleepily, obvious that he thinks we are okay, despite my saying nothing except cuddling close. My head and emotions are battling one another, and dried tears are still stinging my face as new ones threaten to fall.

Maybe it's a lack of experience in life and love, or I am an immature child, which is why I can't understand this. Arrick has always cared about people, and I know this is at the root of why he is just so willing to let Natasha hold on, but now with the weeks passing by, I am starting to doubt this as the sole reason.

Natasha had been his life. He loved her. She had been his future. He chose to go back to her before he came for me, and a part of me wonders if maybe, just maybe, he is having second thoughts and is the one who won't let her go.

Chapter 14

School is stressing me out today, Christian and Jenny are squabbling in the corner, and I have had to redraft this pattern a dozen times. My focus is all over the place, and the interruptions by Karen, another classmate, are making me crazy. I should have just stayed home.

I woke up moody and irritable, and when Arrick got up to shower, I found myself lying in bed and staring at his phone, contemplating if he had deleted texts from her. I know it's stupid. I pushed away the temptation to look at his phone, hating that my mind even went there and knowing how wrong it would be. I would go crazy if he looked through mine, even though there's nothing I wouldn't show him. I know I trust him, but my heart and my head are gnawing apart, with her swirling between us. I have so many insecurities from before; his choice to have a life with her and not me. His decision to keep her around, and as rational as I am trying to be about everything, I can't help how it's making me this way.

I haven't told him. Closing up when she is the topic or the focus, afraid to say it out loud in case he thinks I'm a crazy jealous girlfriend. I saw how badly past girls fared by showing their jealous side around him in his past. He literally can't handle it. He's not that type of person. He doesn't get jealous or tolerate it either because he doesn't understand it when you're supposedly in a stable relationship. Something he said to me in all seriousness, like he didn't even see the connection at all. I felt like poisoning his coffee that day.

In the last weeks, he has been the perfect boyfriend, minus the lack of sex and occasional shithead remarks that make me wonder which planet his brain hibernates on at times. I love him so much sometimes, and other times I wonder what goes on in that pretty head of his and if committing murder is legal if 'idiot boyfriend' is the cause.

Despite all that, he's sweeter than I could have ever imagined. He pampers me and indulges me, even when I'm being childish and trying. What started as only seeing each other a couple of times a week ended up being together every night because he would show up to sleep beside me or talk me into coming over when I was done with my sewing homework. Somehow our days have become more and more integrated into each other's lives in a brief time without even trying. He's taken me on every type of date imaginable, and, contrary to the guy I used to see with Natasha, Arrick never has his hands off me.

He always holds my hand, puts his arms around me, and kisses me anytime he feels like it. Publicly too, usually a lot. He's not shy about adoring me and manhandling me wherever we go or whoever we are with, and he does seem a lot happier and more like the Arry he used to be before he moved out here. He looks more relaxed, back to being less cool and emotionless on the surface towards everyone and more chilled out. Even his friends have noted and commented on it when he isn't listening.

I know all of that should tell me that I'm making him happier than she ever did, but I can't shake it or shift it. This pit of heaviness is like a black cloud on my sunny day that lingers and threatens to ruin everything. I feel like there's a part of his head that I have no access to and in my stupidity, I am convinced that's where he harbors all his little Natasha memories and feelings away from me.

I haven't even told Emma about this, despite calling her every few days and talking the sex and other stuff through. I know she will tell me I am being dumb, even I know I am, but I can't help it. It's been growing over the weeks, and now every time I see him near his phone, no matter the reason, I assume it's her. Or if he runs late from work or the gym or disappears into his study to send emails. I keep telling myself it's irrational, but it's there, stuck inside me, clawing away at my sanity, making me crazy inside.

It's becoming this monster in the room that only I can see. Always lingering in the shadows.

I'm beyond terrified he will wake up one day and say he misses her more than he missed me and leaves me for a life he lost. I constantly worry that I'm not giving him the parts she did, and maybe he will realize the novelty with me has worn off.

"Ugh!" Jenny slams down a pile of fabric swatches on the table and slumps down opposite me. Making me jump as I was lost in my head and driving myself into insanity again on this dumb topic.

"My sentiments exactly." I huff without taking my eyes off the chalk line I'm drawing across my bodice pattern, changing the angle slightly to better fit my mannequin. I hate making cotton first drafts of clothes. So much adjusting and redesigning makes me impatient to get to my fabric choice and the finished result. I need to feel calm at this stage, not inwardly cursing out my boyfriend and contemplating life.

"Please tell me yours is male-related too, and then I will feel less like an idiot ... In fact, it won't be. Your boyfriend is perfect!" Jenny sighs again, catching my eye this time, and I smile softly. Putting down my chalk.

"Nate?" I press. She has been 'casually seeing him' since my sister's party. Apparently, they are only sex on tap and going nowhere kind of deal, but it's obvious from our frequent group nights out that Jenny is falling for him while Nate is still being Nate. Acting like a single Casanova who shows her a moderate amount of attention but not what she wants. The nights out have been awesome, yet his attention towards her seems to run hot and cold, and she never seems to know how to behave around him.

"I know what we are. He doesn't exactly promise me anything different. It's just ... he acts so into me when we are alone, and then when we're not, it's like I don't exist. He rarely texts or calls me, and I always have to initiate it." She sighs heavily, gazing at me sadly. I wish I had some optimistic speech or line to give her, but I have only witnessed the same thing, and Arrick never seems to have an opinion on it.

"I know ... don't say it. You told me, and I said I was fine with just a fuck buddy while I got over Mark." She looks like she's about to burst into tears, and I lay down my chalk and sit down to face her properly, realizing she needs an ear right now to get this off her chest. I paste on my most understanding and gentle expression and hope I have the wisdom to give her right now. I am hardly an expert on happy relationships.

Clearly!

"Sex makes everything messy!" Christian interjects, leaning between us with a furrowed brow, obviously listening and looking super fly in black today. Lately, his love life has been much more settled, his boyfriend finally coming out and joining us all on our little group get-togethers.

James seems to get on with Arry and Nate and the other guys and their girlfriends who come along. I love our extended circle of friends, having known all of Arry's male friends for a long time and now getting to know their new women and extended friends. It feels right, as though I've found where I belong, and no one mentions Natasha. Even though they all know Arrick was with her before showing up with me on his arm as his girlfriend instead of the best friend. Christian, Jenny, and James now seem to slot in seamlessly with Arrick's friends. It's like they always were.

"Agreed." I raise a brow at him, and we nod in unison. I still haven't admitted to them that we haven't even gone down that road again or that I don't even know if I want to. Half of me does, half is scared, and my emotions are still all over the place concerning even trying again anytime soon. I think this whole Natasha thing is messing with me. As much as it frustrates me that Arry isn't trying to get me to try again, a part of me is glad in case I freak out. If it really is down to trust, and even Emma thinks it is, then this messy Natasha hate I have going on will screw it up and make him think I will never be able to go there with him. I'd rather not try if that is the outcome.

"Maybe it's time to cut him loose, Jen. Accept it's going nowhere, and you'll get hurt if you keep sleeping with him." I frown harder at her. Knowing Nate as I do, I know he isn't going to stop messing around and settle down with one girl. Unknown to her, he brought a girl back with us a few nights ago from a bar where we met up. He had sex with her in Arry's spare room and left early the next day. It wasn't hard to guess what they were doing.

She was a screamer, and Arry laughed at the noises while I growled and threatened to castrate the bastard before he drowned them out with some music. Okay, Arry had to wrestle me to stay in bed and remove all the sharp objects I found to go and end the screaming noise in the next room. He laughed mainly at me and my rage and then had to talk me down from a psychotic turn. He finally only calmed down by drowning out the grunting porn fest with very loud music that finally let me sleep.

"I think I'm falling for him." She eyes me woefully, and my heart sinks, hating that I could have predicted this and knew she would get hurt. She got over Mark way too quickly and left herself open to this jerk. Of all the people to fall for in the whole of New York, I stupidly let Nathan near her.

"Don't do that. He is so not worthy of you. He's a slut. He won't change and trust me. You probably aren't the only girl he has hanging on." I know it's harsh, but I need her to stop this before he hurts her. I need her to know that he has been sleeping with other girls too. Probably frequently.

"I know. He told me. He never hides it, and I have never told him that it bothers me. I kind of told him I was seeing other people too so that he wouldn't think I was falling for him." She looks desolate as Christian puts an arm around her and throws me the 'yeah, that was never going to work' look over her head with a dramatic grimace. He raises a brow, looking a bit murderous, and I have to agree, if Nathan were around right now, I would maim him with my fabric scissors.

"Toxic relationships make you lie to hide your feelings, babe.

Cut him loose. You're not you, and you're acting out a part to keep him. You're girlfriend material, a one-guy girl, and he's not for you." Christian lays it on thick, squeezing her half to death. We catch each other's eye and almost nod in unison.

Nathan isn't right for our girl. She's a keeper. The kind of girl you marry and have a ton of babies with. She was never built for this crazy shitty world of games and casual sex. Nathan is jading a sweetheart with a pure soul for his own sordid ends.

"I keep telling myself that, but when I try and not text or call him, I miss him crazily." A tear fills her eye, and I feel like ripping Nate's head off. She is the last girl in the world who needs to fall into the arms of one emotion-sucking sex addict like him.

"Let him go." Christian and I agree in unison, staring at her with real love, so sure that this will end no other way. I know the agony she is in and can relate to her pain. I wish I could reach in and take it all away for her.

"I know, I know ... okay. I do." Jenny stifles a sob, and my heart melts. Moving around beside her at the table and mirror Christian's pose on the other side of her. Arms around her as we both hug her tight. Increasingly aware that I'm getting more touchy-feely nowadays,

I find that touch and affection aren't abhorring me in the same way anymore. I don't know if it's because of Arry or if I'm still moving on emotionally. I catch Christian's eye over the top of her head, and it's clear he's thinking the same thing I am.

She isn't falling for Nate, she clearly already has, and the bastard is already breaking her heart.

"When he takes me home after bowling tonight, I just want one more night, and then I'll tell him it's over ... I promise." She cries softly, not convincing either of us. Makeup streams down her rosy cheeks as Christian reaches for a fabric swatch and dabs her eye. I sigh down the reality because I know she will do no such thing. Mark got away with being a shitty boyfriend for two years because Jenny is too easily led, too accommodating when it comes to her heart, and too weak to dump anyone until they ditch her.

Nate is chewing her up, and the day is coming that he, too, will spit her out, and I hate that I can see this. I hate that someone as beautiful and kind as Jenny is at the center of such a shitty man's coldness. It's the first time I've ever felt a genuine dislike for Nathan Andrews!

Seething under the surface for hurting my friend. Christian mops more of her makeup off with the cream-colored velvet, and I suddenly realize what he is holding.

"That better not be the swatch for the design board we are supposed to finish today?" I glare at him frostily; our current project is almost done, and these marks go towards a final grade on this segment of our course. The fabric he's lifted looks a lot like the one I spent hours sourcing for our mood board.

"Shh. A friend in need. We'll just say it's grubby as it's urban chic." Christian gives me his sassy smile, shamelessly unconcerned that he probably ruined our whole board and weeks of work. I grit my teeth and then sigh in resignation.

A friend in need!

I roll my eyes at him over Jenny's head and take the swatch from him, using it to wipe the mascara streaks from her cheeks instead, and think, 'screw it.'

Chapter 15

"We're running late from this fight promo, baby. We'll meet you at the alley, maybe twenty minutes after you get there. Nate says can you tell Jen too." Arrick is on the phone, surrounded by background noise and sounding cheerful. I'm already home, where he was supposed to meet me, and getting ready, and I sigh heavily. Irritation rises because he's never late, and Nathan can go fuck himself, as far as I am concerned. Still not pleased with the way he's treating my girl.

"You suck. You know how much I hate getting cabs alone at this time of night. Tell Nate to text Jen himself. I'm not his secretary!" I snap a little harshly. I'm not really mad at Arry, just irritated that it's going to be another hour before I see him, and all day I have only wanted a hug from him. So listless and all over the place with my emotions, and he always makes me feel much more grounded. It was a shitty day at school, thanks to everything going wrong today, and I need some real TLC from the boy who knows how to make me feel so much brighter.

"I know, gorgeous, and I shall. The guy needs to man the fuck up and stop being such a pussy when it comes to women. I promise I won't be too late and will make it up to you." He sounds sexier on the phone today, more husk to that manly tone, his voice deeper since he's trying to keep his cell close to his mouth to blot out all the noise of the promo event they are at.

"In what way?" I ask saucily, knowing fine that sex is still off the table. Not sure how else men intend to do any making-up with sexy tones when there's no sex. It's still a source of eternal frustration that sends my head into gaga land.

"Tomorrow, we spend the full day, you and me, and do whatever you want. Saturday, so there is no school, and I have no training before my flight to LA on Sunday. We can stay home and vegetate or go anywhere you want. You have me for a whole uninterrupted day." He sounds smug down the phone, sure that he has offered me a more acceptable token of love. An entire day is a rare thing, to be fair. Neither of us has one at the same time that often.

"Uh, uh. Remember I need to get up and do that thing at 9 a.m.? It will take me an hour." I sigh, deflated that I'm ruining our first entire day, just to be. I have a school open day to attend. The fashion academy is hosting an event for new students, like a sign-up day, and I must man a stall for an hour as a favor for a girl who's going to see her doctor first thing.

"Okay, so I'll take you, pick you up, and then we can have our day." He tries again, muffled a little as he's moving around, and it sounds like someone speaks to him in the background and draws his attention for a moment. I pull off my leggings from the day, pace around barefoot on the carpeted floor of my bedroom, and haul out clean underwear. Sexy new buys: we may not be doing the deed yet, but he does like to get me into my underwear at bedtime, and it doesn't hurt to keep him interested in what can still happen.

"Uh, uh, again. Christian is collecting and dropping me off because he never stands me up and shows up late, unlike you! He's helping too. You can have me after that. He's off to see his man toy afterward anyway." I smirk down the phone, satisfied that I'm giving him enough of a hard time to keep him on his toes. I smile as I hold up a lace-infused navy set that leaves little to the imagination and put it beside the shoes I want to wear tonight.

"You never warned me way back when that despite him being gay, I would still have to share you. I might rethink beating him after all ... Okay, baby, I will make you breakfast, and then when you come home, we will figure out what we're doing for the day." He sounds happier, cheerful like he is most of the time nowadays, and a little tired, if I'm being honest. Some nights he doesn't let me fall asleep until he pesters me by making out and pointless half-the-night conversations about everything and nothing. Last night we stayed up till dawn discussing the finer points of New York cuisine. I have no idea why we even do that crap. I can't complain, though really. I love lying in his arms, listening to that sexy voice, and giggling my nights away with him. I can't imagine it any other way.

"I suppose ... if I must." I sigh dramatically, smiling when I hear him chuckle softly. Picturing his face and those to die for dimples make me want to squish his face.

"Are you ever going to let up on me? Even a tiny bit?" He jests, knowing he gets it way too easy and I should be harder on him. He just has to smile at me sometimes, and I'm all his.

"When you deserve it, I guess. Now go. Let me get ready. I have bowling to go to and might meet a hot guy who sweeps me off my feet." I sulk down the phone mockingly and catch sight of an alternate pair of shoes on the floor I might want to wear instead that have been dumped there mercilessly.

"Just make sure his surname starts with a C, or there will be hell to pay. I love you, Sophs." He seems to sound louder, moved to a quieter spot and a little echoing now, as though he is in a passageway.

"You're such a loser." I sigh with a smile, pulling another soft laugh from him.

"You will say it again one day, you know. I know you still do." Arrick turns serious for a moment, and I deflect. The conversation is a little too close to the bone, and I am unwilling to face the fact that I have been unable to say it to him since Leila's dance. That part of my heart is still curled up in hiding, waiting to see if it can.

"If you say so. Get off the phone. My arm's getting sore." I sigh and pout even though he can't see me. Rotating my shoulder and switching ears.

"Are you naked right now?" Arrick sounds completely smug, back to his cheeky self and the little sexual innuendos he throws my way more frequently nowadays. Even without sex, he likes to act like there is some.

"Ugh, that's it. I'm hanging up." I don't even stop for an answer, hang up the phone and toss it on the bed, eye rolling at him yet unable to suppress the laugh and smile he has pouring out of me.

That boy!

I pull my dress off and walk to my wardrobe in my underwear, picking up a casual pink dress that I have worn a couple of times to the movies and the day he took me to the aquarium. It's cute and flirty and looks good on me. Currently one of my favorites. It's enough dressed up for a night socializing and yet dressed down enough for bowling.

My phone beeps on the bed, so I automatically pick it up. Seeing Arry on the screen, I can't resist the heart-swelling reaction as I swipe to my inbox to see his text.

I love you, beautiful. Wear the pink one. xxxxx

I smile, despite myself, at my cute boyfriend; sometimes I feel like pinching myself to remind me this is real, and he really is mine for keeps. Well, on days I'm not super glum over the whole no sex and the still hanging on Natasha thing. Still, right now, I kind of love him a little bit more than I used to. My heart is doing a great job of letting him in a little more every day, and I guess I am starting to trust him in small ways over time.

Not that he gets to tell me how to dress, though.

I throw the pink dress on the bed defiantly and look for another in my endless sea of clothes.

Chapter 16

I stand laughing at Christian's awful attempt to get the ball down the ten-pin bowling alley with the help of Jenny. They are both equally poor at this, and Claire, one of Arrick's friends I have known a long time, is standing laughing beside me. She loves Christian and seems to find him equally amusing. Her short sassy red hair, framing an elfin face, and almost lavender grey eyes, are homed in on the two of them, mirroring my amused expression.

"Chris is way too hot to be gay." She appraises him bending over, and sighs hopelessly. Despite being married to Jason, she does have an eye for a nice ass. I like Claire. She's one of Arry's oldest friends and has been around this group as long as I have known him. She is married to Jason, another long-termer, and is this group's unofficial mom and dad. Everyone looks to them for advice.

"Trust me. He's way gay. That much drama would never be found in a straight man." I giggle as we both watch him grab Jenny's ass rather ruggedly, grasping it boldly to push her along with the ball, his idea of helping keep her straight. Jenny squeals, batting at his hand to keep her dress down, modestly covering that sexy body, and drops the thing on her foot. The following yelp is smothered by Chris's hand on her mouth as he dies laughing and tries to apologize without drawing attention to the fact he probably just broke her foot.

The comedy double act isn't unusual to see, I witness this hilarity almost daily at school, and I love these two even more because of it. It's like sibling love and hate in the cutest way.

"There you are." Arrick's voice encompasses me at the same time as he spins me and meets my mouth with a kiss, taking me by pleasant surprise. His hand instantly cups my face, and the other slides around my waist, so I have zero opportunity to react. He leans in to tilt me back, pushing the kiss to a little tongue action. Heating me in full view of everyone he knows and devouring me with 'God, I missed you' lip action before breaking away. He leaves me breathless and very hot with that little maneuver. Knowing fine well, it's the reaction he always gets and hits me with a sexy smile still practically attached to my mouth. I have to tame the inner tingles and uncontrollable urge to slide my hands under his shirt and feel out that sculpted abdomen. He has no idea how crazy with longing he can make me with just a swift kiss.

Still makes my toes curl every time.

"Gray dress? Trying to tell me something?" Arrick's eyes scan the jersey dress over the slouch boots I opted for instead of his favorite of the moment and sexy heels. I only raise eyebrows in a challenge and feign innocence poorly.

"I don't know what you mean!" I narrow my eyes with a smirk. I don't know why I still feel the need to do silly things like this. I guess a part of me is still punishing him in subtle ways, even if I am wrapping my arms around his neck for that much-needed hug I've yearned for all day. Relaxing finally into the only place I ever want to be.

"I love your little passive-aggressive stands, baby. It reminds me to keep on my toes where you're concerned." He grins, squeezing me, fully encircling me, and tightly bringing us together as he moves in for another kiss. Someone makes loud vomiting noises to our left and completely ruins the moment.

"Get a room." Nate chuckles at us, suave in navy tonight with freshly trimmed hair. I swat a hand at him and notice how his eyes immediately scan out toward where Jenny and Christian are still trying to throw one ball between them. I swear he looks positively nervous for a moment and then turns and walks off, my eyes suspiciously following him.

"What's that all about?" I nudge Arrick, who seems to be still focusing on my mouth and push him a little to indicate Nate. Still trapped in muscular arms, holding me tight with no intention of letting me go anytime soon.

"Who knows? He's a guy ... we're all fucking weird regarding women." He shrugs, smiling in that dazzling Hollywood special as if that's going to excuse either an answer and I screw up my face at him.

"I forgot you were also an emotional cripple with an aversion to drama." I point out. More truth in that statement than I like to admit. Even I know he's a guy who will bury his head when things get messy and avoid conflict until it passes. Growing up as a kid, when Jake was making his family's life chaotic taught him he hated getting caught up in an emotional mess. I wonder how much of that is to blame for the fuck up he made of things between us.

"Yet somehow, that made me perfect for you. Go figure." He chuckles, screwing up his face to match mine and laughing heartily when my expression drops to a complete deadpan when I click on his sarcasm. That I clearly attract over emotional drama.

Asshole!

He leans in and covers my glare with another swoon-worthy kiss that makes me forget to knee him in the balls and instead get lost in how good that tongue always feels in my mouth. I don't think I will ever stop having butterflies from how he kisses me. He knows how to make me feel like I am the sexiest and most beautiful woman on the planet when he does. Moving back and leaving me light-headed and giddy, still wrapped up tight in our happy cocoon, Arrick frowns past me at my friends and shakes his head.

"Maybe next time we pick something the two of them can do." He laughs and hauls me back with him toward the seats. Arm around me possessively, and I notice he has brought me a fresh Pepsi refill and a hot dog with a side of fries. Despite the constant lectures and always telling me to order healthier options, he indulges my diet.

"Aww, you love me." I grin, picking up the food, and throwing fluttering lashes of adoration at him with a grin.

"I clearly do ... I even bought you this." Arrick pulls a bag from his jacket pocket, a flat, striped paper bag I don't recognize, and take it from him. Opening carefully, I realize it contains a wrapped cookie in rainbow colors with a sticker that reads.

Magical Unicorn Cookie

It's a colorful, chocolate and candy stuffed cookie in supersize, and it looks like he brought it back with him from wherever they were today. My heart does a happy little skip and almost melts with the gooeyness of how incredibly cute he can be when I least expect it.

"Aww, Arry, I thought you put me on a candy ban?" I throw my best loving look, knowing fine well he has tried several times to do that and failed spectacularly.

"Like anything I ever try and enforce works with you." He winks at me as Nate shoves him from the back rudely, almost making him bang facially with me as he is so close, and turns both of our attention to him.

"One of you two take the shot. Jason has teamed you as a pair."

I turn and look up at our names on the screen for the next shot and smile merrily at the little names linked together as one. Stupid, juvenile, but whatever floats my boat.

"The Dream Team ... You are so going to get your ass kicked." I poke fun at Nate, pointing my poky finger in his face and almost getting him in the eye. He bats me away with a scowl meant to intimidate until Arry raises a mock slap as if to say, 'try it, buddy, and I'll hurt you.' It only encourages my smug side, and I stick my tongue out at Nate instead. He shakes his head at me, knowing my bodyguard is more than capable of breaking his face. Then, he is instantly distracted seeing Jenny walk by quickly, avoiding looking his way; he turns to follow her without hesitation.

"We'll see." Nate winks back at me over his shoulder and then disappears after my girl as she heads for the bar at the back. Arrick watches him too, looking like he isn't even surprised by Nate's slinking after her. He lifts his beer from beside the food I am happily stuffing in my face over his arm. I try to ignore it and hope Jenny really has the strength to end things tonight.

"You show them how it's done, beautiful. Make me proud." Arry pats my ass affectionately and gives a little nudge towards the alley, despite my handful of fries that I gracefully dump in his hand. I don't hesitate, secure in the fact he has taught me how to throw a strike for years. I'm his little prodigy, and he knows it.

Picking up my size bowling ball, I wander to the perfect spot, limber up like a pro, and wiggle my butt while glancing back at him, watching me with a smile. He gives me an encouraging wink. Eyes homed in on me like we are the only two people here.

I lean into the swing, down low for the let go and give my practiced bowling throw, the ball sliding out at speed and a straight line down the center to a perfect strike that has an eruption of cheers from our group of friends. Inwardly I swell with a "YESSSS" moment, giggling and acting like the cat who got the cream. I jump up and down in satisfaction giving a little squeal. I have not lost my touch before turning and trotting back to Arry's open arms. He's equally proud of me, grinning crazily as he picks me up, planting a kiss on my mouth with a smile. His arms are crossed and held tight under my butt, so I'm sitting at his abdomen level, much taller than him.

"That's my girl, perfect, as always." He keeps me up with my arms around his neck, legs bent so my heels are kicked up, and he carries me back to our table of junk food with his eyes on mine.

"Like there was any doubt?" I giggle, unable to tear my gaze from that face which melts me in every way. Something out of the corner of my eye catches my attention, spying someone over his head and I start tapping him subtly s my joy fizzles away with the recognition.

"Arry, put me down." I nudge him again, instantly bristling, then take hold of his chin and turn his face towards Natasha's approaching figure across the back of the hall. Through the crowds of milling bowlers, like a bad mood walking into a happy day. Instantly feeling like we shouldn't be flaunting ourselves like this as it just looks callous to everyone here, and the last thing I need is her playing the victim while spoiled brat Sophie acts like a jealous baby.

Arrick slides me down to my feet and lets me go slowly, sliding a hand over my dress to smooth it down and depositing a chaste kiss on the corner of my mouth. Obviously, he feels uncomfortable about her presence too, and I'm in too much of a state of surprise to react. I didn't think she would come here. I guess it's not hugely unbelievable, though, as these are her friends, and someone had to tell her we would all be here tonight.

"I better say hi, or else it will be more awkward. You want to come?" He turns to me in complete seriousness, which makes me almost blanch. I blink at him for a full three seconds, like he has completely lost his mind. I don't even have space for the hints of green-eye hatred while my brain is on 'What now?'

"Umm nope ... Think I'll stay right here." I frown at him sarcastically, as though he has lost his mind, and can't help the spike of anger when he walks off towards her and leaves me here. That spike of jealousy hits hard because he did what he said he would do, yet I expected him not to when I said I wasn't coming. I know I was the one who pointed her out, so we wouldn't rub salt in the wound, but I never thought he would willingly go over there and speak to her while he has me standing like a spare part over here. That erratic inner rage rises again, and I scowl at his progress across the floor toward her. All internal happy bubbles burst, and I'm back to thinking my boyfriend is the biggest idiot on the planet sometimes. I know it's dumb ... but I am beyond livid.

Stupid Sophie, get a grip!

I glare at his back as he wanders towards the group of people who have arrived with Tasha, relieved to see they're not mingling with our friends and not part of this group after all. I guess there's hope that she won't be coming over here to mingle and play, and we might lose her again sooner rather than later.

"Is that the competition?" Christian slides in, dropping an arm around my shoulder, and glares. He knows fine well about the Natasha thing, and I guess the venomous look of 'die bitch die' probably crossing my face is pretty obvious to him. I turn a scowl at him, his eyes fully zoned in on them across the room with a look of loyal hatred. Not impressed with either her or Arrick.

"Nope. According to him, there is no competition. Sure doesn't look like that now." I pout, turning back towards the group of chatting friends, all taking the piss out of Nate as he makes a throw. He isn't bad at bowling. He just likes to turn clown and make everyone laugh and is trying to throw the ball back through his legs with a stupid expression on his face. Jenny is laughing, despite herself, and the wink he casts her way makes her blush and glance away rather obviously.

Nate wanders towards me after finally taking his throw and surprisingly smashing a strike, grins at me, and pinches my cheek in passing.

"Green is not a good color on you, kiddo. Arry ain't a guy that deals with it either." He reminds me and wanders off to pick Jenny up and throw a kiss on her, unusual for a guy who normally keeps his dates hanging on him and acts like he doesn't give a toss. I start to wonder how much he feels for her after all. He is happy with his crappy bowling score and being weirdly affectionate for a fuck buddy.

I scowl his way and catch sight of Natasha throwing a hug at Arrick in the background. All smiles and doe eyes, and he seems to endure it rather than give one back, but I spin away regardless, in a rage again. This time I cannot control the wave of hate towards her for even touching him. The urge to stomp over there and kick her multiple times in the face overwhelms me.

"Fuck you." I spit under my breath, unsure which male it's intended for, and seething so bad I almost pierce my palms with my nails. Christian lets me go, throws me a pained expression of solidarity, and turns too.

"Calm down. He is one hundred percent head over heels for you. She's history, and it's pretty obvious to everyone. Arry would never go back there." Claire cuts in, coming back to my side, and nudges me softly. Flanked by the two of them and Christian smiles at her.

"Smitten kitten, alright. He manhandles this puppy more than most men handle their family jewels." Christian beams at me with

181

that deliciously wicked face and then saunters forward to retrieve his drink, leaving us momentarily alone. I frown a smile after him, not sure if what he said is meant to appease me. He is a funny one.

"I hate that he was with her in the first place," I admit stupidly, suddenly realizing this is the first time I have come out and said it to someone. Strange that I picked Claire. She's never been someone I confided in. I always liked her and felt at ease with her, though.

"We all know Arry. All saw what they were like as a couple. You have nothing to worry about, babe. He's just being him, not an asshole like most men here. Right, Nate?" Claire tosses Nate a challenging look, no doubt an ex-conquest of his from years ago, and he grins back. Throwing an arm around Jenny's shoulder with an uncaring shrug.

"What was he like with her?" Christian asks innocently, returning to my side with a fluffy pink cocktail in his hand that is dripping with glitter. I elbow him in the ribs, warning him with a scowl that this is not a cool topic, especially when I am in a head-ripping mood. I'm brimming on the psychotic here with a torrent of heavy rage waves ripping through my soul, despite the calm façade I have going on.

"Ooh, me, me, me." The small blonde girl named Anna, sitting nearby and listening in, shamelessly jumps up and joins our little gossip group. Sniffing out a hint of turmoil, no doubt. She seems like the type of girl who is always in the fold of a good drama.

"I'm totally in on this." She giggles childishly, leaning in conspiratorially and very clearly in her element. I regard her coolly and realize she's one I have met before but hasn't been around for long stints. I wonder what she could know to be honest.

"Anna is the gossip queen." Claire eye rolls with disdain then laughs as Christian switches his arm from me to her and smiles wider. Giving her the 'you are my new BFF' devious look and smarming over her a little too obviously. He is a shameless flirt when he has someone to extract information from and probably even more of a drama lover than Anna.

"Spill it, Sista." He winks at her and hits her with his sexiest 'I know I am hot' jaw-dropping smile that seems to melt her into a gooey puddle. She obviously missed the 'I am Gay' T-shirt he is wearing and the pink cocktail to hand. If James were here tonight, I am pretty sure he could be straddling him, and Anna would still fail to see the signs.

"Completely not happy. I mean, look at him, and look at her. Totally unmatched in every way. Arry is a wild little thing, seriously good in the sack ... According to rumors." She blinks at me innocently, blushing a little and looking a little panicked that I may beat her around the head. I do not want to know if he did or didn't bang any of these women here. I don't want that thought to cross my mind at all, but I know it's likely he has at one point. Most of the girls in this group came from dating one of them and stayed when they formed real friendships or started dating the one they stayed with. His past is his past and will not get to me at all. I have no desire to be upset over stuff he did before me. Ironic, seeing as I can't seem to do the same with Natasha.

"Why have you never given us these details, lady?" Christian frowns my way dramatically, demanding to know why I'm holding back how good he is in bed when I don't know. Not that I will ever admit it to any of them. I shrug coyly and make a locking motion across my mouth as if to say, 'A lady never tells,' and he slowly narrows his eyes at me.

"Go away." I turn and try my best to ignore them as Christian prods Anna for more details, coaxing and questioning her with his eyes. I try to turn off my ears and avert my attention because I do not want to be a part of this, but I can't help but listen in.

"She totally hated that about him. She's a bit of a prude, not that into sex. It's a wonder he stayed loyal for so long, considering he went from almost daily kinky banging to probably monthly, dutiful missionary style, judging by how pissed off he always seemed." Anna seems to be relishing her audience, and now another new girl has joined the mix. Someone I don't know. I think her name may be Susie or Sandra. I ignore them all crowding in for the juicy tidbits over my boyfriend and his ex and gawp at the fact that none of them thinks this is inappropriate in the slightest.

I stop and think about how different Arrick seemed over the last two years and don't like to think it came down to sex or lack of. My head immediately jumping to our sex issue and wonder if he wishes he could find a normal girl. I pick up my food from the table and nestle between Jason, Claire's husband, and Dave, Anna's man of the night. Both are glued to their phones, silently watching a basketball game. Oblivious to the conversation happening feet away, I stuff more food in my mouth and stare at the little brood of gossipmongers, trying my hardest not to listen or even react. I know Arry would hate this, them all sitting and dissecting his personal life, he's always been so private and introverted when it comes to emotional stuff, and I can see why. I hate it too, and feel annoyed on his behalf.

"So, he wasn't getting enough kinky or regular sex, huh? She does look a little 'sex after marriage' type." Christian glances across at her again, and I want to throw something at his head for being so obvious and encouraging this bullshit. I hate what they're talking about, but I would hate to make that known, like some jealous immature girl who can't accept he has a past. I keep quiet and pretend to be absorbed in my food, feeling sick from what I'm learning and adding to the weight in my chest.

"He's obviously getting a lot of kinky sex now ... judging by his constant good mood of the last month and his inability to stop pawing Sophie." Claire cuts in, throwing me a wink. She seems equally unimpressed with the topic and eyes them all with a stern maternal frown. I recoil inside.

I know she thinks she is reassuring me because she is a lovely girl, and none of them would ever assume he wasn't sleeping with me, seeing as he never stops putting his hands all over me. They all know we've been inseparable, and he's had some of them over for late-night movies, and they know I stay over and share his bed. It's only natural to assume we have ourselves nightly aerobics, especially with his reputation for having a high and adventurous sex drive. But all she has done is make me obsess over the fact I'm not giving him anything of the sort. Not even dutiful monthly and boring sex. Nausea rises in my stomach, and I push my food down with difficulty, that gut-wrenching pit of anxiety forming in my chest that threatens to flatten my lungs and close me in an airtight box.

I know he said sex wasn't a big deal and we would come to it again in time, but it's all that is going on through my head now, thanks to this little lot of nosey assholes and the fixation on his sex life.

If he was that unhappy with her, how much did sex play a part?

"Hey you, move over." Arry's voice catches me off guard as he slides in beside me in what is now an empty seat, putting an arm behind me as he steals some of my fries. I notice the group break up and disperse at his return, guilty as sin and scattering to the wind as Claire gives me a shaking head sigh. I hand him the bowl, suddenly so nauseous that I can't even stomach looking at them.

"You can have them. I'm not hungry anymore." I push the hot dog his way too, and his face tightens in reaction to my refusal of junk food. A huge neon sign that something is off.

"What's wrong? It's not like you to turn down food?" He leans in and steadily brings his face to mine, so he's almost nose to nose, trying to get me close so he can dissect my expression. Gazing intensely at me.

"I'm just feeling a bit yucky, that's all." I pick up my Pepsi to wash the food out of my mouth and try not to push him away when he kisses me on the cheek. That old urge to recoil from touch when I'm upset, only I know I'm being stupid, and he has nothing to be blamed for. He looks completely gorgeous, even for being a thick shithead sometimes, and those concerned brown eyes are boring into my skull and making me feel worse.

"You want me to take you home?" He feels my face as though checking for my temperature, and I pull my cheek away in irritation. Agitated as hell that the walls are closing in on me, I need to breathe.

"I'm fine." I bite snappily. Then heat intensifies in my face at how I am being; prize bitch comes to mind. Especially when he is doing nothing but being an attentive boyfriend like he always is. I sigh heavily and push myself up from the seat to get some space and get my head together. Avoiding his eyes on me and knowing if I keep this up, we will have another Natasha-related altercation in which he will make me feel like crap once more. I don't want to fight with him. All I wanted tonight was for him to make me feel less messed up and cuddle me in. Now I don't even want him to touch me.

Why am I such a weirdo?

"Take our next shot. I need to go to the bathroom." I can feel his eyes on me as I stand, pushing out of our seating area and heading for the ladies' room alone. Knowing this is stupid, and I am punishing him for basically nothing. Even though he was dumb enough to talk to his bitch ex and start this idiot bad mood of mine. I feel completely gutted suddenly, upset, and closed off again. No idea how to even deal with myself at the moment, so how can I expect him to?

Pushing through strangers and walking into the small enclosed space for air, I open the door to the ladies bathroom at the back of the huge hall. Strolling in confidently, if not heavily. I walk to the bank of vanities and look at myself in the mirror. Hair sleek and perfect, makeup flawless, and a dress doing a lot to make me look like a twenty-something sex kitten with long legs and curves for once.

I look like a girl who is probably giving her boyfriend the best sex of his life. Sassy and bold with an air of capability, I feel like a fraud as I stare at my reflection numbly. I still have the grace and airs of a girl who knows how to have fun, the cheeky youthful face of a girl who knows how to work sex to her advantage, and the body of someone who gets a lot of attention whether she wants it or not. I look the part, yet he isn't getting the package he probably thought he was. It just makes me feel worthless.

The cubicle door behind me opens as a girl walks out with her head bowed. I look down from her reflection in the mirror and rummage for my lipstick to touch it up while I'm in here, stalling for time so that I can simmer a little and not cause a major bust-up with Arry when I go back out. Trying to claw back my sanity and bring some calm back to my muddled brain.

"Sophie?" Natasha's familiar voice startles me, and I glance up in alarm, unsure how to react, when I catch her staring at me in the mirror with wide-eyed shock. The last time I saw her properly was the morning after Leila's party, the only time before that was the night she caught Arrick and I making out while I was naked, and his mouth was on my breast. I blush instantly, suddenly unsure how to behave or what to say, so I go for a little smile instead. My eyes glued to hers in the mirror. I drop my lipstick into my bag and fumble to close it, knowing I should make excuses and get out of here.

She looks me up and down slowly, taking in my outfit, hair, and face with slow deliberation and an expression that tells me nothing. I do the same and notice how odd she looks. Her clothes are too tight and short for what I'm used to seeing, and she wears far more makeup than she ever wore. There's a sort of trashy look to her entire style that seems messily pulled together.

Her hair has been highlighted, so it's not as deep brown, a few inches shorter, and she's wearing heels I owned, like five seasons ago when 'slut chic' was a thing. She looks like a bad attempt at being me in my wilder stage, only with less class and curly hair.

"You look ... happy." She says almost bitterly. Pulling her bag up and laying it on the vanity beside me as she starts fussing with her appearance. Mirroring me, but the atmosphere is suddenly heavy and strained. She has tried to sex up her style, which looks wrong in many ways. Like she's playing at being someone else, matched with the wild drunk haziness in her eyes, makes me a little wary of her. I don't know this version of her at all.

"I ... umm ... yeah, I guess." I stammer awkwardly, the urge to up and run coursing through me, but I stand my ground. I've never fled from a real fight in my life, and I will face her head-on if this is how it plays out. Not that I want that, though. Despite my issues with her and Arry, I still would rather have some civility between us if I must be here now. As hard as this is, I still owe her some apology too, even if she doesn't accept it. And as much as I dislike what she was to him and that she's still clinging on like a bad smell, I still harbor some sorrow for how it went down. Especially knowing her father is dying. That clinging guilt inside of me that drives me insane is gnawing at my gut and cooling my temper successfully.

"Look, Natasha ... " I stop when I catch her glaring at me in the mirror frostily. No confusion in the spiteful and hateful look she is focusing on my face, and it takes me aback. I didn't know she could pull this level of nasty from her arsenal of pretty and sweet expressions.

"Don't, okay? Whatever dumb fuck shit is going to come out of your mouth ... just leave it. Nothing you can ever say to me will make a difference to how I feel about you." She slurs. The swearing, the nasty tone, all of it is like a complete slap in the face from the girl she was before, and I wonder how much is the alcohol she has consumed and how much was waiting inside of her all that time. If sweet Natasha was an act all along to keep Arry under her thumb and this here is the real her, showing her true colors.

I don't want to think she could be that manipulative. Arry may be slow on the uptake in some things, but I know he's insanely good at reading people sometimes, and he wouldn't have been blinkered for two whole years with just an act of sweetness.

"I only wanted to say I was sorry, that it was never meant to go the way it did." I blurt out, somewhat in shock, and she sneers at me cruelly. I honestly cannot get my head around this version of her, and suddenly, I don't feel quite so sorry anymore. The fire in me ignited when faced with a snippy hostile tone and looks that act like daggers in my skull. This isn't some sweet, vulnerable girl facing me down, it's a hardened bitch who hates me, and I am all up in that for a takedown.

"Sure ... Whatever. You spent years trying to get him, and you finally did. Can't believe I never fucking saw it until it was too late. You're a manipulative spineless whore who uses sex to get what she wants from him. I don't even want to know how many times you two fucked behind my back before I caught you. I was so stupid not to see it, and you both deserve each other... Don't worry though, pretty sure he knows where I am when he gets bored of sex on tap from a slut and wants someone more substantial." She snarls again, only this time her voice hitches, and she stumbles in her shoes, catching the counter to steady herself. I inhale a lungful of alcohol breath coming off her. I resist the urge to shove her over and get satisfaction from watching her tumble off her heels. Instead, I bite down and grit my teeth, clenching my fists into my bag to hold the temper bubbling inside like hot lava.

"You know what? I was trying to be an adult about this but fuck you." That good old Sophie temper snaps at how she is being, insulted that I was only trying to be nice. I pick up my bag and sling it on my shoulder, making a point of fixing my hair and checking my appearance to show I will not be moved to hurry because of her.

"Maybe if you were fucking him to satisfaction, he wouldn't have looked elsewhere, Tasha. Clearly, something was missing if he had to come to me." I snarl back, complete bitch mode executed and not caring if none of it is true. I know I owe this girl a sorry, but I'll be fucked if I'm going to stand here and take abuse from a snarly-faced bitch who has been mercilessly stalking my boyfriend for weeks. I left, and she lost him anyway. That is not down to me. That is down to him and what he wants.

Which is obviously me!

I turn to storm off and halt in shock as she bursts into a flood of tears in front of the mirror. So unexpected and like having a bucket of icy water thrown over me to cool my heated jets. Her bitchy tone dissipates, and she is nothing but a blubbering mess, grasping for tissues to stop her makeup from pouring down her face, and I don't know how to react. Anger bristling, temper engaged, yet that underlying guilt for her eating away at me and making me stand rooted to the spot when I should be storming out of here. I should be throwing back 'I don't care' and sassily butt-swaying my way out like a Diva. That's what younger Sophie would do.

"Look at what you did to me." She sobs into her mound of tissues pitifully, like a broken child who has just seen her kitten get run over. "Look at what I have become." She picks up another wad of tissues and rubs her face manically, staring at her pathetic reflection and sobbing more at the chaos staring her back in the mirror. I turn and take in the mess she is making, feeling stupidly responsible and cursing my inability to embrace my bitch side fully at any given time. I sigh heavily, walking into a cubicle to grab some more and bring them out to dampen in water before handing them to her to clean her face. She regards me for a moment as though I have lost my mind and then takes them cautiously, suspicion evident and yet a tiny hint of gratitude that I even care enough to hand her them. It hits the guilt spot a little harder, and I could honestly punch myself in the face for being so weak sometimes.

"I wasn't having sex with him. Nothing else happened between us. Not until long after you two broke up." I say with a sigh, hating how pathetic this makes me and not caring anymore about scoring points. I'm not that bitch, and I don't ever want to be. I've had a lifetime of being around bitches, and I despise all of them. She glances at me again and sniffs a little, the hate on her face calming and hints of the girl she used to be shining through. That air of vulnerability that seals my fate hits me in the gut harder, and I have to look away to regain composure.

"Really?" She seems like a wounded puppy in the reflection staring at me, and I cave completely. As much as I dislike everything around us, if I knew her only as a girl I met in the bathroom, I would probably hug her and console her about her idiot ex for letting her go. I hate complicated. It just bursts my head.

"Really. We kissed a couple of times and nothing else, and then he chose you, and I walked out of his life." I look away from those interrogating eyes, rummage for wet wipes in my bag, and hand her the whole pack to get her focus off me. Damp tissues are smearing what's all over her face into a grey sludge, and I have no desire to watch this girl look more pitiful with every swipe. I turn on my heel to leave her to her face and go to walk away, pretty sure there is nothing more to talk about anyway. We will never be friends. We never were. I don't want the added burden of this conversation on my heavy heart tonight, and I don't want any more reason to convince myself that I am immature when it comes to hating her presence in our lives.

"I'm sorry about what I said to you. I trusted both of you. This wasn't how my life was supposed to turn out." She sniffs again, voice trembling and weak from behind me, and I weaken some more, heart sinking and body deflating. Hatred for her waning and guilt reigning supreme when faced with genuine heartbreak; I hate that I'm this easy to manipulate at her gentle hands.

"I'm sorry it came down to you or me. It was never the plan. I'm sorry you got hurt that one of us had to." I reply sadly, with genuine remorse in my torn tone. Hating the heavy pit in my stomach that is for her. I don't wait for a response, my eyes misting and face aching with trying not to cry, as I walk out of the bathroom at speed and head back into the bowling alley to get away from everything she makes me feel.

People are in my way, making me even more agitated. I spy Arrick and my friends across the crowded room, still in the booth laughing, having fun, and generally oblivious to what's taken place. It feels surreal, and I'm no longer in the mood to be here.

"You look serious." Nate's voice startles me from the left, carrying a tray of fresh drinks, beers mostly, and I guess they are all moving onto alcohol now everyone's had enough food. For some reason, every social occurrence with this lot turns into a few drinks when evening hits, not that I mind. It's just that I'm not in the mood anymore.

"Natasha was in the bathroom when I went in. Not exactly the best moment of my life." I shrug, knowing Nate can be a good ear when he wants to be. Despite his 'screw everything in sight' personality. I don't know why I'm sharing when I don't want to regurgitate it. I guess I needed to say it, to let it go.

"Wanna talk about it?" He offers, nudging me towards them, but I hesitate, seeing Arrick laughing and pushing Jason over a seat in the clearing. It makes me fold and start moving towards him, forgetting everything and seeing my beacon of calm and stability ahead. He is too alluring not to want to go to when I feel this shitty; he makes it better. His laugh alone has me wanting to be back beside him, wrapped in those arms he always throws my way, and I go into blinker mode, setting my sights on where I need to be.

"Nope. Just forget it." I smile at Nate tightly and then focus on the body calling to me like a siren, and it only becomes more alluring when he catches my eye and throws me a sweet little wink and smile. That little finger gesture that says, 'Come here, baby,' and I'm powerless to do anything but obey.

Chapter 17

Arrick half carries me, half walks me backward from the elevator, mouth glued to mine as he kisses me passionately. His hands are all over me, and things are getting steamier than they have since Leila's party. He has my hair all messed up and in my face from running his hand through it, using it to tug my head to one side as he angles in. Giving me about the most body-melting kiss known to man. His tongue seems to be doing a whole new thing with mine, and my insides are going to self-implode with the amount of scorching fizz going off. Fingers roaming one another, not looking where we are stumbling and fully focused on making each other as horny as humanly possible without physically putting our hands in each other's pants. We bang into a wall, then a table, giggle without breaking our connection, and his hand skirts up under my dress to cup my ass and guide me a little more directly into his apartment.

We are both drunk, been pawing and flirting for the last couple of hours when we all moved to a club after bowling. He had me sexy dancing against him on the dancefloor, grinding saucily and unable to keep his hands from straying. He changed my mood from downhearted and deflated to happy and party-ready in only one long, slow smooch and flurry of his hands skimming my body in the alley. Since then, I have been wrapped around his neck, unable to be parted.

The cab ride home was equally steamy as he pinned me against the seat and kissed me relentlessly. My libido set loose with the amount of alcohol we drank, and my hands braver than they have been since that party. Arry drunk horny, and inhibitions wavering. Things were notching up all evening, heading for a complete hormonal explosion, and now we're back at the apartment to carry it further. His hands boldly slide up my thighs while I open his shirt buttons, hinting at more than a make-out session brewing between us, and I'm all for it. There is no doubt, no confusion about the inner stirrings of my body and the way I'm crying out for him to be inside me.

All night, it's half the reason I drank so much. Dutch courage.

My head telling me to get over this hurdle and give my poor man a girl who actually gives him sex. He clearly needs it after what I listened to, and I don't want to be another reason he has a less-than-satisfying life. All night I felt fragile and vulnerable, what with Natasha showing up. She kept trying to infiltrate our group and making Arrick more toned down in his attentiveness because he didn't want to rub it in her face. He let loose when we went to the club, and the pent-up 'behaving himself and keeping his hands off me' ended. He made up for it by barely keeping his hands to himself, and I love it.

He sucks on my bottom lip, running his fingers into my hair to angle my face again, lifting me with his other hand so my legs automatically go around his waist. I straddle him standing. I have no bearings on where we are going, too busy playing tonsil tennis with his mouth, those perfectly soft lips pressed into mine, and he tastes so good. My eyes are closed tight, and lost to what an amazingly good kisser he is. No matter how he kisses me, it always feels like this, and seems to press all my buttons effortlessly, igniting any response he wants from me. My body is on fire with the aching need to have him all over me, skin tingling and head empty of everything except the need to be joined to him in every way possible.

I giggle when I'm dropped on my back on the couch, separated for a second before he is right there on top of me again, nestling between my open legs, warm hands sliding down my calves and pushing my shoes off for me while he recaptures my mouth. His kissing is more on par with that drunken night, with a hint of real Carrero passion coming through and blood heating up on his end. I love the little hints into what he can be if his real unleashed side gets to play. It's obvious he holds back with me, always aware of pushing me too far, yet it's always there. Bubbling under the surface like a hot devil wanting to come out to play.

He moves on top of me slowly, taking his weight on his arms as he slides fully against me, moving to my throat with soft grazing kisses. His hand cups my breast through my dress, and I close my eyes at the sensual contact. I let my fingers wander over his chest and shoulders, one hand finding its way down to his hip, then over that tight ass, groaning when he nibbles my throat, and his pelvis grinds in against me. Waves of lust are sweeping from him, yet I know he is holding back, still being gentle and overly cautious, and it has the same effect as trying to rein in the ocean.

So far, there is nothing but that ache of desire to get him on top of me and lose myself in him. I want him to unleash that inner animal I know exists. I moan and writhe at how good his hands feel as one slides under my dress at the thigh, sliding up to my hip where my lace panties lie, stroking my skin deliciously, and I mentally urge him to keep going. Pushing, edging for more, yet knowing he is still holding himself in check, fully aware of where he touches me. I get hints more and more as we continue to be together, and part of me knows that if he opened up and let go, he would probably be more than a competent lover. He will probably blow my mind.

I want my mind blown.

Taking that as a hint that he is open to more than making out, I slide my hand between us, down his now naked abdomen, and start pushing lower, kissing him, teasing his lips with my teeth. His mouth entangled with mine.

"Sophie." He breathes, breaking a hair width apart, catching my hand with his, pulling it from between us, and placing it beside my head on the pillow. He moves back to kiss me, but I turn my head in disappointment, so he can't.

"Why are you stopping me?" I pout woundedly, wanting him to go with what's happening, relax and let this occur naturally, especially as I very clearly want it.

"You know why." He moves over me to kiss me again. I'm unwilling to stop getting things heated even if he has no desire to go any further, and I hold my tongue, hoping that I can urge him to change his mind if we keep going. His body is very pointedly, indicating he wants it too. I can feel his erection in my groin, even if his head tries to stop it. I resign myself to shut up and see if I can coax him with seduction rather than words.

I turn back, getting lost in how he starts teasing me again, letting my hand go so he can go back to running his fingers up the outer edge of my thigh and under my dress. Edging closer, stroking my skin sexily. He seems lost in the moment again so quickly, skimming my naked skin and gradually edging his pelvis into mine with every moan and arch I make.

I get lost in how we grind, erupting into a million sensations as his body fits into mine snugly. I taste every part of his jaw and neck, moving to keep unbuttoning his shirt. He buries his mouth in my throat, pulls my dress neckline down a little, and trails a kiss over the curve of my cleavage seductively, nibbling gently and getting more than a little aroused against me. I can practically feel his erection trying to burst free from his pants. The way I'm crushed against him, he's rubbing into me, so it has me clawing at him as tingles hit my pelvic floor. Stimulating my clit and pushing me to extreme horniness.

I recognize the feeling from that night. The start of an eruption from within amazes me that even though he isn't doing anything, I can feel one starting. Crazily sensitive down there. Either that, or he knows how to touch me without touching me. I wonder if he is doing this deliberately. If this is why he is pushing for more, even if he has no intention of having sex with me. Knowing he can make me climax in other ways with some frontal grinding.

Arrick lifts my leg at the knee, pulling it up to bend around his body so he can rub it into me more intensely. Hitting me very directly with his "bulge" so that I cry out rather than moan and get a smile against my mouth as a reward. I lose any doubts that it is exactly what he's trying to do. Panting so heavily that I can barely kiss him now, the effort of not having some womanly explosion consumes me. In time with mine, his hot breath hits me on the cheek as he increases the pressure and speed of rubbing against me. I'm more than convinced he is trying to make me cum now.

Sneaky ass!

Letting go to slide his hand under my dress and up to cup my breast through my bra as he captures my mouth once more. Kisses more frenzied, bodies completely wild for one another, and looking to anyone watching like we are fully having sex with the motion and noise coming from us. It's obvious he is extremely horny and has me that way too. Squirming for release from the craving inside me just to do it already. He probably thinks he will cum from over-horniness if he makes me climax, and it will satisfy us both, but I want more than an orgasm this way. I want him to get naked and show me what I've been missing in the last month. It's obvious he has skills, and it's about time I got the benefit of having a boyfriend who spent years honing them.

Feeling braver as he escalates things, I grab his free hand and push it across my thigh towards my underwear, which is now on show since my dress has hitched up my abdomen with his wandering fingers. He tenses and pulls back, stopping his grinding rhythm for a second, but I catch his wrist and hold it tight. Refusing to back down when this is something I want more than oxygen. He breaks away to look down at me, gorgeously turned on with dilated pupils, kiss swollen lips and messily ruffled hair from my clawing fingertips, dragging in a breath that makes his shoulders heave and naked chest expand rapidly. I don't think I have ever seen him look so crazily sexy.

"Don't stop ... I trust you. I know you'll stop if I say no. Stop holding back. It's frustrating." I whisper through short inhales into his mouth, kissing him hard and slipping my tongue over his so that he can't talk, getting lost in this and urging him to carry on. I am so close to the brink of internal climax, but I want it from him being inside me, not like this.

He relaxes on top of me a little, his hand moving up under my dress again and over my breasts slowly. Tensing as doubt gets him. He stops and looks down between us for a long moment, so many thoughts and emotions passing over his face as he lightly draws patterns on my skin with his finger. I can almost taste his turmoil, that quick brain torn between wanting to have sex with me and the protective part, wanting not to hurt me. I couldn't love him anymore if I tried.

"Say no ... Promise me! If anything doesn't feel right, Sophie. Even the tiniest doubt, then stop this." His eyes meet mine, deadly serious, and I nod, leaning in to kiss him again. Arrick hesitates, assessing me for a moment even though I'm kissing him. As though trying to decide if he should or shouldn't, he finally closes his eyes and kisses me back. Pushing against me and losing himself in me once again, going back to the way his body fluidly moves with mine.

His hands come up to cradle my neck and face, angling to deepen the kiss to panty-twisting levels, and I realize in that single moment just how much my boy has been holding back. Hot kissing to scorching kissing in a flash as he lets go a little. His groin meets mine harder as euphoric heat starts enveloping me faster, making me tense and move higher up the couch in reaction with a gasp. My mouth is a new plaything for him. Lip sucking, tongue caressing, and generally making every part of me combust with that hidden skill. A talent he has been keeping from me until now. I'm swept up hopelessly and realize he has only had me simmering until this second, and now I am consumed with new levels of insane need.

Arrick's hands move down to my thighs and pull me up so I'm wrapped around his hips snugly as he nestles tightly against me. Body molding heavily to mine, maneuvering me so I can feel every pulsating inch of his desire between us. He has access to my upper body without leaning on his arms. He pushes my dress up to my bra to expose it fully, still tasting me, then my jaw and neck, grinding against me, igniting a switch inside that has me moaning and arching to him wantonly. Excitement goes crazy inside me as I realize I am finally getting exactly what I want, and it only intensifies the sensation.

The way our bodies are pressed together, his hardness fits tightly against me in ways that have me writhing around as he moves against me deliberately, knowing how to get a woman ready when he has his eye on the goal. He slides his hands under my butt, between us, to the outer edge of my lace underwear. His mouth back on mine, leaning forwards over me, flitting from my throat and cleavage to my mouth in small bursts. My hands roam him, unbuttoning the last buttons low down on his shirt to reveal a sexy tanned torso, achingly perfect abs, and that one side of tattoos and sleeve that is as sexy as sin.

I trail my lips down his throat when he leans into me again, nibbling and tasting his skin like he is tasting me. Aching to be fully naked and feel him against me in every way possible.

He slides a hand further between us, along the top edge of my lace panties, and pulls his face away. Opening his eyes to look into mine, focusing on me, nose to nose, as he slides his hand lower and into my underwear slowly. Watching me with obvious concentration and a hint of wariness as I hold my breath in anticipation. Watching his eyes move from mine to my mouth and back as his fingers slide down over their target makes me flinch with pleasure. My lips part with a gasp as his warm skin connects with me between my thighs, and he circles me deliciously.

I groan as he slowly glides his fingers up and down, feeling me out, testing my responses, and making me squirm wildly. His breathing becomes more labored as his pupils dilate. He seems to watch for any sign of rejection, seeing only my inability to withstand how good this feels as I close my eyes, bite my bottom lip and squirm about in sheer ecstasy at his massaging touch. His mouth finds mine again, tongue in as he slides his fingers under the fabric's edge and inside me so slowly it's almost torture. I moan out as he penetrates me, panting, overwhelmed at how amazingly good he feels, arching to let him have better access and pushing against him hard.

He slides inside of me fully, his thumb massaging the front of my sex as tingles, waves, and crazy aching sensations consume me. Feelings that make me claw at his shoulders and arch underneath him. He dips his head to my throat, kisses me, sucks gently, and drives me wild with the intensity of finger-banging me into oblivion. Unable to control myself and not caring about how I am reacting. I have never felt this crazy yet so lost at the same time. My body yearns, crying out for more and unable to control anything I'm doing.

His fingers are raising my body temperature and heart rate to explosive levels, and the building crescendo and fireworks are so close to erupting. I can barely hold myself together and arch crazily as my body is gripped with need, almost on the verge of a body-ripping orgasm.

The harsh ring of his cell breaks the sudden ecstasy of the moment and kills my buzz as it invades my brain and snaps my eyes open. He curses under his breath, pulling his fingers from inside me, and starts moving around to fish his vibrating cell from his back pocket in angry agitation. He pulls it forward, glares at it, and sighs before tossing it aside. Almost automatically, I spy her name on the glowing screen and turn back to him with a frown, anger spiking stupidly inside my stomach.

It's still ringing as he tries to come in for another kiss, but something inside me snaps. Something that has been building all evening after seeing her arrive, lying dormant under my happy fuzz since being aware of her presence in the bowling alley. Maybe being brought to the edge of this mind-blowing ecstasy and then halting abruptly has sent me over the edge.

I push him off and pull myself to the side, pick up the phone, and red button it to reject her call before throwing it at the opposite chair in complete erratic rage. Cursing her under my breath for ruining this moment for me, like she ruins fucking everything in my life. Arrick tries to pull my face back to his softly, but I resist him. I cannot look him in the eye when this much disappointment hits me hard, and I'm struggling to control Psycho Sophie from kicking out inside me.

"Baby?" He soothes, leaning in to kiss me back into submission, smoothing a little of my obvious temper tantrum to get me back under him. Still, the stupid thing starts ringing again almost immediately, and this time, in my drunken stupor, I pick up my shoe and throw it at the cell phone in complete rage. I score a perfect bullseye, and it falls to the floor with my shoe in rattling silence, unclear if I just smashed, or killed, his cell.

I don't care. I picture her in my head and want to assault her with my shoe too. Stab her seriously tiny, little doe-eyed fucking face with any of my knife-edge stilettos.

"Sophie, what the fuck?" Arrick half snaps, half laughs in disbelief, but she has completely killed the mood, and I'm being the asshole I always am when I'm hurt. Unable to return when this inner demon breaks free and acts like a petulant, spoiled kid in meltdown.

"Screw it ... screw you, and fucking screw her." I push him back hard, so he falls back against the couch, and I slide myself out of his embrace. I pull myself up, pull down my dress angrily and start stomping toward the bedroom without a backward glance as fire consumes me for a whole different reason.

Irrational, drunk, and being an idiot, seething inside that we were so close, and there she was, like every time, popping up to ruin everything. Like a damn infernal constant black cloud on my parade, who opens the heavens to a downpour any time she catches a tiny ray of sunshine in our life.

"Answer your fucking phone. You know you're going to," I yell at him in rage as his cell starts ringing again. Storming into his bedroom and slamming the door magnificently, a picture falls off the wall with a crashing thud in the room I just left. Tears blind me, and I feel overwhelmed, like a class-A psycho for overreacting. We were so goddamn close to something people take for granted as normal every day, and like always, she goes and fucks everything up for me.

And he lets her! Every goddamn, fucking stupid, asshole time.

Arrick opens the door seconds after me and stands there staring at me as though I have completely lost the plot. His face is calm, but he has that tell-tale tense muscle and square jaw of being pissed off that makes me want to scream at him. His shirt is wide open and looks too inviting, even though I am in no mood to go back there. I ask myself why I can't go back out there and continue when he's looking like that, but I can hear the ringing again in the room behind him, making me a hundred times worse. I glare at him coldly, like I hate him, even though he hasn't done anything wrong.

Like every other fucking time, I act like a completely insane, jealous psycho and take it out on him.

"What was that?" Arrick seems mildly irritated, but I know him better and can see the suppressed anger as he tries to keep his cool. As drunk as me and swaying on his feet a little. I guess stopping men mid-sex makes them grumpy too, as he looks pretty pissed, in his subtle but annoying way, not his normal cool and controlled, understanding sober Arry.

Asshole.

"Nothing. I don't want to talk to you. Go away." I wipe the start of my tears with the back of my hand, not even sure why they started, and glare past him as the phone finally stops vibrating across the wooden floor like a massive irritation. Hating that she made me feel this way with just a bloody call. Starting to lose it where she is concerned; this goes beyond minor or major jealousy. She's getting into my head and making me crazy on new levels of insanity the longer this goes on.

I can feel him staring at me as I try to think and impulsively throw a cushion at him in a bid to block him out, unable to have him look at me that way when I know I'm the one being mental. I'm suffocating inside, and my head is so crammed full of conflicting thoughts that I want to rip my brain out.

"Go away." As the rage dies, I snap childishly and tearfully and start feeling embarrassed and ashamed of my epic meltdown. I should be apologizing, I know this, and he's looking at me like I should know this, yet I can't. There is that tiny little stubborn mini-me who wants to slap him about the head, shake some sense into him and tell him once and for all to make her disappear for me.

"Why the fuck are you punishing me for her calling? Am I answering the fucking phone, Sophie?" He's getting more pissed by the second, fueled by my behavior, and as much as I want to shake myself and tell myself to stop acting this way, I can't. My heart's breaking with everything I have been thinking about in the last month. About sex, about her. Alcohol always makes me more irrational and unable to cope with this kind of shit. It's why I got so much stronger when I cut out drinking so much. I always end up this much of a mess when I drink, and Arrick always ends up like that.

It's like the straight-thinking attentive part of him gets replaced with pig-headed and impulsive, quick to anger, and a lot less lucid, and right now, we are not a good mix. We don't gel well with each other when drunk and pissed off. We never did. He reminds me of Jake at his worst when he is like this. Jake can be an asshole when he's drunk too, and it's about the only time I have ever seen him argue with Emma over pointless shit or made her cry.

Drunk Carreros are assholes!

"If you don't know, then I'm not telling you. Go away, leave me alone." I sulk. Being a juvenile, deflecting his question because I no longer have a straightforward answer that would hold any weight to explain my behavior. His eyes bore into me, and I cannot stand it anymore, unable to stay in this airless prison with him. I push past him to leave the room, but he only catches me by the waist and spins me to him.

"So, you get to turn psycho on me, and I'm just supposed to fucking guess? Or wait! Leave my own fucking apartment while you have a tantrum?" He snaps at me, gaining a push in the chest as I fight him off. Hating how he's being. Glaring at me with that green-infused, cold deadpan of his reigniting the angry part of me, which had started to curl up and hide in shame.

"You always let her ruin everything." I bawl at him, pushing harder when he only pulls me back for the second time. Not letting me go, refusing to let me storm off and walk away from this fight.

"What am I letting her ruin? We were more than capable of keeping going. Her calling changed nothing. I wasn't going to answer it. I wanted to fuck you. You are the only one stopping that." He bites, anger ripples, face no longer calm, and angry Arry on show. I don't like it, and the age-old whimpering kid in me stands up to become the dominating personality. I can feel the tension coming from his body, radiating outwards like heat from the sun, yet I glare at him, wounded by his stupid words.

"Don't call it that." I slap his hand off me as his grip moves to my arm, and I manage to dart away enough to escape back to the lounge without his hands getting hold of me again, but he follows fast on my heels. In a rage, a dog with a bone mode, unwilling to let this go like I want him to.

"Why? It's what it is. A fuck ... It's sex, not exactly the be-all and end-all of a relationship. You are overreacting to this crazily." He doesn't exactly yell. He angrily snaps in a slightly raised tone, but it has the same effect, and I can't even comprehend how much of an asshole he's being to me over this.

Who the hell are you?

"How can you say that? Sex matters! It mattered when you weren't getting enough of it from her. Is that why you have a constant porn channel on your TV?" I throw at him, thinking back to one stupid button flick that revealed a whole porn menu on his TV box not long ago. Head a tumbling mess of irrational thoughts and trying to piece together some sense in the crazy emotions consuming me. I'm hurt and angry, yet also in pain like he's wrenching my heart out by being a completely different person to who I need.

"For the love of God, woman ... You realize I have like four mates who stay here regularly, and they all download porn because they are guys, and that's what guys do. Do you want me to say I have never watched it? I have, big deal, and sex with Natasha isn't relevant in any way. Sex with you ... it was happening, Sophie. You are the only one who flipped out and stopped it. I don't even get what we are even fighting about."

Arrick is yelling at me now, properly, the way I am yelling at him, completely oblivious to my tears, despite always claiming he can't stand to see me cry. It wounds me more in my crazily sensitive frame of mind, and I now feel real hate for him. Real blood boiling 'I cannot stand to even look at you right now, you fucking asshole kind' of hate. It surprises me that I can have this much venom for someone I love so much. He's making me crazier than anything

Natasha could do to me.

"So now you're pissed because I stopped it? Because you said If I wanted to stop, I could, and now you're getting fucking angry at me. And I'm supposed to feel secure with you?" I sob loudly, wounded and confused, my head full of nonsensical chaos and drunken stupidity clouding my thoughts. My words are like daggers, thrown with intent and poison at someone I don't like very much in my current state. He reacts to the tone as much as what I say, narrowing his gaze icily, obviously feeling the same level of disillusionment with me.

"For fuck's sake ... Don't twist my words. It's not why you stopped it. You stopped over some jealous irrational bullshit because Natasha dared to call my cell. Something I had no fucking control over and no intention of answering." Arrick swoops down and pulls off his sneakers, throwing them across the room angrily as though curbing the urge to hit something or someone, and buttons up his shirt for no apparent reason. Glaring at me with equal dislike and fuming with a rage that matches mine. I feel, at the moment, that we are completely broken and falling into disrepair, and it kills me inside.

"Go fuck yourself ... or her ... I'm past caring anymore." I bite back cruelly, my heart ripping in two, and I turn to look for my shoes so I can walk out and leave him here. Before the tidal wave of emotion, soaring up overwhelms me, and I can no longer function with the pain he can cause me. I know he has the ability. He did it once before.

"Is that what this is? You think I want to go back to fucking her. How many times do I need to tell you, Sophie, I chose you? I'm tired of repeating that every time you get jealous like this. It's exhausting to have to backtrack over this shit constantly." Arrick sways on his feet again, runs a hand through his hair, and sits down on the nearest chair, putting his head between his hands as though he either realizes he's too drunk or maybe to try and calm his temper. "I can't deal with you like this. We're both drunk and angry. I'll sleep out here. Just go to bed." He snaps at me coldly, clear he's decided he doesn't want to put up with juvenile Sophie and her meltdown anymore. Sitting back to stare right at me with no emotion on show and a dismissive wave of his fingers, like I'm an obedient little puppy.

Soooo mixing me up with his ex fucking girlfriend once again!

"Did you leave her because of me or because you were already looking for a way out?" I blurt out through tears, thinking only of the things the girls said about his sex life with Natasha, about how he never seemed happy. The tidbits of their gossip filter through and come back at me out of sequence as I try to remember what they said exactly. So consumed obsessively with this now that it's all in my head swirling around, clouded logic, coloring everything.

"What kind of question is that?" He looks at me, completely baffled as to how my mind works like he no longer knows me. Dumbfounded that he thinks I could be so stupid, and it makes me worse as I hate him so much more.

"Anna said that Natasha didn't have sex with you very often and didn't like it. You weren't happy with her. If you left her for me ... is that what will happen to us?" I sob pathetically, glaring at him insecurely, my heart shredding with this possibility. Not even sure what I need him to say anymore. Now my brain is on a one-way road to complete hysterics.

"Arghh!" Arrick roars out angrily, rubbing his face, and jumps to his feet, pacing past me while blowing out air and storming to the kitchen as though he cannot get his head around me anymore. It's clear he is starting to lose his shit in every way. I know the signs, and I should leave him alone to go simmer and cool down when he's like this, but I just can't. Every part of him is tense and rigid, his movements angry and aggressive, his face tight and jaw angular as he grits his teeth. He yanks the fridge door to haul out a beer and looks for an opener as he bangs things around.

"Answer me!" I scream at him hysterically, losing the plot and feeling like my insides are caving in, despite all logic telling me to back off and shut up for ten minutes while he simmers. Arrick slams his bottle down so hard that it overflows with foam and spills everywhere. He grits his teeth harder and turns on me aggressively with insanely pure green eyes that burn into my soul. Two fiery-natured hotheads caught in a drunken battle where emotion has tipped it all to volcanic proportions, and he looks terrifying to me like this.

"You think fucking is the issue here? That sex is the problem and solution to this whole stupid mess?... Fine, Sophie, let's solve it right now. If you think this relationship depends on me fucking you, then let's put it to bed once and for all. Literally... I mean, we were practically there anyway. Let's fuck!" He explodes at me, walks towards me fast, face murderous with a biting tone, and hauls me over with him back to the couch by the arm cruelly. Managing me like I'm some weightless toy, not like he normally touches me.

He marches me at speed to the couch and pushes me down a little hard so that I fall back and land clumsily on my ass. I'm stupefied, heart pounding through my chest as adrenaline rushes me and renders me momentarily breathless and pliable. Shocked into submission at how he's being.

He makes it like he will get on top of me, looking like the devil himself. I yelp in fright that he would even manhandle me like this while fighting, that he is acting this way, looking completely disconnected from anything I have ever known about him, and regretting not giving him space after all. My anger drops to instant fear, and suddenly I don't even know him, no longer safe with this person in front of me, and I begin choking on my panic as it consumes me.

"Take your dress off, and I will fuck you right now." He stands over me, tone biting and cruel, looking nothing like the guy I trust and love. Caging me in on the couch as though waiting for me to obey. He's angry, aggressive, and emotionally detached, eyes glowing green and brow furrowed. My heart flips over, terror running cold in my blood. I make to get up, sliding over to get out of his blockade and move away from him, but he catches me and hauls me back to him hard. There's nothing gentle in the grip he has on me, and my blood runs cold in my veins, my body beginning to tremble that he means to do this to me

"You wanted to have sex. You think it's going to fix this fucking mess, so get undressed. You want this. Keep pushing me to do it. So

I'll fucking do it!" He snaps coldly at me, his face expressionless, and my insides crumble. Shaking my head weakly as fear overtakes my voice, and I can't formulate a single word.

My Arry isn't here. Some cruel asshole with a stern look in his eye is telling me that, like it or not, I am about to be fucked, and it is doing nothing but making my body recoil in terror. So many conflicting emotions and fears flit into my brain and collide like a tidal wave of emotion. My hands start to get clammy; my body goes cold as I breathe heavily, with the realization that I am on the verge of an anxiety attack. The walls are closing in, and the one person I always trusted to help me through, and keep me safe, is looking at me like he hates me and is the cause of all of this

"You want me to take it off?" He sneers at me, bends down to grab the hem of my dress, and yanks it up as instinct overtakes me. Sudden blinding fear and panic hit me hard in the chest, heart racing, brain crashing, an impulsive. Instant response from years of having to defend myself somehow connects as I start lashing out at him. Blind fury and tears to stop whatever is about to happen to me. Lost in the crippling flashbacks of pain, oblivious to my whereabouts anymore and crying out in anguish that I am back there, alone and afraid, and he's about to hurt me in the worst possible way.

* * *

I can hear someone screaming and yelling, but it's so far and disconnected from me that I can't even begin to find them or where it's coming from. There's strong muscle around me, arms gripping tight, warm skin on mine as I try like crazy to fight back, completely lost in my internal darkness and the memories of shadows and pain, so much pain. So completely consumed in the fight to keep myself from being broken all over again with no hope of escape this time.

Like a flash of light, a trickle of clarity, I'm suddenly on the floor with weight on top of me. Trying to haul off the arms against every part of me, fighting tooth and nail while tears pour down my face.

"No, NO ... NOOO!" I'm screaming hysterically. I am the noise

I could hear so far away. It was me; I was the screaming girl in the distance who sounded like dogs were savaging her. It snaps me into instant silence, then whimpering as I realize I'm not back in that dark room with the rancid air around me suffocating me. Encased in strong arms and solid steel restraints made of muscle that weren't hurting me at all. I sob and gasp and take a moment to fully come around, from hell to here, as lights trickle into my self-inflicted darkness.

The walls recede, then cave in as I stumble mentally, darkness taking control again as I panic, and I am no longer aware of what's happening again. All I am is the sheer terror, fear, and crippling suffocation of an attack. My face soaked, and coughing so much, I start retching. I'm still fighting hard to save myself from a pain I never want to return to. I can't let that ever happen to me again. I won't let anyone do that to me.

I'll fight. I'll always fight.

"Sophie, baby ... come back to me. Please stop. Sophie, I'm sorry. Baby, look at me, we're home, you're safe, it's me. Listen to my voice. No one is going to hurt you. I swear." Arrick's strained voice comes at me through the haze, torn and gentle. Raw with emotion. My real Arry's voice. That calming wave of security was not the monster who tried to hurt me back in the dark.

Holding me down, his nose comes to mine softly, trying to pull me out as I wriggle and fight off my attacker in various memory stages that make me blind to my reality. Lost in being held down and beaten into submission, unwilling ever to yield or let him take me.

"No, no ... no means NO." I sob over and over, fighting until my limbs go weak and I can't fight anymore, my brain letting go of the dark cloud that's keeping me locked inside my head as exhaustion drains every ounce of me. His face comes into soft focus, so all I can see are hazel and green eyes, bringing me back into the light. Calming the craziness of my head enough to get me back slowly. Appearing above me like a sudden awakening from a terrible nightmare. I can barely breathe, panting and gasping hard, choking on my tears in my furious rigidity as I strain my limbs to keep him at bay

"Please stop, look at me.... We're not back in Illinois. Sophie, we're in Manhattan. You're in my apartment, baby. You're safe.... Breathe slowly and steadily. Breathe with me; listen to me. Focus on my voice and breathe...." His soothing tone comes through the panic again, connecting to me on some level, and I lose all resolve. Fight in me dying as fatigue overtakes me, and I realize I am held tight in his arms. His muscles, his strength as he has me taut, so my body is immobile. Gasping and shoving with all my might and strangling myself with the inability to catch my breath. I inhale heavily as my surroundings start to take shape and cough at the sudden rush of air that makes me feel like I might be sick.

"Don't." I croak brokenly, not even sure why I say it, eyes screwing shut as pain consumes my soul. Only realizing I'm still on the floor of Arrick's apartment when I lose all ounces of strength and finally give up the fight. Coming to, aware of the hardwood beneath me, cold and solid and very real. Starting to get my bearings once more as I flick my eyes open, sniffing hard, still struggling to catch my breath, and the familiar apartment comes into view.

Arrick looks devastated, holding my wrists and body solidly with every part of his. Even my feet are pinned with his legs to control my violent outburst. His eyes are moist, his face is scratched, and he has blood on his bottom lip. A handprint across his cheek.

I don't remember doing that to him, but his heavy breathing suggests he has had a battle to control me and restrain me. The way he is pinning me down means he has tried to stop me from hurting myself again like I used to. I know him, this isn't the first time he's had to help me when I was trapped in the past and lashing crazily. The only way was to restrain and hold me down until I returned from the horror.

"I'm sorry, baby. Sophie, look at me. It's me. It's Arry. I would never hurt you that way. I'm sorry, so very sorry..." He moves slowly, bringing his nose to mine. I flinch away, still caught in another place of darkness and rage in parts of my mind, and stare at him with sheer big-eyed mistrust, fresh tears rolling down my face as I recoil. His expression crumbles. Unconcealed heartbreak waves over the face that I love so much normally, but right now, I can't connect the two.

"I'm going to let you go now ... stay calm. I don't want you to hurt yourself." He swallows hard and slowly takes the iron grip from my wrists as he moves his dead weight from on top of me. Carefully, cautiously untangling his limbs, painfully slow so I can regain control of myself.

As soon as there's the relief of pressure and the weight lifting, I move with rapid speed and newfound strength. Skating backward on my hands and butt until my back hits a solid surface and slams me to a halt, staring at my attacker in terror. I curl up into a ball at the foot of the couch, my back pressed hard against it, eyes wide, watching him like a scared animal caught in headlights. In this frame of mind, I trust no one, no one gets to touch me, and I am barely here. I am ready to lash out and defend myself again, willing to take on any cruel hands or naked flesh that wants to defile me over and over.

I retch as I cough back vomit, swallow the tears and panic, and try to regulate my breathing from frantic panting. My fingers gripped around my legs, so I can be as small as possible and hide from the approaching shadows. My nails bite my skin with the ferocity I hold myself in.

Arrick lifts defensive palms and sits back on his haunches, breathing rapidly, his eyes never leaving mine. So devastated. It claws at my defenses and pulls me an inch closer to reality and away from the foggy dreamlike state I'm halfway in and out of.

"I'm not going to touch you. I swear. I'll stay over here if that's what you need." He sits down lower on the ground, keeping his distance. All I can do is obsessively watch his every movement, flinching, body alert in panic mode, ready to run as soon as I regain enough strength. Knowing how important it is to stay tight until I can get enough energy and strength back. Curling my legs against me harder and closed up so no one can get in without fighting me first. Wrapping my arms around them protectively to shield exposed skin from unwanted touch, crossing my ankles over my most sacred parts as a barrier. I stare at him, cowering inside my head, battling to escape the darkness, trying to pull me back into insanity.

"Don't look at me like that, baby. I can't... I'm not him ... I would never do that to you." Arrick's voice breaks, and his eyes well up. All I can do is try and reel my mind back to where I am and what's happening to me and start to cry silently again. More gently and less hysterical as the realization comes crashing in. I'm really here and not there. That this isn't a dream, that I am sitting in Arry's safe and familiar apartment on the floor, surrounded by broken things that were knocked and pushed in the struggle he had. I blink awake slowly, aware I probably just attacked Arry of all people, as he comes into focus, and I start to really see him.

His mouth is bleeding, and his neck and wrist have ugly scratches that have broken the surface to draw blood in places. There are other red marks that may bruise as they come out. His shirt is torn at one shoulder, blood droplets from gouges under the thin material gaping open. He has a darkening mark over his eyebrow, which pans down the side of his face alongside his eye, and a tiny sliver of a cut on his lip. He looks like he took on a cat and lived to tell the tale, yet I am completely unhurt, unscathed.

Despite my hell hath no fury lashing out, fighting for my life, he must have only restrained me and pulled me down to hold me tight. There isn't one tiny mark on me. I feel nothing in terms of injury, pain, bruises, or even where he held me close; there's no sign of redness. This fact makes me even more desolate about what I have done to him, and I sob as reality finally fully connects. Intolerable guilt crashes through me at a hundred miles an hour like a lead weight now that I'm finally returning to reality.

"No means No!" I whisper robotically, like a calming chant that I used to repeat to myself repeatedly, un-focusing my eyes to concentrate on the blur of my tears and rock gently to soothe my agony. Locked inside my head to find my calm. This is how I did it when I needed somewhere else to go and endure what was happening. It's nonsensical, but it brings me a sense of control.

"You're right ... No means No ... It will always mean No, baby. No one has a right to ever do anything to you that you don't want. I will never cross that line, never make you afraid again. I'm sorry."

Arrick soothes at a distance, raising his brows in the most heart-wrenching sign of regret, his voice wobbling with the emotion he is trying hard to keep in check, but I can only feel the deafening pain of my heart pounding through my head. Holed up tight within me, protecting my body. Poised like a timid animal in a trap.

He slowly, apprehensively, moves towards me on his knees a little and freezes when I immediately tense up. Instincts and senses are not fully recoiled. I'm still perched on the edge of a knife, trying to calm myself and get a grip on reality. I'm not with him fully, not yet.

"I'm not going to touch you. I swear. I just want to check you're not hurt and that it's my blood on your face." Arrick's eyes move to my cheek, and I lift my fingers to where he's focused, wiping something wet, and look at the red streak on my fingertips in complete shock. It's like a smear of shame, a huge slap in the face of what I have done, and I break into a million pieces, uttering a soft wail that I have his blood on my face, like some wild rabid animal that would wound him.

A horrible, cruel, evil, impulsive girl who could physically hurt him that way. Injure my protector, my soul, and reason for living. I start sobbing harder and bury my face in my knees brokenly. Unable to look at him, so ashamed of this little bitch who lives inside of me eternally, her need always to lash out and hurt people, even when they try to love her.

"Sophie, let me look. Let me see. I won't touch you. Just let me see." His soft voice, trembling badly, is over the top of me now, pleading, begging, his body heat caging me in. He moves around me, trying to angle in to look at me with his hands on the floor, so he doesn't physically touch me and yet also trying to give me space and not cross the barrier I have placed around myself. I flicker my eyes up, heart breaking and needing more than ever to feel back in his arms where dirty awful things don't happen to me. Where I know he won't let anything bad happen to me.

I reach out impulsively, launch, and lasso myself around his neck, crying into his chest as his arms come around me tightly. He pulls me into his lap as he securely buries his face in my hair and cradles my head against him protectively.

"I'm sorry, baby. So fucking sorry... I will never scare you like that again. I don't know what I was thinking... Forgive me, *Mimmo*. I love you so much, Sophie. I would never do anything like that to you. I couldn't hurt you that way for anything. I'm a fucking asshole." His voice is torn, ravaged with emotion, and there's moisture on his cheek as I find his face to rub against mine. Trying to wrap him around me like the security I always need. Aching to forget the darkness and find the light once more. Unraveling completely.

"I'm sorry, I didn't mean it. Please don't hate me.... I didn't mean it. I didn't." I sound like a broken child, vulnerable and small, wiping my face clumsily with the back of my knuckles and crying when I see more blood smeared across them. Unable to face what I've done to him and break my heart simultaneously. So much remorse washing through me, shame, regret at everything I've done.

"Shh ... don't, baby, please. Here ... let me see." He tilts my chin up to him, brushing back my hair, and scrutinizes my face, wiping his fingers over me and removing traces of blood from across my cheek. His eyes are intent on searching my face and neck, and the relief which washes over him is undeniable.

"It's mine ... Thank God." He sighs heavily, squeezing me in forcefully, emotion flooding his beautiful, angelic face, eyes filled with unshed tears. "I would never forgive myself if I made you bleed. I would never hurt you. I never want to hurt you." He rests his forehead against mine, breathing me in as we both sit and try to regain equilibrium, still locked together on the floor and oblivious to anything but each other, wrapped tight and entangled almost unnaturally.

"Sex doesn't matter, Sophie. It never did. I will always be with you and love you, even if we never go down this route again. I don't need it. I just need you. I didn't leave her because of that... I left her because I didn't love her anymore if I ever really loved her at all. I was ... I am, in love with you, in a way that doesn't even compare, and I want to be with you, only you." Arrick pulls my face to him so he can press us close, eyes locked, wiping my face still and trying to reassure me. Ever loving and back to the guy that I trust and adore. Bringing some silence to my ravaged brain. I'm exhausted, wiped out, and so very shaky and fragile. Like the rug has been ripped out from under my feet and left me free-falling.

"Don't hate me." I croak through tears, scared that I will lose him for doing this to him. His words are lost on me, and all I can see is the evidence of how I attacked him, hating that I could do that to him. My fingers impulsively try to trace the wounds I gave him, but he catches my hand, sucking in his lip to remove the flow of blood, and pushes my hand to his heart instead.

"I could never hate you, Sophs. I made you do this. You have nothing to be sorry for. Never be sorry for protecting yourself, even from me. I've had a lot worse from being in the ring. I'm tough enough to take anything you can throw at me, baby." He leans in, gently kisses me on the forehead, then moves to my mouth, grazing his lips over mine. I taste his blood, but it doesn't affect me the way that slimy prick from months ago did. His blood made me gag and feel disgusting. Arrick's tastes like my blood taste like nothing that would repulse me, a part of him that doesn't affect me. I let him kiss me again as though he, too, needs the reassurance. I can't respond, though, and pull my hands free to trace the marks on his face when he moves away.

"Don't ... I deserve them and more." Arrick pushes his forehead to mine as he lifts me with him steadily, gathering me up and cradling me like a child. He carries me towards his room, holding me tenderly close. He walks us into the bedroom and gently lays me on the bed, running a hand over my hair as he gives me an intense look. Pulling his shirt off over his head and throwing it aside as I watch him in silence, tears subsiding as he grabs a fresh T-shirt and pulls that on over the claw marks evident on his shoulder and chest. He moves me over so he can get beside me and pulls me close to him once more, his heat absorbing me and gently cradling me into his body.

"I'm sorry." He runs a hand across my face and wipes away my tears, holding my face to his, an arm around my waist, and keeps me close. Emotional exhaustion is taking over. I'm drained so suddenly like there's nothing left of me, and I'm starting to numb it all out like a dream that never really happened. The human body's defense system.

"I'm so tired," I whisper breathily, wiped out from the outburst and aching to lie in his arms and close my eyes, forget all of it. To let go of any of this shameful bullshit I just inflicted on him.

"It's okay, go to sleep. I'm right here. I'll take care of you, always watch over you so you can stay safe." Arrick kisses my forehead softly, gently tracing my cheek with his caressing fingers. I close my eyes against his throat, held tight and secure in the only place that ever felt like a real haven for me, even if minutes ago I thought he was someone else.

I bury my face against his strong neck and breathe in his smell, the familiarity of his skin against me, and the perfection of his encircling embrace. Finally, safe and calm, and I never want to lose this moment of complete stillness to go back there again.

Chapter 18

"Shit ... I'm seriously going to be late." I'm running around looking for my shoes and trying to get myself together before Christian picks me up for the school open day. So not with it. Still half drunk, feeling like shit and needing way more sleep. Trying not to dwell on last night, and Arry has not brought it up. He's acting like it never happened, although we haven't had a second to think since I opened my eyes. He is trying to help me and keeps getting in my way, clucking around me, clearly still in protector mode.

I'm not a morning person, I have never been, and I'm so unbelievably irritable this morning. The after-effects of last night and dreams filled with horrid memories left me exhausted and raw. I know I must have been crying out in my sleep. I woke several times to Arrick calming me down, pulling me close, stroking my face, and telling me he was there.

I want to throat-punch everyone this morning, maybe not him, but everyone else. Aggression levels are abnormally high, and I feel crazily out of my head and should have stayed in bed.

"Here. Calm down. You have time." Arrick hands me my shoe, his tone deliberately steady and cool, and I hop around, trying to get it on. We barely had a moment to talk this morning. From eyes flying open when I realized I had never set the alarm, to falling out of bed into a room that was still spinning. I ended up face down, hanging over the side precariously with the duvet around my ankles, Arrick trying to pull me up from behind while laughing at my hopelessness and not helping in any way.

"I hate you." I curse at him for no reason other than he's getting the blame for the state I am in, as he was the one plying me with booze all night, telling me to let go as he would take care of me. I'm never listening to him again, and I think we need to talk about the amount of alcohol we drink together when we are out. I'm starting to see a distinct flaw in our compatibility when we get that way.

"Sure you do." He smiles at me with that annoyingly morning brightness of his, a lot less dead than me, and, thankfully, all those marks on his face from last night have almost faded away. There are abrasions and the odd healing bump, but all the redness is gone. I straighten up and look at him pointedly.

"We shouldn't drink. We act like assholes when we do." I guess this is my way of apologizing to him without apologizing. And my pathetic way of trying to broach the subject.

Lame Sophie.

"I am more than aware of that. Although the times we have, the first half of the alternative to fighting was pretty good." Arrick winks cheekily and then sighs and runs a finger along my jaw. He is right. The moments of not freaking out and not fighting had been more than good, and it makes me want to experience it with him all the more, torn that alcohol is the devil's work. I mean, he only ever loses his inhibitions about touching me that way when he has had a few, and I want to know what it's like to have him make love to me without all the mess that happens around us. Even after last night, I still want that with him.

I wonder if that will ever happen now.

If the first time freaked him out for a month, I have no idea what last night will do to his head. He is in an ultra-protective mode. Gentle and fluffing around me like a mother hen, making me feel a little suffocated today. I know that means overthinking, and an over-logical brain will put the brakes on anything else for a long time.

"You need to eat." He points me in the direction of the kitchen, to which I haul my unicorn cookie out of my handbag and wave it at him childishly.

"Sorted." I grin and see him curb the urge to have a go at me, sighing instead and holding his tongue. I guess last night had some perks. After all, he doesn't want to upset me this morning and is putting up with tremendous amounts of irritability and bad behavior from me.

"If it weren't for you coming back here at ten, I would make you eat something else. I'll make some food as soon as you get back." He frowns at me and moves to the kitchen while I attempt to get my damp hair in order. I had no time to dry it from my quick shower, and my makeup is all at home. I hadn't thought about getting ready when I met him at the bowling alley from my apartment. Luckily, I have some clothes here and found something casual to wear with low-heeled shoes I left behind his couch. The fact I'm a lazy, messy ass who litters his entire apartment all the time with all my belongings is a good thing, now that I think of it. The buzzer goes, and I curse at the time once more.

"I need to go, that's him, and we'll be late if we get caught in traffic." I grab my bag and coat, push my cookie into my pocket and turn to give Arrick a quick kiss. He catches me by the face and sinks a far dreamier smooch on me, making everything stop for a full minute. The kind of kiss that makes every stressful feeling melt away, down to your toes, and leaves you a little breathless. He pulls back and rubs his nose against mine gently.

"I love you." He smiles at me softly, full hazel eyes this morning and looking like my idea of heaven. I go to say it in response but hesitate; that little inner me is holding back, frowning, and I bite my lip a little unsurely.

"You're lame." I blurt out instead, deflecting stupidly, with a smile, and see him break into a smile too.

"So close that time." He grins, and I roll my eyes to hide how horrible it feels to withhold those three little words from him. Hating that after everything, I still can't just say it to him, even though I know I do. I wave my bag in the air to kill the awkwardness, I now feel as I run for the elevator without a backward glance.

* * *

I rest my skull against the cool chrome wall of the elevator and count the seconds it takes to get back upstairs. It feels like I have been gone for days, not an hour and a half. I want to go back to bed and lie down and sleep. My head aches, and the last hour was hell on earth as new students pushed and chatted incessantly in the crowded hall. My feet are killing me, and my clothes stink of the crappy perfume that Christian was walking around spraying at everyone to make them give him space.

No idea where the boy comes up with this stuff. Spraying a piss-like scent around you is a good way to make people leave you alone. All it did was give me a migraine.

The elevator pings open as my eyes close, and the sudden smell of food makes my mouth water, reminding me that Arry said he would make me food for when I got back. I glance up, expecting to see him happily playing with his pots and pans in the kitchen. Instead, the apartment is eerily silent, scarily dark, like he's shut all the blackout blinds and closed off all light to make it pitch black. I swallow nervously and hesitate before stepping out.

I wander in warily, seeing the fire is on low and illuminating the living room, and he's placed small candles all around the lounge to give off a romantic ambiance, which is so not an Arry thing. Walking forward, my eyes start to adjust as I realize more candles are dotted around the apartment, like small fireflies creating a sense of whimsical coziness and appearing strangely small. It makes my heart catch in my throat as I take in how pretty it is and focus more on the dullness of the light.

"Arrick?" I call out warily, not sure if I like this darkness and hoping he is still here and hasn't left me to wander around like a weirdo. That would be plain odd, a little cruel too, if he has just upped and gone out to leave me wandering in the gloom.

"Here, beautiful." Arrick appears behind me, giving me a small fright and making me jump as my stomach lurches into my throat. I giggle in stupid relief as his hands slide over my shoulders, removing my jacket and kissing me on the neck from behind. He must have been tucked out of sight in the dining area by the window.

I nosey around and see the table from this angle, nestled behind the wall, and it's all lit up with more candles and place settings for two with what looks like two boxes on the table. He takes my bag, slides it down my body, hands skimming me lightly, and then pulls my shoes off by lifting one foot at a time. I wrinkle my nose down at him and obey, touched by his cuteness and so glad to get them off. I adore him so much at this moment. My heart is doing a little butterfly dance and relaxing internally. Fatigue is forgotten and replaced with genuine warmth.

"What's all this for?" I watch him as he straightens out and comes to face me. Kissing me lightly on the mouth, his face lit by the flickering lights nearby and almost unrecognizable with the shadows cast on us. His very familiar smell is all around me, intoxicatingly so and soothing me in every way.

"My other girlfriend, you better leave. She's on her way." He grins, running his thumb over my cheek, and I mock sucker punch him in the abdomen with the back of my hand. He flinches slightly, grinning down at me, still gazing at me lovingly.

"Ha ha," I reply flatly. He strokes back my hair and kisses me again, this time more seductively, sucking my lip between his and angling so I can't do anything except surrender as he teases my mouth open a little. Cupping my face with large warm hands. Breaking away after sending my body into tingling mush, he rubs his nose against mine softly. His eyes are still glued on mine and barely a hair's breadth apart, so his breath fans my lips.

"Sometimes I forget, Sophie, that underneath that very feisty façade is a girl who needs a special kind of TLC. I take for granted that you love me when I should be making you fall in love with me all over again. I forget that you're not as tough as you make out." Arrick wrinkles up his nose at the face I'm making.

Tears sting my eyes that he can be this sweet to me after how I behaved last night. That he has this kind of romance in him, for a guy who seemed like he would always be too cool and emotionally distant ever to pull this card when he was with Tasha. My stomach aches with the sheer overwhelm, and my hands tremble involuntarily.

"You don't need to do this." I sniff softly as tears catch in my throat. Overcome suddenly, as this was the last thing I expected when I was in the elevator coming up here and dead on my feet.

"This is exactly what I should have been doing from day one. You're not that kid anymore, but you're still as fragile and easy to hurt. I forget that kind of stuff when faced with my strong, sassy diva, and last night reminded me how much I should be protecting you from everything and everyone, sometimes even me." Arrick swallows hard, emotion hitting him too as he takes my hand in his, caresses the area under my thumb with his, and lifts it between us, nodding towards the dining area and pulling me towards the table.

"Come on. Told you I would feed you. I know that's the surefire way to get into your heart." He smiles back at me, a little too suave and confident today and much more rested than me. I let him lead me to the table, and he pulls my usual chair out for me to sit down. The candles illuminate everything over here, and I spy the familiar boxes in the middle of the table with a sudden gasp as I settle in and let him slide me back in.

"Nancie's?" I pull the box forward impulsively and rip it open to be hit with the smell of the most amazing breakfast ever. Disbelief hitting me in full force and confusion that these could even get here.

"Blueberry and banana waffles with pecan sauce? How did you get them in the city?" I squeal, sticking my finger straight into that heavenly sauce and right into my mouth with a grin. Sheer delight runs over me, and my toes curl from that divine taste. Arrick has walked around and slid into his seat facing me, pulling his own box towards him.

"I made Jake fly them with him as he was coming to the city anyway. We may need to heat them, but I got you a shake too." He smiles at me with unconcealed adoration. "I figured I owed you more than a sorry for last night." He stands up and leans over the table, avoiding a burning candle, to kiss me, looking mighty pleased with himself. Everything seems to swarm at me so suddenly, hitting me with a ten-ton weight of emotion that he did this for me. Even after last night, after how I reacted and what I did. That he loves me this much.

I break into a sob immediately, unable to contain the sudden rush of emotion at the unexpectedness of it and the heartache hitting me hard, that sometimes I don't deserve him in any way, shape or form.

"Baby, what is it?" He quickly slides his seat out and comes around the table to kneel beside me, hauling me against him, smoothing back my hair, and cradling my face against his throat instantly. I can barely breathe for the gasping cries that have overcome me, hurting my soul and twisting me up inside.

"Don't ever leave me. Don't go backward." I cry uncontrollably through howling sobs. I feel utterly emotional. Heart shattering, insecurity at an all-time high from everything, tiredness, hangovers.

"*Mimmo,* I'm never going anywhere unless it's with you. Is this because of last night? I love you more than life. How many times do I need to say it to you? You are all I want. I won't ever leave you." Arrick leans against him, sliding arms around my shoulders and kissing me on the temple, cradling and rocking me gently. His tone soft and soothing, reminding me of how many times he has held me this way to calm my upset, soothe fears or give me support, and yet all my brain focuses on is the one time in my life that he didn't.

"You did, though. You did leave me. After you said, you wouldn't." I whimper uncontrollably, tired, unstable, and having some hormonal breakdown based on an unexpected romantic overload from the sweetest boyfriend in the world. Technically, this is all his fault for knocking the wind out of my sails with this surprise.

I hate that my insecure scars from before are ruining it right now. Tears blur my vision and break my heart. Arrick catches my face with a hand on each side, molding my cheeks, and pulls me to him so I can't turn away, bringing my forehead to his in the flickering light so that I can make out his eyes on mine.

"I regret that every day, Sophie. Even now, because those three months of not being with you killed me and hurt you. They ripped me apart in every way imaginable, like a constant agony I couldn't fix. I know I left you alone, baby. I wish I could undo all of it and go back to the beginning and always go with my heart and fuck my head. I hate that I did that to you, that I did this to you, but you have always had me. I would walk to the ends of the earth for you, Sophie. You have to see that. I always would have." Arrick's eyes glaze with moisture, his voice breaking at the sheer intensity of his words. I don't doubt the regret. I don't doubt that he really loves me, yet this constant fear that it's a dream, that his heart is still torn, lingers like a gnawing knot inside me every day.

"I don't want to feel like this anymore." I sob into his arms, curling myself into him, burying my face against his throat and breathing in his very smell, willing him to take it away. To help me understand why I feel this way and what's wrong with me.

"It takes time to forgive someone for hurting you. Especially hurting you the way I did. I know what I've done and understand that it affects how you feel about us." Arrick sits up and brings my face to his. Kissing me softly again and brushing my hair back.

"I'm trying," I mumble ashamedly, as though I am somehow failing him for feeling this way. Know I am. He does everything he can to make me feel loved and cherished, even when it goes against who he used to be. I've never seen Arrick as demonstrative and publicly affectionate with anyone as he is with me. Not even his own family.

"It's not up to you to forgive me, baby. It's up to me to earn it ... no matter how long that takes. Come on, leave this for now. I think you need to unwind a little bit. You're tired and emotional and maybe need to have a little breathing space to get your head together. You have barely had a minute since you woke up." Arrick pulls me to my feet and pulls me with him towards the bedroom, guiding me surely, through the darkness, making sure I don't trip on anything as we make our way through the enchanted room.

He's right. I'm emotional and tired and feel crazily strung out after last night. I love that he can always read me, but at the same time, it only makes me worse knowing he can sense that somewhere inside of me, I still doubt him and can't fully let myself go yet.

He leads me into his bedroom, which is illuminated by a soft glow from lights coming from the open bathroom door. I make a little sobbing noise as I take in his bathroom, sparkling with candles and a full hot bubble bath. All ready for me to climb into. He has the jacuzzi function turned on in the tub to keep it hot and bubbling, and little flower petals are floating around on top, giving a sweet aroma to the room. The bathroom smells like my favorite bath bomb, and the boxes on the counter with the branded names tell me that's what it is. He's been a very busy boy for someone who only had two hours of my absence, and all I can do is gawp like a dumbfounded freak, wondering when and how he planned all this.

"Arry?" I say breathily, grabbing his hand and squeezing it, so in awe of all this and completely blown away. I notice the glass sat by the side, already for whatever I want to pour into it, and the book I have been reading sat on a shelf over the tub. He anticipated my needs and set it all up, and I can't stop the wave of heartfelt tears that hit me again.

"You're my Princess. It's about time I started showing you that." He picks up my hand and kisses my fingertips so tenderly, gazing at me with unconcealed love and smiling softly before planting another kiss on my mouth and lingering for a second to savor it. Letting me go and making a move as though to leave.

"Where are you going?" I stop him with a hand on his arm, and he smiles at me again.

"I didn't set this up to pressure you into anything. I'm leaving you to relax for as long as you need." He kisses me on the forehead and goes to move again, but I don't let him. The intimacy of this scene, the romantic way he's being, just fuels my need to have more of him. If his touch can eradicate heartache, then what would full possession of me do? If I let him take me in every way possible. His touch holds the key to saving me from myself in many ways.

"Who's going to give me a shoulder massage and wash the bits I can't reach?" I flutter lashes at him shyly. Not wanting him to go elsewhere and leave me with my thoughts. He is the one who makes the doubts go silent. I don't need time to myself. I need more time with him around me, holding me tight and making all of this okay again.

"I guess I can hang around and do that." He grins at me. Moving back to stand in front of me and slides a hand on my hip with a look of mischievous happiness. Every part of me is aching for him now, my heart is a little less fragile, and a part of me that knows I need more from him than I have been getting is in the forefront of my mind.

"Probably make more sense, you know, if you took this off and got in too?" I shrug quietly, tugging at his T-shirt while watching his eyes home in on my mouth. The air around us is starting to charge, even if this was innocent a moment ago, but I know what I'm asking for. My head may be messy and emotionally stupid, but my body is already aching for something he started and never finished, even though it ended badly.

I still remember how the good bits felt and want to explore more of that. I want to know if his joining me in more ways than touch can end the constant ache of something missing inside me. Cure me of these insecurities which keep ripping us apart.

Arrick doesn't say anything, smiles at me, and then pulls his top over his head in one easy movement, that flawless physique on show. Rippling lines of toned muscle and dark art, and my stomach flips over with the sight of it. His body never fails to get my heart racing, tracing the fine line of fair hair up his abs until it blends to smooth skin and then meets the scattering across his chest. He's so much sexier than he was as a teen; losing that air of boyishness and growing into maturity increased his hotness. He was always cute, nicely toned, and sexy, yet he came into his own after twenty-one.

"Better?" He smirks cheekily, watching the progression of my fingertips and tensing his stomach with every tickle and caress. I watch it mesmerized, longing to see the rest of him even more so now.

"Umm ... you know these really should stay dry. Best if they come off too." I tug at his sweatpants and smile when he leans down and slides them off without argument, so he is only in a pair of very sexy fitted boxers and nothing else. It's not hard to see why women go gooey for him when not much is hidden. He should never be shy

225

about the package he is carrying anyway. It works like a switch, hitting me right in my pelvis, and the instant sizzle of horniness hits me hard. Pressing my knees together as my throat suddenly gets dry. With the lack of light, Arrick's pupils are already large, but now his eyes look so dark and consumed with unveiled lust that it changes his whole face. His body gives off new vibes as though he can already sense what I will ask him for.

"Seems a little unfair that I get to keep my clothes dry while this dress looks dry clean only." He leans in breathily and rubs his nose against mine to deliver a kiss, sexily delicate and heats me easily. I turn around so he's behind me, moving my hair aside so I can peek back at him coyly and guide his hands to my back to urge him to take it off.

I let his hands go as he slowly unzips it, stopping to kiss me on the back of the neck as he goes. His warm hand slides the zipper down and then slowly and gently pushes the dress off my shoulders, caressing my exposed flesh as he goes so that my eyes flutter shut at the contact. It pools around my ankles on the floor, and I step out and kick it aside without looking. Lost in the feel of his touch on me, tracing patterns across my shoulders and down my spine sensually. There is no doubt that he's turned on, yet I know he won't do anything about it. In that, I can always trust him.

"I'm awful at taking my underwear off," I whisper huskily, looking over my shoulder at him and seeing the same lustful glaze in his eyes that I'm sure mine have too. For something that started sweet and romantic, the air is sizzling with sexual tension, and he doesn't hesitate to unclip my bra and slowly slide it off from behind, kissing my shoulder and then easing my panties off. My body is churning with need, every ounce of me vibrating with impatience and desire.

He smooths them down my legs and then removes them one foot at a time, casually throwing them on top of our clothes on the floor. His eyes scan my body and devour me shamelessly. His hand skims the curve of my ass, yet he moves both to my waist, trying to tame his urges and stay in a safe zone.

He lets me go, bends behind me, and I realize he is taking the last of his clothes off so that we are completely naked while sober for the first time. The memories of Leila's party are hazy, and we had more darkness than this, so we could not appreciate each other in our natural splendor. I don't feel nervous at all. I feel desirable and safe, my skin tingling with his soft touches as he comes back to stand up behind me. Trembling with how different it feels to have him against me, skin on skin, and completely aware of every touch. Heightened senses and crazily alert.

He runs his fingertips down my neck, erupting in a million sizzling goosebumps as he slowly trails them down my spine and across one of my butt cheeks. I can hear the change in his breathing, the charge between us in the air.

"You're the most beautiful girl I have ever known. I can't believe that you're mine, that I get to touch you like this. Get to kiss you every day. I'm so in love with you, Sophs. Every single tiny inch of you." His voice is in my ear, low and sexy, tickling my neck, and I close my eyes to the sensation of his skin on my skin again. My heart erupts at his words, and I want to turn and throw myself into his arms and kiss him to death. I want so badly to tell him how much I love him too. I pray that the mental block stopping me from that one tiny detail can be cured with one final step in bringing us together properly.

Every part of me longing with a desire to feel the way he's making my neck feel. I want to feel him inside me, to have that mouth back in places he brought to ecstasy before. I want it more than oxygen right now, and every yearning ache has me tensing in anticipation, a need so strong I may scream if he denies me.

"Make love to me," I whisper it so surely, yet so breathily, I don't think he hears me at first. His hand pauses on my back as he registers what I have asked of him. I was so sure he knew this was where I wanted this to go until this very second.

"I don't want to put you back there." His words come out painfully, with so much emotion, and I can hear how torn he is. Despite his touching me and his body sending every signal that he wants this as much as I do, he is still trying to look after me.

I love you so much.

"Try for me, please. I need this to heal, to feel normal." the tears well up inside, afraid that he won't take this further, and I need him to. I need to feel like I can be everything I should be in a normal relationship, to be a normal woman. That I can be to him what he deserves, he needs ... despite his reassurance that he doesn't. I want to show him how much I love and trust him, and I need to do it where words fail me.

Arrick slides his arms around my waist and kisses me on the neck. Pulling me against him so I can feel his body against every inch of mine. That delicious sensation of our naked bodies completely engaged and only fuels my longing for more from him.

"Does it feel like I don't want to try?" He smiles against my shoulder, and I must admit there's a hard wedge up my back, nestled above my butt in a pretty obvious way. I giggle, both nervous suddenly, and because it is unexpected, the humor in something so serious as this.

Arrick turns me slowly to him, moving back a little and putting space between us, yet moving in to kiss me gently. He grazes his nose against mine, hands coming up to cup my face as he leans down to bridge our height difference. He pulls me against him, so my hands go up and around his neck, and his kiss deepens passionately, molding to me, moving with me, and I let my tongue slide to his to initiate more. I am fully aware of his rock-hard self against my pelvis, I can barely ignore it when it's that obvious, and yes, for a moment, I doubt I'm equipped for it. As horrid as it is to compare, my mind does it automatically and abhors myself for it, but he's well endowed. I wonder that I even managed it once before.

"I want you so badly I can almost taste it, but I don't want what happened last night to happen again. Ever." Arrick sounds so torn, looking at me as though he doesn't know what to do. I trace his lip with one finger and focus on his eyes deeply, still caught in his embrace and confident in what I want.

"If you don't make love to me, I may self-implode. Last night doesn't mean anything. I don't want to remember or see it as a reason for not trying. I want you so badly that my body is turning inside out, and we can't keep going on this way, letting it build up to be something more than it is." I reply surely, with no hint of apprehension as I gaze at him persuasively. That tiny muscle flicker in his jaw, knowing he's fighting himself and losing his internal battle, as the look of sheer longing overtakes his face. His eyes get heavy, and his gaze moves to my mouth obsessively.

I mean, it's probably a good move to get naked to convince your beau to have sex before hitting him with the request. All the scales weighed heavily on my side. I lean on tiptoes and capture his lips in mine, kiss him with eyes open and focus on his, teasing him with my teeth as he crumbles before my very eyes.

"No one has ever made me so crazy like this that I can't function." He replies huskily. Losing the air of confusion, and I know I'm winning. I may not have his skills of seduction and sex, but I do know my boy and how to get to him in ways no one else can. Secure in my ability to have him sway to what I want.

I let my fingertips trail up the back of his short hair, scraping my nails gently in his scalp as his hands move down and encircle my waist, pulling me in and up so I'm lifted into him, and my feet leave the floor. Feeling his body against mine, the look on his face tells me this isn't going to stop. I wrap my arms around his neck and get lost in a kiss he started the night before. Groaning as he massages his tongue against mine and parts my lips so that he can devour me freely. The passion I met briefly is back in full control, and the side of him I know that dwells deep inside showing a little face.

We start moving out of the bathroom and into his dark room with a few easy strides. He lays me down on the bed, kissing me, caressing a palm over the full length of my body from the collarbone, over my breast, down my abdomen, and between my thighs, so I gasp and arch under his tender touch. Then down one leg, moving away as he turns on a nearby lamp, giving a little illumination, and I blink at him with a smile. He sets my body alight with that unexpected trail, and a surge of dampness around my secret areas that I know means I'm turned on too. Heightened senses are already at play, and anticipation turns me into a bundle of hot nerves.

"You like the lights on?" I watch him, wondering if that's normal for men when it's consensual. I'm not sure if I want it that way, and figuring that lights might be a good thing.

"I want you to be able to see me, always. So you know it's me." He frowns, reminding me of the first time and what I said to him about not being able to see him. My heart warms unexpectedly, gnawing a little in real love-sick tenderness. He comes to crawl over me on the bed and nestles beside me instead of on top of me, stroking his hands down my body, exploring every curve gently as he does so with careful touch and erupting so many more sensations until my skin goosebumps all over.

"I see you," I whisper back quietly, smiling at him encouragingly as I do so, my voice almost non-existent, and he gives me that beautiful, sincere, stomach-melting smile that weakens every part of me.

My beautiful, sweet boy.

Pulling my face to him by the chin, he returns to kissing me gently, slowly at first, easily moving into more intensity, fire spiking as he slowly slides over the top of me fully. He slowly and deliberately maneuvers himself onto my body gently. He uses his knees and hands to cage me before coming down to nestle on me, watching my expression the whole time as though looking for any signs of change. I can feel his apprehension, his need to take care of me, over his need to have sex with me, and I kiss him for it.

I trace out that sculpted body, legs parting so he can get close, and it's completely different from having him against me naked like this, even though he has been here once before. Somehow being sober changes everything about this.

I'm more aware, it's more intense, and now instead of feeling like he's only on top of me to curb an urge, I feel like he's joined me with a need to love and be close to me.

His skin is hot and smooth, and he smells like he always does, a mix of body spray, familiar cologne, and his smell. That in itself could seduce me effortlessly; he has no idea how much power he has over me with things that are seemingly nothing to anyone else. He breaks away and rubs his nose against mine, locking my eyes seriously, the second wave of doubt hitting him like a predictable, typical Arry as his head brain takes over what his body wants.

"You sure you want this, Sophie? We don't need to. I don't need this." He appraises me carefully, eyes so dark in the shadows he is casting with the light behind him, but I can see every line of his face perfectly. That deep husky voice washes over me like hot liquid, and I feel completely relaxed with him.

"I do ... I want you. Maybe you should turn your phone off, though." I frown and look away, hating myself instantly for that tiny insecurity coming out like that. Feeling instantly pathetic and hating that I even said it. Even despite everything I am feeling, that would jump in between us to kill everything.

Great way to start a fight and end this all again. You're an idiot.

"It's off. Since you texted you were coming home, it's been off. No interruptions ... it's staying off all day." He nudges me with his nose and smiles, kissing me on the corner of the mouth to bring me back to him. I turn back as a small smile breaks over my face. Heart restored, insecurity pandered to, and just us in a naked clinch, ready to finally take this further. Feeling somehow lighter, knowing he even thought about that one tiny detail, and he isn't going to let her come between us this time, not today.

I lean up and kiss him, meeting zero resistance, and he follows my head back down to the bed with a kiss that sparks another instant fire inside of me, knowing exactly how to smooch me into complete submission now that he has figured out what works.

I don't ever want to lose this between us, lose the ability to have him kiss me this way. No one has ever made me feel like he does with something so basic, addictive, and right. His kisses are my idea of heaven; I could do this every day. He has no idea how much more he can affect me since we added kissing into the mix, gentle intimacy, and caresses. He owns every part of me so effortlessly.

His hands skim my body, gently feeling me out, barely grazing my skin with the softest of touches, igniting a fire across my skin that has me aching almost instantly. I let my fingers trail his carved shoulders, feel out his muscles and his strong neck, angling my body to match his kiss, and yet distracted by what his hands are doing to me.

When his hand skims across my thighs and up the inside of my leg slowly, I arch impatiently, eager to get beyond this and have him with me, move past the parts that always get interrupted, and be one. I wriggle into him, urging him to go faster and be less gentle. He breaks the kiss to smile at me.

"You know I can feel what you're doing." He laughs softly and catches my lip between his, kissing me by softly sucking it sensually, erupting another bout of crazy strong urges to be doing it already.

"Maybe you should get on with it then." I smile back, pushing my body to his impatiently.

"Trust me ... this will feel much better if you let me work you up to it. I need to make sure you're ready. No cutting corners." He lowers his head and trails small pecks down my throat, silencing me with the sheer pleasure it gives me. His hand finally making its way between my thighs and finding me willing to comply, silencing the protest I was forming about his needing to hurry up. His finger circles me, enticing me to open my legs a little more, and then has me squirming and arching my back with whatever he does down there that feels divine.

It feels like he's circling, easing me open softly and probing gently. The sensation of what he is doing has me moaning and grinding into his hand impulsively, with no shame or shyness, arching under his attentive touch and clawing at him desperately. My stomach tingles with the effort, and my legs itch to curl up. I start panting as the tip of his finger slides inside of me slowly, not far but enough to almost send me over the edge.

"I'm ready ... Just ... Arry ..." I writhe and moan, unable to contain the building chaos that almost has me begging him, to stop the agonizing torture of drawing this out. My heart is pulsing crazily with need. He chuckles into my ear as he shifts position over me, maneuvering his body between my legs and bringing my face to his. He kisses me on the tip of the nose, pulls his hand from between us, braces himself on the bed over me, and looks down between us. Focusing on my face intently, drawing my gaze to his as he slides in against me softly, I know he's going to do it.

I pause and hold my breath for a moment, locking eyes on his as he mouths a silent "I love you" to me. I bite on my lip, slide my palms to his shoulders impulsively, in case I need to stop him, some control if I can't do this, and encourage him with a smile.

He slides into me so slowly it's almost unbearable, eyes steady on mine, and the sheer concentration on his face makes me break into a giggle that is completely wrong for the moment. It feels amazingly good, though, like I want to squeeze my knees together and make him push further inside of me. I smile when he moves into me some more, almost as though he psychically knew what I was thinking, and despite the wave of complete fullness and the urge to moan, another giggle escapes me.

"Don't look at me like that." I prod his cheek in a bid to get his face off mine, and he only smiles wider and pushes a little deeper, making me gasp, and now I'm wondering if he is even done yet. That seems like an awful lot of sliding in, and my body might not manage more, even if it does make my legs go weak and my toes curl. My head immediately jumps to images of impaled women with heavily hung devils, and I wonder if it's physically possible to be too small for your boyfriend's equipment.

"You're killing the moment, Sophs." He leans down and catches my mouth with his, pushing my lips apart to kiss me as he fully eases his way into me, the last tiny thrust. My body stretches and fills in a weirdly unique yet wholly satisfying way, moaning as he moves slightly against me, and spasms of pleasure course up my stomach.

Definitely fits.

Gasping a little that the first time we did this, he clearly only went half in, and now I'm experiencing every inch of him, and 'Oh, my God' is the only thing my brain can repeat to itself in utter happy surprise. I instinctively slide my hands around behind his shoulders, gripping on, straining to control myself and pull him onto me. My body moves with his as he slowly finds a gentle rhythm and glides within me, sparking another wave of new and equally delicious responses. I fall to pieces and let out a long moan, burying my face in his throat. He lifts his face again over my head, his throat vibrating in my face as he talks to me.

"Are you okay?" He stops mid-thrust and waits for an answer, which only snaps my eyes open, and I lean my head back to glare at him in outrage

"SHHH! Now, who's killing the moment? Stop stopping." I scold him, moving my hips, so he slides into me again and then moan as the sensation intensifies, completely satisfied that he is doing as he's told for once. Arrick closes his eyes, and for a moment, he seems to try and reel in control. Opening them again, he bites on his bottom lip and moves against me with a little more sway and intensity to the way he glides in and out, and I catch my breath. Gasping as the feelings soar through me and kill all conversation dead. The heat pulsing in my pelvis has spread to every part of my lower body, and the only thing that is going off in my brain is just how amazing this feels. It's all I can focus on.

My hands turn to claws without meaning to, raking my nails down his back as he repeats the move that has us both moaning out, breathing labored. Getting lost as he comes in for another kiss, but like some demon inside of me has been unleashed with what he is doing to me, I cling to him with every thrust, every groan and moan, hands roaming his entire back and shoulders, even gripping his ass when he starts to move with more purpose.

He rocks in against me, hands cupping my face and bodies completely in sync. Locking eyes on me, making me crazy with how much my body wants to explode from the one million overwhelmingly amazing sensations ripping through my core with every confident thrust from him. He looks lost in what we're doing. He cannot keep his eyes on me as they get heavier and shut, tipping his jaw into my neck and breathing against me hard when he ups the tempo and I lose control.

What starts as slow, romantic sex, easy movements, and eyes locked turns hot and hard and completely out of our control in what feels like seconds - because I turn into some crazy wanton devil who wants more than soft romantic sex.

Like a power of frustration being unleashed in a tidal wave and try as he might to keep what we're doing on the low key, we are soon grinding, panting, and ravaging each another until the bed rocks and the headboard starts thudding off the wall in quick succession. He pulls my knee up on one side to angle into me harder, to help him gain momentum, and soon has me pounded to the bed, the springs creaking, biting his lip while he frowns sexily, clawing at his chest and nibbling any part of him I can reach.

Caught up in a frenzy of hard thrusts, groaning, moaning, as my body erupts in a million explosions around him, an orgasm ripping through me so fast, like before, and it completely takes my breath away. I pant, cry out, spasm, and arch below him, but do not let go when he tries to give me time to recover. I hold him, urge him not to stop, and find the desire returning equally fast to keep going, gripping on tight.

"Don't stop. Not until we both get there." I gasp between moans, his mouth against my face as he rocks back into me at speed once more, finding a natural rhythm between us. Arrick pushes my hands to the bed to control how I'm spearing him with my nails, fingers entangled, head buried in my neck as he thrusts into me with the pent-up tension that has been building between us for weeks. Grinding into me, making me gasp with every thrust.

He's still trying to be gentle; I can feel the way he's holding back, trying to stay in control, and I am willing him to unleash himself. I trust him. I want him to be able to be who he is with me too. I don't believe for one second that my passionate, fight-loving Carrero is a tame lover. I can feel so much more bristling within him, urging it to come out and face me. I want that side to him, to be the one who he lets it loose on and shows me what he's really like.

I wriggle and squirm as the intensity builds again, my body on fire, aching, growing in heat and sensation for the second time, and feeling like I am about to be torn apart with the summit of this climax. I tighten my legs around his waist to control how hard he is pounding. His hands release me as he grabs my thighs and shifts up to his knees, pulling my body with him so he can lever me. Lifting my butt off the bed without changing rhythm. I arch against him, moaning loudly, and reach to claw at him, completely set free and uncaring about how much noise I am making. I find my natural motion, grinding with his body and moving my hips to match the waves of pleasure.

Arrick seems to be starting to let go. Less gentle as he grips me, thrusts harder, and looks a lot less serene and calm than the Arry I know. This Arry seems capable of pushing me up against a wall and blowing my mind with hard sex, yet it doesn't scare me or take me any place except right here. I want it. I want more.

I push my shoulders into the bed as the first waves sweep up from my toes, heat and tingles engulfing me as I arch so far back that my whole spine lifts, and my pelvis is pushed more into his, making me cum spectacularly. I can't contain the wracking explosion that hits me, how my body convulses for the second time, or how crazy wild I go, lost in my ecstasy and release, completely oblivious to anything else.

Arrick lifts me, so I'm catapulted against him mid-orgasm, and I end up straddling him as he slumps back onto his ass. He grabs my hips and grinds me down onto his lap so the intensity doubles, and I cry out in his face. My mouth gapes open through hard thrusts of every wave until my body can't take anymore. Gasping in surrender and am completely reliant on him to hold me up when my body releases the tidal wave. I spear him with my claws as I grip on through the ultimate climax that wracks me from the inside out.

"Jesus, Sophie." Arrick's voice brings me around, and I realize he's back on top of me. I'm flat on the bed once more and uncurling my grip from his shoulders, definite puncture wounds from where I grabbed onto him, but at least he's smiling. He rolls off me and flops back on the bed with a massive exhale that suddenly makes him sound exhausted. Raising a shoulder and looking behind him as he does so. "Baby ... I did not take you for a scratcher. Holy shit, I look like I've been at it with a wildcat... Fuck, that was better than good. I don't think I expected that turnaround. Are you okay, though?" He grins and rolls back to me, kissing me on the mouth as I lie, panting and reveling in the left-over tingles still consuming my body. I can barely breathe, let alone smile or react to the fact I have probably scarred him for life. Permanent disfigurement while having sex is surely not normal.

"I'm better than okay. That felt really ... really good! And I'm sorry." I pant breathlessly, unsure how to feel about the fact that I want to do that again as soon as I recover my breathing, and maybe I should cut my nails off. My body has just met complete satisfaction in a way I never knew it could, and although he did make me cum after Leila's party, it never felt anywhere near as mind-blowing as these two did. I'm floating on cloud nine and feel he should permanently live between my thighs.

To think I have had him for the last few weeks and haven't been making use of this all that time.

Pretty sure if I had known what was coming, I wouldn't have let him out of bed for the last few weeks. At all.

"Don't be. I always did like a little bit of rough. Guess you are the perfect girl after all... I'm happy that it felt good. That's kind of the point." He winks at me, and I shake my head at him, sated, exhausted suddenly, and completely relaxed in every way as though I have just had ten full-body massages in one go. He looks over his shoulder and then under his arm, feeling with his fingers at his back and upper shoulder for the raised marks that are probably glowing viciously.

"How bad is it?" I ask, regaining a little control and struggling to sit up and see. Suddenly feeling guilty that I did get a little wild and may have hurt him. I wasn't even aware that I was doing it, so caught up in passion and mind-blowing sex I had no idea I was marking him like a feral beast.

"Bad? I'm being serious. Nothing is more of a turn-on than your girlfriend clawing the shit out of you because what you're doing works for her." He winks at me, a completely unashamed Casanova move with a twinkle in his eye that makes me eye roll.

"There's something wrong with you." I giggle and flop back down, a little smug that I realize we did it.

We had sex from start to finish and are lying here laughing about it, and it doesn't feel weird or wrong at all. I did it. I got through it. I don't feel anything I thought I would feel, and not once, while he was inside of me, did I compare it in any way or think about the past. I really did it. I'm so happy that I cannot even explain the immense wave of emotion it's causing me.

"You think so? Maybe I'm just man enough to handle you in all your untamed wildness; you look crazily sexy right now." Arrick smiles and swoops in at me, kissing me on the mouth a little passionately. I seriously wonder how soon he can be ready for round two. My little tingly body is already limbering up for another go at my hot stallion.

His fingers trace my cheeks, and he smiles at me adoringly; for the first time in so long, there's a completely relaxed look on his face, every part of him satisfied, and I wonder how long it's been since he had sex. I don't want to know. I want to tell myself that she hasn't touched him since we kissed so long ago, even though I know that's probably wrong.

It doesn't matter. None of that matters anymore.

"Orgasm glow works for you ... I want to do that again." He grins and lets me go to reach across to the bedside to grab a bottle of water. He takes a drink and offers it to me, but I only shake my head and watch him deposit it back where he got it. Eyes glued to that stunning profile and sexy half-smile, he can't seem to wipe off his face and love him so much more than I ever thought possible.

"I'm not stopping you." I smile saucily and maneuver myself to his body, curling against him to move things along once more, high on happy adrenaline for doing this. More than a little confident he could do that to me again with zero bad reactions, as many times as he wanted, every second of every day. I think I just found my new addiction, and I may even love it more than clothes or shoes!

"Maybe once is enough for now. I don't want to push it ... we still need to see how you go, and we also have a hot jacuzzi waiting for us. Then food, and you know how much you love your food. This was a big deal, Sophie. We need to let your emotions catch up and take time to process... Don't think I don't know how huge this is. I do." He ponders my face seriously, hand cupping my cheek and thumb caressing my skin lightly. He looks so protective that I hug him tighter.

"I know. I don't want to ruin it by talking about it, though. Don't make it a thing." I frown and then feel stupid that I even said it aloud, but he nods understandably and strokes my face.

"Come on then. Distraction is always better." Arrick rolls away from me and gets up, holding a hand out to me, obviously in no way shy about being completely butt naked, and for a second, I honestly don't know where to look. Seeing him starker's is completely different from letting him have his way with me naked. Now the lust-fueled haze has dispersed, it does seem weirdly awkward. I blush and look anywhere but at him.

"Really? I can do all that to you, yet you get shy now?" He laughs and pulls me to him by the ankle when he gets fed up waiting. I squeal as he picks me up and pulls me into his arms to carry me like a bride-to-be. At least up here, I don't have to avert my eyes.

"It's not like I've seen you undressed a lot, okay? It takes some getting used to." I am still trying not to look at anything but his face, but he rolls his eyes and grins.

"I am imprinting you naked to memory and insist we both walk around like this daily... I need pictures. Where's your phone? You are sending me naked selfies." He jokes and turns as though he really is going to find it. Looking decidedly wicked and thoroughly serious.

"Not a chance. You think I don't know Nate uses your phone when you're in the ring? He has called me on it before to tell me when you're winning." I hold a palm in front of his face. I'll never let him get a single naked shot of me when his phone is passed around his promo team so easily. I would never face them again, and I don't want anyone but him ever to see me this way.

"Baby?" He looks wounded, seriously disappointed that I'm laying down the law on this. Obviously had his mind set on some saucy nude shots of me, for real.

"Men!! Have sex one time, and they turn weird on you." I giggle at his juvenile expression, how he narrows his frown at me and then puts me down on my feet when we get to the bathtub.

"Get in. It's time for clean fun instead of the dirty fun we just had." He pretends to sulk, and I lean in and splash some bubbles at him with a giggle. I obediently step in the tub and sit down, then shimmy forward when he gets in behind me, the temp is still hot, and the water jets are crazily good on my body. I keep expecting this to turn weird or different, like a looming mood to jump up and ruin it all for me suddenly, but despite what we just did, it still feels the same. I don't feel weird around him or that we did anything worse than cuddling up or kissing. He isn't acting like it's a big deal, and I guess it's making me relax too. Suddenly, instead of this being a huge thing, it feels right like we haven't even done anything major.

"Ahh, stings!" Arrick cringes against me and lifts his arm out of the water to look at the nail marks I left on him, inching forward against me and looking back over his shoulder."

"Stop being a baby. You said you liked it." I pout petulantly, feeling guiltier now about leaving him with scratch marks. Clawing the shit out of him was not exactly something I imagined doing during our romantic first time. The first pangs of something inside me, close to shame, sidle up, and I push it back down with a heavy sigh.

"I do ... it just hurts when submerged in girly-infused bubble water. I need to man up living with you, or next time avoid climbing in a tub meant for you. I'm going to smell like a woman after this." Arrick slides me between his legs as he inches down in the tub, resting his head on the back and leaning me against his chest, holding me against him.

"Technically, I don't live with you. But manning up might be a good idea if all you can worry about is smelling like a girl and some minor stings from little girl scratches... Jeeze, here I thought you were a big manly MMA pro." I smirk and close my eyes, leaning my head against his muscled pecs and closing my eyes as hot water soothes every inch of my aching body. I needed this and feel exhausted so suddenly. Having two orgasmic explosions, one after the other takes it out of you.

"Umm, womanly claw gauges, actually! Maybe you should?" Arrick stiffens a little, his head lifting, and I guess he's looking at me. I pause, too, realizing what he's saying, as it sucker punches me in the gut. I sit up suddenly, turn and glance back at him over my shoulder warily. My stomach flipping over with nerves.

"What?" I eye him suspiciously, unsure if he just asked me to move in or if he is making some weird and vague joke while I'm almost falling asleep.

"Move in with me." He repeats it confidently with a shrug, like it's a nothing suggestion, and I hesitate. So much colliding in my head that I don't know what to say. So much we are still trying to figure out between us. Everything is so new. I mean, we only just mastered proper sex for the first time, and he's talking about cohabiting.

Shit.

"I ... It's a bit sudden, isn't it?" I frown at him and then turn to look at anything but him so I don't fall into complete panic or guilt over being unable to say yes. I lie back against him as he pulls me to him, giving me no choice. His arms encircle me and tighten around me. He shrugs behind me.

"Only if you count us from a month ago, but I don't... I realized somewhere along the way that I have been head over heels for you for a long time. I can't tell you when it started, but I know it was probably before I came out to live here. Not seeing you for weeks put my head into perspective, and I guess I've loved you for much longer than I wanted to admit. I couldn't deny it anymore... Sophie, you're why I never let anyone else come close to getting in, not even Tasha. You always had the part of me they wanted." He slides his arms around my shoulders, kisses the back of my head, and then lets me go as he reaches for a sponge, dips it in the water, and squeezes water over my upper body. That lurch in my stomach at what he's saying nearly kills me. So much love, so much I want to hear, and yet I'm floundering over him wanting more from me, and I don't even know why.

"I don't know ... I need time to think about it ... I mean, we only just ..." I sigh and let out a gust of air in complete deflation, feeling cornered and confused, upset by his confession even though at the same time it makes me want to squeeze him tight. I know I want him; I need him. But there is still that part of me afraid to take the last step off the ledge and give all into this. So much still turning and twisting in my heart from the past.

Natasha is still a constant headache even though he keeps

reassuring me, proving that she doesn't matter, and I know I am fixating on her when I shouldn't be. I thought I would feel more sure than this, that being with him would feel secure. Not always hiding my worries and niggles from him, fearing that he will get pissed at my jealousy and constant need for reassurance. I hate that it's how I feel. I always thought I was stronger than this, but he has a way of getting underneath all that and making me feel vulnerable. It's not that easy to let someone see you stripped bare and trust them not to wound you again when you're struggling to forgive them for the first time. It's complex.

As levelheaded as he can be, he can be a complete ass regarding irrational jealousy. It plays over in my head all the time lately, knowing how much he hates feeling suffocated. I remember a girl about three years ago who called him in a rage after they had been on a few dates because he was snapped with another girl at a premiere with Jake. He hung up on her icily after telling her he was done.

He's not the jealous type, really. That night in the club, he attacked that sleaze, but it was provoked. Generally, he doesn't seem to care if some guy is smiling my way. The last month so many men have approached me when we are out together, and he shakes his head and kisses me to stake his claim smugly; he finds it amusing. Tells me the highest compliment a guy can get is other men trying to hook their woman, so I don't think he can understand how it feels.

"Take as much time as you need. It's an open-ended request. I want you with me, always." He runs the sponge over my shoulders and down my hair delicately. Seemingly unfazed by my sort of rejection and I relax a little, knowing he isn't the type ever to pressure me. Hoping he still understands that maybe I need a little more time.

"I'll think about it." I sigh and close my eyes, head back to being filled with so many contradicting thoughts that I had been sure sex would fix. Maybe he was right. After all, sex isn't the cure for everything.

Chapter 19

"You want it heated up?"

I shake my head. Arrick runs his hand down the back of my hair as I sit at the table with a fluffy robe covering my naked body. I'm completely relaxed, my body sagging, from the hour-long tub, soak we took. The idle chit-chat that was so easy and the twenty minutes of letting him dry and massage every inch of me on the bed were sensual and heavenly, although he did stop my hands from wandering under his towel twice. I feel surreal, completely chilled out, satisfied, and content.

"They will probably taste as good cold." As I watch him wander off, I open the box and empty the contents onto my plate, digging in and smiling at how amazing they taste. He has on sweatpants, but he's topless and barefoot. His back is a little marked up like he's been rolling in barbed wire, and I look away from it guiltily. Not sure if I like what I have done to him. Even though he keeps telling me he likes a girl with claws and assured me several times that he will expect some scratching from now on in.

Arrick returns from the refrigerator with two shakes and puts them between us. Sitting down to eat gives me an uninterrupted view of his naked torso with strong shoulders and perfect muscles that make me weak at the knees with every movement he makes. He looks down, sexy as always, flawless in my eyes, and starts eating too. That gorgeous jaw at work, slightly stubbled today as he skipped shaving this morning, he looks a little more like a rugged bad boy.

"That's really distracting, you know?" I point my fork at his pecs and wave it side to side to gesture to his naked body. He makes my heart rate rise slightly too easily when he's flaunting what he has. I struggle to focus on delicious food when the view is much more appetizing.

"What about if I do this?" He grins at me and tenses his arms in the Mr. Universe. pose, which only makes me roll my eyes and giggle at his weirdness. He is cheekily confident and knows his body does the trick. He even appeared seminude in some men's and women's magazines last month and is evidently not shy about it.

"Yeah, completely lame." I smile and take another forkful, watching him move effortlessly as every movement emphasizes that hot physique, with little bulges and flinches that are strangely mesmerizing. My inner lady parts are heating up and tingling to attention so readily that I press my legs together to try and calm it down.

Who knew a male body could make me drool so much, especially now I know what it can do to mine?

"Don't lie. You are hot for me like this." He winks at me and then picks up his shake, sliding his feet under the table to capture mine and pull them towards him, so our feet are completely entangled. He is cutely affectionate, like always, and one of his little surprising traits that I adore the most. He's like an eternal human cushion that likes to be cuddled up at all times.

"Possibly," I answer evasively, watching him under my lashes as he slides down into a more casual seated pose and keeps staring at me. I try to focus on anything else other than the way he's watching me eat, and I notice an unfamiliar tribal symbol on his collar bone, just above the main part of his chest work that joins to his sleeve, that I never noticed before. Not surprising, really, he's not ever sat naked in front of me while my eyes wander freely.

"That's new, isn't it?" I point at the little Celtic-type line running up his collarbone perfectly, acting like a border to the rest of his black ink. Looking for a distraction from those pecs and those gazing hazel eyes.

"Yup... I got it a couple of months back." He looks down, running a hand over it, and then back at me with a lazy smile. He has so many tattoos now that unless you sit and dissect them, they all mesh to one large dark sleeve of artwork.

"Does it mean anything?" I ask softly, still digging into my food and looking over all his ink appreciatively. It's a part of him I always loved, and I love seeing new tattoos on him too. Some have meanings to him, and some don't. He has a serious addiction to them, much like his brother, yet they suit him like he was always meant to have them.

"Nope. Just liked this one.... Although this one is my notch of another win." He points at the little star among the cluster of stars inside a geometric shape on his inner arm, getting pretty crowded now with all his wins over the last few years. That tug of pride at the little addition, knowing he's good at what he does and loves it. He is a born fighter, even if that's not necessarily a good thing; his ability to be disciplined and focused play a huge part in his success.

"Guess you will be adding another one after this week." I smile, reminding him that he leaves for LA tomorrow for a week-long promo and fight. He is one step away from a championship fight, and I couldn't be prouder of him. At the same time, there is that sinking feeling of dread inside me because he will be gone for a full seven days, and I don't want him to go.

"Come to Miami with me?" He gazes at me seriously, reading my mind, eyes on mine with complete unmovable intent.

"You know I can't. I have assessments all week. I can't miss those." I sigh and, for the millionth time, regret the fact I can't go with him. Arrick is a born traveler, he loves jumping up and going places impulsively, and I love it too. He always makes trips exciting and fun, and despite his constant overthinking, and logical personality, he is impulsive when it comes to spontaneous getaways. I catch him frowning at me and distract him by diverting back to tattoos.

"What does that one say?" I point at one on his forearm, a long line of words crammed small and neatly within another hectic piece that makes it hard to read from here. Arrick turns his arm and looks at the neat row of scrawls.

"It's a Muhammed Ali quote. It says, "Float like a butterfly, sting like a bee." He puts his arm back down and continues eating, throwing me an eyebrow lift to get me to eat too.

"You're strange." I giggle and dig into my pancakes once more. Savoring the bite, loving that he did this for me, and filling up inside with so much joyous feeling.

"Well, I did get your name on the bottom of my foot too, so I guess I am." He glances at me with deadpan seriousness that I cannot judge if it's a joke.

"Wait. What?" I blanche at him in complete open-mouthed disbelief. Little wheels in my head are turning, trying to think back if I have ever looked at the sole of his foot. I cannot recall if I have ever seen a tattoo there and frown at him suspiciously.

"You know, cos you loved toy story so much, you made me see it fifty times, and you kept calling me your Woody. So I figured I would let you be my Andy." He seems completely serious, eating his food again and glancing my way occasionally with a half-smile that I can't read.

"Please tell me your kidding." I drop my fork on my plate and gawp at him steadily, unsure how to feel about that. I don't even!

There are no words.

"Why? ... Don't you think it's cute that your name is on me. I even made sure it was in your juvenile handwriting, like a personal Sophie mark... Authentic." He smiles at me with an infuriating cute boy expression and no telling whatsoever if he is serious, while I'm starting to think he is.

"Noo .... I think it's weird, and why your foot?" I retort, no longer gooey, emotional, and starting to think he is an actual moron for something so lame.

It's not cute. It's weird.

"Because that's how you claim ownership of your toys. I thought you had that movie committed to memory?" He sticks more food in his mouth and taps his fork on my plate to remind me to eat while I keep staring at him.

"You're not my toy, though!" I retort.

"I am now." He winks dirtily.

"Please tell me your kidding?" I can't even begin to contemplate the millions of reasons that a guy having your name on the sole of his foot is neither sexy nor romantic. It's plain odd. It's not something I imagine he would ever do with any girl. Especially not one who wasn't even his girlfriend at the time, and yes, I do see the cuteness somewhere, but it's still a bit, Ughhh.... Lame.

"Why?" He looks innocently surprised.

"It's weird! On your foot Arrick? That means you're standing on me every day." I blurt out, thinking of how many times he stands on it - every second of every day sweats in his gym shoes or pushes it up against furniture where he perches his feet, as though it's physically me on his foot, and so disrespectful. I know I'm weird, I never claimed not to be, and my thought process only points it out to me. Arrick is laughing softly, clearly amused with how I am taking this and not seeing it as I am.

"Wanna see it?" He grins at me cheekily.

"No. I may hate it so much that you might have to cut your foot off... Why would you be so dumb?" I implore him, raising my palms like I sometimes don't even know who he is. I don't want my name to be jammed into gym shoes and sweated on daily. I can't imagine anything more yucky and unromantic than that, like it would affect my physical being.

How would I explain his tattoo to friends or future children who thought it was equally weird?

Arrick lifts his leg from under the table and lifts his foot awkwardly while I try and prepare myself for the moment of grimace at seeing it and try not to look too distraught. He is crazily flexible, thanks to his martial arts training, lifting a sexy muscular leg and showing me a completely tattoo-free sole of his foot. He is grinning at me like a smug douche bag and winking like he is the funniest guy on the planet. I gawp and then glare at him, so not impressed with him anymore.

"You're an asshole," I answer flatly, annoyed, nope, enraged that

I fell for it and could not, for love nor money, tell he was joking.

When the hell did that happen?

"But yet, not dumb enough to tattoo your name on my foot. You love me, though." He shrugs, smirks, and eats more food as he continues to gaze at me, happy with himself and his ability to dupe his innocent, tired little woman.

"I totally believed you; you are a sucky boyfriend, and I don't think I do anymore." I pout, throwing him my best sulky face with an attitude. Glaring at him because he actually suckered me in for once, and I completely fell for it, like a dumb blonde.

"I'll get the tattoo to make up for it." He nudges my feet with his. Now both are back on the floor and continues to smile at me.

Cocky asshole.

"No, you won't! I don't want my name kissing any guy you kick in the face." I throw back, refusing to look at him and stuffing my face completely nonchalantly. Digging into my food to ignore him and still quietly seething at my gullible brain.

"Is that why you hated the idea of it? I'll get it on my butt then." He laughs, throwing me another childish wink, and I frown harder. His butt may be sexy in so many ways, but I do not want my name immortalized on his ass for all time.

"So you can sit on me?" Completely outraged this time as I stare at him in disbelief. He has gone from a romantic, gorgeous boyfriend to a smug, weird ass in about thirty seconds of conversation.

"I like you kissing my ass." He laughs naughtily. Despite myself, I curb the urge to smile and look at my food instead, frowning so hard to fight the tugging corners of my mouth.

"I swear it's conversations like these that make me rethink this whole thing. Sometimes you are like a five-year-old boy." I throw my napkin at him, hitting him in the chest, and he continues to look like a smug ass who thinks he's the best comedian on the planet.

"I think you should get my name on your ass, and we can kiss each other's. Or maybe rub them together." He snorts with laughter this time, chuckling at his own jokes, making him the supreme lame head of the century, and he just lost all credibility.

"I swear I am done with this." I sigh heavily and try not to have some eyeroll epidemic, face aching with the inability to stop a smile from creeping out and trying to avoid the game of footsy he has started under the table.

"Let's get matching tattoos." He leans in conspiratorially, trying to hit me with the Hollywood smile and meeting deadpan nothingness.

"Let's not... I don't want a tattoo." I respond flatly.

"You already have one." He frowns, eyes scanning me as though he somehow thinks it's going to jump up and say, "here I am." Sometimes I feel like we have an age reversal, and it's moments like this that I forget we are supposed to have a five-year age gap in maturity.

"And whose fault is that? My mom still doesn't believe you took me, paid for it, and picked it! You were obviously not the good influence everyone thought you were." I raise my brows and widen my eyes at him sarcastically, that smile itching to be let loose. He is still sitting, picking at his food in the candles' semi-glow, and looks much younger like this.

"Just branding my girl, staking my claim, and they still see me as the golden boy. Years of pulling the wool over their eyes." He gives me a smug smile, the 'I am not smiling yet I clearly am' one. Far too pleased with himself today, and I wonder if it has anything to do with what we did in the bedroom that has him so relaxed and happy.

"Hmmm. Wait until they find out what you have been doing with me now! Bet they no longer think you're such a good boy after all.... How did we get onto the topic of us getting tattoos?"

He chuckles harder, pleased with his bedroom antics, although I am glad he isn't truly a good boy when it comes to that.

"Because I now have an itching for a new one, thanks to you, and I need to find a good spot for 'I love Sophie' on my body." He stretches out, drops his fork, and eyes me seriously. I roll my eyes again.

"Don't you dare! Do you know how lame it is when girls get their boyfriends' names tattooed on them? You would be worse than lame if you did it, worse than a lame girl." I point out.

"So somewhere people can't see it then?" He innocently asks, and I want to smack him on the head.

"Stop it. You're not even funny. Considering you fight half naked and all over the TV when you do, the only unseen bits are not getting tattooed." I stomp my foot, missing his toes by millimeters, and start to get agitated with his so-called playful joke.

"A little bit funny. I can see you smiling. Are you thinking about the bits the other girls don't get to see?" He winks at me again, that mischievous dirty look coming on, and I lose the will to live, a smile breaking on my face despite trying so hard not to let it.

God, he makes me so gahhhhhh.

"Pretty sure there are not a lot of New York girls who haven't, at one time, seen what's in your shorts, Arry." I raise an accusing eyebrow, biting on my lip to kill the grin that is trying to surface. Not really that bothered that he has a past as a man whore anymore. I now see the benefits.

"Ouch, baby. So no to a new tattoo, then? Or just no to Sophie in naughty places.... I kinda like the idea of Sophie in naughty places." He reaches out for my hand, and I bat him away. Looking for a distraction of any sort to shut him up and leave me be about scarring my skin with another mistake. It's not that I don't like the little black rose on my back and the memories of him holding my hand when I got it. It's just I am not a lover of permanent marks on me. Even if he did tell me I was like a little rose, beautiful, but came with thorns if you didn't know how to handle me.

Now I see the symbolism in that.

"What about that one? What does it mean? Please don't say it's weird and vague and has something to do with cartoons?" I point at a symbol on his left pec, giggling at him; off center, near the middle of his chest, trying to get him back to the previous topic.

I don't think I have ever asked about that one, nestled there as though the other art came after. It stands out because its encircled with borders and tribal patterns yet seems out of place, a different style entirely. It looks like Japanese symbols, maybe. Arrick looks down and points to the one I am gesturing to. Seeing me nod, he frowns and suddenly seems to lose all his joking chill.

"Little Warrior." He glances at me warily, frowning still, and I wonder why that would even be one he wanted. Or why his mood has suddenly turned cagey, and I get that slight wary feeling that he doesn't want me to ask. I wonder why. It's not like it's another girl's name, or maybe it has something to do with a girl, and I feel instantly sick at the thought.

"But you're not little." I push, despite my niggles, and look over the mass of muscle of show. He isn't exactly short, either. My gut is telling me to leave it alone, but I am an idiot and cannot. I want to know, yet I don't, and now that we're talking about it, I can't just say it doesn't matter.

Damn me and my dumb head.

Arrick sighs heavily and stares at it for a moment. His face unreadable, and his brows dipped down as though he's thinking about what to say. I'm hit with that tremor of dread and wonder if it belongs to a past girlfriend I don't know about. So sure, he had it long before Natasha was around.

"It's not my tattoo......... It's yours." Arrick's face straightens finally, looking serious and a little elusive. He sits up a little straighter and starts toying with his food, avoiding looking at me. My breath catches in my throat with that unexpected response, and I blink at him, so very still.

"What do you mean it's mine?" I don't know if I should be smiling or confused, unsure how to feel or why he would choose that for me, on his body. He seems to take a long moment of pause, inhaling slowly before even attempting to answer me. Adding to the nervous tension building inside me as I stare at him.

"I got it after he was convicted for what he did to you." Arrick looks uncomfortable, eyes glancing my way, and I put my fork down and really stare at the tattoo again, then at him with absolute disbelief. He has had it for years, and I never thought to ask before, but I don't get why he's never told me this.

Why he would never tell me this.

"Why?" I blink at him unsurely, tears prickling my eyes as something chokes me in the base of my throat. Happiness sliding away to something deeper, painful, yet not.

"As a reminder.... To always keep my little warrior with my heart, close to me so that I can protect her." His eyes come to mine, the brown color flecked with green and heavily emotional. I know he's being completely honest, and it makes my heart ache so much more. A tear gathers in my eye and rolls down my cheek as the realization hits me that he didn't do this for me. He did this for him because I meant so much. It's huge to know that even back then, I had this much of an impact on him. I was still a kid going through the worst ordeal of my life.

"I'm your little warrior?" I repeat numbly, not sure why he even sees me that way. Overcome with the fact that he's had this there all along, and I can't stop the tears from rolling down my face at the point he loves me this much. He always loved me this much.

"I watched you stand up every day in the trial and face him head-on, Sophie. Not once did you ever let him see you break. Even if, after, you cried in my arms for hours on end. It was hell on earth to watch you look him in the face and tell them what he did, it was beyond brutal, so I couldn't imagine what it was like for you. You were so strong. It was you who made it all stop, you who ensured he got what he deserved.... You taught me the real meaning of being a warrior... You taught me that nothing couldn't be overcome, even if it hurts like hell, and you sometimes need to break down to keep going. No matter how many scars it leaves on you, you keep fighting. I have never been prouder in my life." He focuses on me, eyes soft, tone softer, and I break, gasping as a sob hits me in the chest. The full weight of what all of this means. How intense his feelings must have been all these years, and he still hadn't even known it.

"Why did you never tell me." I implore him, trying so hard not to fall to pieces knowing he's carried this with him these last years, always had me on his body, etched over his heart. It's so painfully beautiful.

Arrick gets up and comes around beside me, kneeling on the floor so he can turn my face to his with a hand under my chin, wiping my tears with his fingers.

"It was for me... I didn't want you to look at it and remember what it stood for." He has tears in his eyes too. The momentous weight of this little thing isn't lost on me at all. Hitting me like a freight train that he has always loved me, meaning he had never really been able to love her at all. I couldn't see it any clearer than I do right now, and it's twisting my heart to shreds. Happy shreds, painfully, but good. Crying even though it's not out of sadness.

"You loved me... Even then?" I sniff to try and curb some of the tears, voice a little rough, but he only smiles through his own.

"I did. Deep down, I have always known, Sophs... I couldn't face it. I was scared. I had so much to lose by going down this route. You... I had you to lose, and I figured that if I pushed it all down deep and ignored it, I could keep you the way I had you. Safe and straightforward, no chance of fucking it up." He pulls me from my seat and onto his lap, so I can straddle him and curl myself around him, nose to nose, unable to stop the tidal wave of emotion that's overcome me.

"Were you scared when you chose to stay with her and made me go?" I lock eyes with him, holding myself together a little more and needing to understand that night. Needing to know so I can let it go. He wounded me when he made that choice; I need to understand why.

"I was.... I don't deal well with emotional mess. Drama. I felt my head would explode with all the shit that hit me that night. I did what I do best.... I reversed, locked it all up safe, and tried to put everyone back in their pigeonholes so we could go on and not have to face any of it." Arrick's instantly remorseful, tightening his arms around me and pulling me in closer as though he wants to squeeze it all away.

"You never thought it was pushing me to leave? Ending us?" I look down between us, my heart aching with a conversation we should have had properly a while ago. I have never wanted to address these wounds after that first night.

"I thought you needed me in your life enough to get past it. I didn't think about the after, Sophie, just how to throw a Band-Aid on everything. A quick fix." He presses his forehead to mine, his breath on my face, but I can't look at him while talking about something still so raw to me.

"You hurt me...More than I ever let you see. You made me feel like I didn't mean anything anymore." My voice breaks, waivers, and I sniff hard to stay in control. He kisses my forehead and new wetness against my skin, knowing he has tears too.

"I know, baby. I hate myself for doing that to you, for throwing away everything you do mean to me. I can't stop hating myself for that, Sophs. I know how it looked, what it must have done. I thought I was doing right by everyone and that I would have time to try and salvage something of us... I thought I loved her, but she was just a safety net, a way to hide from what I really felt....... I was terrified of facing that more than anything. Acknowledging this." He sounds so broken up, so painfully honest. It fuels more of my tears as I cling to him.

"So, what changed? Why are you not scared now? Why did it all become so clear when you stayed with her?" I implore him, finally meeting his face and seeing pain mirrored in moisture-filled eyes, making me ache so much more. Strangely calming, though, I watch his face and gentle expression.

"I lost you....... It was the end of the world for me. I was trying so hard to fix something that I didn't even care about fixing, watching myself as though from above and feeling like everything was empty. I thought it would get easier, and then I don't know.... It hit me one day that I couldn't do it anymore, everything was different, and I was barely functioning." He swallows hard, pierces me with such intensity, and wipes more stray tears from my face.

"I was alone, waiting for her to come so we could go for food.... I was channel surfing to find something to watch to pass the time. So my head wouldn't be left to stray or think, and that dumb film about Unicorns you love so much came on screen. I remember sitting down and breaking to pieces as something hit me in the gut so hard, missing you so much that I couldn't breathe. It felt like I was having a heart attack; it hurt so much. I wanted to call you... so badly... I tried and got that beep tone because you moved my cell to your block list. I stared at it for God knows how long, dying inside, unsure what else to do because I waited too long and kept telling myself to give you time. Then Natasha walked in, and my expression said it all." He scrubs his face with his palm and kisses me softly on the cheek, rubbing his nose against me for a moment. I've at least stopped crying, and I am listening, watching him quietly, feeling a little numb now that I have a little more control, but it still hurts to hear this.

"Is that when you ended things with her? Broke up?" I tenderly trace his brow, wanting to understand and forgive him. I need so badly to forgive him for this.

"We were heading that way from day one; she was clinging on and trying to convince me we could move on. It should have been the other way around." He sighs at me, looking like a guy who feels bad about everything.

"Why didn't you just come and see me then? I needed you to come and see me." I lean my forehead back against his, aching and hating him a little as the memory of those months pushes through. Squeezing his shoulders a little with frustration, he made me endure that.

"I stood outside your building more than once, unsure what I would say if you came out. Too afraid to face you. No clue how I would apologize for everything I ruined between us that night... I finally got the courage to wait for you, to take whatever you were going to throw at me. Then I saw you and Christian together, and I figured the worst thing I had been afraid of had happened. That you met a guy who saw what you were worth and wasn't about to lose you, wasn't about to be the idiot I was. I knew I didn't deserve another chance. That I'd lost you..... So, I left. Told myself I owed it to you to let you get on with your life and be happy. That I deserved that." Arrick moves his nose to mine, hands tracing my face as he angles me close as humanly possible. So much translating in a look. My tears have stopped, and my heart is still in pain, but knowing how much he loved me, even then, helps me heal a little.

"I missed you so much. I hated that you didn't try to call me or see me. You just ceased to exist and left me alone." I whisper against him brokenly. A new single tear breaks loose despite thinking they were done.

"You were always in my head, believe that. Every second. I missed you so much that I saw you everywhere, baby. In every blonde girl on the street, every Unicorn stuffed toy I saw on display, every song or movie that reminded me of you. Even passing a sundae store... I wanted to see you, to talk to you... But I was afraid to reach out and have you tell me you had fallen for someone else. I didn't have the strength to hear that. It would have killed me." He buries his hands in my hair, tenderly holding me close, two hearts laid bare, and as painful as this conversation is for both of us, it's needed. I need to know these things, feel this out and finally let the past go.

"I don't get how you could love her if you loved me that much? ... How could you think that you loved her if you didn't? Why you even first thought she was someone you wanted to be with?" I tilt my chin to focus on him steadily, direct in the eye, unsure but ready to hear everything.

"She filled a void, I guess; I met her when I needed more than casual hookups. I needed to feel like I was taking care of someone after I stopped taking care of you, and she was a sweet, vulnerable girl who seemed like she needed me. I felt disconnected and tired of the single life. I missed the companionship of having you close by .... but I didn't see it was related at the time. I guess, looking back, I tried to replace you with a polar opposite who would not be out of bounds to love." He frowns, my heart constricting as I try to digest what that even means. So heavy with so much going on inside of me that I am struggling to breathe normally, my hands trembling.

He chose someone who was my complete opposite on purpose because he felt like he wasn't allowed to have me.

"But we weren't anything back then, and you still had contact with me. You always had me." I watch him carefully, trying to understand how he could think that's what he did. Trying to understand what she ever was to him.

"I moved away. I wasn't getting to see you as much because of life and school. Work and training made it harder to drop everything to see you, and I didn't even know that's why I felt so fucked up. I thought I was just tired of dates and random hook-ups.

I couldn't see the connection, Sophie, so I couldn't understand how emotionally invested I was with you... You saw how I reacted when you told me you loved me. I was so far down the path of denial I couldn't think straight." He nudges me with his nose and gently kisses the corner of my mouth, stroking my face again. His voice so low and husky, still sitting in darkness and lit only by candlelight, our food forgotten, and this moment so much more intense than I ever imagined it could get.

"You never really loved her the way you thought you did? Why did you choose her, then? That's what I can't seem to get my head around. If all of this here shows me that you always loved me, why did you choose to be with her that night in the club?" The tense ache in my tone, the pain in my words. He sighs against me, so very sad, watching me and keeping me wrapped up tight in his lap.

"I grew up watching how much Jake hurt my parents, Sophs. When he went off the rails after my dad's affair. He made an art form of living impulsively, using women for his own ends, and hurting people in his wake, because he didn't give a shit about anyone except what he wanted to do... I love my brother, but I didn't love the pain he caused in those years or the chaos he left in his wake, and I never wanted to be that guy. I didn't want to be my father either when he chose sex over my mom and threw away her love for something new and exciting, and I felt like it was what we were doing. That somehow Natasha would be like hurting my mom as my dad did... It's complicated and messy, and I don't even know how to explain it. I thought I could fix it, so no one got hurt, and I would still be the guy everyone relied on, everyone trusted. I kept telling myself it wasn't right to be with you that way, and I had a world of reasons holding me back.... Fear being the worst. I reacted, didn't think it through, couldn't face reality, I guess." We rest our heads together, both lost in our little mind bubbles at this moment, thinking through all that's been said.

"I know that should make me feel better about her. I know all of that should help me sort my head out.... I don't even know what I'm trying to say." I'm frustrated, flailing at whatever my head is trying to formulate, and feeling very tired from all of this.

"I should have seen what we were, and I should have chased you... Regardless of Christian. I hate that I lost that time with you. I let my head stand in the way of what my heart wanted more than once." He kisses me tenderly, capturing my mouth with his, healing so many little wounds this conversation has opened, making me feel cherished with such a simple act. When he breaks away, I regard him warily, a little secret I know I should tell him while sharing this kind of truth.

"I saw her in the bathroom last night. She spoke to me, kind of." I look away from him and swallow hard. Feeling compelled to confess, seeing as he is being forthright about everything. And she is the subject right now.

"Why didn't you tell me?" His hand wanders up to play with my hair, and I shrug, unsure why I felt I couldn't. I guess knowing how he gets when I react the way I do. I'm hoping after this conversation, I might start to feel differently about her. Knowing how long and deeply he has always cared about me this way, he always loved me. That thought alone can make my heart soar above the wounds he inflicted on me.

"She was upset and angry and a mess. It wasn't an enjoyable conversation, and I kept thinking she was me six months ago. The train wreck drunk girl in a club, dressed to attract any guy that cares and not giving a shit about how she behaves because she's in pain. I just kept thinking... I did that to her." I glance at him, the tears biting my eyes, guilt racking my gut.

"I did. I did it to both of you without meaning it to either. Where do you think the guilt comes from when it comes to her, Sophs? Knowing that you got the way you did because of me, and now she's pretty much reliving your last two years. I've been trying to help her, dealing with her father's insurance company over his med bills, trying to get her to calm down and stop being so reckless." He seems so utterly deflated, making all my jealousy and stupid doubts about him even more unfounded, the guilt heavy within me.

"Does she call you to come to get her.... Like I used to do." I watch his face steadily, knowing the nights I am with him, he has never gone, but I don't know how many nights I am not with him that he may have. Not that there are many anymore, he is a constant bedfellow because he likes to cuddle up with me. Regardless, I tense as I watch for his response.

"She called a few times, usually when I'm with you. I tell her to go home, Sophs. I have never gone out and picked her up the way I did with you. I am not that dumb. It would only give her the wrong idea." Arrick stands up and pulls me with him so he can properly pull me into his embrace, wrapping his arms around my waist snugly against him so I can lay my head on that strong naked chest and listen to his heartbeat as he holds me tight; his face on top of my head.

"Does she think that you'll maybe go back to her if she does?" I squeeze him questioningly, trying so hard to put to bed all the emotions surrounding him, still letting her linger.

"I don't know what's going on in her head. I've told her more than once that we will never go back. That I have already moved on. I think she's not coping; this will eventually get better as she starts to get over me. I think her dad's cancer has pushed her to the edge, to be honest, and she is not herself right now." He sounds distraught, and as much as I still want to tell him to cut all ties with her, I can't.

Part of me sees the mess of her in my head and feels responsible. Part of me looks at how much he feels the guilt about how she is and know it would be worse if I forced him to make her leave us alone. So torn. Selfish and insecure, yet I get it. I know that he loves me now, always did. It should be enough not to care about her in our life anymore.

"I don't want to talk about her anymore." I tighten my arms around him, back to pressing my cheek next to delicious skin with its slight scattering of hair. Lost in how he feels. Still exhausted but feeling more human after some food and a lot of honesty. Somehow knowing more about what he felt for me back then helps me let go of a little of the hurt I have been harboring.

"Me either... This day is about you... and us. Do you want to go back to bed, nap, or watch a movie? ..... Have sex?" He grins cheekily, nudging me coyly, even if there is still a hint of seriousness in his tone. I know he is still lingering on the things we have said, covering it with attempts to get me back in bed. I love him all the more for it.

"Sounds good to me... Maybe not in that order, though." I nudge him suggestively, bumping into his groin naughtily, equally willing to end this far too intense moment and lighten back up.

"I'm not going to just assume I can have sex on tap now that we crossed that hurdle... But I will keep angling for it anytime you're up for it. That was too good not to." He grins and leans in to kiss me hard. Breaking away when we are both breathing a little heavily, angling for sex with a kiss that steamy. I ponder his expression, catching that tiny hint of tension still there.

"I want you to be normal with me, don't overthink it or overcompensate... I don't need handling with kid gloves. I want you to, you know, seduce me anytime your horny. I want to be like any other girl. I want to be normal too." I lock him dead in the eye with every ounce of seriousness I can muster, so sure about this little fact. I don't want him policing his urges and attention toward me. I want the groping, ass pinching, and feeling up Claire and James do to one another. I want him to pick me up caveman style and drag me to bed when we're in the middle of dinner or a movie. I want to feel like he can't keep his hands to himself and has to have me at any given time. I think it's what I need more than anything.

"You're not like any normal girl, though... You're my girl, special and beautiful and way outclass any girl I have ever known, baby. But... you will maybe regret letting my libido out. I have been behaving myself for far too long, and I don't think you should set me loose without boundaries." He chuckles, running his fingers through my hair before cupping my face and leaning in to kiss me lightly on the lips.

"No boundaries.... I trust you. I'll tell you No if I don't want to. I want you to be like you would if I was any other girl you were dating." Arrick presses his forehead to mine, kisses me again, and then lifts me under the arms, so I am the same height as him. He looks at me for a long moment, complete adoration crossing that handsome face before he breaks into the cutest smile, full dimples on show, and melts what's left of my heart.

"In that case.... I'm getting you naked and showing you exactly what else I can do with my mouth and hands."

Chapter 20

"I need to get up." Arrick moves to get out of bed, and I cling on desperately.

"Nooooo... five more minutes." I stick to him irrationally, hating that he needs to get a flight and leave me for a week. We have not left this bed for the last twenty-four hours except to eat and use the bathroom, and I don't want to uncurl from his naked body now. Especially not after the number of times he has shown me exactly what that body can do to me. Shattered beyond belief, glad it's Sunday so I can finally sleep as we haven't done much of that, and my body is tingling with every memory.

"I don't want to leave either, but if I am not on that flight in forty-five minutes, Nate and James will kill me. I have to go, Sophs. I've delayed getting up twice already." He laughs at me, trying to gently uncurl my grip on him and sliding nearer the edge of the bed.

"I hate you," I murmur as he pulls out from under me, kissing me on the head as he lets me go, leaving me lonesome so suddenly.

"I love you enough for both of us." He winks and walks to the bathroom, switching on the shower and coming back to poke his head around the door as I lay here looking at him longingly.

"You could always come in with me." He grins at me in his

devilish way, and I zoom out of bed automatically, with zero resistance, when that body is the reward. Heart doing a little merry dance and lady parts limbering up in anticipation.

All it took was several times letting him loose on me, although actual sex only happened twice... The rest was definitely him showcasing his skills, and I feel things will look up after this. I didn't freak out once, didn't go back into memory or fight him off, didn't have bad dreams or anxiety attacks, and didn't feel any after-effects. Except for a seriously bad craving for more of his attention, he has decidedly created a monster.

I stroll across towards him, completely unashamed about being naked, as his eyes scan me unapologetically. Reaching out to grab my wrist, he hauls me into the bathroom as I squeal at the speed he yanks me to him.

* * *

I miss you like crazy xx

I stare at the text and sigh; he's only been gone since yesterday, and already it feels like an agony worse than hell. I stayed at his apartment last night, slept alone, and hated every second of it. I hate him not being there, and after school today, I am going back to mine to at least try and get through the next six days with only texts, calls and skype to get me through not seeing him.

"Earth calling Sopheee." Christian nudges me, and I "shhh" him as people in the auditorium turn to look our way. We are in a lecture on the history of denim jeans and completely bored with the onscreen 'jeans through the ages' bullcrap we have been subjected to for the last hour. Christian rolls his eyes at me and then pokes Jenny in the back of the head. She is sat in front and throws him back a haughty glare, and slaps her notebook on his leg.

I miss you too. I hated staying there last night without you. Xxx

I text him back, then push Christian's face away as I catch him reading over my shoulder.

"You two are so cute it's actually sickening." He prods me on the cheek, and I sigh at him, pushing my phone under my notebook on my lap. I go back to sketching the dress I have been doodling while listening to the video drone on about the denim industry. The auditorium is semi-dark and packed with a couple hundred students, none of whom seem to be watching this darn thing.

"Jealous much, darling?" I smirk at him, and he narrows his eyes my way. Jumping as my phone vibrates on my lap, I fish for it with an instant smile, unable to think about anything much in the last day except Arrick. His very fit, naked body, and those hours of knowing exactly what sex could be like. I dreamed about that tongue and what it did to me. I think I have a serious addiction and am counting the minutes until he gets home and does it all again. I squeeze my knees together just thinking about it, and my cheeks heat with the realization that I am getting crazily horny.

New for me.

I will be back in bed with you soon enough, beautiful. Keep it warm for me. X

I grin at his message, run my finger over his name, and sigh heavily.

"Text back with something kinky if you want his head on you for the rest of the week," Christian interjects, pushing his face between me and my phone, and I resist the urge to punch him in the head.

"Shut up and stop reading my messages." I push his face away again, and this time he grabs the phone from me, scanning back over all this morning's and last night's texts and smiling at me.

"He really is one smitten puppy, isn't he...Yet seems he is too gentlemanly to start with the sexting. Clearly wants it, though." He raises a brow and turns further away as I attempt to snatch it back. He has no right to be reading all our messages, even if there are now a few hundred.

"Fuck off. You have no idea what he wants." I haul my phone back and glare at him, but he only grins harder.

"I am a man... Gay or not, we all have pretty similar minds when it comes to sex. Arry dear is no different, and would probably like you a whole lot more if you added a little sexual tension to your messages. Imagine the reunion if all he thinks about for the next week is fucking you." He winks at me, and this time I stare at him deadpan.

"He's not like that," I murmur, refusing to believe he would turn into a basic slut and only be consumed by sex above all, even though it's what I have been fantasizing about since he left.

"We are all like that... You will thank me for it. Wind him up... flirt with your boyfriend. If he doesn't play, then stop with the sexy chat and go back to the lovey-dovey yawn fest of PG.........Trust me." Christian waves an airy hand my way, pretending he no longer cares.

I stare at my phone, pondering it for a moment, in two minds about whether I should ever listen to Christian. I feel Jenny's eyes on me and lower my phone to see her looking back at me.

"He's right, you know... Sexting your man makes him crazy horny for you, and when he gets back, he will bang you in the doorway." She giggles and turns away with a knowing nod to take notes on the in-depth way to double-seam denim.

"Talking of men, what happened with Nate on Saturday night?" I lean forward, whispering, and she waves a hand at me. I hadn't seen her until she walked in here late this morning, and we haven't had a minute to find out. I was obviously a little preoccupied ever since that night.

"I'll tell you later." She turns back to watch the video with no real emotion in her tone, so I sit back to stare at my phone again, taking a deep breath. Thinking through what I should say before I send him another. I know he's at some media promo crap to do with his fight in five days, some live stream interview thing that has him waiting around for a couple of hours and will reply.

I'll be waiting for you naked and keeping every part of me, and the bed, very warm. X

I have never sexted anyone before. I have no clue how even to talk dirty, let alone type it and send it off to him, hoping he doesn't think I'm being weird. We haven't gotten to teasing each other overly sexually, either, so this is all new to me.

I stare at the phone for what feels like an eternity before looking up to see the tutor has changed the video to another dreary fashion through the years piece of nonsense that serves no real educational purpose; my phone vibrates, and I almost drop it in fright.

"Jumpy...Someone's feeling guilty." Christian smirks my way, and I toss him a frown and open my message.

I like picturing you naked and warm, definitely in a bed.... Pretty sure you have just made my day a lot harder to get through. X

"He's being safe and lame... trying not to get too dirty and push you into anything X-rated. Give me your phone." Christian pokes his head over my shoulder and snatches the phone before I can protest. I scramble to try and get it back, slapping at his shoulder and leg as he furiously types and ignores me completely. He shoves his palm in my face holding me away and meeting my fury before I finally get it back. Looking down in sheer horror at what he has sent him.

I'm so wet thinking about what you do to me, can barely keep my hands to myself.

"Oh, my God, Christian!" I turn and slap him hard on the leg, and about a dozen heads turn our way angrily and "Shhh" us. Christian flips them off with a defiant head flick.

I am completely livid and start typing a retraction to explain it wasn't me when my phone buzzes, and I pale instead.

Shit.

Tell Christian, Nice try! Sophie...If you want to try sexting, wait until he's not around, and I am all for that. X

I giggle at his response and wave my phone at Christian with a smug look. Jenny is giggling, obviously hearing everything, and shakes her head at us. I show her the text, and she laughs loudly before clamping her hand over her mouth to quieten herself.

"Busted. He clearly knows when it's not me." I smirk, giving him my sassy head sway and clicky fingers that I adopted from him. I reply to Arrick before sliding my phone into my bag out of the way from itchy fingers.

He's an asshole, and maybe.... I think you need to initiate it, though, not me. This is out of my comfort zone. xxx

I kick my bag under my chair, so I don't look at it again and concentrate on class, thinking maybe I should start taking notes if I am going to get anything done this week. My head is not on school, and it really should be. I have three dresses to sew up this week, two tops to draft and fit to a mannequin.

* * *

"So, spill." I eye up Jenny across the table of the lunch hall, trying to pin her down to this topic finally, now we are alone. Christian has gone to meet his beloved in the common hall, and we are having girl time in the lunchroom.

"What's there to say.... I went home with him and somehow ended up staying with him until he left for Miami. We had sex before I left, and when I was in the cab on the way home, he texted me and told me we needed to stop seeing each other. Beat me to it, I guess." Jenny's eyes mist over, and she looks devastated for a second before reeling it back in, wiping one eye and biting her lip.

"Shit Jen, I'm so sorry." I reach out and pat her hand, completely devastated for her. I'm going to fucking maim Nate.

"The weird thing is... I felt relieved because I had been waiting for it since the first time we had sex, knowing it was coming and I wouldn't do it. I would keep letting him use me repeatedly until he broke me." She lets go and wipes her eyes again, only this time a tear escapes, and I want to shake Nate to hell, knocking his brain around that dense skull. He has been stringing her alone for over a month and using her for frequent hookups. Broken his own code and used the same girl until she fell for him.

Fucking asshole.

"I don't know why he let it go on as long. It's really not his MO. He's usually a screw them and forgets them the next day kind of guy, Jen. I don't know what to say." I regard her painfully, watching her cry and feeling like I should be ringing Nate and calling him a fucking asshole right about now. I know I will vent to Arry, and he better say something to his so-called best mate, or I will.

"He told me I was amazing in bed.... I don't get what he thought was so hot. Mark used to say I was crap with sex and made me give him oral more than screwing me. Nate was the one who did all the work. I felt majorly inexperienced next to him." She wipes her face again and sighs heavily. I don't have the heart to point out that this will make things a little tough for a while. We have all gotten into a routine of meeting with Arry's friends and mine and doing things as a group in the last weeks. Anything we do will include both Nathan and Jenny, and I don't think she will be able to handle it, especially when Nate does what he always does and starts bringing other women on the scene.

"You just had the right chemistry or something. You told me he was abnormally good. Maybe you work that way with him." I know I must work with Arry, or maybe he is skilled, as everything he has done has been mind-blowing. I am the inexperienced one who has no clue how to return the favors, although I am starting to find a little confidence after the second time. Like on the scratching thing, though, it's impulsive, and I have filed all my acrylic tips to rounded edges in his absence to save him from more injury, even though he seems to like it more than he should.

Weird boy.

"We had something....... Made me realize I wasn't in love with Mark anymore. Just going through the motions and being a doormat... You know he asked me to get back together?" Jenny shakes her head as though this is the most unbelievable thing ever.

"What did you say to him?" I watch her carefully, seeing a host of emotions run across her face as she pushes at her pasta absentmindedly.

"I told him I needed to think about it. I didn't want any drama if I straight out said no." She sighs and sits back in her chair.

"Isn't he the one who ended things?" I pick up my mug of hot chocolate and take a sip. Watching her, admiring how composed she seems for a girl who has had her heart majorly stamped on twice in a month.

"Yeah, seems something he and Nathan have in common... Dumping me via text. Guess I'm an easy girl to discard that way. That or I am drawn to cowardly assholes." She throws her fork down and sighs again, wiping her eyes and pushing her hair back in agitation, a break to the façade and a slight crack in the shell to how she feels.

"They are both fucking idiots, Jen. You're probably the nicest and most loyal girl I have ever known. You're so pretty too. You deserve a guy who sweeps you off your feet." I'm outraged on her behalf, aching to shake Nate half to death and see what is right in front of him. Jenny is quiet and reserved, a good girl, and loyal to a fault when you deserve her to be. She doesn't draw attention to herself, ever, and hates drama. I have no doubt she has been the absolute dream fuck buddy for him the past month, as she won't voice anything to rock the boat, and he probably assumed they were cool.

"Maybe direct one of the infamous Carrero men my way. They seem savvy enough to treat their women a little better." She frowns at me defeatedly.

"Hmmm, not always. Arry and Jake were both male sluts in the past, and their cousins are just as bad. The downside to being a hot Italian with great DNA is knowing you're a hot Italian with great DNA and using it on many a woman before one pins you down. Trust me. All men are capable of being dogs when they get it effortlessly. They start to think it's owed to them." I frown, pushing my mug away in irritation.

"I'm so sick of being everyone's doormat. I hate all these stupid games and rules and how men think we are so easy to fuck and discard like it means nothing. How can he sleep with me for over a month and then feel nothing over dumping me in a text?" Jenny starts to cry, and my rage ignites. She never cries so openly, especially not in the school canteen in front of a ton of bitchy seniors at another table. I hand her a tissue and scowl.

"You know what? I am about to find out." I yank my phone out and scroll until I impulsively find Nathan's number, hitting call and shoving it to my ear before sense can smack me. Fueled by anger on her behalf.

Jenny's eyes widen in alarm. She shakes her head, slides up, and disappears to the ladies' room, unable to witness this call. Yet she wants to know too, as she hasn't stopped me, not that she could. I guess she even knows that about me.

I watch her go, listening to the long, drawn-out rings and knowing fine that Nathan is with Arry in Miami. It seems to take endless seconds before he picks up, and the noise of a busy atmosphere hits me before Nate's voice does.

"Sophie... Aren't you calling the wrong cell? Arry is being interviewed right now, so he can't answer." He sounds like he always does. Upbeat, confident, and in no way concerned that he just smashed a poor girl's heart to smithereens yesterday.

"No, I'm calling you. To call you a dickhead and ask you why you think it's acceptable to fuck Jenny and then dump her via text after she leaves your apartment. That was the most douche-baggest move of the century, Nate. Even for you." I snap at him angrily and get silence in response. The noise around him seems to change rapidly, as though he has moved somewhere quiet. "Not going to say anything?" I snap again, my temper rising at his lack of conversation. Hating men who feel they do not have to give a response to angry females on their phones. Nate knows me better than to blank me.

"What can I say? Yep, dickhead move.... I didn't have the nerve to say it to her face. I didn't want to see her cry." He sounds much less cocky suddenly, more closed off, the way Arry can get when he doesn't want to talk about something. It grinds on my nerves.

"You're an asshole. Maybe she was already thinking of moving on, and you just beat her to it. Jenny can do much better than being your fuck buddy, and she deserves a little more respect than you showed her. Even her idiot Ex realizes what he lost and has come groveling to win her back. So maybe in the future, stick to one-night stands and stay clear of girls who deserve more! She isn't one of *THOSE* types, and she deserves better!" I'm properly yelling now, so pissed at his attitude that I want to hang up on him and scream.

"Sophie?" He tries to butt in.

"No, Nate, listen to me; you know I adore you. Maybe not today. I have always got on with you, but with this, I am so fucking pissed at you. Text dumping her after using her for sex one last time? You don't deserve her tears. Why didn't you leave her alone after the first time, huh? Isn't that more your style?" I grind my teeth, tap my nails on the table and see Jenny appear sheepishly. Seeing me still on my cell, she turns and heads to the vending machine.

"I.... uh.... Don't tell me she's crying, Sophs." He sounds feeble for a moment, and I soften at him. Still majorly angry, but a hint of the good guy he can occasionally be stands out like a sore thumb. Then I remember he bailed on seeing her cry and dumped her via text, and fury returns.

"Like you care. Yes, she's crying. What did you think would happen? She's not someone who sleeps around, Nate, even though she tried to convince you she was. All you have done is make her think she would be better going back to that dickhead ex who treated her like shit. You showed her that all men treat her like shit no matter who she dates." I know that's not exactly true, but he is making me severely pissed, and I want him to feel like the shithead that he's been to her. I watch her in the distance, fumbling with her coins, trying to look normal and not okay.

There's a long silence on the line, only the background noise, and he finally speaks.

"I need to go, Sophie. I'm sorry. Tell her ...... tell her I'm sorry I turned out to be an asshole. It's not like I didn't warn her we weren't going anywhere." He hangs up before I get a chance to say anything, and I stare at my phone, completely dumbfounded. I shouldn't even be surprised. This is who Nate is and always has been. He is the biggest commitment-phobe going, and I should have known Jenny would only get hurt.

"Asshole, fucking goddamn, douchebag dickhead, of a rodent's ass," I swear venomously at my phone.

I slam my phone down on the table, scowling into mid-air and gritting my teeth. Nate is one of those infuriating men who never talk about anything, except maybe to Arry, but even then, I have no clue how their conversations go, as Arry isn't the type to repeat anything a friend tells him. I know the entire time he was with Natasha, she never knew anything about my past, only that I was adopted and had a crap start in life.

Arry is one of those types of people who never really tells anyone anything that other people confide in him, well, maybe Jake or Emma. Only because he knows that we both confide in them; they know everything about us, and well... Jake is his brother.

I once asked Emma what Arry told her about my sessions and things I told him, and she only ever said "the bare minimum," so I am guessing he has some sort of code about harboring people's secrets or confidentialities.

He'd better realize that I don't count and should be told everything from here on in!

He better open up to me about Nathan, or there will be hell to pay. I am fuming right now. I don't care about any best mate or guy code in this. I am his fucking girlfriend, and he better be straight with me, or he can go to the doghouse and keep Nate company.

"What did he say?" Jenny looks coyly at me as she slides back down, carrying about ten brands of chocolate and three packets of Cheetos. I steal one and yank it open a little aggressively.

"Not much... I Gave him a piece of my mind and got a lame male response. I'm an asshole. Tell her I am sorry... No explanations, nothing. Fuck him, Jen." She slumps down, looking desolate, and gives me the universal eyebrow rise of 'What else can I do?' Taking the bar of chocolate from her pile of goodies and digging in with a very somber expression.

Chapter 21

"Stop laughing. I don't like you right now!" I sulk down the phone, pulling at my shoes on my apartment couch and glaring at them before tossing them away as Arrick kills himself, laughing down the other end of the line.

"Baby? I'm sorry...." He bursts into another hysterical fit, and I feel my temper rising. I am seriously not a happy camper with him right now, and what started as a minor insult has escalated because he is an asshole. He is the biggest type of douche bag known to man, and if he were here, I would make him eat my shoe.

"I'm hanging up on you." I pout, tears welling in my eyes and lip wobbling, stupidly hurt over a stupid text and acting dumb, but I can't help it. He has this insane ability nowadays to hurt my feelings much more easily than he ever did.

"Sophie. Come on.... Don't. I want to talk to you. That's why I called instead." He's still trying to control the giggling fit he's hit, but I am not laughing, even if he is half begging me with a cute, endearing tone. Through laughter, though!

Asshole!

"You called because I didn't reply to your little row of hysterical laughing emojis when I tried to sext you." I snap at him. Completely humiliated that my attempt at flirting with him had ended in him creasing himself in laughter and sending me little crying laughing faces as a response.

"You're cute when you're mad. I wish I could see your face right now." Still laughing, still an asshole. Sometimes I see the whole 'hate and love have a fine line between them.' thing.

"Me too, then you would see how much I am hating on you, and I could kick you in person." I sulk. Flopping down onto the couch and laying back in a slump, pulling a strand of my hair and twisting.

"You can't hate me for laughing at that text... They were progressively getting worse, baby. No matter how much I was trying to play along." Another bout of snorting as he falls to bits again. He really knows how to make a girl feel good. He was the one who started the sexy talk, sending me extremely X-rated messages to get things heated, and then seemingly fell into hysterics the more I tried to keep up with him.

So, sue me for not being well-versed in Casanova slut chat and being able to schmooze with an ex-sex addict.

"Shoot me for being shit at talking dirty.... I just wanted you to think about me." the tears let loose, the tremor to my voice, and I sniff a little. Arrick seems to stop laughing immediately, sensing or hearing the nosedive in my emotions and knowing when it's going too far.

"I do think about you. All the time. Every second. You don't need to send me dirty messages to get me thinking about coming home to you, Sophs. I am going crazy with desperation to get home to you already." He soothes me softly, all jocularity gone and replaced with the voice that makes me feel better.

"You're just saying that because I got upset." I sulk petulantly, feeling like an idiot child, insecurity peeking up with his absence, every day making me more emotional, and I still have two more days to endure. I never knew it would be so much harder once we crossed from friends to lovers, I used to bear his absences a lot, and now I can't even go one night without him.

"I would never tell you something I didn't mean. If you want to get me crazy hot, send me some selfies. You don't need to be naked or doing anything except looking beautiful in them, baby. You make me want you without trying." He says genuinely, that husky tone and sexy voice lowering a tad and sending my insides to mush. Smoothing over my hurt pride a little.

"Maybe I want you to tell me what you want me to do to you...... Want to know that I do it for you." I whisper, a complete insecure freak on show, hating that I am turning into one of those needy girls who needs constant reassurance. The distance is driving me crazy already, and my head is a mess. All I have obsessed about over the past few days is how often Natasha probably called or texted him without me being there to put him off answering. Now we're moved on after our heart-to-heart, making me feel pathetic.

So stupid, I know.

"You do! I'll tell you now if you like... All I ever have are X-rated thoughts about you, Sophs. More so since the weekend. I have a problem and cannot get my head out of the gutter since then." He softens his voice. I can tell he's smiling and sigh at him.

"Just tell me you love me and miss me... I hate that you're not here. It's making me crazy." I curl up on my side and hold the phone close, trying to make him burrow inside my head and wrap around me. I hate how much more I have missed him since we got together. It's worse than hell.

"I love you... Crazily love you. Like, so much that I may have to retire from the fight scene, so I can never leave you again.... And I miss you more. I Miss you so much that I am calling you instead of taking the elevator. I am using the stairs to my next interview so that I can, hoping they don't care that I'm pretty late." He does sound like he's walking. I can hear the echo of his voice as though he is now in a stairwell and smile.

"Keep talking. I might hate you a little bit less." I smile to myself with some satisfaction that Arry always knows how to grovel so well. I can picture soft brown eyes looking calm and clear and the smooth square jaw with his half smile and cool, smooth mannerisms. It makes me all warm inside.

"As soon as I get home, I will come to find you, strip you naked, and do things to you that will make sure you never doubt how much I love you again. Better clear your schedule for a few days. I have a lot of love to show you, baby. A week is far too long not to be able to touch you." I can picture that half smile growing wider, dimples on show, and a wicked little twinkle in his eyes.

"Hmmmmm.... It's maybe working." I whisper, rolling onto my other side and cuddling up to a cushion to picture him against me. Body peeking interest at his slow, subtle seduction.

"Don't doubt that you're in my head every second. I am taking frequent cold showers almost every time I hear your voice. I seriously think we should start having phone sex before I self-implode, or maybe you listen, and I will detail everything I want to do to you." the soft, breathy chuckle and then the noise of people around him as either he enters somewhere, or people arrive where he is.

"If it ends up the same way sexting you did, then I'm out." I point out a little sassily, but my tone has become soft and mushy.

"Maybe I'll call you when I get back to my room later, and we shall see." He says huskily, and I can't help the little naughty thought that crosses my mind, knowing he's about to either leave the stairwell or start an interview. He has my body glowing, my temperature rising, and my knees pressing together, all with the power of a few loaded words.

"Maybe my hands are already warming me up while you tell me how much you want me." I sigh a little as I say it in a deep husky, breathless teasing tone. Smiling to myself as I hear him groan, not in a good way. Thanking Christian in a roundabout way for the insight into my one and only semi-dirty attempt.

"Jesus, Sophie, that is not the visual I need right now when I'm about to walk into an interview. Fuck.... Thanks to you, I have a little something I need to take care of now. I'll call you back later. Love you, beautiful." Arrick hangs up the phone fast, and I burst into instant giggles. Payback for being an asshole and laughing at my sexts. I do a lot better with calls than texts.

I hold up my phone to look at the sexy sleeping photo of him I took before he left and now use as his contact picture; sexy and peaceful, looking every bit poster boy for a dream guy magazine. I sigh and giggle as a text pops on the screen from him.

Naughty girl. Might have to spank you when I get back. X

Spanking sounds.... Interesting. Not that I can imagine he ever would lay hands on me that way, yet a part of me wonders what it would be like if he did. A tiny inkling of maybe a kinkier side to me that I didn't know existed. I am open to trying out something more than straightforward sex when it comes to him. I think I could trust him to do anything to me now.

I smile wider and then sigh and feel deflated again, all at the same time. It feels like it has dragged so far, no matter how much he texts and calls and how many times he sends me weird selfies of what he's doing. Two more days to go. I just need him to come home.

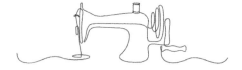

Chapter 22

I throw the pasta and salad in my refrigerator. Bending in to move over the vast amount of junk food and movie snacks I went a bit overboard with and push Arry's favorite bottle of dressing in the door. Counting down the hours to his getting home.

The last thing he texted was he would call when he got to the airport, and I haven't heard from him since. I know the day after a big fight is usually hectic for him. What with reporters, paparazzi, and media vying for his attention, especially after a big win, and I hate this wall of silence. I have no clue when he's even getting here. I lean in further to fish out a bottle of water and straighten up to close the door.

"Miss me?"

The voice startles me, spinning to see him casually closing my door behind him, and I cannot control the squeal that erupts from me. Charging across the floor and launching myself into his arms with a little jump, lassoing him around the neck and hitting him with a week's worth of pent-up passion. I have been waiting a full seven days to give him this kiss, and I go all in.

Arrick smiles mid-kiss, lifts my butt so he can nestle my legs around his waist, and kisses me even harder, completely molded as tongues caressing shamelessly. I break away, showering his face with kisses and nuzzles, being hugged tight and kissed back with equal fervor.

"God, I missed you so much, baby. This has been all I could think about the whole time I was gone." Arry lifts one hand to catch my face and pulls me to kiss me properly, parting lips, tongues caressing some more as he moves a frantic happy kiss into a sensual 'I want you badly' kiss.

I am more than happy to comply, letting my legs loose and sliding down in his embrace, every inch of me in a short dress skimming his button-down and jeans. He feels so good. His smell, his taste, his body. His mouth never leaves mine, hands entangled in my hair, and I get lost in him. It feels like the empty ache I have had all week has just been filled in one brief touch. He breaks away and rests his forehead on mine, gazing at me adoringly, and rubs his nose against mine with a gentle smile, moving in to kiss me again and grinning. Overjoyed to be back with me too.

"What happened to stripping me naked and proving how much you missed me." I poke at his chest boldly, smiling back when he only grins harder. His eyes roam my face as though he needs to take in every single inch of me.

"You don't want your gifts first? Jumping straight in without a massive welcome-home kiss isn't my style... But if you insist." Arrick slides his hands under my dress so he cups my butt in a lacy thong, lifts me to him, and starts carrying me to the couch. Kissing me again as I cling around his neck and angle to get more from him. Pushing my mouth against his so he can devour me with that delectable tongue, making my toes curl. I keep my eyes closed to his every sensation, only aware that he's lowering me to the couch when I feel it underneath me, and then he is on top of me, pushing up my dress as his crotch connects with mine. His mouth is all over me, mouth to mouth, jaw, neck, cleavage, as he pulls my neckline down. His hands roam me crazily as I return the favor.

Heat and need overtake me at searing levels. Crazily hot for him and almost throbbing myself inside out with need. I suck on his exposed neck, pull his shirt open a little and then roam my hands down to unbutton his jeans. We're grinding against one another, heavy breathing, lost in a lust-fueled craze to have sex immediately, and I can almost feel my body gearing up to react quickly.

Arry helps push his jeans down a little, his hands tracing my panties and me, so I moan and gasp at his touch before he tugs them aside, giving him access, and starts delivering teasing circles and subtle probing fingers that make me arch under him. I am more than ready for him and his hard bulge pushing through the gap in his jeans, shielded by boxers telling me he's more than ready to give. He comes back to my mouth, his fingers sliding into me slowly, kissing me as I moan out, and comes back to teasing me with his tongue.

The buzzer makes us both jump guiltily. Arching my back to look towards my front door in upside-down confusion. Arry looks up in the same direction, still very much joined to me and breathing hard.

"You expecting someone?" He smiles, scoops down to kiss my jawline, and teases me into submission, my eyes closing at his touch as I try to think who the hell it could be.

"Hmmmmm. No." I moan out, getting lost in what he's doing to me. Groaning as his finger slides inside me and makes me fall to pieces. That far too expert touch of his.

Like a kick in the head, a sudden thought flies through my brain at superhuman speed, my eyes snapping open, and I react in complete shock.

"Shit!"

I shove Arrick off me so hard, so impulsively, he has no way to counteract, flailing and falling off with a massive thump onto the floor on his back, arms out and elbow hitting the coffee table with an enormous thud that sends everything rattling. He groans on the floor as I dash up in a panic and somehow manage to stand on his abdomen.

"Jesus, Sophie." He groans through the 'ooffft' noise as I recoil my legs.

"It's my parents... I forgot they said they would drop by when they were done in the city. I'm sorry." I pant, face heating in complete panic, pulling my clothes back to rights as Arrick gets up into a sitting posture and rubs his elbow and then his abdomen with a wounded look on his face. I haven't got time to feel guilty right now. I'm just panicking.

"Calm down. Stop freaking out." He groans again, rubbing his arm, and gets up, casually fixing his trousers and throwing me that cool look that is supposed to get me back in line, which has never worked as long as I have ever known him. I widen my eyes right back at him.

"Oh, my God, oh, my God." I ramble, flustered and on my feet, pacing in a tiny circle and thinking of all the possible bad outcomes from being caught on the verge of sex with your best friend.

"Go to the bathroom and get yourself together. I'll let them in." He smiles confidently, guiding me past the couch, but I start pushing him towards my room by those crazily solid abs, knocking him backward, so he catches my upper arms to steady himself, panic overwhelming me.

"No, no, no. You have to hide. They don't know about us...Oh, my God ...What if they can tell what we were doing?" I blanche at him with sheer devastation, and he starts laughing at me. Stopping the progression of my pushing as the buzzer goes again impatiently, I feel like I am freaking out for real. Nerves are churning my stomach up into my throat, and my hands are getting crazily clammy.

"Sophie, for the love of God. They won't think anything of me being here or know what we have been doing if you calm down and wash your face. You're looking a little sexily flushed." He leans in, kisses my cheek, and turns me, so instead of pushing him to my room, he's guiding me there instead.

I balk at him in sheer bewilderment over my shoulder, unsure what to do, but he's forcing me to the bedroom now and smoothing my hair from the back. He leans in and kisses me on the side of the face, pushes me the last inch into my room, and pulls the door closed behind me, so I am left standing staring at my door with him on the other side. I seem to shake myself, turn and head for my bathroom, trying not to have some meltdown while in the process of trying to trust him not to give the game away.

I can't face my parents like this; he just had his fingers inside me, and we were about to have sex... Literally, probably seconds away from it. My face heats with even the thought of it, and I catch myself in the reflection and gawp.

If this is how I look when he gets me turned on, then no wonder he likes it. I look wild. Flushed, pupils dilated crazily, and my blue eyes are much more tropical. My hair Is a little flyaway, but my lips look crazily kiss swollen. I have never seen myself looking this way. I look sexual and wanton and immediately get to work patting cold water on the rosy glow over half my features.

I make out the murmur of voices and try to calm down. Arrick knows my parents well; they adore him and will assume he's here to see me or take me out somewhere. He's right. They won't think anything of his being with me. I'm being stupid and panicking because I feel guilty. They won't connect the dots, and I am not sure if I am ready for them to.

I mean, it's only been just over a month, and still finding our way with each other, still trying to get used to being able to trust him again. I also don't know how they will react. All his fears and reasons from before making sense to me now. They might see this as wrong because of what Arry was to me, the age gap, and they always trusted him to take care of me like a brother. I stare at myself, think through all the different things they may object to about this, and see myself visibly pale.

I never considered what my family disapproving of us would mean, what it would feel like and I am suddenly terrified. My heart drops, and my stomach turns over in complete heartbreak. Knowing I could never give him up and go back to before, it would destroy me. I swallow hard, take a deep breath and fluff out my appearance a little. Smoothing, primping, and preening until I look as close to normal as possible while my insides wrench themselves into an ulcer.

I take one last steadying breath and walk through the door leading me to my parents. They are all walking to the couch, obviously having had pleasantries in the foyer, and my mother smiles widely at me and then turns and squints at Arrick.

"Interesting shade of lipstick you're wearing." She smiles. I glance at her, wondering why she would think my coral lipstick was odd as she bought it for me. I then realize she's rubbing a thumb on Arrick's neck, and I die a little. Heart stopping mid-beat.

He's wiped my mess from his mouth, but there is a clear trail of smudges down his throat and under his collar, and he falters. His perfect poker face is only betrayed by a tiny flicker of the brow, and he refrains from looking my way.

"You know us? Carry on and act weird sometimes. Smothering her is kind of my thing." He laughs jokingly, and I feel my dad's eyes on me questioningly.

I hate it. I hate that he's trying to cover for me, lying to them, when he never lies. Hate that they're now both looking at me with a hint of dubious and probably wondering why I never am open with them. Why, after all these years, I still never tell them anything of importance or share myself with them the way I do with him. My mother's eyes flicker to me, hovering in the door, and I break so easily.

"We're dating... Please don't be mad." I sound like a feeble child, blurting it out impulsively when caught like a deer in headlights. Small and scared, my eyes fill with moisture. So frightened about the back lash I am about to get and terrified they may make him leave. My dad frowns at me and then at Arrick, then steps forward and pats him on the shoulder with a smile.

"About time... Only took you six years to finally see sense." My dad grins, and Arrick breaks into a smile too. He seems to exhale with relief visibly. My mother's eyes are still trained on me, giving nothing else away as to what she is thinking, and I begin to tremble under her scrutiny. The relief from my dad's response cannot stop the fear I am feeling waiting on hers.

She slowly walks to me, runs a gentle hand over my cheek, and tucks hair behind my ear.

"We gave up hope when he got with Natasha...... Sophie, why would we be mad?" She smiles at me gently, her soft face crinkling pleasantly. I swallow hard, emotion choking me as a tear runs down my cheek.

"The age gap.... It's Arry? I don't know... Maybe you would have thought it was weird or wrong." My voice trembles and I feel Arrick looking at me, his calm hazel eyes on mine with a supportive smile, as my dad pats him on the shoulder again. All manly like and pulls him into a hug that knocks him off balance. I stare into my mom's eyes and inhale fast when I spot the hint of a tear filling her eye.

"We have hoped for so long that you two would move past from a sort of sibling bond to more. We have always known he was exactly what you needed." Her voice is strained with genuine emotion and happiness.

I let myself cry a little. Her nurturing fingers brush away my tears, and then I throw myself around her in a tight hug. Completely overwhelmed and needing this.

"I love you, mom." I gush at her and revel in her tight hug, squeezing me tight and pushing my face back so she can kiss my cheek. She looks at me as though I have just given her the best Christmas ever, and I am aware of how very little I do shower her with hugs.

"I love you too, my little Sweet pea. You will always be my baby. My little wild child." She grins at me with unconcealed joy.

"I second that." My dad chimes in, and it's now I realize he's beside us, pushing my mom away gently so he can lean in and kiss me on the head. Arrick is standing back, giving them space, and seems at a loss as to what to do with himself. I can see the utter relief on his face that they are really okay with this. Despite saying it didn't matter to him anymore, I know it does.

"Guess we should go and let you two get back to.... your evening." My mom smiles gently, a little awkwardly, and my dad chuckles.

"Mmmm, Hmmmm." My dad winks knowingly, and I inwardly cringe, wishing the ground would open and swallow me whole. It's clear that they know we were not just playing scrabble or something equally innocent before they arrived.

"Does your mother know?" My mom turns to Arrick and blinks with raised brows.

"No. Not yet. We were giving ourselves time to adjust... Guess I should now, huh?" Arrick gives my mom his Hollywood smile, reserved for special occasions when he wants to completely charm the pants off someone, and I eyeroll.

He's such a schmoozer sometimes.

"I think so.... Dare says she will be happy to get out for a new hat. She's been praying for this day as long as I have." My mom is beaming, a little too smugly, so I wonder if their knowing so soon is good after all.

"Pressure much," I grumble, realizing my parents are probably about to marry us off and set up a new home beside them to fill with grandchildren.

I think not.

Arrick slides past them and stands beside me, sliding his arm around my waist, which I instantly push off awkwardly. It's one thing to tell them we are dating, but a hell of a difference to let him touch me in front of them. I am so not there yet.

I hear him chuckle under his breath at my reaction and elbow him in the abs to warn him to keep his hands off.

"We will be off... Come for dinner soon. I think telling your mom face-to-face will be nicer. We won't tell a soul until you both come home." She smiles at me adoringly, and my dad nods in happy agreement.

"No, actually... Mom. Maybe you could tell Leila and Ben and the rest of them for me. I can't face either of those two having the older sibling, birds, and bees chat. Leila would traumatize me for life." I follow them to the door, Arrick close on my heels as he runs a finger down my spine, stopping mid-way down one of my ass cheeks with a pinch. I try to slap him away without making it obvious; he knows what he's doing, and I turn and give him a little scowl that is only met with a grin.

Sometimes he's like a child.

"If that's what you want, I'm sure everyone will be fine.... Some of us predicted this a long time ago." My mother has suddenly come over all misty-eyed and weird, and now I want them to leave before this gets awkward for me.

"A heads up would have been nice." Arrick jokes, coming beside me as we get to my main door. My dad opens it and steps out to the foyer with a last kiss on my head. My mom follows suit and joins him outside.

"You were always a very clever boy. Why would you need us to point out that Sophie was meant for you? See, you got here in the end." She pats him on the cheek, then wiggles a little come here finger at him so that he bends to get her motherly peck on the cheek. "See you for dinner soon, call your mother, and we will set it up. A proper family get-together." My dad smiles, and I grimace, that moment of horror, imagining them all sitting around a big huge Carrero Huntsberger table and staring at us adoringly. I go to say something in a complete knee-jerk reaction, but Arry cuts in, placing a hand on my butt and squeezing so that I am shocked into silence.

"We will... I'll need to go home and see my folks anyway. Have a good trip home." He seems too cool and chilled out for someone who almost got caught banging a girl by her parents.

My parents gush at him, say their last goodbyes, and stroll down the hall, waving back every few steps until they are out of sight. Arrick pulls me back and shuts the door, fully sliding his arm around me.

"They totally knew we were fucking." He winks at me and then dodges fast when I make a slap for him.

"I told you to stop calling it that! And no, they didn't... They don't think I do that stuff." I point at him, right in the face, with a scowl, my head caving with mortification in case they really did know what we were doing. Shame coursing through me that my parents know what I let him do to me.

Oh, God, no.

"They know I do that stuff. Your mom caught me once........." Arrick sops mid-sentence as though suddenly realizing what he is saying and stops, completely sheepish, that cute half smile and 'oh shit' expression that crosses his face. I eyeroll at him.

"Relax, Casanova... You were never shy about your sexual antics. I am more than aware you are well-used goods." I pat him on the arm and walk past to retrieve my water. It's still sitting in the kitchen, and needed to un-parch my throat, knowing fine I am only drinking water nowadays because of him, and he hasn't even noticed.

"Hey! I'm not well used... Refined, honed skills." He follows me, grabs me by the hips, and stops me mid-step, nuzzling my neck from behind and slowly kissing his way up my jaw. Moving my hair out of the way with soft fingers. I close my eyes and surrender to him, my body sagging into his as the heat from before the intrusion resurfaces quickly. Forgetting everything except his touch.

"Want to experience the skills I acquired, on the couch?" He asks softly, huskily against my skin, making every wanton urge stir in a nano second.

"I wasn't complaining... I happen to appreciate you took time to master a craft." I whisper breathily, tuning back into the previous state of 'take me now.' He is way too good at this, making me surrender with such simple motions and soft words. His tongue traces my ear, and I bite my lip to curb the urge to moan, pressing my knees together. He smiles against me, knowing he has me exactly where he wants me. Reading my body language and subtle tells and acting accordingly.

"Let's christen it... Think it's time I showed you how many ways we can use a couch and prove I can still rock the Casanova crown." He breathes in my ear, bending in behind me to scoop me up, and carries me backward with a kiss on my mouth.

Chapter 23

Arrick slides down from his position behind me on the couch and slumps on the floor, using it as a back rest as I flop sideways and stretch out on the full length of the sofa. Feeling his head and hair nearby and pushing my fingers into the spiky hair on top. He leans into my hand and sighs heavily, equally worn out and breathless. My heart is pounding from exertion, and every single part of my skin and inner body is tingling. Neither of us has a stitch of clothing, yet my body heat is through the roof, and I generally feel like I could sleep.

"Jesus, baby... My little porn star. Who knew I would find a girl who matched my stamina? I almost bailed because I thought I would have a heart attack mid-way through. Now that.... Was worth missing you for a week!" He turns and hits me with a boyish smile, catching my eye from his angle as I can only try and regain my breath, calm my racing pulse and seriously luxuriate in the marathon of positions he introduced me to.

It wasn't like any other time he's made love to me. This time was all sex. Primal, unleashed, pushed by having been apart, and for the first time, I can tell he let go and showed me what he's got. I was right about his unbridled passionate side to him. He's a demon when he lets go, and my body hasn't an inch left that didn't meet some part of his. I didn't know sex in acrobatic positions could feel so good, and I found my favorite is when he gets behind me and we both stay upright.

Somehow intimate yet also so goooood!

He has left my skin pink and sizzling and taught me a thing or two in the last two hours. It only makes me love him more now, seeing that every other time has been gentle and controlled and fully aware of my every noise and mood. This time he gave his all like I was any other girl with no seedy past or fragile scars to worry about. I needed him to be that way more than I knew I did.

I giggle at him, running my fingers through that sandy, sexy as-sin hairstyle. All short back and sides but long enough on top to grab onto, which I did, several times. He's a lot less scratched up since I had my nails rounded out, but he still bears my marks on various places of that tanned body.

"You have been holding back on me." I tug his hair, and he gets up, sliding on top of me on the couch and nestling comfortably into my body. Propping his elbow at either side of my chest so he can rest his chin on his hands over me, eyes skimming my breasts.

"I haven't wanted to scare you. Didn't want a repeat of the first time we ever tried. Finally, figuring out what triggers your reactions means I can relax. I can read you better than you think sometimes. Learning the little tells that I never used to notice when it comes to this." He leans down and kisses my left breast with a cheeky smile. His touch can still make me burn, even if he just satisfied me in many ways. Our bodies fit so perfectly together.

"I trust you... I know that no matter what, I can always stop you... That no means something." I glance away, sudden emotion catching my throat when on this topic, and gaze at the wall of books and memorabilia I have been filling my shelves with lately. A mini fluffy Unicorn Arrick brought home for me is sitting on the coffee table, sticking out of his backpack, watching us.

"Tell me how your week was." Arrick changes the subject, sensing my uneasiness, and I turn back to him with an adoring smile. His eyes trained on my face, committing me to memory and looking at me as though I am the most perfect girl he has ever laid eyes on. My heart does that gooey melt thing that he causes, and I sigh back at him with complete devotion.

"You know how my week was. You texted and called me endlessly." I giggle, pulling his face forward with two flat palms and strain to kiss him. Meeting those soft lips perfectly.

"You know, maybe I missed something." He kisses me again before I flop back down and stare at him lazily.

"Me... You missed me." I point out with a grin, poking him in the cheek playfully and then tracing that strong jawline tenderly.

"I did." He nods in all seriousness, grinning at me again, and I sigh and trace his seductive mouth with my fingertips. I love his smile. I always have. All perfect Hollywood white teeth and manly kissable lips. He has the kind of mouth that makes you want to eat him.

I love that he always seems to be smiling nowadays. It's one thing I missed a lot in the past couple of years when he seemed to get more and more emotionally cool and serious. Like he was maturing and losing the fun boyish part of him that has since made a comeback.

"I barely noticed you weren't here." I raise a brow with a deadpan tone, smirking at him as his grin stays put, all sexy dimples and flawless lines. Not convinced at all.

"That explains the constant little insecure 'Ohhh, I need you home. I miss you Arrrryyy', texts." He mimics my girly voice and clutches his heart dramatically. I slap his shoulder and shove him, but he barely moves, catching my fingers and pinning my hand to the couch.

"They were for my other boyfriend. I just mistyped your number." I screw up my face at him, and he mimics me looking crazily cute. Annoyingly childish at times, but in a way that I go weak for.

"Better up my game then. Make sure you ditch the other and devote all your attention to me." He nudges me with his groin, and I am shocked that my lady parts react with a 'yes please' moment of their own accord.

I think I have an addiction.

"He is a hard act to follow. I might not really be that into you." I squeal when he moves up fast, his mouth nibbling my neck and holding me down mercilessly. His body deliberately crushes me to the couch, so I can barely move, and I wiggle to get him off.

"Well, we both know I am the only one making you cum several times a day. Besides, your other boyfriend is gay. He can stick with your love of clothes and shoes and breaking your credit card. I will stick to satisfying the parts of you that need a straight guy." Arrick lifts his chin and grazes his mouth against mine, relieving the pressure of his weight from me once more.

"I do love Christian." I giggle at him as he rolls his eyes, mocking or stealing my favorite gesture. Not sure which.

"I kinda figured you did. Especially as he keeps texting me to try and wind me up about what he's getting up to with you in my absence." Arrick lifts his brows and smiles as I instantly blanche.

"What? When?" I giggle, surprised, knowing fine well Christian would do something like that to wind Arrick up. Lately, they have become good friends. He talks to him a lot when we are out as a group, I know they text and call each other too, and they even went on a guy night out with Nathan not too long ago and met Christian's elusive man for pool and beer.

"Likes to keep me on my toes and remind me you're within his grasp if he just switches up his sexuality." He raises a brow, completely unbothered by any Christian threats.

"He's so naughty. I'll have to punish him for that sort of behavior." I laugh a little more, enamored with how funny my friend is. Arrick shakes his head at me, looking serious so suddenly.

"Don't. I like that you finally found friends you let in, Sophs. Instead of just hanging with me and mine. You learned to trust people outside the family and finally let other people matter to you. I like both a lot. You finally met people worthy of you, and knowing they are there for you when I'm gone is all that kept me sane this past week." He rolls me to my side and then nestles beside me to face him, tucking my hair behind my ear and coming nose to nose with me.

"You, obviously, are not the jealous type." I point out.

Something I have always known. I often wondered how two brothers could be completely different regarding this stuff.

Jake is a green-eyed demon who jumps on any guy who looks Emma's way. Even gay ones. Arry only seems to get pissed if men cross the line and try to go beyond showing an interest in me.

"Not generally. I do have my moments with you, though. Guess I am not insecure and never really have been. I don't feel threatened by other men, baby. I've never known what it's like to feel that way in a relationship because I know you're all mine. I know you would never do anything to hurt me in that way. Trust is a two-way thing." He shrugs at me, completely open, and for a second, I'm slapped with a pang of guilt. Knowing fine well that I don't know how to feel when it comes to Natasha.

I know I trust him, yet at the same time, I can't get past her. Can't ever get that niggling horrible black dot from inside of me where she is concerned, and listening to him now makes me feel shitty as a person.

I guess he can't understand insecurity or jealousy because he's never experienced them. He's never had his heart broken like that or found a girl cheating on him in any way. Never been dumped either. He has nothing to ignite that kind of insecurity from his past. It explains his intolerance of the green-eyed monster if he can't empathize. He doesn't understand it.

"Did Nate tell you I called him?" I bite my lip, changing the subject quickly to deflect how uncomfortable it makes me feel. Watching the tiny, almost non-existent flecks of green in his eyes, wondering where they go when they are like this. Fully chilled out and completely content. It's the only time his eyes are ever truly hazel.

"He did... Told me feisty Lil Sophabelle gave him an earful." He laughs, always offering encouragement for my sassy side. I think he likes it a lot more than he lets on and is not one to ever tell me off for being petulant.

"And?" I nudge him impatiently. I want to know what he said after my call and his feelings about my girl.

"And he's Nate... He doesn't talk about his feelings very much, even to me. I know he is acting weird around the Jenny thing, to be honest. I think he feels something for her, but he's unable to go down that route." I watch his eyes for any hint of evasiveness and see none.

"So he's another Daniel Hunter, a Jake, or even you a few years ago? Another man with cold feet, who shits a brick when real feelings come along." I frown at him and get nothing but a smile in return.

"Oh, the jaded heart of a bruised girl.... Don't I get brownie points for manning up in the end?" He leans in, so our faces are touching, leaning against me adorably, obviously trying to get away from the topic of Nate.

"No. You took way too long to do it and made me more jaded in the process." I push my nose against his and then back off to scowl at him in jest.

"I know, baby... Nate's, just, Nate.... He acts like an ass, does stupid shit then takes a while to process things. It's why we get along. We're too alike. All week all he's done is knock back women. I think his head is on the girl he left crying in a cab, and it's making him feel messed up." He shrugs, clearly not interested in delving into his best friend's emotional psyche if it doesn't directly affect him.

"Knock women back? So, you two, when you're out there living up the fighter life, really are having randy girls throwing panties and phone numbers at you?" I eye him suspiciously and catch that tiny glimmer of wickedness. My heart is torn between feeling insecure about this happening and knowing he wouldn't go there behind my back. That slightly uncertain me, who wonders that he might if someone better came along.

Someone without my temper or my insecurities, or my scars.

"They don't get near me. That's what Nate is for. I have security and an entourage like a proper little diva. So, you can rest that pretty little head, knowing that Nate fields off horny women hence why he gets all the offers. My eyes are only for you, always for you and this right here." He pulls me in tight, angling to dodge my nose, and plants a kiss on the corner of my mouth. Smiling at me as he does so and winning me around effortlessly.

"It better stay that way, or else I will cut it off." I scowl harder, only half joking as he firmly slides his arms around me. My heart a little fragile with subjects like this after years of men who thought nothing of betraying me.

"Duly noted." He kisses me softly, more intensely this time, and that twinkle of 'I will never hurt you' in that smooth, beautiful face.

"He really has been knocking girls back all week? What about that girl from the bar he brought home?" I fully dissect Arry's expression, knowing he might not tell me anything if Nathan asked him not to. Trying not to get distracted by the little kissing touches he has trailing down my neck.

"He told me he regretted drunk banging that chick and didn't know why." He mumbles from my throat, more interested in what he's doing than what he's talking about now. I surrender to the sensation and close my eyes, but my mind won't be swayed that easily.

"Meaning?" I blink at him as soon as he stops, sighing because he knows I won't let up, sitting myself up a little to prop my head on my hand as Arrick traces my collarbone softly, so close to my face.

"Meaning.... He's probably more into Jenny than he can admit, and ditching her has made him realize it. Give him time, Sophie. He's not someone who ever followed his heart with just one girl. I've never seen him turn down sex the whole time we have been friends, so maybe, who knows? He may surprise you yet." Arrick is way too cool and lenient for someone whose best friend is a heart-shredding man whore. One who deserves castration.

"Hmmm... Who says he even deserves her after how he ended things? That was an asshole move." I sulk petulantly, watching that set of eyes trace my neck and shoulders as his fingers do, his touch caressing me into tingles.

"I told him that.... I gave him a tough time, trust me." Arrick seems to realize his attempts at placating me with sexy moves aren't working and comes to rest on the throw pillows beside me. Instead of tracking my skin, he curls up with me, pulling me down to snuggle.

"Why are men such assholes? I surrender to him wholly with zero resistance.

"Hey!." Arrick prods me, and I only bat his hand away with a giggle.

"Even you have been known to have asshole qualities. Definitely not as perfect as I like to think you are. Especially when you're drunk. I don't think I like you drunk." I raise a brow. I have been pondering bringing this subject up the whole time he was away. Not sure if I am overreacting but still. We suck as a couple when we are alcohol-fueled.

"I can be okay drunk. We've just had a couple of rough sessions ... I promise I will cut down next time we go anywhere and not be an asshole. You become an emotional wreck when you drink, and I can see why it escalated everything in the past... Maybe we should both go easy at our next social outing. Tipsy sex is as good as drunk sex." He smiles at me, eyes on my mouth once more, and I know he's already thinking about how quickly he can recover, even from two-hour sex sessions. I wouldn't say no, but I can tell he will not push it any further. There is still that part of him that is cautious with me.

"Agreed. I hate fighting with you." I sigh and nestle in against his throat, loving how even naked, he feels inviting and safe. Nothing is wrong. Nothing is making me feel shameful about this at all.

"Me too. Especially when we could be doing way more satisfying things." He wraps his legs around mine tightly and bodily squeezes me until I half giggle, half cough with the effort to breathe and push him away with a grunt. Arrick untangles us with a kiss on my eyebrow and a smile that signals he's getting up.

"We should get dressed, get up and eat. I want to take you to my apartment to sleep tonight. I have to sign some papers Jake's sending over, and I need to deal with something." He sighs and then yawns, clearly now suffering from delayed jet lag and exertion, and it's all starting to catch up on him. I glance up and catch that tiny flicker on his face, something he's not telling me, an elusive look, and my heart sinks.

"What do you need to deal with?" I push his stomach with my

palm as though to urge a response. He sighs and gets up, leaning over me as he climbs off the couch and plants a kiss on my head. He gets up, picks up his discarded clothes, and turns his back on me.

"I'm paying for Tasha's dad's med bills. His insurance fell through, and I felt like it was the least I could do. She texted me the number, and I need to call the treatment facility." He carries on picking up our clothes, pulling his own on, and keeping himself turned away because I know he is trying to play this off as nothing. Stop an ensuing fight.

"So she's still texting and calling you then?" the heavy thud hits me in the chest and almost winds me; He hasn't mentioned her calls or texts since that night. All week he has kept her out of our conversations. He stiffens, body language moving to the defensive, and I try like crazy to control every single tiny thing going off inside me. Hating that one little word from him concerning her makes me feel sick and stupid. My blood runs cold, and my heart erupts in a flurry of anxiety.

"Sometimes." He sounds evasive; for the first time ever, I feel like he's lying to me. I don't know why but I get an odd sensation from one little word that I cannot quite place. It makes me want to cry, but I push it down hard.

"About her dad or......?" I pause, not sure I really want to know what she talks to him about anymore. I hate myself for the flood of pain and insecurity that overtakes me now. Arrick sighs and looks over his shoulder at me.

"She knows I'm with you. She avoids mentioning it. Just her dad, basic stuff, like how she's getting on.... Pleasantries. Nothing that means anything." His voice is tighter, although I can tell he's trying not to let this turn into something, and I hate that I am making it something. I swallow the wave of emotion away and try to plaster on indifference.

Something touches my arm, and I turn to see him holding my clothes out to me. I take them and avoid looking at him, getting up and unraveling the bundle to find my underwear. I turn away from him to fasten my bra and hide the single tear that fills my eye.

Blinking it out fast and despising my insecure idiot self. Hating that I can tell myself a million times that she means nothing, and then it all goes to shit so easily. I know the weird vibe I got is why it's escalated to tears, and I know his sudden need to be cool and distant is because he's picking up on the jealous vibe. Still an issue for both of us then.

"I'll go sort us out food. Take your time." Arrick sounds closed up and moves away. I guess he's already dressed, and I continue focusing on getting dressed slowly and silently. Hating that without fighting, it feels like we are, and he's suddenly so very far away from me.

Arrick sighs dramatically.

"I love *you*, Sophie. I'm not going to fuck that up. You need to let this go. Give her time to move on by herself." He's pleading, my heart shredding that he has no concept of how this feels.

Why can't he understand why I would have insecurities about her?

I don't respond, just look at what I am doing and keep doing it.

For someone so smart, sometimes he's such a dumb ass. In his head, as understanding and perceptive as he can be, I guess he figures confessing he's always loved me means it takes it all away. That showing me he loves me daily means I shouldn't have any reason to be jealous.

Chapter 24

I yawn for the millionth time in the aquarium and blink at the bright light of a flash nearby, body heavy and achy from too much today. Arrick walks behind me with his arms around my waist, pushing my tired body like a child.

"Maybe you need a nap before we get dinner." He nuzzles his nose against my ear from behind, pushing his knees into my legs to keep me walking, and holding me up bodily. To anyone watching, I am behaving like a stroppy kid who doesn't want to walk around anymore, and I don't care. He has walked my legs off after keeping me up half the night with his undying libido after a week's separation. Taken a million selfies at various tanks and ponds and tired me out on some pedal boats for an hour. I am beyond shattered and never good when I am tired. I resort to being a five-year-old kid in a temper tantrum when I can't be bothered anymore. Completely flaked out and unable to enjoy any more of this day without some shut-eye.

"Maybe you should leave me in bed and go without me." I yawn again; this time, he stops, lets go to walk in front of me, turns his back to me, and encourages me to hop on. Which I do, wrapping my legs around him and arms around his neck while I cuddle in.

Glad to be off my feet as nearby onlookers throw us disapproving looks. A woman with two children glares at us when her kid asks why she can't get a piggy ride, but Arrick throws her a winning smile, pats my ass with the hand he slides back, and then returns to holding my thighs up and keeps walking with me. I'm an effortless weight to him, yet it seems it doesn't even break his stride.

"Not a chance. I have seen the dress you brought over with you, and I am not missing seeing you in that tonight." He squeezes my thighs and starts walking faster, skirting people as he maneuvers towards the nearest exit, having to watch my feet sticking out and saving poor children's passing faces from impalement.

"I'll wear it to bed, so you can ogle me when you come home." I yawn and rest my head against his, closing my eyes to snuggle up and sigh heavily. So much fatigue in one little body is so not good.

"I want you with me. I hate going out without you, baby." He bumps me higher on his back for a comfier grip and walks on at speed, finally heading toward the neon signs to leave.

"You're a horrid boyfriend. Forcing me to socialize and go clubbing when I am wasting away with tiredness." I whine to no one in particular, and Arrick answers with a "Hmmmm" of disinterest.

"I'm pretty sure I don't care right now." I can almost feel his smirk as he carries me out of the metal gates that lead to the carpark area, still bouncing me along and getting cute looks from other couples we pass. We look so adorable to non-moany people.

"Why am I even with you?" I mock huff at him, poking his cheek with my finger and sighing loudly as if he is the cruelest person alive.

"Because you love me to death, and no other man alive would put up with your stroppy ass the way I do. Or piggyback you home because you're too diva to keep walking." Arrick gets us out into the crowded car park and drops me on my feet when he finds his car. Holding me up as he can locate his keys in his jacket pocket and beep opens the locks.

"I only love you sometimes, like when you let me go to bed and stay there. I'm tired, Arry." I huff, whine up at him with soft sleepy eyes, flop around dejectedly when he positions me in the car, and lift my feet into the footwell.

"Do I need to buckle you up too, or are you capable of that?" He sighs, leaning in to kiss me on the mouth and ruffle my hair. Used to this side of me, but patient and indulgent. I lift my hands pathetically, and he sighs, leaning in, and pulls my belt over me, clicking it in place with a kiss on the cheek.

"You suck. I don't like you anymore." I flop sideways, so my head rests against the door frame, gazing up at him like a puppy, and give a dramatic exhale. He shuts it and comes around to his side, getting in and pulling his shut. Arrick buckles his belt starts the car, and revs the engine, adjusting his mirrors before he notices I am still scowling at him.

"Sure you'll love me again when I let you nap. You can crash on the couch while I cook dinner. It might make you smile again... Sleep and food are your two favorite things in the entire world." He mocks flatly, completely unphased by my overly dramatic teen behavior. He's seen me this way a million times on a million different days and has oddly never gotten annoyed with it.

"I have a third now.... And nope. You're making me get up to dress up and spend a night with your friends in a noisy bar when I could just have a long bubble bath and a smoochy movie in your bed. School holidays could be put to better use than lying dead with a hangover." I try for Bambi eyes and seriously wounded animal behavior, but he tweaks my cheek with a cute look and winks at me infuriatingly.

"The party animal in you really did die, didn't it, baby?" He smiles my way, again with a ruffling of my hair, before maneuvering the car out of the parking space carefully, avoiding milling pedestrians.

"She retired happily." I retort.

"What good is having a sexy as-sin girlfriend if she makes you go out solo? I want a trophy wife that men can hate me for." He raises a brow my way with that devilish wink before turning back to the road and so very handsome with full-on concentration.

"I may have to hurt you," I warn with a low tone and steady deadpan gaze on his face. Not impressed with pretty much telling me he wants bimbo arm candy for a girlfriend, only as an ego boost.

"Well, we both know I like that, so feel free. Not sure you'll get your nap, though." He grins cheekily, and I slap his shoulder with a flat palm.

"You're an asshole sometimes. I forget what I ever liked about you." I sulk now, grumpy from being overly tired. Now I am hungry too, which makes me 'hangry.'

"Jesus, you're a stroppy one this afternoon. You're lucky I am probably the most chilled and tolerant male on the planet and don't carry out my desire to suffocate you." Arrick wriggles in his seat and fishes in his back pocket, one hand revealing his phone, buzzing crazily as he pulls it out.

He glances at the screen and red buttons it before dropping it in the car's center console. I catch sight of the illuminated name before it blanks out again and see it's Natasha. Biting my lip, I turn away and stare out the window before he sees I noticed.

"Sleep for you, cooking for me, and then we'll see how you feel, okay?" Arrick looks my way seriously, catching my eye for a second so that I look at him, a flat tone and no hint of anything other than continuing a conversation. I push down the tidal wave inside of me and try not to turn into a crazy bitch.

"Yeah, whatever." I shrug airily. Still pretending to be absorbed in the view outside, I turned back to and jump when his hand rests on my knee.

"I love you, beautiful." Arrick is watching me and the road simultaneously as I let out a long sigh of defeat, faced with adoring and cute. I really can't be pissed at him.

"Fine! Okay! Stop giving me puppy eyes. I'll come to your stupid, whatever it is." I am dying to get home and lay down, I hate feeling this wiped out and blame it half on a bad night's sleep and half on the fuzzy head and runny nose I feel coming that I'm sure Christian has inflicted on me. Diseased freak he is with his damn cold. As if to prove the point, I sniff again and wipe my nose with my sleeve.

"Are you getting sick? If you are, then maybe we should stay home after all. I don't want you getting sicker." His eyes scan my face, looking concerned and instantly paternal, and it soothes my ruffled feathers a little.

"I'm fine. I just need sleep. I feel out of whack and touchy. If I had periods, then I would probably be having one." I point out blatantly; my contraception injection means I never get them at all, but I do occasionally get symptoms of having them, and I wonder if this is part of why I feel so tense today. Emotionally overwhelmed when Arry was nothing but sweet all day. Taking me out one-on-one, holding my hand, and kissing me endlessly. There's a stuffed sea lion in a bag in the trunk from earlier and about three bags worth of tourist crap that I just had to have.

The aquarium is one of my favorite places to visit, but as it's a bit of a long drive and takes an entire day to get around, we only come occasionally, and I felt the need to splurge. Not that it cost me anything. Mr, old fashioned. He wouldn't allow me to use my card for anything.

"I love the fact you don't. It means you're never off limits... Maybe I need to set my watch for this time every month, so you get a free keep-out-of-jail card for being a pain in the ass." He flicks his eyebrows upwards in a cheeky gesture, and I roll my eyes at him again, instantly back to irritable.

"Ha ha. I can never tell when you're being serious or being an ass." I slump back down in my seat and lift my feet to his dash, practically curled up. He frowns at me but never says anything about how I use his dash as a footrest. He never has, even though Jake practically rips my legs off for doing it in his car.

"Usually, I'm being an ass because you're easy to wind up, and I enjoy it. Part of being my girl, so get used to it." He reaches out and pinches my cheek to be met with a hand slap.

"I want a massage." I pout in an irritable mood, being demanding when I should be giving him one for the tough time I always give him. I am getting too used to Arry indulging me in every way, pandering to me. Not that I can blame myself, he has done this for so long that I blame him for the spoiled baby I have become. He always encouraged me to behave like a little madam around him.

"Not sure... If it gets you to sleep, fine, but lately, they all end up in sex. I think I've tainted you." He winks, and I shake my head at him.

"Well, either would make me sleep, so, you know, I'm easy." a naughty smile creeps across my face, and instead of pouting, I find myself sliding my hand over the console to curl over his thigh. Solid, muscular thighs that make me think about climbing on his lap.

"When it comes to me, you are." He casually picks up my hand and replaces it on my lap, grinning at the furious look I give him and knowing he is as bad. All I have to do is say his name in that husky pleading way, with big eyes, and he's on me like a dog in heat.

Not that I'm complaining.

"I wouldn't get so cocky, might just go to bed alone and not bother coming at all with that smug ass attitude." I prod his shoulder, so not impressed with him rebuffing my advances.

"You know you want me. You have very little control when it comes to that." He looks a little too sure about that as he moves down in his seat to adjust his jeans. I get a little smug when I realize why. He can hide so much but never the start of an arousal.

Easy!

"Stop being smug, asshole. It's not endearing." I raise a haughty eyebrow his way, half smiling at him because I can't help but like him, even when he's being his confident, cocky self.

"I have every right to be smug. You can't keep your hands off me lately. I'm not complaining, Sophs, but all I need to do is look at you nowadays, and the panties drop." That one gets another Casanova wink, and the inner stubborn me uncurls to stand up to him. She doesn't like when he gets too big for his boots... or, err, pants.

"Maybe I'll implement a sex ban, seeing as your so overworked and so sure of yourself." I sit up, and cross my arms across my chest and legs for good measure, sizing him up as though he means nothing to me anymore. So petty. Sometimes I surprise myself.

"Try it... See how long you can last before I get you naked and moaning for me. Begging me to fuck you." He smiles, the hot shot of smiles, that 'I know you better than you think', glance and the infuriating way he rests his hand casually on the wheel like he knows he's got this. I again narrow my brows at his use of that vulgar term, hating how crass it is.

"Okay, I will. From this second until further notice. I'm not giving you sex. You can try all you like, but I am not yielding to you." I pout, sticking my chin in the air and smirking like a diva.

"Wrong thing to say to me. Never challenge a Carrero, baby." Arrick pulls the car into a turning, looking away before his attention is back on me. I realize he's heading off course to home, heading into an underpass off the freeway and turning into a tunnel at a faster speed until we slot into dimness. He stops the car suddenly in a darkened tunnel, unclips his belt, and gets out. Like a flash of decision, so fast I don't even have a moment to think about it or what he's doing.

Coming to my door seconds later, he opens it, leans in, unclips my belt, and pulls me with him. Moving me forward to close the door, pushing me back to lean against the car. Standing close but not touching, he tilts in, so his mouth hovers over mine. Runs a single finger from my knee up along my inner thigh slowly.

I'm wearing a comfy knee-length dress with boots, so he has fully naked skin on show to torture with caresses. Tingles erupt as he comes to my dress's short hem and slowly teases upwards. An instant bodily reaction I have to him, knees tensing, lips parting as I ache to kiss him suddenly. He stays still, eyes locked on me, not inching this further.

"What are you doing?" I blink, whispering, inching towards his mouth so he can kiss me, but he tilts back and smiles.

"Trying all I like." He says smartly, his husky, seductive tone giving me goosebumps, his lips parting, and pupils dilating. It's clear he wants sex, but he's playing with me. Proving a point.

"I said no sex. I didn't say no to kissing." I frown huffily, pushing his chest away, so I can cross my arms again, glaring steadily at him.

"I think all it will take is a kiss, so I'm giving you a sporting chance at not breaking your ban." He is far too sure that he is going to make me cave. I will so not break with a kiss. I have way more resolve than that when it comes to him.

"Smug... Cocky. Fine! ... Here." I lean in and kiss him softly, meeting no resistance, then slide my hands around his face and kiss him more passionately. His body comes to mine and presses me to the car as he gets lost kissing me back. It takes only a second to ignite the fire that's been growing between us in the last weeks, instantly aching to have him inside me, even though we're out in God knows where in an underpass. At the same time, heavy traffic flies overhead and rumbles deafeningly. Arrick breaks away, his eyes heavy with lust, and rubs his nose to mine.

"I don't think I can handle a sex ban. You've ruined me with explosive fucking." The defeat is in his tone, his eyes, and the way his hands are roaming me already. Sliding my dress up enough to make me tremble in anticipation, hands already skimming my hips under my skirt.

"Fuck it! Neither can I." I yank him back to me and bring our mouths back together, pulling his jean buttons open and shoving my hands in his pants feverishly, overcome with lust. I search him out and then groan as his hands find me, lifting me to pin me to the car as he pushes a hand into my underwear. I bite on his bottom lip and suck hard as he pulls my underwear off to one side and seems to lose all control.

There's no foreplay, no real working up to it. Just two people going crazy with desire. Lost in need to have each other and caught in the moment. He pushes inside, lifting me by the thighs and making me moan with the way he slides inside. Noses together, eyes locked as he thrusts into me. Both of us are panting with the way it's happening. My arms are around his neck, and clawing at him already with how good he always feels within me.

Arrick kisses me hard, sucks on my lip, then rams me against the car harder so he is deep inside me as I gasp in pleasure, moaning around him. I pull open his shirt, nibble at his jaw and neck, rake my nails down the exposed flesh as he thrusts into me aggressively, heated, banging against the car, and I don't care who hears us.

We have never been like this, even with the marathon of kinky sex positions over the last few days. We have never had a fast-heated quickie without serious make-out and foreplay coming first; this is all a basic, primal need. We have never physically been rough with one another like this, minus my claws, but this is some unspoken need to do so. Loving how much he is throwing every raw urge he has at me. I throw all my inhibitions to the wind, clawing at him, bite his lip harder and cry out so loudly a flock of birds scatter away from nearby trees.

It lasts only minutes, so hard my body is pressed into the smooth metal roughly, leaving marks on my skin with steel fingers, and my gauges on him are drawing blood, but I like it. I lean back, so my head rests on the roof of his car as the waves of ecstasy climb up through me like hot waves. I dig my nails under his shirt at his muscular skin to feel myself piercing him. The car rocks behind me with the force of the sex we are having, shifting with every thrust.

Arrick's grip bites into the flesh of my thighs in reaction, a slight moan from under his breath, pushing me up harder, faster until I can't contain it anymore. One final scream as an orgasm rips through me, and I cling to him crazily as the biggest all-consuming spasms of climax rip my body apart. However, this doesn't feel like any I have had before. This feels more intense and different, stronger and body-racking, and completely screws me up physically with the intensity.

The sudden drenching between us makes me look down in complete shock. I'm pretty sure I just peed myself mid-orgasm, and it instantly snaps me out of the afterglow. Arrick looks down too, finding his own release as I did, and smiles at the obvious something all over us. His trousers and my shoes are soaked, and I'm utterly mortified.

"What the hell?" I can't move from the way he has me perched as he pulls out of me. It's disgusting and completely mortifying, and I have no clue why he is even smiling at me like that. My face is set in a grimace, and I'm silently ashamed, utterly cringing in ickiness.

What the hell just happened?

"You came, baby... Like properly came." He grins and slides me down to my feet, pulling off his shirt over his head as though this is a completely everyday thing, leaning down to try and help clean me up. I don't know what to do, staring at this like it's the worst thing ever. Immobile because I feel so.... gross.

"What? What does that even mean? That's disgusting." I have heat creeping up my face, completely mortified that I would do that in front of him, on him. How can he even be dabbing at my legs and not recoiling in 'eww, my girlfriend is disgusting,' like I am? I have lost all composure and am utterly embarrassed in front of him of all people.

"It is not! It means you're one of the very few women that can have a female ejaculation, and you just made all my Christmases come at once. I feel pretty accomplished right now." He hands me his shirt and slides his belt off, throwing it in his open car window and attempting to minimize the mess of his pants with the edge of the shirt I am now holding. I stare at it with complete abhorrence. His pants are soaked like someone threw an entire bucket of water over him.

"I didn't... Pee?" I ask numbly, thoughts of Emma's baby waters hitting me months back and looking at what he's doing with that same grim expression as that day.

"No, you didn't *pee,* baby. You had a very real orgasm. Meaning I was doing something completely right. I think this proves my theory that I am the guy for you. Not every girl can do this." He looks so fucking happy, and I keep staring at him like he has lost his ever-loving mind.

Why did I get the weird one?

"Why are you smiling? We're messy and wet, and now you don't have a shirt." I point out, not sure this is ever going to be a good memory at all. Standing dry, dress back to rights, and staring at my half-naked man looking as if he's high.

"This is pretty much what every guy aspires to do during sex... I think I just earned a permanent crown of sex god." He walks to his trunk and pulls out his gym bag, stripping behind his car quickly into his change of clothes without one care about who might see him. I watch him strip naked without two shits about it and frown.

"You're weird. This is weird." I follow him, handing over the drenched shirt, seeing as I am mostly untouched. He had my dress out of the way, and my underwear pulled aside.

"My little Climaxer." He chuckles and winks at me with a smile that almost takes over his entire face. Clearly very happy.

"Eww! Arry, don't call me that; you better never tell a soul that I did that." I pout at him irrationally, scared that other people might hear about what I did. Still not entirely convinced I didn't just have some weird, weak bladder moment that is utterly vile.

"Aww, come on baby, I have to be able to tell the guys I made you cum like a waterfall. You're so innocent sometimes. It's crazily cute." He pulls his new T-shirt over his head and throws his other clothes in the trunk, leaning in to plant a kiss on my mouth.

"Don't you dare!" I gawp up at him in complete alarm. A sudden thought hitting me in the head so suddenly.

"You tell them about us having sex?" I squeak, completely betrayed and hurt that he discusses what we do with Nate, Jason, or any of his friends when I am not there. Panicking as Arrick's smile drops.

"Hell, no! ... Why would you think that? I mean, they know... I train topless, and your nails are brutal. Plus, I think the fact I'm always in a good mood is a dead giveaway. Men make sex jokes; I swear I tell them nothing. I've had plenty aimed my way from your little sexy scratches and bites. I think everyone is jealous that I got myself a beauty who gives me a wild sex life." He smiles properly, no Hollywood charm or 'I'm hot' just genuine, 'I am so happy right now', and I relax a little. Something inside calming down that he genuinely seems to have liked this and knowing he wouldn't betray me by boasting to his mates about what we do.

"I do?" It's not like I can compare what we do to anything or anyone normal. My past taught me about being used and hurt, and I try never to go back there. I only know what we do together always feels good and right. I can't tell if it was always like this with other people. I don't know what normal sex with other people is like. I have no comparison.

"You have no clue how amazing you are. Sophie, if you ever doubted that sex between us was going to be an issue, stop.... Because you are the best sex I have ever had, there's no comparison. You blow my mind every time we do this." He catches my hand when he closes the trunk and pulls me around, leading me to the passenger door. Stopping and turning me to him, brushing back my hair with his fingers and kissing me softly on the lips.

"You're just saying that because I peed on you, and I'm embarrassed," I mumble childishly, still not sure this is a good thing. Feeling strangely shy and looking down at our entangled fingers.

"Fuck no... I want you to do that every time. I will be aiming for it. Baby, you have made my fantasies for the dream girl come true. Sex with you is better than I could ever have imagined. You're amazing. You completely let go and trust me to take care of you. There are no real boundaries with what you let me do to you. I know how huge that is.... I love you so much more because of it." He pulls me to him and kisses me again, only this time with a little teasing tongue, leaving me breathless and wanting more before opening my door and guiding me inside.

"I don't know what to say." I settle in the seat, watching him automatically lean in and buckle me up.

"An I love you wouldn't go amiss occasionally." Arrick eyes me warily, and I frown, looking away with a sigh. Of all the things I am still having a hard time with, it seems so dumb that something I used to say to him so freely now sticks in my throat. He moves in against me and kisses me on the cheek.

"I get it, baby. It will come. When you feel like you trust me like you once did. I love *you*. That's all that matters." I catch the tiny hurt tone in his voice and look up at him sadly, wishing I could cross that last barrier and tell him that I do.

I really do.

Chapter 25

I roll over and open my eyes, completely refreshed after sleeping so long and the smell of food drifting my way. I sit up on the couch and blink at the tv, still playing on low, the noise of Arrick clanging pans or whatever's in the kitchen, and gaze over the back of the couch to watch him.

He's been making Ragu sauce by the smell of it, his moms' recipe, and I can see the pasta on the counter. He made his own. She used to teach me how to do all that stuff when I was younger too, but I never had any real affinity with cooking. He seems to enjoy it when he's in the mood, and everything smells heavenly.

I don't know what time it is, but the skyline over by the dining table looks too dark to be early evening, and I wonder if he's changed his mind about going out tonight with his friends.

I know Jenny is meant to be coming, but Christian is with his boyfriend tonight and won't be making a show of himself. We are celebrating Arrick's win, and his next fight is a championship try at a belt. He could get a real title after this, launching him as a fighter among the people he admires. Nate set up tonight as a celebration for them both, as he's the one who got Arry this far.

He's worked hard to get here, and I know that even though he jokes about retiring, he loves what he does. He keeps Carrero Corp in his back pocket so that when he does retire, he still has something to do besides spend money and rely on wealth. Arrick will never be one of those men who sit idly by a pool and let life pass them. He's already booked us on three or four trips over the next months, in my school term breaks, and he's taking me to Austria soon to go skiing before Christmas. Just the two of us.

"I'm hungry." I yawn and call out to him while stretching my limbs like a contented cat; he spins his head and instantly smiles at me.

"Hey, sleepyhead. Do you feel better? Food will be ten minutes still." He has a towel over his shoulder and looks hot and flushed from slaving over a cooker all afternoon.

Love my domestic man when he looks like this.

"I do.... But now, I'm starving." I get up and wander to the kitchen, wearing one of Arry's button-downs as a sleeping shirt over fresh underwear. We showered when we came home, seeing as I left such a lasting impression on both of our clothes, and I am still not entirely sure it's the wonderful thing he claims it is.

I curl up in the arms that outstretch to me, snuggling in as he kisses me on top of the head and squeezes me against him. He feels hot and clammy from being in the kitchen with the steam and heat. He smells more like his antiperspirant than normal, so I guess he's been sweating it out while I acted like a Disney princess and conked out in front of Jurassic park. I let go of him and move past to the bread bin, where I stashed my open family-sized bag of Cheetos last night, and pull them out to graze.

Arry turns from stirring the water and dumping the fresh pasta in and frowns at me. Switching the bag in my hands with a breadstick in a fast swipe gets him a major glare.

"Hey." I go to snatch it back, but he holds it up over anything I could ever reach and then dumps them on top of the refrigerator, which is like seven feet tall.

Douchebag.

"You only need to wait minutes, besides.... Cheeto's Sophie? You're going to turn into one at this rate." He scolds me gently, smacking my ass to move me as he leans into a cupboard for bowls.

"Why do you always do such mean stuff to me?" I shove his hand away when he tries to pinch my cheek on the way back up and jump up to reach the bag of snacks like an adolescent. Failing miserably because I am vertically challenged, and Arrick shakes his head at me.

"Yeah, wanting you to eat healthier is super mean. What an awful boyfriend I am." He rolls his eyes, and I smack his ass, this time for his cheeky retort and for stealing my mannerism.

I own the eyeroll in this relationship.

"You are!" I point out, slump back against the chrome door, and bite the end of my breadstick in defeat. Crunching noisily to be annoying.

"You know, when we have babies, or even when you're pregnant, I won't be so lenient on what you eat." He turns to me, deadly serious. I blink at him, completely stunned, and the blood rushes from my entire body in a split second.

"What now? ... Arrick, why did you say the B word? We don't talk about the B word or the M word... Isn't that like the number one cardinal rule of Arry?" heat creeps up my face, and I gawp at him in disbelief, stomach churning over in nerves at this sudden surprise attack. Arrick turns to me with a soft look on his face.

"No. It's just we never used to because we weren't the subject. One day there will be the M and B Sophie. Neither of us is ready for that, but I think about that stuff with you. I know where my future lies." He seems so sure, says it in such a matter-of-fact way, going back to scooping or ladling or whatever the hell he is doing over there with his back turned to me, without any other reaction.

"You do?" that tiny waiver in my voice betrays the fact he's going to make me cry, and his posture changes, his head turning over his shoulder to look at me.

"Of course, I do.... I want you to finish school and get onto whatever career path you want, Sophs, but one day, I want to marry you and have kids. Even if I'm the one who has to be the mom... You know, cos you're domestically challenged and all." He smiles at me, and my face crumbles, a tear rolling down my cheek as bittersweet pain hits me right in the chest.

I hate when he's this randomly sweet and catches me off guard. Completely rips the rug out from under me, and I never know how to react.

"I thought you never wanted any of that stuff with anyone. You always said you didn't think about any of that. If I remember right, your exact words were quote, 'the thought of babies and a wife put the fear of God into me.' Unquote." I blink at him still, wiping away my moment of weakness, heart racing in both panic and yet something more. The thought that he would completely change that for me, and I want to break into massive sobs and wrap myself around him. Arrick puts down the spoon he's been holding and comes to me, placing his hands on my shoulders, and gazes at me adoringly with a long, slow exhale.

"The thought of any old wife and anyone's babies, sure... But you, and ours... No fear in here at all. Only the sad thought that I fell in love with a girl who thinks Cheeto's are one of the five food groups, and uses bath towels to dust, occasionally... Or the fact, I'm pretty sure you didn't mean to dust at all... I think you probably assume towels live on the coffee table when you're done with them. And you leave your shoes on any surface they land on, daily." He smirks, kisses my temple, and then returns to retrieve the pasta from the boiling water.

"Why do you always ruin something so sweet with something extra, not sweet." I blink at him, wiping my face and throwing a kiss on him from behind, recovering from the tenderness and hitting his neck because I am barefoot and he's not bending for me. Completely blown away by what he said and know he's lightening the seriousness of his statement because neither of us is ready for the M talk yet. Especially not me.

How can I marry a guy I can't even tell I love yet?

"You know.... because I live with you, and you rubbed off on me. You have made abrasive love an art form." He winks, again, sass in place of love sonnets, and I eye roll.

"Thanks. I feel so proud! .... About that...... Ummmmm. How much do you like your spare room?" I finger the hem of my shirt nervously, pushed to do this now because it's been on my mind and seems like a good topic to slot it in. Watching his strong shoulders move under that sexy fitted tee as he does the chef thing over there.

"If you're planning on a sex cave or an Xbox room, then I am all for it." He turns to me a little, cheekily smiling, leans in, and kisses me, completely missing the subtlety of my hint.

"I was thinking pink.... Maybe a lot of sparkles." I blink at him nervously, watching as he goes and scoops the last of his pasta out of the water into a colander thing and turns the heat off on the sauce. Preoccupied and not getting the heaviness of my tone.

"You want a pink sparkly sex room? I don't know if that will do it for me, baby." He glances at me, completely confused. Head clearly on what he's doing and not what I am saying. Although my topics are usually random, he probably thinks I am off on another weird tangent.

"You're the only one thinking of sex rooms here.... I was thinking of ...You know? That if I'm going to move in, I would need to bring my sewing room." My heart skips a beat as I finally verbalize what I have wanted to say for days and kept losing my nerve.

"Mmmmmm." he is only apparently half listening and answers vaguely before he seems to frown. Arrick pauses with moving the pasta to plates and looks at me twice. Face finally registering on that extra little glance. "Moving in?" For a moment, I truly believe he's maybe changed his mind. My stomach drops to my toes, but then the smile that breaks across his face, like a sudden beam of light, soothes the pop of pain that went with it.

"If the offer is still there?" I sound so scared, completely out of my comfort zone, and Arrick drops everything he is doing to pick me up and kiss me hard. It's so sudden I yelp in fright and flail my arms before gripping on tight. A clumsy kiss, bashing noises, and I manage to bang my teeth on his, hardly the sexiest of moments, but it makes me giggle away the nerves as he cradles me against him tightly.

"Offer is most definitely still there, baby... You can paint the whole apartment pink and fill it with fluffy cushions if it means I get to come home to you every night." He spins me around, hugging me tighter and kissing me again, grinning like a crazy person, and it's infectious. I giggle back as he slides me down to my bare feet but keeps a hold on me, hands sliding down to cup my ass cheeks through the thin shirt.

"I'm bringing my unicorns." I point out sternly. I'm making it clear before he faints when I box up my three million fluffy roommates.

"Didn't expect anything else, even if there is an army of fifty now." He kisses me again, obviously very happy with my decision to move in. Not caring about the Unicorn army, either. Yet!

He hasn't seen them in their entirety, all in one place like I have.

"And my complete collection of shoes. I may need another wardrobe, though, as yours is *so* not big enough." I raise serious brows his way, knowing the importance of my walk-in and the sheer lack of one in Arrick's room. Just breaking him in gently for what he is agreeing to.

"I will sacrifice any room in the house to keep your shoes and dresses pampered, baby... I'll even buy another floor if we need to expand down the ways. I want you here, always." He lets me go to wander back to what he was doing, content and smiley still. I'm suddenly bursting with happiness too. He dishes sauce over the pasta in the bowls and stoops to pull garlic bread from the oven, winking at me as he does so.

My cute boy.

"You may need the cleaner to come a little more often... I don't do cleaning or cooking, or, you know? ... most adulting stuff that is normal for girls." I shrug unapologetically and know fine and well that he is forever cleaning up my apartment when we stay there, being a bit of a neat freak. Arrick is forever loading my dishwasher and emptying my trash. He should understand this before the big move-in, in case he regrets it or thinks I might miraculously turn into Martha Stewart or some normal female. He should know he's getting a fully-grown child with bad habits and a lazy side when it comes to cleaning.

"Nothing new there, then. I would never have picked you if I wanted a domestic goddess." He slides the bread onto another plate and puts all the pans in the sink behind him. Smirking and still looking a lot like a guy who hasn't changed his mind.

"We really doing this?" I blink at him nervously.

Last chance to run for the hills, handsome.

"Sophs, we have been doing this from the morning of Leila's party. You've just been slow on the catch-up." He kisses my cheek as he passes by and starts to gather up plates on a tray, looking a little too at ease with this.

"Don't take up snoring. I may have to smother you in your sleep if I have no escape from sharing a bed with you." I warn, slightly panicky that maybe he isn't thinking through how serious this really is. It's a huge decision, taking over half or more of his man cave and making it a little less 'guy.'

"I promise not to take up snoring." He smiles happily. No sign of any confusion or doubt or niggles. Infuriatingly cool and calm like always. Satisfied that he isn't in shock, misunderstanding my very real intentions and obviously with the program.

"Good, I think that we have that settled. Guess you just need to paint my room pink, and then I'm all yours." I pat him on the top of his head and stroll off toward the dining table to remind him how hungry I am.

"Wait? ... I'm painting the room? You know I can afford a decorator, right?" He pauses what he's doing and gazes at me, looking a little disturbed, his tone on the shocked side.

Yeah, that right there!

"Ummm, noooo. It will mean more if we do it; well... you. I want to see you use a drill thing to build stuff. I think that'll be hot." I point out, sliding into my chair, so I can watch him in comfort and see him waiver. Feeling strangely evil at this moment.

"You don't drill anything to paint a room, Sophs... I mean, I will do it if you want me to. I helped Nathan decorate his apartment, so I am pretty good at all that *stuff.* I figured you would want it done professionally." He shrugs, goes back to sorting out the tray, and lifts it.

"You're a professional fighter. Close enough. Perfect." I smile, quite happy with myself for that one.

"Is this some passive-aggressive punishment for something I can't figure that I've done?" Arrick frowns at me suspiciously, but I shrug. Watching him making his way towards me, he is so effortlessly sexy at times, and it makes me sigh and curl my toes.

"I'm thinking pink with wooden flooring, white furniture, and a wall of hanging rails for my finished pieces. I need a blackboard, too, for the design stage. I like the idea of an old blackboard like they had in old schools." I scroll off the list of things I have been daydreaming about when I snooped in the room the other day and try to picture where it will all go.

"Should I get a notepad?" Arrick comes to the table, lays the tray in front of me, in the center of the table, then goes to his side unit and fishes for silverware. He hands me a spoon and fork and sits down to face me to eat. Passing me a bowl and taking his own, leaving the tray with the bread between us.

"Maybe. I want a chaise lounge; your room is much bigger than mine, with more space for girly stuff, like mannequins." I help myself and dig in with relish, it smells amazing, and I am about famished already. So hungry that my mouth is watering.

"Mannequins? Is this a studio we're building or an actual store?" He seems momentarily worried.

"Tailor's dummies! I have one in my size, but I need more if I make different-sized items. A store is in the five-year plan, not yet." I raise a brow at him, and Arrick looks completely blank.

"Five-year plan, huh? Sophie's store? ... Designer extraordinaire... Career girl in fashion. I like it." He smiles, eyebrows meeting with that cute half-smile dimples galore. He looks down and scoops sauce on his bread before stuffing it in his mouth.

"You better? ... You're going to fund it." I grin at him and catch that small dimple get stronger as he fully smiles and then regards me with a long, drawn-out smirk.

"Don't worry, baby... Carrero Corp has your back. We will be seeing you at New York Fashion week soon enough." He winks, throwing me that winning smile that takes my heart.

Chapter 26

I'm still smiling as I'm led hand in hand across the hall of the nightclub towards the inner entranceway. Arrick has his phone to his ear and is trying to locate his friends, now we are here, almost two hours later than intended.

Arrick made good on peeling my panties off after teasing me mercilessly after dinner. He made love to me when we were supposed to be getting ready, but that turned into another marathon of assorted positions, and now we are seriously late. I am starting to think he might be right about matched stamina. I even made him sweat this time, and he gave up before I did. Calling a time-out and having to lay on the bed with me on top to finish what *he had* started. It was my first time being in control, and I think I liked it the most.

I'm eyeing that tight, firm ass in black jeans, his upper body encased in his leather jacket, over a dark grey shirt. From here, he looks like a swoon-some cover model for about any sexy male product currently trending.

I am a super lucky girl.

He's scanning around at milling people, my fingers entangled with his, while Nathan tries to direct us to another VIP room in a club we have never tried, on his cell. There are three flights of stairs down here, and he pulls me towards the middle ones.

"Sure, we're in the foyer... Yeah, up to the left. See you in a second." He hangs up and turns to me with a smile, another kiss hitting my lips softly. He hasn't been able to stop kissing or touching me in hours, evidently happy that I am finally moving in with him. I can't wipe the smile from my face either. It all feels so right.

The club is noisy, smoky, and loud; crowded to the max with people in the party mood, and he has to forge a path, pulling me close and putting his arm around me as he squeezes us through to find our party. He leads me up some stairs, and we soon find our way to a slightly quieter, cordoned-off area with a roped-off entrance. The bouncer nods his way and pulls the rope off for us to pass with a smile. Arrick nods back and guides me protectively.

"Mr. Carrero." He closes the rope behind us and lets us walk towards the crowded small bar surrounded by Arrick's friends. I grin at the fact he is getting more known in recent months, and his face seems to be gracing more billboards than ever before. Although I am glad he isn't being pestered by paparazzi yet. I know it will come, though. Arrick squeezes my hand, pulling me to the group of rowdy people as we are enveloped into hello's, back slaps, and handshakes from all the familiars.

Arrick lets go of me for a moment as Nathan gives him a typical male hug and back pat, and Arrick turns, pulling me forward into the crook of his arm, hanging it around my shoulders casually. I lean in against him and rest my head on the place where his shoulder meets his chest.

"Late for your own celebration? You fucking suck, man." Nathan scolds him with a grin, giving him a naughty, knowing nod.

"I was busy." Arrick smiles and takes the beer handed to him with a grin and shrug; Nathan gives me a glass of red wine, and I smile thankfully. Watching Arrick's profile with complete adoration tonight. He always looks so much sexier in jeans and buttons downs with his jacket; that face seems more tanned, and his eyes lighter in contrast to dark colors. I love him in sweats and tee shirts too, but tonight he is giving me serious butterflies, and panty-twisting urges dressed like that. I wonder if it's because he worked me up to fever-pitch heights before we came out, and I'm still relaxing in the afterglow.

"Yeah, sure you were. You know, Sophs, this guy was never late for anything, ever, before you! You are the worst influence on him." Nathan leans in, catches Arrick's collar, pulls it forward to peer down, and catches sight of fresh love bites across his collarbone on the non-tattooed side. Arrick shoves him off with a laugh.

"Shut up." I smile, knowing fine and well it's Arry who wouldn't let me get off the bed while his face was between my thighs. He started the whole thing.

"You are the worst girlfriend ever." Nathan laughs at me and tilts his beer, nodding to my abilities.

"Or the best," Arrick smirks dirtily and winks at me, making me giggle, despite the creeping blush up my face. Pretty sure they are aiming blame at me when king libido was the one making all the moves. He also taught me how to make a love bite, and then I had to practice with him to master the art.

"Keep it up. You might convince me that I can hack the one girl, guy thing." Nathan laughs, but it comes across as far more serious, and I eye him up warily.

"She said she was coming after eleven when she gets off her shift at work. If you like her, Nate, then stop being an asshole." I point out, and Arrick breaks into a smile, nudging at his best friend with a small shrug and a 'my girlfriend's direct' look.

"I need to be drunker than this if I have to grovel tonight. Just tell me she didn't take him back, Sophs?" Nathan looks completely panicked. Face paling as he seriously ponders his plan for her arrival. I shake my head at him, a small part of me glad that he is even contemplating this, but still, a huge amount of me feels the need to lecture him for all the shit he's put her through the past two weeks. She has been a mess. Christian and I have tried everything to cheer her up, shocked that she fell to pieces over Nate and never Mark.

"No, she didn't. Not really going to jump back to a guy when she's been sobbing over you, is she? Why are you waiting for her to arrive? Man up and text her, Nate. She's suffered enough... I swear if you keep fucking this up, I will personally maim you." I softly punch him in the shoulder with a little more grit than I intended to. Still pissed that he's why Jenny has been a moping hell, and her work at school has been horrendous all week. She would have been better off taking sick days.

"Now I see why you always look like a cat has eaten you for breakfast. Sophie is terrifying; I can only imagine what she does to you during sex." Nate smirks, dodges another slap aimed at his head this time, and keeps grinning.

"Keeps me smiling. Pretty fucking awesome sex." Arrick shoves his shoulder playfully, and I slap both in the abdomens for talking about my sex life like this. It's embarrassing, especially acting like I beat him or harm him crazily; it's just a few little marks and the occasional nibble.

He needs to man up.

Nathan turns around to answer something someone else has said. Arry brushes back my hair, leaning in low so that his breath tickles my neck as he moves in to kiss me and flutters his nose across my cheekbone, giving me instant tingles.

"You look amazing in this dress; crazy sexy. Yet all I can think about is taking it off again." He swoops further around my face and, this time kisses me seductively, sucks my bottom lip lightly, and grazes his teeth across it. I relax into him, always so ready to surrender to him in any way. My insides are stirring with heat, always letting him devour me.

He pulls me against him and slides his arm around my back so we are front to front as Claire appears behind us and starts asking him about something he has been helping her and Jason with. I lean my head against his throat as he leans back, face turned towards her, and cradle my drink. Leaving them to talk while being held tight in his arms, facing off to the opposite side.

More of his friends are sitting at tables at the side, overlooking the nightclub on a sort of hanging balcony. It's much like the club I last saw Camilla in. I let my gaze wander around the semi-dark space cluttered with people and seats. I pause when I catch the eyes trained on us from a shadowy corner. Two women are standing side by side and looking our way steadily. At first, I bypass them as strangers, but as my eyes adjust to the dark room and flashing disco lights, I realize with a sudden thud in my chest that one is Natasha and hardly concealing her hatred at that moment.

I stand up quickly, pulling myself free of him, lifting my glass to take a drink as he loops my hand in his with my change of position. Casting a glance at me while still talking to see why I'm moving. I smile at him and wave my glass as if to say, 'taking a drink,' and he returns to Claire. He's completely oblivious that we are being watched.

I frown and turn back to Arrick, eyes still across the room as I try to act nonchalant and turn to him slowly. My mouth is met with a kiss so suddenly it almost knocks me over. Claire has moved on, and he kisses me a little too passionately while I know she's watching us. I try to push him away, but his hand slides behind my neck, teasing my mouth open to turn the kiss into something hotter. Arrick is very hands-on when he drinks, and even though he's only started, the club seems to have him in the mood to make out and sex me up a little.

"Arrick?" I talk into his mouth, trying like crazy to capture his face and pull him away. He tastes like beer, like him, only half hearing me under the music around us, and finally pulls back to frown at the fact I am not kissing him back like I normally would.

"What's wrong?" He leans in, touching his nose to mine, and frowns harder when I shrug his hands off me that are sliding around my body. Looking concerned at my behavior.

"Natasha's over there, staring at us," I say into his face as he tries to catch my chin and throw another kiss, overly frustrated that I'm rejecting his attentions and slow on the uptake. He gazes at me for a second, eyes registering, then over me and scanning the room. I guess he sees her too, as he comes back to my face and kisses me on the cheek before letting me go and sliding my hand in his instead. That tiny frown that he saw her too and now feels equally uncomfortable.

"Sophie ... Wow, check you, baby, you look freaking amazing." Gary, an old friend of Arrick's, appears beside us and kisses me on the cheek before Arry can say anything else. I smile at him, holding down the urge to wipe his assault from my skin. We haven't seen him in over a year. He is not one of the regulars in this crowd. He worked in Australia for the past few months, and I guess he caught wind of Arrick's party tonight. Apparent that he's home visiting again.

"Thanks, Gary, you're looking well. Australia must agree with you." I lean in and receive my half hug, something all his friends do. And pull back when he aims a little close to the corner of my mouth with a second kiss, a hand on my hip with a little too firm a grip. It gives me the sudden recoiling urge, and I glance at him warily, tensing my hand in Arry's.

"You look about ten years older than the last time I saw you; fuck me, you're hot as hell." He moves back with Arrick's hand on his chest, firmly removing him from my space. A little smile of warning as Arry pulls me back against him tight and lassos an arm around me. Clearly getting my signal and dealing with him. He may not be prone to jealousy, but he knows when I need him to protect me.

"Back off, Briny, this one's taken, and if you so much as attempt a kiss at her like that again, I'll break your face." Arrick smiles, but it's clear he doesn't like the drunken way Gary is clinging onto me and inappropriately swaying into me. His eyes have done a full body sweep of me more than once. Arrick removes him from my hip and pulls me back another inch to widen the gap.

"Calm your pants, Arry. It's pretty clear she's off limits, seeing as you have been manhandling her since you walked in. When the hell did that happen? I thought you were shacked up with ...." He nods off towards the corner of the room, and Arrick throws him a murderous look.

"Nothing like coming out with the most obvious statements, ehh, Briny? This is what happens when you fuck off for months on end and don't keep in touch." Arrick sounds mildly pissed but swigs his beer and shoves the other guy in the shoulder with his bottle in a friendly manner. Weird vibes suddenly, and I stand stiff and unrelaxed between them.

"Does that mean Tash is back on the market?" Gary winks, making me tense, and I want to shove his bottle down his throat, but Arrick shrugs.

"Guess so. Not that she actually liked you, but sure that won't stop you." Arrick throws him another smile, slides his arm down low on my back, and tugs me, so I am encircled in his protective space with a clear show of 'hands-off.'

I immediately stare at his profile for a reaction, to see if it bothers him that his so-called mate wants to make a play for his ex, but he gives nothing away. I'm uncomfortable being scrutinized from afar while he has his hands on me, and I'm not too fond of the way Gary is now leering at me like he can't get over the change.

"How about we go dance?" Arry says softly, smiling at me and being my savior in one smooth move. Ignoring his friend and offering me a respite.

"Yes. Definitely." I smile and sigh in relief, glad for any excuse to get out of here so I can relax again. I don't see myself enjoying this night if it continues like this.

"Watch these. We're going down to dance." He orders Gary, handing off our drinks to the table nearby before catching his fingers in mine again and leading us back to the rear of the room and the direct stair down to the club. This feels like that club I was in the night Camilla tried to drug me, and I look around uneasily, trying to push that memory away.

Arrick glances back as we get to the stair and catches Natasha watching us. He frowns and then smiles before he leads me onwards. He's trying to act like it doesn't matter, but the odd waves of uneasiness that come off him only put my nerves on edge.

He helps me navigate the stair slowly, sliding a hand over my ass and pulling me against him when we get to the bottom, and he leads me across the floor to find a place to dance. He's always been a great dancer and has buddied me over the years, so I look forward to getting in among the bodies already bouncing to the beat. I squeal when he tugs me by the hand into the crowd with a yank and pulls me in to get moving, clearly back to his normal playful self now that he isn't monitoring his behavior from prying eyes.

* * *

Arrick pulls me with him to a nearby row of seats in the corner by the corridor doors. We thought we were going easy on alcohol tonight, but we are probably much drunker than we intended. Caught up in the night and his friends, it's easy to lose track of what you consume until it hits you hard in one fell swoop. I'm feeling beyond tipsy, everything swaying softly, and that ultra-merry, 'I am so drunk' dream quality has me all giggly.

I've danced my legs off with Claire, seen Jenny for all of ten minutes when Nate swept in and dragged her away, and haven't seen her since. I don't doubt it's all kisses and roses, seeing as he picked her up over his shoulder, put a hand on her ass, and took her off in the direction of the private VIP rooms. Neither has come back in hours, so I am going to assume they left together. No doubt I will get a text sometime tomorrow explaining her disappearance and his. Christian sent me a dozen selfies from his little party for two. It seems they are drunk in a hotel and effectively using an empty swimming pool.

I slump down on the seats and lean back, tired and fuzzy, glowing with the warm sensation of alcohol consumption and feeling better down here away from the VIP lounge. We have not strayed back upstairs in almost three hours, and I get the distinct impression he's keeping us away from her, even though he hasn't mentioned her.

I saw him check his cell a couple of times when we were at the bar. I guess she has texted him, and I am trying not to let it get to me. I know he didn't respond to her if it was even her, but I'm a bit pissed that even here, seeing me with him, she still tries to get between us. That I am letting her.

Let it go for one night.

"We should think about heading home soon." Arrick slides in beside me, leaning across me so he can get nose to nose, and angles in for a kiss. Far too appealing with that soft hazy drunk look on him, eyes heavy and lips ripe for smooching.

"Really? Are you tired, Mr. Carrero?" I smile sweetly, rubbing my nose against his as he teases me with an almost kiss, his fingers gently tracing my lips. His eyes are focused on my mouth, and for the last half hour, he hasn't been able to keep his hands off me. Most definitely get the vibe that he's thinking about going home to get naked. I'm on board with that. He has my body tingling with his attentions; gyrating and grinding into me on the dancefloor, fueling me with alcohol, and letting me hang around his neck, making out to slower songs, has me more than eager. I'm completely relaxed, ready to take all my clothes off and climb on top of him.

"Not tired, baby... Crazily horny for you and thinking how good you look out of that dress." He leans in the last millimeters and kisses me seductively. His lips meet mine perfectly, parting and easing his tongue against mine. Cradling my jaw in his hand and pulling my body to him so he can run his free hand up my thigh and under the edge of my dress to cup under my butt. I moan against him as his hot hand warms my skin on the cool seat, edging my body to his so that I mold against him, smiling when his other hand skims my throat and across the curve of my breast teasingly, and he squeezes.

"Get a fucking room!" The nasty bitchy tone makes us snap apart, and Arrick looks over his shoulder to glare at the female voice behind us. It isn't a voice I know, and I'm surprised to see a random girl I vaguely recognize standing beside us. Hands on hips and glaring at me icily. I try to place her face and can't. Tall, slim with jet black hair and soulless grey eyes.

"Back off, Miranda. Go back to wherever you came from and keep out of it!" Arrick snaps, gently holding me close, hand back on my throat, body still caging mine protectively.

"Your heartbroken ex-girlfriend doesn't need you flaunting your hussy in her face. It's fucking cruel, Arrick!" She sneers directly at me, looks me up and down, and snorts before dragging her eyes back to his face.

"Miranda, we stayed down here knowing she would stay up there... What else do you want me to do? We broke up... I moved on with my life. I'm sorry that we socialize in the same circles. I am not trying to hurt her, but I moved on." Arrick stands up and offers me his hand to move, obviously intending to avoid this kind of drama, but Miranda stands her ground. I can tell by his posture that she's getting to him on major levels, but he's trying to ignore her and keep the cool he's famed for.

"It makes me sick watching you, so I can't even imagine what it's like for her. It's fucking incest! Dumping a sweetheart for some trampy little girl who's been trying to break you up for years under the guise of a little sister. What the hell is wrong with you?"

She has a serious attitude when it comes to me, even though I don't even know her; death glare and nasty, vile scowls from behind his back aimed at me with such clear hatred. My temper rises, but I know he won't want me to react. He will want to deal with this and keep things from escalating, so I bite my tongue and try to avoid looking at her. Trying to control that inner demon in me as best as possible by squirming around, taking long, steady breaths, and counting to ten.

"What the fuck? This has nothing to do with you, so how about you back off and go console her instead of starting shit here?" Arrick yells at her, losing his temper faster than I even anticipated, and I blink at him as he turns on her. Seeing, really, the first tell-tale signs that he's a lot drunker than I thought, and that does not bode well for her. All his normal controlled composure is a little flighty when he's like this.

"I'm her best friend, and she's been sobbing all night because you cannot keep your hands off the tramp. What is she, Arrick? All of twelve? You threw away an amazing girl for some little whore, who drops her pants on a whim." She storms forward to face him, so close facially and spitting venom. I glare at her hatefully, so consumed with the urge to yell something back and fight every inch of myself. I sense the shift in his mood, the vibes of aggression building and standing up too. Ready to either take her on or hold him back.

"Stay here. I'll only be a minute." Arrick turns to me snappily, leans into my face, kisses me on the mouth, and then turns, catching the fiery girl's arm, and aggressively drags her with him to a corner across the room. He turns on her and lets her go, and I can tell immediately, even from here, that he's having a major go at her. He looks angry as hell. His mannerisms are that of one very pissed Carrero, and she seems to be yelling back at him stupidly. My insides crumble, and I know this is our worst possible scenario. The last thing we need is his mood to set off while under the influence. I get an almost foreboding heavy pit in my stomach. I sit down again shakily, watching with complete numbness, unsure what to feel about anything she said or the fact that she has him murderous right now.

"Shock! Miranda and drama; funny how it's always hand in hand." Claire sits beside me and nods her way, eyes trained on them in the shadowy corner with no look of surprise. I'm relieved that I'm not sitting alone and smile at her, some little thanks. My stomach is churning, and my hands are shaking at that little scene.

"You know her well?" I ask out of curiosity and watch as Claire, a seasoned party girl, downs her drink in one go.

"So, so. She used to come out occasionally with us when we did couple things. She dated Colin for a while. She's a bit of a poisonous one, and I never got the relationship between her and Tash, to be honest. Chalk and cheese. None of us ever warmed to her, so we were glad when Colin dumped her." Claire throws back her short red hair from her eyes, casting a navy-blue gaze at the woman with complete indifference.

"*She's* her best friend?" I follow and try not to watch as Arrick is seemingly going crazy at her; he doesn't look like him, frowning, scowling, animated in whatever he's saying, and she seems to be pushing all his anger buttons. I recoil internally, a pit of unease at his being drunk and her setting him off, and try not to dwell on it.

"Yeah, probably the reason Tasha is now dressing like a whore and drinking her life into oblivion while trying to make Arry jealous. Sad that she took the unclassy route to break-upsville." Claire twists her glass in her hand and sighs heavily. I turn towards her with a snap of my head and blink. Not sure what she means by that.

"Trying to make him jealous?" I blink again, looking from her, then to Arry across the room; he's still arguing, and then back at

Claire. He hasn't mentioned anything about that, only said she was being mature and talking 'pleasantries.'

"Yeah, you know. Showing up in Miami and trying to get Nate to sleep with her for a reaction. Low blow. She's turned into a fucking mess, and I think it's that one there who's filling her head with this nonsense about making Arry jealous and shit. Natasha was never that girl. I think her dad being sick has sent her over the edge." She shrugs and throws me a supportive grimace but pauses when she catches what I assume is an ashen expression on my face. I'm openly staring at her with a crushed look of complete betrayal.

I feel like someone has punched me in the stomach. I stare back across the room at him and suddenly feel sick that he hasn't told me she was in Miami with him. A thousand things run through my head as tears sting my eyes, and I want to wail physically. That he would even keep this from me, and that day in my apartment, when I felt like he was lying or being evasive.

This is why! He was with her, there, without me! .... And he never said a single thing about it.

Why?

"She went to Miami?" my voice breaks as I stare at him, anger and betrayal ripping across my heart, a deep aching heaviness that hurts so much I can barely breathe and hold my shit together. Tears sting the backs of my eyes as I struggle not to react.

He always swore he would tell me everything, always did tell me everything, and now I am finding out he spent all that time in Miami with her. His ex-girlfriend, who means nothing to him. In all the texts and calls and even when he came home... Never once mentioned it.

"Shit... Sophie ...I thought he would have told you. I'm sorry. Nate mentioned it to Jase, and I assumed you knew." Claire looks distraught and stands up quickly. Suddenly uneasy, looking incredibly guilty and sheepish. "Fuck.... I will go away before I put more foot in my mouth and Arry strangles me. I'm sorry, Sophie." Claire takes off, looking his way, and I realize it's because he's coming back to me; Miranda shouts after him as he waves her away, looking glacial.

I get up, turn away before he sees the tears threatening to spill down my face, and take deep breaths to calm the rage swirling inside me. I am completely devastated and feel like I did back when he chose Natasha over me. I want to lash out at him, shake him. So consumed by devastation and trying so hard not to fall to bits in this club. My whole body shakes, and I am close to lightheaded and passing out.

I feel his hands on my waist and pull away from him instinctively, agony slicing through me as he tries to turn me. His touch burns me painfully.

"Hey... Sophs? What's wrong?" He turns me, but I shrug out of his arms defensively, not wanting his hands on me and refusing to look him in the face. If I let loose, I may self-implode. It's all bubbling up inside of me like a torrent of anger. So much going on inside me, burning explosively, and I shake my head at him, barely containing my outward calm. "Baby? ... What is it? Is it what she said? Because you know that doesn't mean any......." His face, looking so goddamn honest and endearing, makes me snap crazily.

"Why didn't you tell me she came to Miami with you?" I bawl at him, yanking my hand free as he tries to lasso my wrist. Shoving him away when he tries to catch me and feeling only worse when his sudden falling expression and paling pallor tells me it's true.

"I ... Who?... Sophie... I didn't go with her. It's not like that. She showed up in the last two days." Arrick lifts his hands to brush my hair back, and I slap him away, fire coursing through my veins. Hating him with a passion that I never thought I would ever feel again. That face I love so much is the last thing I want near me right now.

"So now you're lying to me? Keeping secrets? After everything? Over her? Do you have any fucking idea what that does to me?" the tears break down my face, and I swipe them away angrily, glaring at him. Hating that he could make me feel this much pain so easily. Again.

"No... I didn't lie. I would have told you eventually .... Just not anytime soon while you're still like this about her. You're overreacting about this." Arrick drops his hands and moves away, equally riled, even though he should be groveling and not acting like an asshole. It sets my teeth on edge, biting down to curb the tidal wave of tears behind the surface.

"Like this? Pissed because your ex-girlfriend came and spent two days with you when I wasn't there?" I spit at him, seeing red, jealousy eating my insides out, and a million stupid things running through my head. I wonder how much time they spent, how far it went, and if he did get jealous when she tried to hook up with Nate. So many insecure stupid little thoughts like a floodgate ripping through my brain. He narrows his brows, taking on that icy distant look of emotionless cool.

"Jealous! ...Over nothing! I barely saw her, Sophie. She showed up... I was busy with interviews and my fight; she got three minutes at most, then Nate fielded her elsewhere and left me to it. I didn't see her alone at all. You're being stupid. I don't need you starting on me too." Arrick lifts his hands and makes an 'arghh' gesture, obviously still bristling from his fight with Miranda, and I'm getting the brunt because *I'm* being 'difficult.

"I'm being stupid? Yet you're the one who hid this from me?" I retort, shoving him in the abdomen because I'm fueled with so much rage towards him it's spewing out in aggression. That inner need to hurt people around me is barely contained, and I am trying so hard, aware of eyes nearby and around us, of strangers in this club seeing a little drunk domestic. Self-preservation makes me unable to react fully.

"I knew this is how you would be, so I never told you... Sue me for not wanting to fight! For knowing how irrational you get when her name is even mentioned." Arrick snaps; his tone has deepened angrily, that furrowed Carrero glare that has him looking fierce and his jaw almost angular with rage. Intimidation at its finest, yet it's lost on me. I am so caught in my own pain that there's nothing but fury.

"You don't think I have a right to feel insecure about her? That I shouldn't trust you when it comes to her because you are clearly incapable of letting her go?" I snap in complete disbelief, tears filling my view and anger searing my heart.

"For fuck sake.... No! Not when I have spent weeks doing

everything I can to make you see that you're who I want; you're who I love. I don't know what else to do.... I can't stand when you get like this." His eyes on mine, deathly dark; in the club's shadows, it's hard to tell the color, but it's obvious he is as angry at me as I am at him. In his stupid fucked up idiot's head, and I can't believe he feels justified in this.

What planet are you from?

"You're an asshole. Sometimes I hate you so much." I push past him to walk away, too angry to stand here with him and bicker while he can't see beyond his own nose, can't see the pain he inflicts on my fragile heart, and he spins too.

"Probably, but you're fucking unbearable sometimes. Fuck this shit. I'm going to get a drink... I'll be at the bar with Nate if you decide to grow up." Arrick storms off, looking like he would easily go twelve rounds with any idiot who got in his way, and disappears into the crowd in the direction of the bar. The tears hit my cheeks, and I turn the other way, fighting myself on this and trying to claw up my wall of numbness that died somewhere in the early days of being his. Heading to find a bathroom, I will myself to stop myself from falling apart.

I won't let him hurt me again, not like this. Especially not over her.

* * *

"Sophie?" Arrick's voice comes up behind me, and his arms slide around my waist. I try to push him off, but he doesn't let me, he turns me instead, and I turn my face away impulsively. I don't want him to touch me or look at me. Still majorly upset and pissed at him, and the last thing I want is for him to give me shit over my jealousy. I feel like I can never believe anything he ever tells me again. I spent an hour on my cell with Christian in a drunken mess, sobbing down the phone while he calmed my hysterics, and he only agreed with me on every front.

Arrick is the fucking dick head in this.

"You're drunk, and I'm taking you home." His tone has

completely changed, but he's still blatantly pissed. He is manhandling me out of a duty of care, but he has no real affection in how he's pulling me. It feels like those nights he showed up out of obligation to rescue me, and I shove him away. Abhorring the touch that is not doing anything for me right now. "Stop acting like this, and come on. I'm done with this bullshit, and I'm leaving. You can come or stay." He tries to bring my face to him, holding my chin as more tears sting my eyes, and I wriggle my arms free to get him off me. Fighting him in every way.

"Leave me alone." I start to cry, but he sighs and clenches his jaw. Gritted teeth and no love in that expression at all, his body is bristling against mine.

"Fine. I'll tell Nathan to bring you home later. I'm out." He lets me go and turns to leave me here, and it hurts like my insides get wrenched free. Crumbling from an angry wall of stubbornness to a wounded, broken child in need of his presence.

"You're just going to leave me here?" I start sobbing and follow him, anger dissipating and desperately pathetic, suddenly scared that he will leave me alone here. I don't want to be left alone. I can't breathe at the thought that he will walk off and leave me here.

"Right now, yes! Because I'm drunk and being the asshole you hate, this will only kick off if we stay together. We don't do well like this, and I can't handle any more shit tonight." Arrick turns and sees me crying openly. I can feel the tears dripping off my face, broken in so many stupid ways, not knowing why I even need him to stay with me, and he falters. Coming back to me, he lifts his hands and starts wiping my face, still closed off but softening a little, losing the edgy ice from his eyes.

"Don't. Look, let's just go... We'll go to bed and deal with the fallout when sober. Neither of us works when we're like this, Sophie. This is turning into the shittiest night ever, and I want it to end." He pulls me into his body and slides his arm around me protectively; even being an asshole, he is still trying to be my good guy, and I waiver a little, even if I am still so heart-achingly mad at him.

So many emotions are ripping through me, and I want to go

home. I sway in his arms, trying to fight him still, wanting his presence but not his touch, exhausted and done. Tears slip freely, so I don't fight him when he guides me to the quiet hall. I want him to make this feel better, to take away the gut-wrenching pain he has caused in my heart, for it to go away. I want so badly to cuddle him, yet I also don't. I'm too drunk, too emotional, and being stupid about this. I need to go home and sleep.

"Let me go. I can walk. I don't need you touching me. I don't want you touching me." I try for one more attempt to get loose from him, but he turns me into him more as I try to get free. He says nothing and keeps me walking until we get out to the corridor, to the cloakroom, to get our jackets. He lets me go as he fishes for our tickets and goes off to collect them, leaving me standing there. It's almost empty out here as it's still early, and few people are leaving. I stay rooted to the spot, wiping my eyes and breathing myself back to calm.

"Toddling off home for some incestual sex to keep your man, are we? Never took him for the perverted type." The bitchy voice makes me glance up to see Miranda carrying coats, heading towards the little frail drunken mess slumped in a corner that I realize is Natasha. She straightens when she sees me and wanders over to her friend, eyes glued on me viciously. Wiping her makeup-smeared face, her eyes passing me to Arrick in the background, she starts to right herself. She is so obvious it's pathetic.

"Look, just go away, okay? I don't know you, and I don't need this. What does it solve? You're not going to make him change his mind. He is with me, and that's how it will stay." I snap, drunkenly swaying on my shoes and wishing he would hurry back and deal with this foul-mouthed bitch. I can only hold my temper so long, and now, how I feel, I might stab her in the face with my shoe. I glare at both, brimming with hostility.

"I trusted you." Natasha sobs at me, giving me an evil look and grabbing her coat from her friend to hold in her arms. Squeezing the life out of it, still acting like the poor innocent victim, except, unlike the night in the bathroom, I no longer care. She followed him to Miami to do God knows what, and she can go fuck herself for all I care. I have zero remorse where she is concerned anymore and see this as a war between two women now. Not about to lay down and let some bitch try and take him from me.

"I'm sorry... What else can I say? We both love him... but he chose me. I'm who he's happy with, and you need to accept it." I lift my hands in defeat, cornered and defensive, so not able to deal with this and already a mess from fighting with him. My skin is prickling, and my anger is barely holding it together. I am trying to be mature and do what he wants me to, even if I hate him.

Be a grown-up, turn the other cheek, be mature, and show everyone you're not a little spoiled kid anymore.

"Did he? Pretty sure he stayed with me.... Then when I couldn't forgive him, he went looking for his second option." Natasha spits cruelly, and I don't know if it's what she says or if the sudden change in her makes me screw up my face in disbelief. Reminding me of her behavior in the bowling alley bathroom. Like a sucker punch of realization that it was not a one-off.

"Who are you? Were you always this person hiding in the depths, huh? ... Some nasty, manipulative bitch that pulled the wool over everyone's eyes? All sweetness and love, yet the claws are certainly coming out now, aren't they?" my body bristles as both girls sneer at me. Miranda looks about ready to spit at me with an expression of utter disgust. Natasha has an air of smug hostility about with her narrowed eyes, and I see it clearly. It's almost always been an act.

"Aww, bless, she thinks she can act like an adult and get into a grown-up argument. Go find your playpen, Button. Leave the big people to sort things out between them." Miranda laughs at me, coming forward aggressively, and some guy saunters in behind her.

"Ready to go?" He slides his hand around Natasha and eyes me up sleazily. His slimy slow crawl up my body makes me instantly hate him. Another perverted asshole with a ticket to make women's skin crawl.

Classy man, you have there, Tasha.

"Whatever. I am above this. Have a nice night." I turn to walk off, trying to do the right thing for once, and lift my chin high and come face to face with Arrick coming in behind me. His eyes are immediately on the group behind me, and he is clearly unhappy. He looks like rage personified.

"What the fuck did you say to her?" He snaps at Miranda. The Carrero glare on full force, and he slides my jacket around me and moves me aside robotically. Putting himself between us as stares her down aggressively. Even I know that sober Arrick would have dismissed this and walked off, leaving the cool side of him to counteract this heated conversation, but drunk Arrick is in confrontational and emotionally charged mode.

"Don't even act surprised that we're all wondering about your Pedo tendencies, Arry, Love... Is she even potty trained?" Miranda laughs coldly, flicking her hair in a sassy way, and throws her eyes at Natasha, who seems to have reverted to coy and feeble in his presence. The little victim doe-eyed act that he's always been a sucker for. I can't believe what I'm seeing right now.

Manipulative little cow.

"Fuck off, Miranda. This is getting seriously old. Do you have no control over your mouthy mate, Tasha?" He throws a glare her way, and Natasha turns on the tears. Whimpering pathetically, and I have the urge to rip her hair off now. I haven't felt this much consuming hatred since I faced my father in a courtroom at sixteen.

"She cares about me way more than you do. At least I know I can count on her to be there for me. Where have you been lately?" She sobs and pushes in against him, placing a hand on his arm that gets me riled up, and I grab it and push it off again. I catch the icy frown Arrick slants my way, and my temper ignites. Biting on my lip to curb the urge to curse him out.

"Don't start with the emotional blackmail. How many guys stay in touch with their ex to ensure they're okay? How many would keep dealing with stuff for you and help you with your dad's hospital bills, huh? I'm trying to care, Natasha, but I'm also trying to live my life with Sophie." He stands his ground, removes her fingers when they return to his arm, and knocks them away. I'm still raging at him, but a smug eyebrow raise hits my face. I seriously want to 'Hah!' at her.

"By pushing me out... Avoiding my calls, ignoring me when I fly hundreds of miles to see you?" She cries, sobs broken by gasps, and a great little act of having an emotional breakdown. My eyes roll, and I push down the one hundred and ninety-nine reasons I should punch her in the throat right now.

"Stop stalking him then... Maybe he would care more if you gave us fucking breathing space. For the love of God!" I snap impulsively, instantly regretting the outburst when I get a cold glare from Arry, still trying to be commander and chief in this little drama. I glare right fucking back.

"Sophie, stay out of this. I'm handling it. Go over there." He points off to one corner bossily and riles my temper. My stubborn side connecting, sadness replaced with that part of me that he knows better than to activate. He should understand better than to be an asshole to me and then think he can tell me what to do.

"Don't fucking tell me to go away. For her." I snap at him angrily, eyes locked on one another in a fierce battle, and neither will back down. I'm losing the tearful side, and all fight is up in here, brimming like a cyclone needing release.

"That's not what I'm doing. I need you to walk away, so everyone can stop being assholes, and we can all go the fuck home." He grinds through clenched teeth, and that brow lowers dangerously. He is so on the edge of an all-out snap, and even I experience a little lull in bravado.

"What's the matter? Worried I may strip naked and try to seduce him the minute your backs turned. Oh, wait. That was you?" Natasha spits at me from her standpoint. Losing the act while his back is turned and forgetting herself for a moment. Hand on her hip, bitchy tone, and bitchier face.

"Go fuck yourself. He clearly wasn't all that in love with you if he ended up with me." I snap right back, pushing past him to face her, but his arm blocks me and wraps his other around my waist. Hauling me in front of him and keeping me tight by the shoulders to control me. Natasha walks sideways to face me, putting herself back in my face, dismissing his presence entirely. I guess it's because she is either really riled or she realizes he isn't all that enamored with pathetic, soft, doe-eyed brunettes. He is choosing to wrap his arm around the sassy, 'I will beat you to death with your own bag,' blonde."

"Maybe he just knows a whore when he sees one." She sneers at me, up and down, like I'm some tramp, yet she's dressed in a cheap hooker dress and stripper heels that look like they came from a Walmart reject bin.

I slap her hard across the face, impulsively; enraged by how close that sneering bitches is to mine, when she leans into me, breathing almost in my face. I yelp when a male hand grasps my wrist over her recoiling body.

"What the fuck you bitch?" In a bizarre couple standoff. The stranger appears behind her, holding her with one arm and my wrist in the other.

Arrick moves in a flash. I don't see it or manage to get my head around what happens, just that I am let loose, and he's on the other side of me in the blink of an eye. My hand released, and he has the guy by the throat, pushing him back into a pillar at speed and looking like he's going to rip his head off. He is in fight mode, body poised to take on an opponent, and has the death grip of a terminator going on.

"Don't ever fucking touch her. Ever! ... No one ever gets to touch her." He snarls, terrifyingly cold, sinister even. He looks scarily dangerous, and even I don't know how to react to this version of him; the guy doesn't know how to respond either and seems limp as Natasha turns into a screaming banshee and hurts my head with her instant wailing.

"Stop it! Stop it! Let him go." She grabs Arry's arm and starts hauling at him, sobbing as Arrick drops him back on his feet and tries to shrug her off. His eyes still piercing the other man's sheepish face as he recoils from the terrifying, crazy guy with an insanely strong arm.

My temper explodes in my chest as she starts hauling him towards her, trying to get him to cuddle her. Pulling his arms and body to her to get him away from the other male and sobbing against him pathetically. Miranda starts fussing over the guy and glaring icily at Arrick.

"Nice, Arrick. Fucking well mature. Love how your little girl makes you behave." Miranda throws his way, hauling the man off to one side to get away, still staring over and muttering viciously. She ushers his shell-shocked face to one side and gives us distance.

"She's poison to you. She's toxic, Arrick. Don't you see how much you're changing? She has you blind to it; come back to me. I still love you and can forgive all of this if you return to me. We can make this work again. I know you still love me too." Natasha is wrapping herself around him, riling me to fever-pitch rage that my jealous, insane side cannot handle. I can't take it anymore. What was numb shock at the fast reflex of his maneuver is now raging fire as I haul her off him by the hair and drag her backward hard, flying to claw her head off.

"Stop touching him. He's not yours anymore." I yell at her, pulling her so fast she stumbles backward into me, and I resort to shoving her away hard. Arry grabs me quickly, disentangling me from her and leaving me with a handful of curly brown hair as she screams, hauling me to him to calm the violent outburst.

I want to pound her into the floor with jealous rage coursing through me. It feels like I have snapped, and every ounce of hurt, heartbreak, and insecurity that has built in me for weeks is pouring out in one massive black release of psychotic behavior.

Inside, deep down, that inner fury child who never quite learned how to control the hell cat inside of her lets loose. I try and rip at her, claw and squirm, kicking out to vent every ounce of rage and hatred at the one thing that has been fucking my head for weeks. I hate her so much I can taste it. Consumed by some inner demon that only sees red and rage and a longing to smash her face.

Arrick starts grappling with my body, trying to catch the limbs that break free and lash out at her, bucking and fighting him harder than I have ever fought anyone in my life.

"Sophie, calm the fuck down. Natasha, NO, I DON'T!!!...Go home! Everyone go the fuck away and let me take my girlfriend home." Arry's trying to haul my fighting body with him, struggling to hold me, breathing heavily in my ear as he tries to lift me from my feet and restrain me. I kick and lash out to reach her, but she keeps sneering at me, making me a thousand times more murderous.

"This is what you want? Some crazy uncontrollable brat, who makes you act the same? .... Really excellent choice, huh? Good luck with having a normal life with her. You downgraded from me, and your life will always be like this if you stay with her." She's lost the air of vulnerability, and it's all becoming clear now. The way she can switch it on and off is like a tap. She *is* manipulative, and I am only just seeing it. Years of pulling the wool over his eyes, getting in his head.

I lash out again, trying so hard to kick at her face, almost getting my leg that high and heels missing her skull by a fraction, but Arrick wraps his arms around my shoulders, pinning my arms down, and lifts me to the side away from her.

He's struggling to control me, sending me off the charts while restraining me. It's one thing I have never been able to handle as I fight him and wriggle, getting increasingly panicked that I can't get loose from his tight hold on my upper body. I turn my efforts on fighting him instead, all rage directed his way. Freaking out at having my arms pinned down, anxiety and black rage consuming me to get free. Flight or fight kicks in, and all my senses know is that I am being held hostage and must escape.

"I made my choice. Now let me live with it. Just go away." Arrick yells at her, and her face crumbles, tears pouring down her cheeks, but he no longer cares; he's too busy trying to reign me in while making me worse. He swears under his breath as I buck and twist, throw myself into him so that he's knocked back a step, but he still doesn't let me go. Ignores my cursing and shouting at him.

"Let me fucking go!" I scream, using my legs to try and push against his to hurt him enough to let my arms loose so that I can stop.

He grips me tighter, almost disabling my breathing ability, and starts maneuvering me to the main doors.

"Sophie, fucking stop it." He jerks me hard, shuddering my mouth to snap shut, and I bite my lip, flinching as pain shoots through my face. It stuns me into a moment of submission that sees him let me go, and I realize there are a few feet between us all now, and Miranda starts waving and clapping her hands in sarcasm from far behind. I turn on him, slap him in the chest, shove, and hit him in shocked frustration as he bats me off and gets pissed at me for the backlash.

"Take her home to bed like a good big brother. Help tuck her into her little cot. Hellish little fucking psycho." Miranda calls out and attracts all my venom away from his defensive maneuvers instead. I pull off my shoe to throw it at her face, but Arrick grabs it and my wrist, twisting it out of my hand and yanking me with him. Taking it from me.

"Go fuck yourself," I scream at her and him. I don't even know anymore. Blinded by my inner thoughts and feelings, tears again pour down my face, and I have no idea when they even started. My chest is caving in, and my heart is aching so much that I think I may die. I'm a sobbing mess of sniffing, tears, and a torrent of verbal curse words.

"For fucks sake. Will you quit it!" He hauls me after him less than gently and ignores my tugging and twisting of his hand to get free. He's dragging me by one arm like a kid taking an epic freak out.

"Let me go," I scream at him, tugging at his harsh, biting grip on my wrist, seeing my skin turn red where he is holding me, and digging my fingernails under his to claw loose.

"Let me fucking go." I try to hop while I reach for my other shoe as a weapon, but he disables that too, taking it from me as soon as I get it in my hand and holds both by the heels away from me. Still pulling me along, I dig bare feet into the ground to try to stop him. Both my hands are held in one of his as he hauls me with him and doesn't even falter. I hate him with so much venom at this moment. I don't want to be with him. I want him to let me go, to leave me alone.

Stop fucking touching me.

As soon as we get outside, he looks down at the sidewalk, then at my feet, turns, and scoops me over his shoulder, igniting a second bout of psycho and fight in me. I throw myself into a second hurricane tornado of violence and try like a feral beast to escape him.

"Sophie, for the first time in my life, I will actually spank you. Will you stop fucking fighting me!" Arrick snaps at me, gripping me so harshly it makes me yelp in fright, and I fall quiet. The threat of being smacked sounds real, like he means it, and I recoil inside my head. It's not being said in kinkiness or jest this time, and I wonder if he would. Silenced by the thought of him hitting me, knowing I should never fear that from him, there's a part of me that does. Memories of what it feels like to be kicked into a corner punched, and repeatedly slapped until your fight and fire die out, and there's nothing left but a sobbing, broken little girl.

He puts up with so much, takes so much from me, and never snaps, but maybe he could, especially after tonight.

He finds a cab fast and practically tosses me in, taking a moment outside on the sidewalk to try and calm himself. So much aggression and fight in that strong body, bristling and simmering behind that set of cool eyes before he gets in. He slides in beside me and moves closer, but I turn and shove him away with my feet and hands. Beyond pissed and needing space, still sobbing brokenly and hating him with every ounce of fire left in me.

He glares at me and grits his teeth but says nothing. Just moves away again and slams the door shut before barking his address at the driver. He lifts a hand to his head, rubs his face in agitation, scrubbing it through his hair, and looks away.

Feeling messed up, hysterical, and stupidly irrational, I shove at him with my foot again. I want a reaction, yet I do not know what kind I need, playing with fire because he has me so messed up in the head. I can't stand the crippling agony, fighting with the all-consuming rage inside of me, and I know I should let this simmer and release some pressure, but I can't help it.

"Do you still love her?" I cry, "Is that why you lied to me?" It's all falling out of my head, an uncensored, gibberish emotional mess, sniffing back tears, wiping the flood from my face, and failing to stop it. He clenches his fists in his lap and snaps around to glare at me.

"Don't be fucking stupid. I didn't lie.... You need to stop this shit. I'm warning you... I don't know how to handle this right now. Just leave me be to cool down and let me alone." He barks at me, glaring angrily, and there is no hint of love in that expression. He looks like a stranger, detached and cold, nothing in that face I even recognize as my Arry.

"Why did you say you made your choice, and now you have to live with it? Didn't sound like someone who is where he wants to be." I sob, taking bits and pieces from my head and trying to make sense of them, aching and messed up with all of this.

"You're remembering it out of context. Look.... Right now, I know I am drunk, and this... US.... we need to leave this alone until tomorrow before it gets a whole lot worse. With you this way and me like this... Just leave it alone. I'm begging you, Sophs. I'll sleep in the spare room, and we won't fucking do this to each other again. No more booze, ever." He pushes my foot away from him harshly, cradling my shoes on his lap, and turns away, his jaw tensing and every muscle twinging in his face as he grits his teeth.

"Fuck you." I bite angrily. Hating his decision to blank me out like I'm worthless. Needing to do something, anything, to alleviate the pressure inside of me that has me on the verge of an all-out explosion.

"No, Sophie. Fuck you! I am sick of trying to convince you that I want you, sick of dealing with this shit. Maybe I should take you home and leave you there instead. It'll be better for us if we spend tonight apart." He snarls at me, pushing my foot away again as I attempt to childishly shove him once more, no clue why I am 'poking the bear'.

"You know what, you're completely right. I should go home, away from you, while you go run after her and make sure she's okay. Run after the girl you obviously still love more than me." I bite sarcastically. Tears dripping onto my naked collarbones and making me shiver. I realize my coat is no longer on him or me. We must have left it wherever it fell; only he is wearing his. I hadn't even noticed in the drama, and I'm left in a strapless dress and nothing else.

"Hey? Can you take a left here, buddy? Change of venue."

Arrick taps the driver, completely ignoring me, giving him my address when he nods, and we turn in the direction of my apartment. Making it clear he meant what he said about being separate tonight.

"Pretty much admitting that's what you're going to do." I slap his shoulder, leaning forward to reach him, and see him tense, but he doesn't react, grits his teeth, and turns to me coolly.

"If that's what that crazy fucked up head of yours tells you I'm going to do, then we should end this here........... Pull over at the building with the red door." Arry leans forwards as my building comes into view quickly, we were only seconds away, and I let loose.

"Don't say that to me... Don't call me that." I barely wait for the car to stop before I yank open the door, blinded by tears and complete heartbreak, and jump out without any awareness of my safety. Dragging ass across the road at speed, even with bare feet on the harsh tarmac, and almost getting hit by a car in the process. The honk of the horn doesn't even phase me. So blinded by rage and sadness, I'm not paying attention.

"Sophie, for fucks sake." Arrick is hot on my heels and pulls me back as a second car narrowly misses me, grabbing me by the arm and then pulling me against his body. Turning me to him with another tug and yanking me the last gap to the sidewalk outside my house. He motions two minutes to the driver across the road, making it clear he has no intention of sticking around.

"I hate you." I lash out at him, but he dodges and shoves my shoes in my chest so that I automatically grip them. He hands me his spare key to my apartment because I never brought any with me tonight, and I sob some more. My insides are turning to chaos, and I can no longer think straight. All I can see is that he's leaving me alone ...again. After everything, all his promises, all he said to me. How many times did he swear he would never do this?

He's doing it again.

"Here. Go to sleep. We're drunk, and I'm not doing this now." He lets me go and makes to move away with a complete lack of anything in his demeanor. The deadpan, emotionless dick head who hurt me so many times before. My lungs can barely inflate, pain in my chest stabbing through me at unbearable levels, and I want to hurt him even an ounce of how he hurts me.

I throw my shoes back at him, getting him in the jaw with one and following with another 'Sophie crazy lash out,' hating him at that moment. I see red and want to wound him as he wounds me. So many scars on this heart at his hands, and I can't take it anymore. Lashing out and aiming slaps at his face in uncontrolled hysterics. It's like some venomous inner psycho possesses me, and I can't control myself.

My hand collides with flesh, stinging my skin, biting on my lip as I put my full fury into an attack. Gasping when he viciously grabs me by the wrists, shoves me back hard, and pins me to the brick wall of my stair, panting and angry in my face. He grips me so tight he hurts me in a way he never has, and I let out a little whimper of fear, gasping at the bite of his grip.

The realization hits me that I finally pushed him this far and start cowering away, regretting the impulsive need in me always to hurt, and now faced with the consequences of doing it. The blood drains as my body runs cold and shocks me to instant silence and surrender, eyes wide as I stare at him in complete terror.

It's like a bulb goes off, and his face drops suddenly. His grip on my wrists instantly loosens, and his body and face lose that terrifying ferociousness in a second of clarity.

"What are we doing? Look at us." He lets go of my wrists and moves away from me, gawping in horror at me, lifting his hands, looking at them as though they are alien to him, and then back at the red fingerprints on my arms, clearly visible in the light. He looks instantly disgusted at himself, and I feel nauseous that I could push him to hurt me, even if it was only in a grip.

I pushed him; I am always pushing him.

"This isn't us... this isn't me." He seems shocked that he could, even if he only restrained me, and I break my heart at the expression on his face. "Maybe she's right? Maybe we are toxic for each other?" He says numbly, mildly shocked, softly to himself, more so than at me, and no longer bristling with anger. He moves further back, and that part of me that tries to shield me from pain finally claws up and rears her bitchy head.

"So, go back to her then. You're perfect little domestic housewife. You clearly had a much easier life with her." I spit through tears and racking breaths, rubbing my wrists to remove the burning feeling of where he hurt me and hating that I'm doing this. Saying what I don't mean, wounding, biting out at him.

"You know what? I did... So much fucking easier than this." He glares at me, no caring whether his words hurt me anymore, with no hint of my Arry left inside. I have pushed him to the brink, and he's looking at me like he could never love me anymore. It rips me apart, so I feel part of me die.

"Then what's stopping you? ... I clearly am not...Go! ... Fucking go!" I sob through panting breaths as anxiety starts to cripple my lungs, but I don't want to show him my weakness. Venom in place of angst scowls in place of sorrow. Self-defensive, protecting myself from the pain he can and will inflict. "Why do you always choose her?" I blurt out almost in afterthought, head a train wreck, and can no longer formulate any logic. He scowls so hard that his eyebrows practically adhere to his lashes.

"Sophie! I always choose YOU. I'm sick of this bullshit over her. How can you even say that to me? All I do is show you that I love you." He growls at me, clenching fists in mid-air, snapping so suddenly that he makes me jump in fright, nervous, edgy, and afraid of his unpredictability.

"Why won't you just cut all ties then?" I sob, pleading, wanting him to give me that one thing and needing it more than ever. It's what I need more than air, no matter how many times I try to fight it, reason with myself, and convince myself that I'm being immature. I will never let this go.

"I've been trying. You know I have. I don't know how else to do it without being a complete asshole... You can't fucking attack people like that. You physically attacked her, Sophie." He scrubs his face with his palms and paces in a circle before coming back to face me, keeping his distance, still looking at me like he wants to throttle me and no longer knows me.

"She deserved it!" I yell in his face, refusing to back down when she's the subject, still hating him for lying to me and keeping secrets. My head chaotic and gripping my hair in complete frustration. He makes me so crazy that I can't think straight, breathe, or stop this consuming aching pain inside me.

"You need help. You're not right in the head." He leans into me, snarling it in my face in a manner that I would never associate with him, venom in every word, and I recoil as though he has slapped me in the face.

"Fuck you... fuck you.... I fucking hate you. How can you even say that to me?" I wail, a return to violent, racking sobbing, and he doesn't seem to care.

"Because you're fucking crazy." He shrugs so coldly, so hatefully. I see red and fly for him, aiming a slap at that smug face that seems to spear me with a glaring scowl. He catches my hand mid-hit, throws it aside, deflecting me with fast reflexes, and looks at me like I am nothing to him. I completely break.

"I don't ever want to see you again. I don't need you. I never fucking needed you. I won't care if you go back to her... I want you to go back to her... GO! FUCKING GO!!!" I turn into a blubbering mass of hysterical sobbing, pushed over the edge with one cruel sentence from him. Killing every single ounce of my heart in one fell swoop and pushing him away with the force of a tsunami.

"I'm leaving anyway. Maybe this was something we should have never started." He shrugs coldly, devoid of every emotion. A stranger before me who turns his back on me and steps off the sidewalk onto the road without a backward glance.

Arrick starts to walk away, and I crumble, my heart dissolving when faced with the reality that this is really over. Panic courses through me, even through the fog of crushing pain and tears.

He's leaving me, for real. Not a fight or a cool down.

He's leaving me; for what I have done, what I said.

My Arry, my heart and soul, my haven, the love of my life. He's had enough, and he's walking away from me. After all, he said he would never do. My heart stops, my anger crashes, and all that is left is that desolate pain of a little girl who always needed him.

"I didn't mean it. Arry? ... I didn't mean it. I'm sorry... I do need you." I sob and gasp, unable to control my breathing as panic hits me hard in the chest. I follow him as he moves across the road, a whimpering pathetic version of myself, reaching out to him. He keeps walking steadily without looking back at me.

"Sometimes walking away is better for everyone. Go inside... I need breathing space. We both do... I need time to think." He sounds cold and detached, yet I still follow him, reaching out, scared that I know he means it, that this isn't just a fight. Fingers catch his jacket as he moves towards the cab. Suddenly back to being childlike and afraid, vulnerable and in pain, and reaching for the one person I need to save me.

He always saved me; I need him to do it now.

"Don't.... Don't leave me alone." I sob, clinging desperately to his clothes. He pushes my hand off with a backward swipe and gets in the awaiting vehicle, closing the door and turning away, so he doesn't even look at me. He taps the driver and keeps his eyes and face turned forward, blocking me out, even when I place my palm so desperately on his window and let the tears fall faster and harder. Struggling to breathe.

The car pulls away, leaving me standing in the street sobbing and alone. Watching it fade into the distance with the most all-consuming, breath winding pain, destroying what is left of my sanity. I throw my bag after the car and then sit down on the sidewalk like a hopeless mess, trying to pull myself together before the panic attack makes me fully blackout.

Chapter 27

I pick up my bag and wander across the street to collect my shoes, looking up at my apartment with cold emptiness. I'm numb, my feet ache, and tears stream down my face. I wander slowly into the building, letting myself in and getting up to my floor via the stairs. It's deathly silent, around two am or thereabouts, and I try not to make too much noise that will disturb my neighbors.

I only sat on the cold sidewalk for a minute or so before self-preservation kicked in. My numbness made me move and walk inside. I can't stop sobbing, but I feel dead inside. I don't think I can handle this pain if I sit and ponder it, so I have decided to walk anywhere, anyplace, until my legs fall off so that I do not sit here and cry over his leaving me.

Again.

When I get into my apartment, I throw my bag, coat, and shoes aside, find sneakers and a hoody, pull them over the top of my dress, tuck my hair behind my ears, and head back out. I don't want to be here surrounded by everything that reminds me of him.

The unicorns he bought me are lying everywhere. The memories of every part of this place he has inhabited or touched, or even that one of his jerseys, are hanging on the handle of my bedroom door.

I pull my phone from my bag and turn it onto silent mode, not that he'll call, but it's part of how I'm feeling. I ponder leaving it behind, but he has ingrained into every aspect of me for so long that I should always have it with me in case I need help, and I take it, despite myself.

I don't want pings from my social media or anything to infiltrate my head right now. I want to walk and cry myself out, so I will come back and sleep and try to forget all of this. I don't know what I will say to him when I see him again if he ever sees me again. I don't know if this was a fight or a breakup anymore; it's all such a mess in my head, and I can't think straight.

He seemed like he was emotionally and physically closing the door on me. I'm not sure how I come back from that anymore, especially when I don't know if I can ever trust him the way I want to. Knowing she was in Miami has hurt me irreversibly.

He left me again. I'm so heartbroken and mad, and yet empty.

I know I overreacted and acted crazy. Jealousy and insecurity were spiked. Knowing he fueled it by keeping the fact she came to Miami from me. It still hurt to think he would do that, how he couldn't understand why this would upset me.

I have every reason to feel insecure when it comes to Natasha. He has no clue what it's like to feel this way or how much it screws you up inside. I know I just acted like an idiot, and more so when that stupid bitch Miranda started on me. But he has to see his blame in the final eruption of everything I have been holding inside of me.

I'm done with drinking; I always make an idiot of myself and get way too emotionally volatile. It's great until something sparks us off, and then we are completely wrong for each other. We can go either way; either lust-crazed, all over each other, crazily in love, or at each other's throats and hurting one another stupidly.

I get outside and make my way down the steps. Tears making my face ache, and my head hurt. I want to get myself together and not feel anything; maybe if I sober up, I can calm the chaos, and right now, I just want to walk. The streets will be quiet now, and the air will do me good and help the alcohol work out of my system for a while.

* * *

It's been an hour or two. I'm not sure anymore; the sky has lost the darkness, and we are moving into dull grey light. I'm freezing. My nose is numb. My legs are like Jell-O from my walking in the last few hours. Shivering, I decide I should head back to my apartment to heat up and maybe think about what I will do if this is really it for us. It must be nearing four or perhaps even five am, and it's dumb for me to keep walking the streets all night like some sad homeless nomad.

I pull out my phone from the pocket of my hoody to check the time as I walk the street. Signs of life start around me as the garbage trucks and traffic get a little more frequent, and people start milling around with early morning chores. I skip over someone sweeping out a shop door and swipe my screen.

My heart lurches when I see seventeen missed calls from Arrick, ten texts too, even voicemails, which he never leaves. My stomach lurches with sudden butterflies of fear. I stare at my phone, unable to contemplate even reading them or calling him back while I'm still a mess and my hands are numb, yet I don't know what to do.

If he's calling to end things properly and give me all the reasons we are not working, then I don't know if he would try this hard. Maybe he's calling to have a go and fight some more, chew me out on exactly how I behaved, now that he is soberer and knows I will be too. My hands tremble, and I stare numbly at his name in duplicate on the row of missed calls, so broken up inside.

I'm only a few blocks from home where I can face calling him back and have somewhere to sit down if this is truly bad. It's not like him to try calling me so many times when I don't answer, especially if he assumes I'm in bed asleep, so it can only be awful, possibly telling me all the reasons he wants to be free of me. I wonder if he would properly break up with me over a phone call and shake it out of my head. Afraid to think about this in case it starts another wave of tears.

I turn a corner and walk into a girl looking down at her feet with a hood pulled over her head, dressed in black and obviously homeless. She walks right into me, even though I try to dodge her, with an 'ooft' and then skips out of the way with a mumble. I slide my phone back into the pocket of my hoody protectively. It's not uncommon to be mugged in this city. She looks like a street kid, a little unkempt and possibly dodgy.

"Sorry, I didn't see you." I turn and glare back at her as she keeps walking at speed and doesn't look around. The strong English accent from under the black hood is crazily familiar.

"Camilla?" I call out impulsively, the head of the hood spinning as the face, which I haven't seen since that night in the club, turns my way in surprise. Wide-eyed and free of makeup, Camilla looks like a lost child and stares in open-mouthed panic.

"Sophie!" Her pallor loses its little color, and I stalk towards her, seeing nothing but rage and anger bubbling up from somewhere deep, and after a night like mine, she gets the brunt of my turmoil. I punch her square in the face without a single ounce of thought.

Arry would be proud of the perfectly poised and formed knuckle duster I deliver, just as he taught me. Sending her reeling on her ass across the path, her hood knocking back to reveal that bright red messy hair that stands out like a beacon. She grabs her face, blood instantly running from her nose, and then begin shaking my hand manically as pain sears through it with an alarming speed.

Hurts like a mother fucker. How the hell can he punch men and not react?

I think I may have broken every one of my knuckles and maybe my thumb as a stinging, dull ache spreads over them alarmingly and knocks the fight out of my sails. I clutch my hand to my chest in agony and yet still feel a little satisfied with the sloppy mess on the sidewalk

"You bitch. I think you broke my nose." Camilla tries to yell, but it's muffled by her hands and the fact she has red liquid running down her face. I feel strangely better at my little release at finally getting to hit someone, even if that does make me a shithead.

She deserves worse.

"I think we are pretty fucking even! That's for trying to drug me and leaving me to be raped by some power-mad fuckwit. You're lucky I don't stomp on your head." I snap at her and shove her with my foot to goad her to get up and face me. Arrick always told me I should fight fair, and if this bitch wants to get up and go, I am so in the mood to have a girly punch-up. I've enough anger to expel, and she has earned my wrath.

"You're fucking crazy... What the hell is wrong with you?" Camilla scrambles to her knees and starts crawling away like a coward, unable to face me, and I roll my eyes. She's using her sleeve to rub the mess from her face and smearing blood across her cheek.

"Get up! I'm not going to touch you if you're going to act like a fucking girl and be this pathetic." I follow her and watch in irritation as she uses a lamp post to get to her feet and scowls my way.

"Go ahead... Save someone else the bother." She bites back as tears stream down her face, and I frown at her angrily.

"What? Are you trying to make me feel sorry for you? You have a fucking nerve, Cam... After what you did? I hope you rot in hell." I turn to walk away, tossing my hood up and still nursing my hand. It's burning like hell and already starting to bruise, and I could use some ice. It's another reason I'm happy to walk off and not hit her again. Arry must have hands like steel if this doesn't bother him. I seriously need a medic. I think the pain in my hand is enough reason for another bout of tears.

"I'm as good as dead, Sophs.... If they find me, then I'm history." Her pathetic voice follows me, and I can't help myself from turning. Despite hating her, my curious side gets the better of me. That desperation in her voice claws at my gut, the weakness of my non-asshole side.

"What the hell are you talking about?" I glare at her, trying not to care, but she seems so desperate that, for a moment, I waiver in my rage for her.

"Drug dealers. Criminals... I don't mean low-key street pushers; I mean the big-time, Sophie. Mafia-type men who think nothing of slitting your throat for not paying up." She starts to cry, pathetic little silent tears rolling down her face, and I'm torn between keeping on going, forgetting I ever saw her, and turning back to her. It's clear she wants someone to listen, and I'm sorry she picked probably the only girl in the city who doesn't care about her anymore.

I'm so beyond not caring.

"Why? What did you do? Don't think for a minute this makes me forget what you tried to do to me... You tried to get me raped, Camilla... You left me to be raped... Is that what you do? Let men rape and abuse girls like me?" I yell at her, stomping back, despite my inner protests, and face her now she is back on her feet. So much anger still bristling inside me, and I need to know why? Why she would do that to me?

"No.... You were .... Revenge... I told you I was a bitch when I was pissed. You left me high and dry, and I was angry at you. It cost me dearly for that apartment, meeting you in the city... All the time I invested in you. The other girls do it willingly, for drugs, and the men pay to have a good time with girls who are a little more class than street pushers." She sniffs, wipes her face on her sleeve, and lets go of the mess. Sadly, it's not as bad as it looked, just a bloody nose and a little redness, and I doubt it's even broken. I'm disappointed in myself that I couldn't even inflict a broken bone on her.

"I recognized one of them. Her family has money. Why would she need to offer sex for drugs?" I ask drily, hardly convinced that her little story is legit and she's not playing me for sympathy.

"Not everyone's parents keep supporting them when they become a problem... You're one of the lucky ones. The girls get hooked on my product, and when mummy and daddy stop paying, they become one of my party girls. Sex on tap for wealthy men who get to do whatever they want to them. Lucrative little business deal until I took on the wrong girl." Camilla cries some more, then wipes the tears away coolly, that strength I know returning and pulling herself up a little straighter. At this moment, I still hate her, and I can't seem to move. Staring at the way she self-composes but still looks utterly hopeless.

"Someone fucked you over?" I raise my brows in a very non-surprised way with a deadpan tone.

"Left me high and dry, took my product and money, and

screwed me over. Left me unable to pay my debts or fuel my girls."
She's completely desolate, as though this is the worst thing to
happen in her entire life, but I feel nothing for her. I don't know if
it's the emptiness because of what's happened with Arry or what she
did to me, but I struggle to feel even an ounce of warmth.

"Karma, Camilla.... I have no sympathy for you." I sneer at her,
satisfied that someone got what they deserved for once.

"They will kill me if they find me. I'm getting out of the city, out
of the state. Going anywhere, they can't find me. I owe them too
much money, and they don't like lame excuses." She's rambling at
me. I'm probably the first human contact since she went into hiding;
by the looks of her, it's been a rough few days. Her clothes are
grubby, not her usual classy style.

"What happened to your parents? Was that all a lie? Was there
ever a rich family and a house in the Hamptons?" I watch her
warily, trying to piece this all together. My head going back to
before, and everything I thought I knew about her.

"No....... I'm a runaway from London whose smackhead mother
used to pimp out to dirty drug dealers to keep her in heroin. I was
hustling street corners from the age of twelve to keep her in supply...
I ran away as soon as I saved enough, and well... here I am." She
raises her brows with a sarcastic smile that screams, 'broken little
girl' for a moment, that tug of empathy gets me low in the gut. One
tiny little hint of someone I can maybe understand a little, looking at
her and wondering how much of her cold heart was created by scars
from a childhood she didn't deserve.

"We're not that different, you and I, but I would never use
people as you do. Even if I did end up homeless on the streets
instead of with my family." I pull back the sympathy. Despite a little
deeper insight into why she is the cold bitch she is, I still hate her
too much to care. Just can't forget what she tried to inflict on me as
payback.

"Well, good for you! Some of us must survive in any way we
can. We don't all have a rich family to sweep us off to happy ever
after. Some of us are dirt poor and left to run again, even after
everything we try to build for ourselves." She lets out another sob.

Feeling sorry for herself is wholly unattractive on that normally beautiful face.

"Building a life based on the suffering and abuse of others is not an admirable success... You deserve this. I've no sympathy for you having to run." Girls like us don't continue the circle of abuse. We learn to rise above it and help others... But Camilla is another type of beast who uses her pain to close her heart off to other girls and does to them what was done to her. She has more issues than I do, and her trauma runs deeper than I allowed mine to.

"Easy to say when mummy and daddy keep you in a lifestyle, right? Fuck off, Sophie. You have no idea what it's like to be scared and hungry and running for your life." She scowls at me and moves to walk off, dismissing me with a cold glare.

"What the hell would you know? I've been all of those things and more. They adopted me at fourteen. I was a runaway, living on the street, fending for myself, and hiding from someone who raped and beat me daily since before I can ever remember it starting. Don't fucking tell me what I don't understand or can never empathize with. My father made me run for my life; either he would end up killing me, or I would end up killing him." I snap at her viciously, choking on the raspiness of my voice, full venom on show and no hint of weakness anymore when talking about that scum bag. My scars concerning him are toughened now, not open gaping wounds, and it doesn't hurt to say this out loud.

Camilla stares at me in open-mouthed astonishment. The penny is finally dropping as to why I am how I am. She sees in me what I saw in her. Some kindred, who maybe in another lifetime, could have been real friends.

"I'm sorry... I never knew." She backtracks pathetically, stunned by what I said and momentarily at a loss for words. A tiny hint at the human within her before she closes it back up and snaps the ice queen back in place.

"Like it would have made any difference to you... Just go away. I'm done here." This is going nowhere, and I don't want to be involved with her problems or the mess she's made. I truly think she has made her bed and needs to lie in it. If only to save so many girls from what she does to them.

I turn to walk away from her, throwing back a nasty glare, a parting goodbye in a way, seeing her turning to walk off too. The end of the fake friendship we never had, and I walk into a tall figure who has come up behind me. I smack into a hard, tall body blocking my path and recoil with an 'ouch.' Making to apologize when he cuts in first with a dangerous tone that halts the breath in my lungs.

"Going somewhere?" He snarls at me, grabbing my arm with an odd accent as I try to back away; I turn in panic towards Camilla, a million things racing through my head in that split second. Thinking the bitch has somehow set me up again, but she's being manhandled by two more men, dragging her into the alley nearby, kicking and fighting hard, and I realize this isn't her...This is what she is running from.

My heart leaps into my throat, blood draining from my face, and I impulsively make a run for it, instinct telling me to get the hell away from this. He hauls me back effortlessly, as though I am nothing more than a piece of paper, and cruelly wraps arms around my upper body.

I try to struggle, turning and twisting to break free and aim a kick at his shin with my full fury and strength, but he's too strong and fast, grabbing me around the face and waist to get more control and hauling me after the two men in the ally. Lifting me off my feet so I can only kick my legs out and try and buck in his arms. He squeezes me tighter and almost breaks my ribs, suffocating me with the palm pressed to my mouth so I can't even yell out or bite.

My heart is beating fast, my face aching with the force I am being smothered, as we are trundled into a black car parked in the shadows, and I realize they must have seen her and come around behind us to park here. All the while we were standing arguing, the men she was hiding from had spotted her and that tell-tale bright red hair. This is my fault.

Shit!

I'm thrown into the car's back seat as Camilla is thrown on top of me, a man caging us at each side as a hand comes to my throat to pin me back against the seat and keep me still. I automatically freeze, knowing that fighting here is futile and these men think nothing of putting a bullet in your head or a knife across your throat. I don't have to know who these people are to understand the danger I'm in. Obedience is what they are going to get. Sense tells me to stop fighting.

"Well, well, Camilla, my love." The heavy English accent, so like Camilla's, comes from the front, a husky male tone, as a man in the passenger seat turns to face us. He's wearing black shades, a stubbled middle-aged face, dark shaggy hair that's semi-groomed, and an expensive leather jacket. "We've been looking for you, Love." He smiles at her, and it's completely sinister, a crooked, evil smile that does not bid well for either of us. He has an air about him that he is a guy you do not piss off.

"Tyler. I haven't been hiding. I've been trying to get your money." Camilla's turned white as a sheet, with a wobbling voice and clearly terrified. Losing all her poise and mannerisms as her accent gets a little shaky, dropping its upper-class edge and sounding less refined. I stay painfully still, regulating my breathing so that I don't fall into a panic attack, and try to keep my head. Everything inside of me is poised in fear; all I can keep thinking about is how much I need Arry right now.

"Bull shit, don't you think we know you've been giving us the runaround? We've been watching the bus and train depot for days. Actually, we were on the way there to check early-hour departures." He smirks as though there's something funny about that and keeps those shades trained on her. I can feel the eyes of the man beside me, watching my every breath. The one holding my throat tight and doing a visual sweep of my legs under my dress. Sickness and fear sweep through me, yet I stay completely still, knowing that if this goes the wrong way, I may be subjected to my past all over again, and I can't fall to pieces.

"I need more time. I'm trying to get the money. I've had bad luck; I need more time." Camilla's sobbing, her face bruising where it looks like one of them has slapped her, and blood pouring from her nose still where I hit her. Complete numbness overtakes me, that old me, climbing into the depths of my head, where I know I can endure so much. Scared and terrified, this weird sense of calm has come over me, dampening it all, and I'm already trying to look for ways to get out of here, to escape. My eyes skim every door and person around me for a possible maneuver. I don't care if they keep her, she deserves whatever happens to her, but I will not stay here to be abused or murdered because of her.

"I've been patient. It's been a week since you checked in, a week past the payment date, and we've not heard a fucking thing from you. Imagine my surprise to be driving along the street, and there you two were. Having yourselves a little girl brawl. What's up, Honey...She holding out on you too?" He looks in my direction, and I scowl back, inner fire spiking at being goaded and berating myself for a stupid reaction.

"Please, Tyler...I can get it, I swear. I just need a few more days." Camilla continues with more tears and pleading, yet somehow it all sounds like a well-practiced act. I glimpse her way, and I can tell they're crocodile tears.

"Really? Can't seem to get it in the past weeks, yet suddenly you can get it in two days... From fucking where, Cam? It's fifty grand!" He laughs sardonically, and so do the men around us like this is some joke, and they cruelly want to drag this out and are deriving pleasure from it. My stomach drops when I realize this has become as much my problem as hers, and I only have a way out if she does too.

"From me... From my money. That's where we were going, to get money from my family." I blurt out, my heart racing and tears blinding my eyes. Knowing that if there's any hope, then it comes from the fact I can have them paid off. Fifty grand isn't an outrageous amount for my family.

"Really? And you have that kind of cash, do you, princess?" He looks at me dubiously, sarcasm in his tone as he takes in the sneakers, the party dress that's now dirty from sitting on the road, and the grey hoody which belongs to Arry. I guess my face is a mess of tear-stained makeup, and my hair has probably seen better days after my hood got tugged down in the struggle. I think I probably look a little homeless, much like Camilla's 'on the run' get-up, despite this dress being couture and costing more than every outfit here.

"No, but my family does. I need to make a call. It's pocket change to them." I strain against the biting grip on my neck as he regards me silently for a long agonizing moment. My heart is pounding in my rib cage so hard I can feel the pulse in every part of my body.

"One call, and you can get fifty grand here?" He's sneering at me and raises eyebrows at the driver, who seems to chuckle; so far, he has never turned our way, but I see his eyes in the rear-view, trained on me. Camilla whimpers something about Huntsbergers, and he strains to hear.

"What did you say?" He barks at her.

"Her family are rich...... Huntsbergers.... They're billionaires in the Hamptons." She blurts desperately, her eyes on him pleadingly. I wonder if she knew that before she conveniently met me in the hair salon that day. Made a play for me in every way.

"Why didn't you say so, sweetheart? Didn't realize we were sitting with a little pot of gold here. Hampton's royalty!" He laughs dryly, again his flanking men and the driver chuckle too, enjoying this sarcastic power trip a little too much. I can barely catch my breath, but I'm keeping my cool, trying to keep my head together. My body is tingling with adrenalin now the initial shock has worn off, and I'm thinking through all the possible ways we can get out of this. Who I should call if he lets me? My heart already knows.

"Take her out to play while I talk to blondie here, don't mess her up too much. She might be of use after we get paid." He nods again, and Camilla begins screaming as she is dragged backward out of the car by the hair and throat, taken out of sight to the rear when the door is shut on us again. Her voice is muffled with a cruel hand, and I shudder. Panic spiking, so I grip my hands together to curb it.

It's almost like a reminder that this will not end well if I can't get one of them to transfer or throw so much money at these people that will satisfy them. Head screaming with the doubts that I can even pull this off. I don't have that much in my own account unless

I let my allowance build up. I don't have time for that. I'm scared that he won't be there for me, won't do this for me, and I have many doubts about what I still mean to him.

"Please, don't hurt her. I'll get your money. Please, I just need my cell." The biting grip on my throat tightens, and I can barely swallow or breathe. Holding still as a statue in fear and knowing it's not wise to make this worse.

"Phone?" Commanding in an icy cold. He barks at the man holding me.

"In my front pocket." My hands have been motionless by my side, and as I go fishing for it but the man yanks it out instead, skimming my stomach as he does so with careless hands that make me recoil. My body shudders at the touch. Coiled and afraid, tense.

"So, who are we calling, Darlin? Better not be someone who is too quick to call the feds, or else they won't find their sweet little princess intact again." He warns, his shades focused on me so I can see myself in their darkness. Seeing me, my reflection, and I look awful.

"Arry, he's listed as Arry. He'll get the money. I know he will." I tremble, rushing out his name with a shaking voice and knowing he will come through for me despite everything tonight. He has too. When I truly need him, he never lets me down and has access to billions of dollars if he needs them.

If you still care? Please, please. Help me.

He takes my phone, swipes at my screen, eyes flicking to the first screen, and grins.

"Oooh, you had a little lover tiff. Seems like he's been trying to get hold of you for a while. How many calls does a guy need to make before he gets the hint?" He turns the phone to the man beside me to show him the list of missed calls and texts, Arrick's face in the background. Both laugh, and then he sneers as he turns it back to hit call, putting it to his ear to listen to it ring before he pulls it away. He holds it out to me, the hand around my throat loosens but doesn't move away, and I keep my eyes trained on the shades, motionless as they point at my face.

"Any talk of police and your sweet little neck will be slit, Honey.

Make sure you remember that." He turns on the speakerphone and holds it in front of my mouth. I nod calmly as it rings and pray he's there, pray to God that he will be on the other end. That he's not asleep or left his phone in the lounge and gone to bed like he normally does. Every part of me willing him to know that I am not okay right now. My heart is in my mouth, and nausea sweeps through me as cold fear drifts up my legs.

"Sophs?" He answers in only two rings, relief sweeping through me at the sound of the only voice that matters to me. He sounds wide awake too, considering it is still before six am; he's husky and stressed, and I wonder if it's because of me. Tears hit me as soon as I hear him, and I want him here so badly, to be with me, protect me, and save me.

"Arry." I sniff, so glad to talk to him at this moment, overcome with emotion suddenly and aching for him to come to get me. I don't want this to be the last time I ever hear that voice again.

"Where are you? I've been looking for you for hours... I'm at your apartment, Sophs. Baby, come home. I'm here. I came back for you not long after I left... I'm sorry for what I said, how I was. You just need to......." He sounds broken, torn, and ravaged, much like the version who dragged me to his mother's garden at Leila's party, and my heart crumbles. Picturing him as emotional and upset, and I want to hold him. I love him still, even when he makes me hate him.

"Arry, I need your help." I cut him off, trying hard to sound normal, but my voice shakes so badly I can't control it. Ignoring what he's saying, even though it makes me ache, in a bid to get him to listen to me as eyes bore into me. Aware of the faces trained on me and what I need to do.

"What do you mean? Where are you? What's wrong?" His tone is alert suddenly, that hint of concern shining through now that he realizes there's something more important than making up. He can hear my fear and knows that something isn't right.

I love you so much.

"Arry, please, listen. You need to listen to me." Taking short breaths as panic sets in, the sudden thought that maybe I'm asking too much, and he can't do this. I know getting your hands on that amount of money at short notice is difficult. It's not even daytime. I have no idea how he's going to do this.

"I'm listening, baby. Talk to me. Tell me what you need." He sounds calm suddenly, the fighter in him taking control and seemingly completely cool. I know him better now. This is Arry trying to disconnect emotionally, so he can handle whatever it is. His sixth sense tells him this is serious.

He does that. When he can't deal with stuff, he cuts off and handles it with the part of his head that doesn't feel as much.

"I'm in trouble, and I need money." I blurt out, but the sleazy boss slides off his shades to reveal deep brown eyes and eye-rolls. Turning the phone to himself, he kills speakerphone and puts it to his ear instead, winking at me nastily. Obviously too impatient.

"Listen, buddy, as sweet as all that was getting. I haven't got time to beat around the bush. You sound like a smart guy, and I'm guessing this little bundle of blonde pussy is your woman. She needs fifty grand here within the next four hours, or I will start posting pieces of that sweet ass to your address. I suggest you don't dawdle, Love, and call us back when you have the cash in hand. Don't think about getting fly and involving the boys in blue, cos I will put a bullet in her fucking head." He smiles at me as I hear the low mumble of a deep voice at the other end, my heart aching for Arrick to be here. Hating that he'll be melting down at what dickhead has just said to him. Knowing how this must be affecting and picturing him going into freak-out mode as soon as he hangs up.

"Don't worry, Love. If your boyfriend comes through with the cash, you won't join her back there. She's learning a good lesson. Never fuck over your supplier." The overly muscular slime ball, gripping me, chuckles in my ear as the brown leather jacket still talks to Arrick. I glare at him, still aware that there's a lot of noise coming from far behind that sounds like she is getting a going over, and even I feel for her at this moment. I try to ignore it, not to picture what it feels like and hope she's as tough as she seems.

"Fine by me, Mr. Arry, we shall rendezvous as soon as it's in your hands." Slime ball sounds cheerful, smug even. I zone back into what the smarmy prick is saying to my boy and frown at his over-familiar use of a name he isn't allowed to utter.

"Carrero." I correct impulsively, having no idea why I even feel the need; it's ridiculous, given the circumstances, and I see the immediate change in his face, like a little tiny flicker of the penny dropping.

"Carrero?" He pauses, that smirking sleazy tone dropping with the phone still attached to his ear and the flicker of eyes to the man sitting close to me as though questioning him for confirmation. I can make out Arrick's tone on the other end. He must be confirming his name, as the blood visibly drains from the boss man's face.

He motions for the man holding me to let go suddenly, waving his hand anxiously and not so smug anymore. I don't understand; as soon as he releases me, my hand automatically goes to my throat to rub away the traces of his fingers where they have been, and I pull my arms around myself protectively.

Boss sleaze turns and gets out of the car, clicking his fingers, and the asshole holding me follows. Leaving me alone with only the driver, I watch as they stalk off to the side and huddle with another man in a suit. Still holding my phone to his ear. Looking from man to man and then motioning toward the back of the car.

Moments later, Camilla is tossed in beside me, her face more of a bloody mess and completely disheveled. She has taken a beating, and I immediately try and help her clean the blood off her face, but she pushes me away. Like me, she abhors touch when she's in that defensive mode inside her head, and I leave her be, understanding her at that moment. Feeling sympathy for what they have done to her, but knowing weakness will not do either of us any good.

I turn and watch the men outside instead and realize something has changed. None of them seem so smug anymore, and my phone has been handed off to someone else while the brown jacket is on his own cell, pacing like a maniac. I watch the man talking to Arry and see him finally hang up, looking sheepish, and he nods at the other man. He hands my cell to brown jacket and then looks at the other men gathering around with a worried expression. Huddling together and looking so desperate.

"Somethings wrong," I say impulsively, and Camilla looks up, following my gaze and staring at them outside. The driver shifts in his seat, and I immediately home in on him

"Why does the name Carrero suddenly change everything? I blink at him innocently and catch his narrowed gaze back at me in the mirror. The frown and then glare, and yet he remains silent.

"Carrero? As in Alexi Carrero?" Camilla turns my way with a gulp, pulling my arm and attention to her. Her face ashen as though I've said something awful. I'm completely confused.

"Arrick's cousin? What has Lex got to do with any of this? How do you even know who he is?" I feel surreal, unsure of what is happening, like I'm in the twilight zone. Losing all sense of anything else while confusion reigns dominant. I have known Alexi as long as Arry, nothing sinister or terrifying. I don't get the connection at all.

"Wait, you're related to the Carreros?" Camilla seems equally shocked, and I shake my head. Watching her completely awed expression and trying to get my head around why this even matters.

"Arrick Carrero is my boyfriend. I grew up across the road from Jake and Arrick. I'm part of their family, and Jake Carrero is my godfather. What has any of this, or Alexi, got to do with anything?" I frown at her, turning my body to her. My eyes are now on her for answers as she seems to know more than I do.

"Alexi Carrero is like the kingpin of New York... These goons are small fish compared to him and his family. Everyone knows them. If you're a Carrero or mean something to them, then Tyler majorly fucked up. You're talking about small-time crooks pissing off the mafia." Camilla wipes her face, straightens herself a little, and leans forward to the driver with an air of menace, narrowing her swollen eyes at him in his mirror. "Isn't that right? You are all fucked when Alexi finds out you manhandled Arrick Carrero's girlfriend and threatened her." She has her sassy tone back, obviously finding something to be smug about, despite our predicament, and I can't even get my head around this.

I mean, I always knew there were rumors that some of Arry's family were into organized crime, and there has always been some dodgy evasion from Arry about his dad whenever the topic is raised.

I never for a minute thought Alexi would be involved in this kind of shit. He is so normal and loving, and I've spent a million family dinners and barbecues with him. He's like the rest of them. Charming, suave, okay, maybe more of a loner and a bit standoffish and cool compared to his cousins, but with a lot of good genes and a wild playboy side. I know him well enough to see that he has a good heart underneath.

Or so I always thought.

The driver remains silent, but his whole body seems stiffer, eyeing us and remaining impassive as he can. The men outside are all on cell phones and murmuring among one another, and I wonder why they aren't letting us go.

"If they are so afraid of Alexi, why aren't they opening the door and letting us walk away?" I stare at her in complete angst, so wanting to be done with this now and anxiety rising that this goes so much deeper than I thought it would. If Alexi finds out, all the Carreros will become involved, and I have no idea how this will play out. The family is huge. I'm in so much shit from them after this; Giovanni will spank me for getting caught in this kind of danger.

"You're kidding, right? They called your boyfriend and threatened you, making it clear they have you. They know how fucked they are, and the only way to make it right is to deal with this face-on. I bet they have Alexi on the phone right now... groveling like bitches and trying to retract anything they said to your boyfriend." Camilla is finding leverage in this situation, and despite the mess of her face, she is trying to sort her clothes and hair. She has swelling eyes and is clearly worse for the wear, yet her inner fire is still there. She has found her way out, and the realization has her brimming with confidence.

"So, they just keep us? Until when?" My head is racing on how crazy Arry will be going, how panicked and scared he must be, thinking that something awful is happening to me. The thought of him knowing I'm here keeps me calm, knowing he's probably on the phone with Giovanni and Jake right now, and probably Alexi too... Trying everything in his power to get me back. I know he'll make sure I'm okay, whether he wants to be with me anymore or not.

He will always take care of me. I know he will.

"They will have to arrange a proper handover... Take whatever punishment they have coming. If they dump us and run, they will be hunted down like dogs. There's a code you don't break, and I think they've just broken it." Camilla slides down in the seat and holds her ribs, laying her head back to try and breathe and sniffing through her bloodied, swollen nose. I watch at her for a moment, then sit back too and try to reign in the craziness of my head, try not to count the minutes. We all fall into silence as I watch the panicked scrambling of the men outside. Not sure what else to do but sit here and wait. A part of me knows I am no longer in danger, that his name alone is enough to protect me when he's not here.

I jump when the car door is opened, and another suited man gets in, sitting in front and doesn't even look this way. Another suited thug with a skinhead and a whole neck of tattoos peeking out of a tailored black suit. Hugely intimidating and adding another layer of fear to my already thin nerves and shaking hands.

"We've got to go to the club with them and wait for further instruction." He mumbles to the driver, and I glance at Camilla in sheer panic. Somehow knowing we are being moved and taken elsewhere seems to set my fear back on edge. Heart racing, blood running cold, and the unknown looming ahead of us.

I was starting to calm down, becoming sure that the name alone would keep me safe. Yet somehow, knowing they intend to take us somewhere else for God knows how long terrifies me. I thought this would be over by now, yet it feels like it's only beginning. Moving us, taking us somewhere else, it seems far more sinister and real suddenly, and I can't contain the nerves hitting my gut with force.

Camilla looks completely useless; she is in no fit state to do anything except lay very still and gaze at me with large eyes. The blood has drained from her face, and I can tell she is in a lot of pain. Her breathing has been getting more and more labored the longer we sit here, and I wonder if she has broken ribs or worse. I'm starting to feel concerned about the depths of her injuries.

I want to ask them questions, yet something inside me tells me to be quiet and do as we are told. Trust that he will get us out of this, and pray we don't get touched.

When the car starts, I grip Camilla's hand tightly, looking for comfort in the oddest of places, and she squeezes right back. All bravado and confidence, a mask, and she is clearly as scared as I am. I'd never clung to another person when I was young, enduring what I did, but somehow, knowing we both share so many hideous scars; we may need each other to get through this if everything goes wrong.

The rumble of the car as we pull off lulls us into tense silence; the men in front don't say anything more, and we edge away from the men loitering in the alley. I catch sight of Tyler and realize he still has something that belongs to me.

"Wait. My cell?" I snap impulsively, and the man in front holds it up in plain sight over the top of his head. I reach for it, but he yanks it away fast with a 'tut tut' and chuckles.

"You'll get it back when we make the switch. Until then, shut up, be a good girl, and don't make this worse." He slides my cell back out of sight, and I sit back, still clinging to Camilla, watching the New York streets slide by as we hit early morning traffic. Sick with anxiety and trying to keep picturing Arry in my mind's eye and praying he doesn't let me down.

We pull up to a looming dark building in a back street that I don't recognize. It's hard to gauge where we are, as they seemed to take us down a route of back alleys and shortcuts that messed up all sense of direction. We have hit downtown, but I can't be sure, and the building above us looks industrial. Blacked-out windows, even in the early light, grimy, old, and foreboding.

The door clicks open beside me as a new face, another suit, another set of muscles leans in and looks at us with a disinterested eye.

"Come with me, both of you." He reaches in and offers me a hand, but I slide out, skirting past him, and get onto the street without touch. Camilla looks like she is trying to follow but whimpers and moans under her breath. It's clear she can't get out unaided, and the man clicks fingers over the top of the car, motioning men on the other side to handle her as I am pulled off by the arm ahead of them.

"Wait, I need to wait for her." I try to argue and twist in his grip, but it only tightens, and he throws me a warning look.

"This will go much more smoothly if you don't cause me any hassle, girly. I'm not one of Tyler's men, and it will do you well to behave." That stern look and no-shit tone have me recoiling within myself, and I immediately simmer down to allow him to guide me into the building. Something about him intimidates me crazily, and I realize I'm still in as much danger as I was. My safety relies on Alexi and the Carrero's reputation, and it feels like I am being pulled deeper within the folds of things I shouldn't be messed up in.

He marches me into the dark building, revealing a seedy strip bar that is surprisingly already open. A half-naked woman is gyrating on a pole that is sat up on a huge box in the middle of the bar, with men already perched on stools and leaning over drinks. Their eyes are glued to her bouncing breasts, and I look away in complete discomfort. Hating that of all the places I have been brought to, it's a seedy joint full of sex and perverts.

My stomach is in knots, gripping me tightly, my body is on high alert, and I have no idea what I should be doing. Silent and obedient, hoping it will all be over soon, I must trust that my Carrero men will come for me.

Please come for me.

He leads me through the bar, past the dancer and straggling men, and through a dark door to the side. It opens into an office that's crowded and cluttered. A huge desk in the middle of an overly packed room of furniture, cabinets, and overflowing files, and I'm forced down into a seat by the wall that faces into the room. He keeps walking to the desk and sits awkwardly in the large leather seat, looking completely out of place, and I get the distinct impression this is not his office at all. He seems too pulled together and groomed for this shithole.

Moments later, the door is opened, and Camilla is dragged in and dumped on the couch opposite me by two men, her face white as milk, tears in her eyes as she muffles cries under her breath from pain, and they leave her there to wallow. Nodding at the man who brought us in and depart quickly, pulling the door behind them. I glance at her, checking to see if she's okay, and see she's already closing her eyes to try and internalize it all. She's panting, sweating, and I start to feel sick, worrying that she might not make it waiting for Alexi.

"I think she needs a medic. Tyler's men did her over." I look at him imploringly, appealing to the gentler side, but he smirks at me and shrugs as though I'm insane.

"Better tell your boyfriend that when he comes for the handoff." He leans back in the chair, creaking as it goes, and sticks two expensive, polished shoes on the wooden surface uncaringly, pulling off leather gloves that I didn't even notice he was wearing and throwing them casually on the table.

"When will that be? How long do we need to stay here?" I watch him nervously, trying to keep my cool and not fall to pieces even though I really want to. None of this seems real, this can't be happening, and I have never been more afraid.

"As long as it takes! Alexi is a busy man, and he's coming here from elsewhere. The last thing he needed to deal with today was problematic little girls getting themselves in all sorts of trouble." He sneers again, and I get the distinct impression that he isn't on Tyler's payroll at all. He seems a little cozy on the first-name basis of the man they were all trembling over. I swallow hard to try and rid my dry throat of the parched dryness and stare at him questioningly, sitting upright in the leather tub chair I'm on.

"You work for Alexi?" I'm shocked; not only that this is the kind of man he deals with, but his lack of care that I mean something is astonishing. Considering the fear Tyler and Camilla seem to have for him.

"No... Let's say we are on the same side of a very big club and have been known to rub shoulders. I'm here as a favor. Keeping you cozy until he gets here. Safe from Tyler's handymen." He slides his feet back down and pulls himself upright, walks across to a dusty shelf of books, and looks through the titles, pulling one aside and dragging out a hidden bottle of booze. He reads the label, turns, and throws it across to Camilla with precise aim and a grin.

"Here, sweetheart, kill the pain and stop your little friend here from having some sort of caring epidemic." The bottle hits her in the stomach and sends her into a yelping recoil, curling up and clutching her ribs before it slides to the floor with a dull thud, and I glare at him in disgust. I have no idea who he is, but I hate him. He has no compassion and his treatment of a wounded woman has me thinking murderous thoughts. I hope Alexi beats him half to death with that stupid bottle when he gets here.

There's a knock on the door, a head pops in and motions to him, completely expressionless, and I get nothing from the look that passes between them. He says nothing, a nod, and then he walks towards the door and leaves, closing it behind him without a second glance as though we are of no importance at all. I get the impression he isn't happy about babysitting us and wonder why they didn't let us go back in that alley.

We could have been in a cab to the hospital hours ago.

As soon as the door clicks, I'm on my feet and speedily cross to her in seconds, pulling the bottle from the floor and trying to help her to sit. Pushing cushions behind her head to get her comfier. Focusing on this is all I can think to stop myself from going bat-shit crazy.

"Don't." She croaks between breaths, and yet I still persevere.

"Sitting up a little will mean I can help you drink this. If it dulls something, then it has to be worth it." I maneuver her, so I can lift her head, unscrew the cap and help her drink the neat vodka a little at a time. She coughs, chokes, and shakes her head at me, trying to signal that she cannot drink it.

"I can't... it hurts too much. I think they broke most of my ribs." She's breathing so shallowly, closing her eyes tight in pain, and I want to cry for her. I once had two broken ribs and know how painful it can be. I hate that we're stuck here like this, that I'm helpless to do anything for her.

"It will help. I promise you." I know because, at twelve, it was how I dealt with the pain from self-treating those same broken bones from my father's drinks cabinet. Hospitals would have asked questions, so my mom never took me. My bruises, marks, and state would have alerted so much suspicion.

I shake it out of my head and try again with the liquor, holding her face as she tries to drink, taking smaller sips this time; she turns her head away when she can't anymore, and I swallow down the urge to burst into hopeless tears. I have to keep telling myself that they are coming.

"Why are you helping me? After what I did?" she croaks, swollen eyes barely open enough to look at me, and I regard her with so much in my head. Trembling, trying to stay positive.

"Because I am all you have right now. We're in this together. I can't watch you suffer. That's not who I am." I sit on the floor, cradling the bottle between my knees as the tears fall. Hopeless at where we are, in this dirty room, surrounded by strangers. I never imagined for a minute that I would ever be locked in a place that meant she and I only had each other to rely on. She is the last person in the world I would ever trust to help me, yet I can't let her suffer.

I just want to go home.

"I'm sorry for what I did.... If it means anything, then... I am." Camilla croaks, grimaces with the effort, and watches me with slotted eyes. The bruising and redness are so bad now. The swelling seems to be getting worse over time. I catch the hint of emotion in her voice, realize my tears are making her upset too, and try hard to pull myself together. My problems of last night, what happened with Arry, seem insignificant compared to this, and I want him here.

"I'm sorry I punched you in the face, even if you did and *still* do deserve it. I know that's why we're here... if I had just walked by and left you to it, then we wouldn't be here." I sniff back a fresh wave of guilty tears and wipe my face with my sleeve. Seeing the smeared makeup residue and can only imagine how bad I look.

"They would have caught me anyway, and there is still a good chance that I won't walk away from this. I still have a debt." She sounds completely resigned to the fact that I'll be allowed to go, and she knows fate has finally caught up with her, but I shake my head. If the reason we are still in their grasp is money, then I know the

Carreros will deal with it.

"Arry won't let anything happen to you... Alexi will take you as part of whatever deal he makes because he'll assume you're my friend. Alexi won't let anything happen to either of us." I assure her, so sure in my family and knowing their hearts. I know they won't let her be left behind in this. They will bring her out with me and get her help.

I'll make sure they do.

"You're probably the first real friend I have ever known... Sad, isn't it? And look what I did." She laughs softly, then groans as pain splices through her, coughing up a little blood that sends me into instant panic mode. I start to fumble with the bottle, almost spilling it, and rush to kneel up so I can tend to her in some way.

"Shit, Cam... I don't know what to do. You need a doctor." I get up on my knees so I'm higher and start using my sleeve to try and wipe her face, try with the booze some more but give up at her first rejection. She seems like she doesn't want to do anything anymore, and I can't let this happen.

"Lisa...... My name is Lisa; not exactly the name of a budding rich kid, right? I guess someone should know it, in case, you know...." She trails off and looks away as fear courses me that maybe she is dying. That they messed her up inside, and she's bleeding internally. I instinctively place a palm on her face and curse when I feel how cold she is, how her skin is clammy under mine, despite being in a warm place. I get up impulsively and stalk to the door, determined to bang the shit out of it until they get her help, but I freeze as the man from before swings it open and walks in to face me, his gaze completely blank at me standing a foot away from him.

"Going somewhere?" He snarls down at me, still cruelly cold and uncaring, and I falter in his presence.

"She's coughing up blood. She's really hurt." I shake in front of him and try not to beg, but it's so hard to be the picture of strength when everything is falling apart around you.

"Not my problem. It's Alexi's. Get your shit together. We're going to meet them."

* * *

It seems like an eternity we sit in here, the windows steaming up until they are too foggy to see anything clearly, and Camilla has managed to get her breathing under control. It's obvious she is in a lot of pain and trying not to move much. Stiff, immobile, and focused fully on not moving a muscle.

They put us in another car and moved us somewhere new. Another back-street alley, another group of terrifying men, and I'm starting to become so dizzy and weak with lack of sleep and food. It's been hours. It feels like days since I watched Arry get in the cab, and I have no idea what time it is anymore. It's become so surreal that I don't even feel afraid anymore. Caught in a dreamlike state like this will never end.

Movement through the misty window catches my attention, and I can just about make out two black four-by-fours entering the front of the alleyway. The driver's eyes flicker in the mirror, and I turn to look behind us automatically to see what he sees. Another two identical four-by-fours pull up behind us, so we are all trapped in this narrow lane with no escape. It seems like the cars start spewing more men than could be in the vehicles as soon as they stop, and they all make toward each other. I nudge Camilla gently and nod with a head gesture.

She sits up a little and glances around slowly, taking in all the new vehicles. She's been quiet, no more blood to be seen, and it doesn't seem to be getting worse since they put us back in this car. She looks out of her head now, some of the booze taking effect from earlier.

"Guess your cavalry is here. Those are Alexi's cars and men. Not that I have ever met him, but I've seen his entourage before." She croaks, finding it hard to talk, and slumps back down with a heavy exhale. I hold my breath, afraid to hope, afraid that this is real, and watch silently.

A familiar and welcoming sight saunters out of one of the cars, looking like the big mafia boss in a black overcoat and perfectly groomed hair. That tall, foreboding, familiar, handsome sight is strong with Carrero DNA. Strong, muscular, and like this, completely different from how I normally see him.

His men part as that Carrero swagger confidently moves him towards Tyler in a manner that screams power. I get a sudden rush of warm relief hit me in my throat, the unwelcome sob as tears hit me hard, and I couldn't love Alexi more than at this moment. Never been so happy to see him in my life. My nerves are so taut that I feel like they just broke, and everything starts to fall around me with sheer relief.

Through a foggy windscreen, I can barely define him from Jake, but I know that he has the palest grey eyes, rimmed with almost black, a defined jawline, and a flawless set of Carrero features. His tailored clothes molded on that tall Lothario body, his jet black hair cropped in a neat modern style and groomed, while Jakes has a hint of brown to its darkness. Like his cousins, he's another lover of tattoos, but his peek up his neck as one curls behind one ear into his hairline to disappear and one that covers the full back of his hand to his knuckles.

I always knew Alexi was a little sinister if I'm being honest. He has that same coolness as Arrick, and you can never read him, but now, seeing him like this, in a tailored suit and expensive overcoat, there's a tremor of uncertainty. Camilla watches him like a hawk, poised, yet still, her eyes are trained on our rescuer.

"He's something, isn't he? Never thought he would be so young." She watches him steadily move through the sea of men. He is a powerfully built male who screams Alpha and is completely at ease; he glances this way as he asks someone a question and nods.

"He's in his thirties, the same age as Jake or thereabouts," I answer impulsively and jump when the door next to me clicks open.

"Miss. Huntsberger?" A hand comes out to me, and I relax when I recognize the familiar face of Arrick's ex-bodyguard, yet his name eludes me. As a teen, his father insisted on his presence, but Arry ditched him as soon as he hit maturity. I smile and throw myself out of the car and into a relieved embrace, feeling him stiffen with the shock of my unusual affection and pats me lightly on the back. I'm overcome with so much emotion that these are men I recognize, these are Arry's men, and I'm truly safe and about to go home. I cry and weep, let it go into his chest and only start to calm when he gently pats me on the back, leans back, and hands me a handkerchief.

"I've to take you home. Reynauld will take your friend to a medical facility to be treated under the care of Mr. Carrero. Leave this mess to him." I turn back and see Camilla gently helped out the other side of the car by another man in a black suit, one with a heart, and watch as she hobbles away. Clearly, the longer she has sat, the worse she has suffered, and I turn back to grab onto the arm of my savior. Relief washing over me and leaving me lightheaded.

I have never been so happy to see anyone in my life, and I'm afraid that he will disappear if I let him go, h My chest is constricting with so much weight, my head aching with stress, and I want so badly to leave, to go home and wrap myself in Arry's arms...If he still wants me.

He walks me towards the cars in front, passing what seems to be a lot of strange men standing around. As we get near that familiar asshole from the strip bar, Alexi turns and glances my way.

"Hold on." He snaps, and everyone stops around him. One command, and literally, the world stops turning. He walks from the group towards me confidently, scanning me with his eyes as he gets to me. Taking in every inch of my disheveled self and makes me feel a little self-conscious. He appraises me with scrutiny, runs a hand over my cheek, wiping a few tears as he tilts my face, and then lifts my hands as he gazes at the purple mess of my fist, frowning angrily. Those pale, almost empty eyes focused directly on the swelling knuckles, and I flounder nervously. Suddenly feeling like I don't know this version of him at all. He is so far removed from the Alexi I know back home. Ice in the air and his deadpan, almost emotionless control, have me afraid of him.

"I did that to myself. I punched Camilla in the face." I blurt impulsively. Those soulless, almost colorless eyes are back on me now, and I feel like this isn't the Alexi I know and love. There is something scarily intimidating about him, and for the first time, his eyes make me think of a hunting wolf. He's handsome, like his cousins, but there's a darkness that I can't put my finger on.

"Any marks or injuries... They do anything to you?" He asks in a low even tone, serious, and I shake my head. Knowing my face must be marked from how tightly they gagged my mouth, but I just want to leave and go home and wash this mess from my skin, remove traces of men's hands from my body and all the memories from today out of my head. His jaw twitches, that same tell-tale mannerism as Arrick, and he leans in, kissing me softly on the forehead, a gentle graze of public affection, reminding me of the part of him I do know, and I relax a little. I have only ever met him as part of an extended family.

"Take her to Arry's apartment. I told him to wait there for her. I'll deal with this personally." The cold, brutal tone, hint of a threat, makes my blood curl, and the silence of the men around suggests that he is not someone you ever fuck with, and I suddenly feel unsure. This is a side of the family I have never known or seen, and my gut tells me that the payback for this little mistake will cost Tyler's men dearly. Alexi looks and acts now like he is capable of so much evil, sending cold fear through me, seeing him this way.

I'm ushered away from him, glancing back as he watches me leave. No one moves or says anything as I'm silently trundled away, guided into the car gently. He turns and throws that Carrero death glare at the dick head who refused to help Camilla, who seems to physically recoil a little before I'm closed into safety and driven away.

Chapter 28

I walk into the elevator with my chaperone and slump back against the cold steel interior, heart thumping through my chest at how Arry will react. Pretty sure he's going to be crazy mad at me for this one. Another stupid and dangerous situation, even though it wasn't my fault at all. I know he's going to yell at me, off the charts explode, and well, after last night, he probably still doesn't like me very much.

My heart's pounding through my chest, nerves eating away at me as we wait silently to get to his floor. Whoever buzzed us in on the other end wasn't him. Some male voice I don't recognize, so knowing he isn't alone makes this even more stressful. The last thing I need is a bunch of witnesses while my boyfriend tears me a new one and probably dumps my ass spectacularly.

I mean, why the hell would he keep wanting to do this, after last right and now this?

Getting him dragged into some crazy, unbelievable bullshit. He's right; I'm toxic and attract all sorts of trouble. I'm a mess, and I'm screwing up his life.

He's better off without me.

When the doors slide open, I'm faced with two men standing casually on guard, both identically suited and booted and looking very Mafia'esque. I half smile their way nervously, getting nods in return, and glance around expecting to see Arrick. They are completely out of place in his apartment, and I'm aware that my driver is following me inside. There doesn't seem to be any sign of Arrick at all.

"I think they were on the veranda." One man nods to me, and I sigh, smiling thanks as I leave them to it and wander towards the back of his apartment apprehensively. On almost tip toes because I'm so consumed with nerves. My heart starts thudding through my stomach, and I begin to shake physically.

I have no idea how he will react, and I'm tense with nerves. I think I may throw up. All my strength saps away, and I'm left feeling weak and shaky as I tentatively proceed. I'm hot and unwell from the stress of the last twelve hours, and I'm pretty sure I may pass out before the hour.

I can see from here the doors are open but voices coming from his study pull my attention in there instead. I pause as I catch sight of Jake and Arrick in the open doored study, in view from where I am, yet neither looking my way, so they don't see me at all.

Jake has his hands on Arry's shoulders, standing facing, but Arrick has his own hands in his hair, clutching the shortness as though he is on the verge of pulling it out. Head tipped down and almost leaning the top of it into his brother's chest. His posture is completely rumpled and loose. They don't see me approaching, but I'm glued to how much he looks, unlike his normally calm and composed self.

Jake is practically holding him up, and he is so slumped it's like he has no life in him, and his form screams of pain. It brings back a wave of heart-wrenching tears, filling my eyes instantly.

"She'll be okay. Alexi won't let anything happen to her. You know he'll fix this and get her out safely." Jake sounds ravaged too. Tears in his eyes fully trained on the top of his brother's head, while Arrick seems inconsolable. His voice is broken when he responds quietly, which only wounds me to my core.

"I left her.... I left my baby girl out there alone, Jake. Hurt and crying. Like an asshole. I left her... I said such cruel shit to her that I didn't even mean.... I was pissed and lashing out. So stupid, so fucking wrong. All I keep seeing is her face, begging me not to leave her, and it's ripping my insides out... I left her... I said I would never. I hurt her again... This is because of me. If I stayed, or kept her with me, then.... if anything happens to her.....I can't forgive myself for this." His voice is like the night he took me to the garden after Leila's party, wrecked and torn, obviously overcome with emotion. Broken like he was when he got on his knees to stop me from leaving.

He sounds alien, and my throat catches with so much raw emotion it chokes me, and I can't call out. Edging further towards them while holding back tears at how much pain my boy is in because of me. I made him like this, and I can't control how much it hurts me, ripping my insides out as I cover my mouth with my hand to muffle my sob.

"You didn't know this would happen. You can't think that way. You have to tell yourself she's going to be okay. It was a fight, nothing more, Arry.... You'll see her again, and you'll fix things." I walk towards them, hoping to catch their attention, unable to say anything, emotion rendering my throat mute and strangling me. I hate that he thinks this is his fault. It crushes my insides with so much guilt because it's not.

"I won't survive without her.... This is my fault. I shouldn't have ever left her. I promised her I would never leave her again, and I fucking did... I deserve to lose her for doing that to her again. She has no idea how much I love her and wouldn't be able to live without her... If they do anything to her. I'll kill every fucking one of them with my bare hands." He breaks and seems to cry as Jake pulls him into his chest, a proper embrace as he breaks down, and I break too; a little sob escaping my throat that catches Jake's attention.

His eyes flick up to me as I get to the door, and relief flushes through his face instantly. I almost see him visibly slump. His green eyes are a little red-rimmed and intense as he frowns at me with a half-smile and inhales slowly.

"Arry? Arry, look up... She's here. Sophie's home." Jake nudges him, and what seems like the longest moment as his words register before Arrick looks up at him and then spins towards me. The sudden shock of relief on his face as he takes a second to convince himself that I am real. I have never seen him in so much pain, and it breaks what's left of me as he comes at me fast. I can't control the tears anymore. I let them flow and stop caring when those perfect Hazels meet mine with so much raw pain.

His face is ashen, tears on both cheeks, eyes red-rimmed and so very green. He looks awful, beautiful, perfect, yet completely awful. I burst into a new flood of tears as he swiftly crosses toward me and scoops me into his arms so fast I can't react. He wraps himself around me so tightly, burying his head in my neck like I'm being confined and having the life squeezed out of me. He hauls me up to his chest and completely cocoons me with a palm cradling the back of my skull, so I'm almost a second skin to him.

I can't do anything else except slide my arms around his neck. He even has my feet off the floor with the strength of his embrace, and I hug him back tightly. Clinging on desperately while Arrick almost crushes me with need, finally, in the one place I have longed to be all night and day. I close my eyes as emotions swarm over me, through me, and make everything stop hurting.

He's still sniffing into my neck, making me feel horrendous that I reduced him to this. I can feel the wetness from his tears on my skin as his face comes to my cheek, pushing himself against me with ragged breaths.

"I'm sorry, baby. I'm sorry.... So goddamn sorry." He gasps between quick inhales, crushing me so much that I'm finding it hard to breathe, but I don't protest. His hands cup my face as he pulls me hard against his mouth, kissing my cheek and eye, and jaw clumsily, planting lips anywhere that comes in contact and showering me with the heartfelt adoration of a crazy person. He lets go to slide me to my own feet to wrap his arms back around me again and squeezes me doubly tight, almost winding me fully with rib-cracking strength.

It's the kind of hug given in desperation when someone really is happy to have you back with them and can't control how it feels. I don't mind the bone-cracking as long as he doesn't hate me anymore. Obviously still loves me if this is anything to go by.

I cry silent tears and cling on desperately, every part of me wrapped in the one safe place I never want to leave ever again. Enveloped by everything that I love about him.

"I'm so fucking sorry... I love you so much, Sophie. I thought I was never going to see you again." He lifts his head to push his forehead against mine, not caring that he's stifling tears, his voice broken and trembling, and I find comfort in it. Knowing that I mean this much to him, that he loves me this much, even when I've been awful, violent, and undeserving. I have never seen him this way with anyone else. He isn't the type of guy to fall apart easily, yet his body vibrates with so much relief after what I assume has been a night of hell.

He lets me down properly to cradle my face with his hands, pulling it to him, tilting my head, and kissing me hard. Our tears mingle as he locks lips with me and makes it clear that he has been going out of his mind over me. It's not a sensual or even a graceful kiss. More a push on me, a forced, 'I am so relieved to have you back' sort of kiss.

Every part of his face squishes into mine, and his arms make their way back around me to squeeze the life out of me once more. This time he wraps them around my shoulders and head like he wants to force us into one and never be separated again. I'm starting to think he might crush me to death. It's obvious he still hasn't quite gotten control of his inner emotions and isn't aware of how indelicate he is being with his affection. I cling on, feeling truly loved at this moment like he would never let go of me again.

"Hey. Give an old man some of this." Jake nudges us, and Arrick relinquishes his hold enough for Jake to slide me out of his arms reluctantly. Grabbing my hand and locking fingers even though I'm only parting for a second while 'God daddy' gets a hug.

Jake slides his arms around me, gives me a full proper embrace, squeezes me too, and then kisses me on the forehead as he lets me go. Less crushingly so, and using his sleeve to wipe his own eyes, which are leaking a little manly moisture too. Seems I can make Carrero men cry, and I wonder if I should add it to my CV.

Can reduce big tough Carreros to tears.

Arrick does the same. Wipes his face and clears his throat, then starts drying my face with his fingertips. Pandering to me once more, guiding me back to his circle of proximity, and litters my skin with small kisses as he goes. He seems completely lost and focuses on tasks and touching while he pulls himself together.

"You okay, Kiddo?" Jake frowns at me, and I nod, feeling surreal like I'm no longer awake or here. I guess it's shock catching up on me.

"They didn't really hurt me, just scared me, but then the name Carrero popped up, and I wasn't scared anymore. Seems you lot are a force to be reckoned with." I sigh and shrug and am recaptured by Arrick, pulling me into every inch of his body. His face is against my cheek, wrapping himself like an octopus around me. Returning to death by forced hugs, and pretty sure he's going to crack ribs this time. Jake smiles at him in an endearing 'my brother is overwhelmed' way and ruffles his hair affectionately.

"What's this?" Arrick catches sight of my bruised hand and lifts it with deadly scrutiny as he lifts his cheek from mine. His eyes scan it, and his face scowls to that age-old Carrero glare. Anger spiked that someone dared to hurt me. Instant fire and rage hit his expression hard, and I pull it free quickly and caress his face softly to tame him.

"I punched Camilla in the face... Thanks for never telling me that it hurts like a MOFO, by the way!" I giggle, through tears, somewhere in relief and disbelief, that this has even been my day so far. No pain in my hand anymore, I guess because I am still high on adrenalin and know I will crash later. I'm dreading the later if I'm being honest. This day is going to catch up on me in big style.

"Jesus, Sophie. One night out on your own, you're beating women and taking on drug lords." Jake shakes his head, joking to cover the seriousness of the last few hours, and both stare at me with mixed emotions. Jake is slightly more relaxed, while Arrick still looks like he might beat someone to death. He is poised and stiff, like he can't calm down.

"Camilla?" Arrick questions me, homed in on that one little

point. I realize I have never told him about any of that. After the night in the club, we never really talked about how it came to be, and we never brought it up after we found each other again. I guess the two of us have some explaining to do, and maybe I am being harsh on the Miami thing. Now I'm sober and clear-headed, I can see why he didn't want to tell me. It still hurts that he kept a secret, but now I can understand why.

I am a jealous irrational psycho, after all.

"Long story.... Another time." I curl myself into his throat and sink into his body around me once more, completely attached to me and unwilling to let me loose. He keeps squeezing me and kissing any part of my face or head he gets near. Repeatedly checking that I'm okay by smoothing his hands and eyes over me, assessing, checking obsessively. It feels good. Safe. Needed. Like I'm in the one place I belong, and I finally believe that he will never survive without me.

"I'll give you two kids space... I need to call my wife and tell her where I am before she freaks out. She was still asleep when I left. No one knows, Sophs ... I don't think this is a tale that anyone besides a few Carrero men should know." Jake eyes me warily, patting both of us on the shoulders, moving away a little, and I nod in agreement.

"My parents would ship me back home and mark the city as a far too dangerous place to live alone." I agree, gasping softly as I get another squeeze of death to the ribs, and Arrick picks me off my feet. Obviously, another wave of emotion has hit him, and he's reacting internally. On the surface, he looks relieved, but his green eyes and little tensing muscles in his jaw tell me he's overthinking, overanalyzing, and summarizing how close he came to never seeing me again.

My overthinking weirdo. I love you.

The shock might be wearing off, and now I'm feeling fragile as I realize this could have ended badly. Fatigue washes over me, coupled with nausea because I haven't eaten in hours.

"You're not going to be living alone anymore. You're living here, and we're moving your stuff today. No argument, Sophs... I don't want you to go back to that apartment or anywhere alone again, without me. Ever." Arrick has found the strength in his voice again and frowns at me bossily, endearingly serious, and I shrug at him, placating him while he is still so emotional and fragile. Looking so very stern.

"Was going to happen anyway. Just not today... I need sleep, food, a shower, and some time to get my head around this." Nothing sounds better now than making sure I never leave here again. He's back to gripping onto me like he wants to melt our bodies into one, and I have to accept that he may be a little needy for a while, not that I'm complaining. All I need is to be wrapped up in him too.

"If you two are getting to the cohabiting stage, then maybe it's time you properly told the families that this thing is serious, Arry? Maybe you could both come home and make mom happy in a few days?" Jake gives him the affectionately bossy tone and the slight furrowed look that means, 'I am saying it as a suggestion, but what I mean is you will do as you're told.' I giggle at his lack of subtlety, and Arrick finally breaks a smile too. Both are thinking the same thing.

"Give her time to get over this.... Me too. I think I've aged fifty years in the past few hours." Arry sighs and pulls my cheek back to his face, littering more kisses across my eyebrow and temple. Unable to stop touching and showering me with his affections.

"That's what love does to you, Buddy. God Knows Emma knows how to make me fall to shit sometimes... I'm heading home, but dad insists you keep the security team until all this dies down and Alexi does whatever he will do." Jake is in serious mode, fatherly, and CEO toned. This a hint that the dark side of the family is something he knows more about than he lets on. He ruffles my hair and then his brothers, pulling his head over roughly and planting a kiss on Arrick's temple. Arry throws him a weak half-smile, shell-shocked, exhausted, and completely out of his depth.

"Thanks, Jake... I love you." Arrick lets go of me and gives Jake a proper hug. It's a weird moment, something I don't see very often, and they pat each other's backs in a very manly way. I can't deny their close bond when I see them this way with each other.

"Love you too, asshole. Stop upsetting my goddaughter, or you'll have me to deal with. You know better than this shit, Arry... Make better choices." He pushes him in the shoulder, catching him by the back of the neck to plant another kiss on his baby brother's forehead, and turns to go. He throws another kiss on my cheek as he passes.

"I know.... Trust me... I know." Arrick eyes me warily and hauls me back for another round of squeezing and kissing. Only this time, he lassoes my head with his arm and pulls my mouth against his to stay that way. Not kissing, more face-planting us together and breathing me in with closed eyes. No intention of giving me any breathing space anytime soon. Despite suddenly needing to pee, I am okay with that, although I want to get these grubby clothes off my skin. I slide my arms around his upper body and hold on tight.

We don't see them leave. The first I know when he lets me go is that we're alone, and I guess, like his bodyguard of old, they have gone elsewhere to guard this apartment from a distance. Discreetly, non-evasive.

I know all it will take is a call or even stepping outside to be flanked by men in suits. I remember this from the first years I knew him. When Giovanni was paranoid that his sons would be targets for kidnapping or harm. It makes sense why he would even assume anyone would want to hurt them. There's so much about this family I don't want to know about at all.

I'm glad they are out there now, keeping me safe.

I need to be safe right now. I need to be here and surrounded by normal.

* * *

I walk out of the bathroom, draped in his fluffy robe, free of grime, the city smells, and chaos. Refreshed by the shower, I told him I needed to take alone, and I feel less surreal. I needed some head space to process this stuff, and even though he was reluctant to let me out of his sight, he agreed. As long as I knew he would be charging in if I took too long. I didn't doubt he would.

He's sat on the bed when I walk out, backed up against the headboard, his phone in his hand and his knees propped up holding it. He sees me and slides his legs down, leaning over to put his phone on his docking station, and motions for me to come to him, with complete exhaustion on his face. I climb up on the bed without hesitation, shimmy into his open arms, curling beside him to sit up against his chest and snuggle into muscles that fit perfectly around me.

"Your friend is okay. She's in the hospital under Alexi's care. He says not to worry about her anymore." Arry cuddles me in and kisses the top of my head, and I nod. Filled with relief and getting some comfort for that, at least. I don't want to talk about her. I just want my day to feel normal like nothing happened.

"You decided to camp on your bed and wait for me?" I ask, blinking up at him with a smile. He looks normal now. Like he's washed his face and calmed down his inner chaos and hair. He has fresh clothes on too, and it's only now I realize that he had been wearing last night's clothes when I walked in here earlier. Arrick was never the type to fall to pieces and neglect his appearance; it reinforces everything I mean to him, and I'm hit with that gut-aching gnaw of guilt that I could ever doubt it.

"I wanted to be close to you... In case you needed me." He gazes back seriously, and I'm glad to see that he seems more pulled together and back to calm and cool. He is back to being my Arry. Stable and chilled, he hides the war of emotions below the surface, and I finally feel more at peace. He's my stability, my constant level, and when he falls apart, I suddenly don't know how to be. I never realized before how much I needed that side of him to be this way.

"You're lame." I sigh and turn my face, so I can snuggle against his heartbeat, listening to its lulling rhythm, so utterly drained. I know there's a world of stuff we should say to each other and that I should apologize.

"I know, baby.... You make me lame, though. I know how to make a mess of everything when it comes to you... I couldn't live without you, Sophie." My heart tugs at the sudden raw way it comes out of his mouth, and his eyes narrow a little as he fights back new emotions. I sigh heavily, my heart aching with so much between us, closing my eyes, using his steady breathing and heartbeat to keep me grounded. I hope all this intensity will float away and leave us back to being how we were before any of last night or this morning happened. I want to forget all of it.

"I'm sorry about last night. About how I acted, the things I said." there's that familiar tug in my throat, the inability to talk about this without getting close to tears. All I did in the car coming here was think about how stupid I was. How horribly I acted and how wrong I was to lay hands on him.

Hitting him isn't okay. It's never OK, and I wonder if I need to go back to my counselor to readdress the anger issues. The impulsive need to lash out when pain is inflicted upon me. The aggressive side of me that I have little control over. I know it's CPTSD from my past, but it doesn't make it right.

"Don't, Sophs .... Look at me." Arrick sits up and helps maneuver me to sit up too, so we're face to face as he strokes my cheek. Brushing back my damp hair and focusing his eyes on mine. "You have nothing to be sorry for, baby... I did all of that. I made last night happen. It was all my fault, even the way you blew up and went off the charts." He leans in and kisses my forehead softly, strokes my face, and pulls back to rest against my head, regarding me with a pained expression.

"You didn't make me act like a prized jealous bitch, Arrick." I look away, but he tilts my face back by the chin. Not letting me out and tightening his arm around my shoulders.

"Yes, I did! ... This is all I thought about when I was walking the streets of New York trying to find you... I came back, Sophs, got to my apartment, and thought, 'what the fuck am I doing?' After telling you a million times I never would, I realized that I left you, and hightailed right back to you, baby... I ran all the way because I knew I was wasting time looking for a cab, feeling like the biggest asshole going and knowing I was fucking things up more than I had already. Losing you all over again." He narrows his eyes, furrows his brows, and nudges his nose a little closer, wanting me close enough to feel against his entire face. His husky tone betrays how close to breaking he is, and it only fuels the deep welt inside of me and urges my eyes to mist up.

"You haven't been fucking things up. I have. By being insecure, jealous, and stupid whenever she calls you." I answer softly, full of regret and hating that is how we even got here. If I hadn't acted that way, he would have told me about Miami while he was still there. He would have kept me dancing after arguing with Miranda, and then we would have gone home together and snuggled up in bed, and none of this morning would have happened at all.

"No, stop that and listen to me..... This is me, all on me. I see that now... I should have cut ties from day one of being with you. I should have told you about Miami as soon as she showed up... I was wrong and didn't put myself in your head. I kept thinking doing the right thing was how to play it, and all I was doing was making it harder for you to trust me again... I'll never keep anything from you again, I swear. I need to stop putting my stupid ideas over what you need from me, stop thinking about how it makes me look, and start realizing it hurts you. All of this is because of me. Last night was the climax to you holding it all in for weeks. I know you. You're not irrational and jealous of other women I know... Just her... It should have been a neon sign that I needed to do a better job at making you feel loved and secure, Sophie." He swallows hard, that tinge of upset and emotion clawing away at him as he sighs heavily against me. With so many emotions warring across his face, his eyes have returned to green speckles and flecks that are insanely intense.

"You do make me feel loved. You go above and beyond to make me feel like I'm the center of your world." I try to defend him against himself, truly adoring him in every way and hating that he's trying to blame himself for everything. He can't dismiss the fact I attacked her and him last night. I know I have a responsibility in this too. I can't always blame him for how I behave.

"You *are* the center of my world. You have no idea. When I couldn't find you last night, I called Jake, freaking out... I didn't know where you would go, where you would be. I was beyond crazy with so many possibilities and the thought of how many girls get attacked in the city every day, so he flew out to help look... I must have called you twenty times and begged you to answer. I called Christian and Jenny, and no one knew where you were." He squeezes me a little tighter, lost in memory and distraught at how it felt.

"Seventeen times." I giggle, tears in my eyes, and he smiles, breaking his heart-wrenching expression apart.

"I needed air and time to walk...Clear my head. I kept my cell silent as I didn't think you would call or even come back. I didn't know you were looking for me... I thought you were done." I answer him honestly, untangling myself from him and managing to sit up properly. Overheating from his embrace while in a heavy robe in a very warm apartment. He lets me go but catches my hand and draws it into his, playing with my fingers gently and tracing the marks littered across it.

"That right there! ... Not thinking I would, not expecting that I would. It's proof that I'm not making you feel like you're all that matters to me. I'm failing to make you believe I will always come back for you. No matter what, no matter the fight... I was pissed and drunk, thinking like an asshole.... All it took was walking into this apartment without you, and I realized how wrong this was... I love you...More than I can ever express because I don't know how else to say it. Those three words don't seem to be enough for the level of emotion I have for you. I'll never stop loving you, no matter how mad we get at each other... You make me better. You complete my life; without you, Sophie, I don't know how to breathe or be. I need you more than you will ever know." The intensity of those soft brown eyes locked on mine take my breath away, tears rolling down my chin with the sheer truth behind them. I can't deny how much he loves me when he looks at me like this. How much I need him too. He breaks me apart inside in every way.

"I know you love me. I know that sometimes I make it impossible to love me." I look away from him so he doesn't see how ashamed I am for everything I do to him. He tugs at my hand, gets up on his knees, and faces me. Sliding down to mirror my upright pose and angles, so he's back in my face, kissing me softly on the lips.

"No, you don't. You're far too easy to love. That's my downfall. Even when you're acting out and getting hellcat on me. I love you so much it rips my head apart." He strokes my cheek and brushes a thumb across my mouth, bringing my eyes back to him. "I texted Natasha and told her I was done with her. To stay away and leave me alone... I saw another side to this whole thing last night, a side to her that I never knew existed, and it made me realize that I'm hurting you for a girl that isn't worth the effort... She's gone, she's not going to be an issue, and I blocked her cell number, so she can't even respond."

He searches my gaze for a reaction and I'm overwhelmed suddenly. That he would do that for me, even though I never asked him to. Wanted it for so long but knew my reasons were so selfish, yet he's done it anyway. My eyes fill with tears at the thought that he really is choosing me over her, properly this time.

"Really.... You're done with her?" I whisper, more tears sliding over my cheek. He lifts my chin, brushes it away, and kisses the path it traveled so very tenderly that it warms my insides.

"Honestly ... She can hate me if she wants. I don't care anymore. I only care about you, us, our life, and making you happy. I asked Jake to take over the medical details and deal with her directly. I told him I didn't want to know anymore, and he agreed... He pointed out how dumb I was to keep her involved when trying to get you to trust me again... I know I screwed up, Sophie... Last night was a massive lightning bolt to the brain that finally made me see sense... I know this is all on me. I'm going to do so much better, baby. I'm going to try so much harder." He pulls me onto his lap, not happy with the brief touch he has on me, and pulls my legs to wrap around his waist, not even catching a quick perve under my robe as it splays open to reveal naked me underneath.

"You already make me happy. You don't need to do more. I am happy." I smile when he leans in and kisses me on the mouth more intently, a deep kiss, parting my lips and making every part of me tingle with the emotion it pulls through me. I can never doubt how he feels when he kisses me like this, it's so much more than those three little words, and it heals so many wounds. Lost in each other for a moment and erasing so many tears and pains that we inflicted on one another in the early hours. I completely forgive him for all of that and more. He breaks away, staying close and watching me with unveiled adoration.

"I love you." He lifts my hand and plays with my fingers, eyes flittering down to look at the bruised mess on my hand, gently tracing them with a frown. I know we should talk later about Camilla, but he's my only focus for now.

"I love you more," I respond honestly, without hesitation, and his eyes dart back to mine in sudden surprise. Immediate filling of moisture and a slight furrow of the brow. He falters, swallows hard, and clears his throat, completely overcome.

"You mean that?" He seems suddenly so much more fragile and younger, and I nod. Equally welling up at how he's reacting to something I used to say all the time. Something I always felt for him and hoped he knew I still felt for him.

"I mean it. I always have, even when I didn't see you anymore. I always will." I sniff through a smile as tears let loose again, and then we're both nose to nose, equally emotional.

"I never realized how much I needed to hear it until now.... Say it again." Arrick's voice breaks as his eyes glaze over, and I trace over his lips with my fingertips, loving him so much more than I ever felt possible. Aching to make him feel the way he makes me feel.

"I love you," I whisper softly as his arms come around me, and he yanks me tightly to his body, kissing me fiercely and almost crushing the life out of me once more.

Chapter 29

I lose my courage and turn back to Arrick's car once more. Aiming for the door, he catches me from behind and turns me back, keeping his arms around my waist and shoving me forward to walk slowly with his groin pressed to my ass to help push me onward.

"We're doing this... My mom will probably not react like you think she will." He's trying to get me up the path of his parents' house. The entire drive here, I tried to talk him and myself in and out of doing this. My nerves are frayed, my emotions are a mess, and I'm losing all courage. I feel like I will be sick or pass out and maybe want to stay in his car and hide.

Or go home, we could just go home.

"It's not her. It's facing everyone, knowing that my mom has told them all. That they all probably know the stuff we get up to now. How they're all going to react? It's awful." I beg him, tensing against him to try and stop our descent down the drive. He keeps moving me onwards, not letting me go or backing down. His chest against my shoulders and winning with sheer strength.

"Where's my little warrior, huh? She's fearless in the face of tough times! Pretty sure you can get used to the family knowing that we have sex, Sophie... What happens if you ever get pregnant? Are you going to tell them it was an immaculate conception?" He chuckles and bumps my ass with his groin when I stop suddenly, urging me on and not giving in to me. Arrick is trying to keep me moving. Despite digging my heels in, I push my butt back into his groin to stop him, but he's too strong.

"Keep that up, and I might bang you here, and then no one will doubt what we get up to." Arrick leans back and smacks my ass hard, making me yelp, and I throw around a glare at his face.

"You wouldn't dare. You're not allowed to touch me when we go in... Don't be all like lovey and touchy and stuff. I don't want you doing weird shit that you do, like smacking my ass.... Or you know, being sweet, or lame, or annoying me with wanting to touch me." I scold, suddenly aware that they might scrutinize us in every way and unsure I will be comfortable with affection in front of them. Arrick sighs as I duck away from him and shove his hands off, not ready to have people seeing us all touchy and cuddly when I think it will just weird them all out. It's already weirding me out that they might see it.

"Don't make me carry you, baby. I don't think we'll need to hide anything if the first thing they see is me manhandling you in the door." Arrick yanks me back firmly and pulls me into a loose headlock, squirming as I give up the fight and sigh.

"I changed my mind. I don't want to come with you to see your mom." My tone is fearful because I'm starting to panic. Hitting that age-old childish part of me and sulking, pouting, and whining expertly.

"Yeah, right, you're my human shield. My mom is less likely to throw dishes at me for defiling your innocence if you're standing between us." Arrick smirks, still refusing to let go, but I shake my head hard.

"Nope." I turn and wrap my arms around his waist in a bid to stop him walking, crushing my skull to that wide chest and pleading with little tense nudges; he unravels me, turns me back around, and pushes me in front of him with more force than necessary, that sends me skipping ahead.

"If you don't come with me, I'll be forced to tell her to pick an engagement party date and that you want to give her ten grandbabies. You know she will hold you to it." He grins, and I stop, spin, and stare at him in open-mouthed horror.

"Stop with the B word! ...What engagement? You wouldn't dare!" I accuse, returning to put my hands on his abdomen to keep him from the last few feet to the door.

"I might even have to bring up the M word... So, you better come in and supervise. Who knows what might come out of this mouth if she puts me under the grill... My mom can be terrifying when it comes to you girls and her maternal need to protect you all." He chuckles, obviously smug at his attempts to blackmail me, but I admit, it's working. I don't trust him not to promise his mom big white weddings and three hundred grand babies before I'm twenty-two. I don't like that at all.

Arrick tugs me the last foot towards him and kisses me softly, tilting his head so he can get close and personal. I jump back again, gasping in panic, and dart my eyes around wildly, scanning the empty street for spies.

"Someone could see." I chastise him, fearful of prying eyes and infuriated by his sudden grin. It's going to take a while to get used to letting Arrick be this way with me in front of the people we love; it's not natural for me, and even though Jake got a glimpse, I would rather ease into this more comfortably.

"It would save us all of this drama. Come on you. We can stand out here all-day bickering, but I'd rather face the music and tell everyone I'm fucking little Sophie." He dodges my slap on the shoulder and chuckles at my outrage at calling it that. Hauling me back under his arm and pulling me towards the house, despite my protests and struggles. Arrick isn't taking any excuses. He is intent that coming home is for one reason alone: to tell his parents and face my family as a real couple.

God help me!

Getting me in the front door completely changes my entire demeanor. I revert to scared and wide-eyed, cowering behind him, grabbing his upper arm with a death-like grip as he leads the way. I've no idea how Sylvana will react, seeing as she has been like my surrogate second mom, or maybe third, for years. Suddenly it's too terrifying that she may not approve of this because I know she genuinely liked Natasha.

"I think you're cutting off the blood supply, baby." He nods at my hands, and I loosen them a little. Arrick peels one of them off and slides it into his hand as he pulls me towards the sound of chatter in the day room.

"Mamma.... Where are you?" He yells into the echoing house, and both jump when a voice comes close by from the kitchen to the right instead.

"Right here waiting for you two to come in and stop arguing on the drive." Sylvana is standing with a mixing bowl in her kitchen. A wooden spoon is furiously pounding some batter, eyeing us up with her usual loving face, a raised brow of a woman who already seems to be in the know.

Arrick glances at me, and despite telling me I'm his human shield, he steps in front of me to bridge the gap with his mother. Leaning in to kiss her on the cheek. Sylvana lays down her bowl, pats his cheek, and then moves forward to kiss me on the forehead.

"Do I need to wait for you two to awkwardly beat around the bush and spit it out while I pretend I don't know or are you going to tell me how serious it is?" She says pointedly. My mouth snaps shut, and I recoil behind Arrick once more. Arrick only giggles and gives her another kiss on the cheek.

"Can't get nothing by you, can I? Guess I know who I take after....... Serious, Mom.... I asked her to move in with me, and she said yes... I love her." Arrick doesn't hesitate. He is always at ease with his mother and never fears retribution. That is the perk of being the golden child, the good one all the years, while Jake had been the devil. He dips his fingers in the batter bowl and sticks them in his mouth, throwing me a wink as she bats him away for his dirty habit.

"Well, seeing you kiss her on the drive was hardly a shock. The last time I saw you here, you dragged her off in the dark like a crazed jealous loon when her gay friend was doing an awful job of acting like her boyfriend... Sophie, darling? ..... You left your shoes in my garden and your underwear under my son's bed." She smiles my way gently and moves the bowl out of reach of her son's wandering hands, and lays it behind her on the worktop.

I'm instantly speechless, face flaming as I recoil like she's burned me. Praying the ground opens up and devours my mortified body as shame courses through me. On the other hand, Arrick is smiling, chuckling, and casually pulls me forward into his arm. Like this is no big deal at all.

"Not as fly as we thought we were, huh?" He kisses me on the head, and I wriggle free, shoving his hands off me in sheer awkwardness and slapping his hands away when he tries to catch me again. Grinning at my reaction as Sylvana shakes her head.

"Stop tormenting her!" She smacks him on the lower arm with a warning look and then turns to me with a warm one.

"If he's anything like Jake, the more you make a fuss, the worse he will try to get a reaction. I would get used to being pawed by him. It's pretty clear to anyone you are bumping uglies already. He is a Carrero, after all." She smiles widely, motions to the coffee machine in a 'would you like some' gesture, and seems oblivious to anything wrong.

"Mooom?" Arrick groans. "Wherever you heard that phrase, please never use it again. It's not cool or hip, and it's really cringe. I never want you to say anything like that to me again." He leans back against the worktop behind us, appearing traumatized. His mom is giggling girlishly and sways a hand his way.

"Well, genitals are hardly attractive, and you do sort of bump when, you know? ... Copulate." She raises an eyebrow and then softens her face with a smile that cheeky Jake-like glimmer in the depths, and I realize she is doing it on purpose to get a reaction out of him. Sylvana is naughty, and I giggle too, losing all shame and embarrassment and suddenly wondering why I was ever worried that she would hate this.

"I swear, I'm scarred for life." Arrick groans again, clearly at a loss for words.

"You're not mad?" I turn to her now, little inner Sophie reaching out to her maternal figure and needing reassurance.

Insecurity peeking out and requiring the balm that the Carreros have a way of applying.

"No. I'm not mad, darling child. I'm surprised it took him this long to see the beautiful woman you were becoming." Sylvana reaches out and takes my hand, holding it tightly and squeezing it gently.

"Yeah, took him way too long." I nudge him in the ribs when he comes back up behind me and slides an arm around my shoulders. Feeling a little awkward under Sylvana's scrutiny but leaving him alone to touch me, urging myself to relax and accept that it's not going to stop, and I want to be able to relax with him.

"I didn't fail to see it.... I just didn't think I should ever act on it." He points out defensively, suddenly being ganged up on by two women he adores and deflecting the hard time he knows he will get.

"I can't say it seems odd. You two have always been close, so seeing you being this way isn't new. Don't play with her heart, Arrick... Sophie is a fragile soul and needs stability, not some lothario romance that messes with her head. I know what you and your brother are like." She tuts at him. Arrick frowns in complete disbelief.

"Mom? Jake has been married to Emma for the last five years, and they're solid and happy. I'm more than capable of being in a committed relationship too. You're basing your facts on maybe seven years ago." He laughs at her and meets that scowling look.

"Make sure that's what this is because if you hurt my little *Mimmo* and break her heart, I'll break your neck. There better be a ring on that finger before long." Sylvana is deadly serious, scarily so, and a hint of a momma bear and fiery temper makes me squirm back in his arms a little.

"Steady on. I'm only turning twenty." I squeak in sheer panic, knowing this was going to be a topic at some point, but not thinking she would swoop right in. I want that with him one day, but I have so much to do first.

"Mom, I swear there will be a ring on her finger eventually. Right now, we're living in the moment. She's moving in, and we're taking it from there." Arrick encircles my waist affectionately, his body molding to mine, despite my attempts at batting him off subtly and then giving up again. Somehow her non-reaction makes me relax, and I admit, I like his touch a little too much to ever push it away for long.

"I've never understood you young folks and all this living in sin before marriage. Just get married if you want to cohabit and be done with it." She sighs, contemplative and moves off to drag mugs out of the cupboard despite no one saying they wanted coffee.

"Mom, are you trying to give Sophs a heart attack? She has an aversion to marriage and babies. Give her another five years at least." Arrick laughs, his breath tickles my neck, yet I'm still staring at her as though she has two heads. And as for five years. I think not. My five-year plan has stores and fashion week, not B's!

He better re-think his time scale.

"Why? If my son upsets you, then come to me. I'll kick him in the balls for you." Sylvana wanders back to me, kisses my forehead, and smiles gently. "Although knowing you, my darling child, you're more than capable of doing it yourself." Sylvana smiles at me again, patting my cheek tenderly, and then wanders back to the counter.

"Amen to that." Arrick agrees.

"I've recently discovered I have a right hook." I point out subject change is smoothly applied. Head very clearly diverting from the cringy B and M words and pulling me to safer shores.

"A pretty good one... I have her in the boxing ring, teaching her to kick ass, should she ever need it." Arrick leans his head against mine and sighs.

I went with him yesterday evening for his late session with his trainer because he was adamant that I learn some self-defense moves before we left. He's been clingier to my presence since the night I was grabbed by Tyler's men, not that we talked much about it again. There is some unspoken rule that we forget that it ever happened, and no mention of Alexi or how he took care of things. All I know is he took over Camilla's debt, and she remained unharmed and somehow in the shelter of the Carrero family. Alexi's problem now.

That's where my need-to-know ends.

I wasn't any good when he got me in that ring with him, and he did grab me a million times in a million ways to rile me until I got stroppy with him and threw his stupid gloves in his face. Yes, I was tantrummy, and he was patient and kept talking me back into the damn ring until I mastered one evasive maneuver. Also, how to properly knee a guy in his family jewels. I can now break a pinkie to get a hand off me too. I guess he's just making sure that if I ever get grabbed again, I'll have a fighting chance to get away, and I can't not love him for that.

"Will come in handy then, won't it? When you're being a jerk, and Sophie needs to put you in your place. I'm guessing your arrival is why Cynthia has arranged a mass Carrero and Huntsberger family dinner party tomorrow night?" Sylvana glances at us with a smile, and every ounce of blood drains from my body.

"What?" I told them we were coming, and my mom mentioned dinner, but she never mentioned this. I think I may pass out. My heart stops mid-beat, my breath halting in my frozen lungs, and the instant sweats come over me.

"Ouch.... Guess we better get our glad rags on and behave, baby." Arrick laughs over the back of my head, and I feel sick.

"Oh, my God." I groan, imagining how they're all going to behave. I already have the texts from Leila and my brothers over the last couple of weeks teasing me about my new boyfriend. My family mainly seemed to have taken it well after my parents told them, and I got a lot of non-surprised responses. Rylanne, however, asked me if this was new... He thought we'd been dating for years, and I literally had no answer for the lack of observation on that front.

I'm not worried they will say anything bad; I'm just not relishing how my hands-on boyfriend will behave in front of people that I tend to act more demure around. People I make an art form of appearing non-emotional and non-affectionate in front of.

He kills all of that. Ironically.

"Better hone my skills of feeling you up. Can't let an opportunity like a mass gathering slide by without torturing you." He huskily brushes against my ear, and I know he's grinning. I can feel it. I elbow him in the ribs and turn with a glare.

"I swear you better not. I'll make you sit at the other side of the room and ignore you all night." I threaten, seriousness to my tone and that warning glare aimed at his face.

"Fat chance, I'm going to be glued to you all night, every opportunity to get my hand on your ass and my tongue in your mouth. Might even get a hand up your skirt at dinner, baby." He chuckles, eyes glued to my mouth as he says it, and I shake my head with such an urge to poke him in the eye.

"Arrick Carrero!" Sylvana slaps him across the head softly, getting an instant naughty boy scowl of surprise. Doing what I wanted to and eyeing him up. "That's not an attractive trait. Don't tease the love of your life. Leave her be if she isn't comfortable with public displays of affection." She scolds haughtily.

I laugh at the irony in that sentence. Never did I ever imagine Arry would be on that side of that sentence. I giggle at the complete switch-up in what we have become. He's still my cool and calm outward man, but I know that only seems to be the surface layer he shows the world.

"Nope. I need to cure her. I have no intention of stopping." He shrugs and seems to be trying to prove the point by roaming his hands down my thighs and then back up towards the hem of my dress, but I slap him away.

"Well, I may just leave you to Leila then. Sure she will have something to say about you groping me over dinner." I shove him off with more force, slapping every attempt to haul me back and moving away to glower at him accusingly.

"Groping ... Hmmmm.... I like the sound of that." He winks with a cheeky smile.

Both Silvana and I systematically slap a shoulder each.

Chapter 30

"You will be fine, babycakes. Just man up and seduce him before you tell him." Christian laughs down the phone, supportive as ever, and I sigh. My nerves splayed, my stomach churning and tapping my fingers on the counter impatiently.

"I think he might get mad. Or upset. I don't know." I stare at the apartment wall facing the entertainment unit with its million and one framed pictures of us from the last year. The happy smiling trips and the cute couple snaps from favorite selfies. His lounge looks less refined and manly nowadays, with the addition of throws, fluffy cushions, and a manner of pink and sparkles mixed through all the grey and cool tone things. His domain has slowly been morphing over the months into a girly love pad, and he doesn't seem to care, even though it's not as prim and neat as it used to be.

"No, he won't. He never seems to get mad at you. He will sigh, smile, and do whatever you ask, as he always does. You have that puppy wrapped around your little pinkie, and you know it." Christian is being annoyingly upbeat today. I guess he chose his holiday with James to stay in bed again, seeing as that's all they seem to do now they are officially cohabiting. Much like Arry and I.

Moving in here was the best decision I ever made, and living with him has made us closer than ever. Not that sometimes he doesn't want to string me up for being a messy housemate, but he's easy to placate. I just have to get naked, and he's over it.

"I'm not sure I even want it. I'll miss you guys so much." I play with a strand of my hair, longer now as I've been growing it a little, and stare at its light highlighted color, tugging it in front of me nervously. Trying to curb my nervous tension.

"You know that we shouldn't hold you back. Jenny is leaving anyway. Married with a bun in the oven has redirected her priorities, and what with Nathan opening his own marketing company to promote more fighters. I think she's happy to be one of those stay-home and adore my kids type of people." Christian sighs as I do. We attended the crazily unexpected wedding a few months ago that seemed to come out of the blue after those two got into a very serious relationship and found out she was pregnant.

She's happy, though, and the unplanned baby seems to make her more so. Nathan turned out to be more than capable of being a one-woman man after all and is all for the new life he is giving her, if not a little old fashioned in the whole 'You're not giving birth to my baby until our names match.' I honestly never saw that one coming at all. I think they will make it, though; he seems to adore her as much as she adores him, and he stopped playing games with her heart the second he told her so.

"I know, but I still see her. If I go, then I won't see you both for a year, Chris." a sob stifles in my throat at verbalizing it, and the doubts all flood straight back in, winding me in the gut. I haul over the unicorn mug that now holds cold coffee and play with the handle.

"We'll keep this place warm for you. You need to follow your heart and chase your dreams. You can go places with your talents, Sophs, don't let us hold you back." He sounds hoarse, a touch emotional, too, and I let the tears erupt. I hate that I love them so much that leaving them kills me this way.

"Promise me you'll visit me?" I sob down the cell phone and sigh heavily to get it all back inside.

"I swear. As often as I can. You don't lose me that easily, princess." He seems to be crying too, and the oven's ping alerts me.

"I'll call you tomorrow. I need to take the food out. He'll be home soon. I love you, Christian." I wipe the back of my hand over my face and pull myself together. Sighing heavily and pushing my brain into action with my plans for Arry getting home. Pulling myself together because it's going to be so much worse talking this over with him.

"Good luck. Wow him with sex and then show him the letter." He giggles down the line, and I eyeroll at his typical suggestion.

"It's always sex with you. Goodbye." I laugh at his dramatic goodbye in return and hang up before he drags it out more. I am overcome with apprehension as I move to the oven to remove the food I'm heating. Arry has been teaching me the basics of cooking, as he prepares a lot of what I come home to stick in the oven, but it means we eat better, and the housekeeper is never short of recipe suggestions.

* * *

I nervously dish the food onto plates, watching the clock for him to get home from his evening training and fuss around the table. It's been a weird day. He stayed home late this morning, with me in bed because it's a rare day off for me, and left for work before noon. Whistling as he went because his libido has never failed us in the past year, and he hasn't ever stopped wanting to get naked with me every second of every day since.

That's when I went down for the mail to see him off and discovered the offer from the fashion academy. I've been mulling it over for hours, my head churning itself crazy. Unsure of what to do or say to him, shocked that they sent me an offer.

I'm top of my class in school and earning recommendations by the truckload. I've been recognized for my skills and achievements all year, focused on pushing myself to do my best. This is the payoff, and now it's sitting staring at me from the countertop, yet I don't know what to do.

I fix my dress, smooth my hair, and lay the dressing on the table beside the salad, trying not to overly focus on how confused I am about the offer. I want him to be happy about what I have to talk about, but everything rests on how he will react, what he says when I tell him they offered me an entire year in another place.

Consumed by a pang of nerves as the elevator chimes, signaling his return and quickly fixing the silverware, straightening it all out, holding my palms to my cheeks to cool the flush of heat and paste on a bright smile as the doors open across the hall.

Arrick walks in wearing his grey hoody and sweats and dumps his gym bag down near the entranceway, kicking off his sneakers and smiling my way as he pulls off his sweater. Looking as delicious as he always does and warming my insides with his presence. It never gets old, his coming home is like a warm hug every time, and he's still my most favorite person in the whole world. I still spend every second with him that I can.

"Hey, beautiful, something smells good." He hangs up his top over the array of my jackets, now overtaking the hallway, and makes his way toward me. His hair is damp, suggesting he's showered already, and I get a sense of relief that I won't have to wait to do this. Coming level with me, he eyes the perfectly laid out dinner and kisses me on the neck from behind, catching me in his arms and nuzzling me affectionately.

"This looks amazing, *Mimmo*, but you look even more so. I don't know which I'm hungrier for." He pulls my face around towards him and kisses me passionately, making my toes curl like he always does. It's been a year of being his, and nothing has changed with how much affection he showers me with. How big a smile I get any time he comes home, or how much he likes to take me to bed to find new ways to pleasure me. I thought some of it would wear off when the novelty did, but he is consistently adorable.

Still love you to the moon and back.

"Dinner first, that after. There's something else...." The pang of nerves hits me in the stomach like a kick again, and that little shiver of anticipation that this is a bad idea. Arrick, as always, in tune with me, senses the change and the crease of concern hits that perfect brow.

"What's wrong?" He catches my chin and turns my nose to his, a hair's breadth apart so he can study my face and try and work out why I am being cagey. "What is it?" He looks immediately worried, and I kiss his nose, untangling from him with a breezy smile that's supposed to lighten the tension, but I can't hold it for long. Walking to the counter, I pick up the letter, bring it back, and hand it to him. My brow creased in sheer uncertainty. I can't even formulate what I need to say, and I know the letter will do it so much better. My hands are clammy, and my heart is pounding through my chest as faint fear gets me in the gut.

He takes the letter silently, looking from my face to the paper with deadpan cool. He unfolds it and reads carefully, eyes scanning the words in silence with no expression that clues me to what he is thinking. He only takes a minute to get through it, looking unchanged. Finally, a smile breaks over his face.

"They offered you a scholarship for a year to some French fashion academy?" He beams at me. A real show of pride running across his gorgeous face, yet I still get that tight knot of anxiety biting inside. Waiting for him to realize what that means. "You really are good at what you do, baby. Why is this a bad thing?" He puts the letter down and moves to catch me again, pulling me in by the waist, so I'm against him snugly, molding to him in our unique perfect way.

"It's a year... An alternative to my year here at the New York design school." I frown at him, unsure why he is taking this so well when the letter clarifies that it is in France. Across the world.

Feeling fragile on this topic, and not sure if this is how I even wanted him to react.

"And? The problem is?" He's smiling at me again, a frown creasing his brow, obviously confused with what I am getting at. Not seeing why this would upset me only makes me feel worse. Little insecure niggles are spiking up, even though they are not as bad as they once were. I will always have minor insecurities that arise when I don't want them to.

"In Paris Arry... Not here." I bite my lip and study his expression, waiting for the outburst, but yet again, he smiles and leans in to kiss me with a soft grin.

"Do you want to go?" He asks softly, as though it's the simplest question in the world. I stare at him silently for a moment as tears fill my eyes, nodding and then look away as one rolls down my cheek pitifully, really hurting inside. Arrick tilts his head to one side so he can still see me and nudges me gently.

"And that makes you cry. Why?" He smiles at me again, hands coming up to my face and stroking away the tear with his thumb. Always so gentle with me, so endearing and affectionate. It makes me want to sob.

"I don't want to leave you." I cry some more and bury my face against his T-shirt instead, sniffing as his arms wrap around me snugly, trying to get some comfort from him while verbally he is giving me none. I don't get why this is not affecting him. Why he is so willing to let me go after the year of happiness we've had together?

Our life is perfect. We haven't had any fights or outbursts from the days of Natasha, not since. We seem to work so well and cohabit flawlessly, despite our conflicting personalities where domestic crap is concerned. I don't get why he would let it go so readily when it's ripping me in two.

"Who said anything about leaving me?" Arrick props my chin up to him so he can look at me again, wiping away the tears, only this time, he leans in and kisses me softly. "You think I would let you travel across the world to fend for yourself for a year, baby? You can barely take care of yourself on the odd weekend I have to fly out for fights and leave you for a max of three days... If you're going to Paris, you're stuck with me coming too. You attract trouble like crazy, and I don't trust anyone else to look after you." Arrick rubs his nose against mine, bringing a tiny smile to my face that makes me realize how dumb I'm being. He doesn't see it as a big deal because he isn't letting me go alone.

"Really?" I brighten up as I stare at him hopefully. I feel so stupid that I didn't even think he would give me this option. So sure it had been a case of me having to leave to go to school and him staying here.

"Really! I told you, *Mimmo*, we're in this together, always. I don't need to be here to train. I fight all over the country, and it's only a flight. It's not forever... I'm sure Carrero Corp can do without me for a few months. Besides, it's the city of romance, isn't it? The hell I'm letting you alone out there with your track record of attracting every male who lays eyes on you. You might never come back to me." He kisses me again, this time harder, and takes my breath away with the sheer passion behind it. Arms tight around me and knocking away all my stupid little niggles and fear with one confident lingering smooch.

I love you so much.

"You would do that for me? Leave New York so I can go to school in another country?" I dry my eyes ungracefully and wipe my nose on the back of my hand, unphased by him watching me adoringly. Comfortable in my skin when it comes to him,

"School is important, your future is important, and I already told you; you need to find your feet and place in this world to be happy, baby. It doesn't mean I can't be with you on that journey." Arrick leans in and circles his arms around my butt, squeezing firmly and picking me up, so I'm suspended yet taller than he is. He carries me across to the couch and lays me down on my back, crawling carefully over the top of me and nestling down, so our bodies meet perfectly, caging me in, nose to nose.

"I love you." I sigh heavily, meaning every single word with conviction. Heart full to bursting. I kiss his nose, running my fingers through his short sandy colored hair and raking them gently over his scalp.

"I love you more." He smiles in the heartthrob Hollywood best he saves only for special occasions. Melting me into a bowl of goo and making my toes curl.

"Guess I better accept the placement on Monday, right?" I smile, wriggling under him as he shifts over me and seems to fish around at the side of the couch.

"Right. I'll start apartment shopping when I drop you off. For now, though, there's something else." Arrick moves over me and leans down the side of the couch, looking down as he slides his arm underneath and feels around. I watch him with a furrowed brow of wonder. Confused by his sudden intense look of concentration and what the hell he is even doing. He is so accepting that we just committed to move to another country for a year, yet he is more focused on something under the sofa.

He's so weird.

"What are you doing?" I giggle as he slides further and stretches out more to reach, almost pulling us off the side we are teetering on. I grip his shoulders in case I do meet the floor from the odd angle he has me perched.

"Looking for... Got it." He grins, coming back up, hauling us both back to rights and nuzzling back in, pulling a wrapped box with him. He holds it up proudly with a smirk on that handsome face.

It's a black gift bag decorated with a gold ribbon and strangely Carrero Corp themed. He turns it upside down to tip something out and discards the bag quickly, picking up a package about the size of a ring box, only flat. He pulls back to his knees before sitting comfortably on his haunches and watches me with a very happy expression.

"So tonight would or should have been Leila's anniversary party, right?" He gazes at me with that boyish smile. So much going on behind those eyes as they rest on me, and I wiggle myself up to sit up too and regard him curiously.

"Right, except they all got chicken pox, and it's a month away now." I sit up properly, pulling my legs under to one side in the tight dress, and stare at the brown-wrapped box with a frown of confusion, guessing it's for me. Gifts are something he regularly does, but I didn't expect one tonight. My head is still dancing with delight at the fact that we're going to Paris to continue my studies in fashion, not quite focusing on what he is saying.

"So that means in about three hours, we had sex for the first time a year ago tonight." He grins at me. A naughty twinkle in those sexy eyes brings them alive cutely.

"It wasn't exactly something we finished, but yeah, I guess. This isn't some strange souvenir from that night, is it? Like the cushion cover I left makeup on or something equally weird because I know how lame you can be." I smile sweetly, frowning at him in complete seriousness. Arry has a box of ticket stubs, weird crap that girls normally save from our many dates over the past months, and I think it's odd. His sentimentality is plain abnormal for such a 'dude.'

"Thanks, baby. Very heart-warming to know that, and no. This is a gift for you. Tomorrow will be the anniversary of the first day of us.... I kinda liked tonight's anniversary a little more, though." He winks naughtily, and I eyeroll at him. Obvious that he picked the night he first got to bang me over the morning he made me his girlfriend.

"You would! .... It's always sex with you. I'm starting to agree with Christian that you may be closet gay, though. Normal men don't do all the mushy romantic stuff you do." I poke fun at him merrily, screwing up my nose to match his expression, and we face off each other in a war of stupid faces that has me giggling insanely in seconds. He is the king of weird faces.

"I think that's wishful thinking on his part. Don't think I don't notice you two comparing notes on me when you think I'm not looking." He slides his fingers through my hair, pushing it back off my face with a sweet sigh.

"He agrees your ass is a ten plus... Although he does not like your unsymmetrical tattoos, he thinks it's like some designer, no-no! I disagree. I think it's sexy all down one side." I lift the hem of his top and try to wiggle my fingers underneath to get a cop of that luscious abdomen and peek at his new additions across his waistline. He is running out of body on one side, and now the very sexy line that sits across the top of his ring shorts has been getting some new scrolling text.

"Focus baby.... Presents, not sexy bodies." He smirks, removes my hands, and chucks me under the chin to bring me back to him. I flutter lashes at him and bring my eyes back to the box in hand with a tug.

"Can I open it?" I reach for it, but he moves it above his head playfully.

"I should make you wait the three hours; pretty sure we didn't have sex until after midnight, buuut...... I can never hold anything back from you. Even the fact it's been under here since yesterday has been agony." He smiles again, lowering the box between us and holding it out to me gingerly. He is hopeless at surprises, so he usually makes them short-lived and fast to plan; otherwise, he ends up telling me. I grin at him, watching at me, sighing heavily, and take it graciously with a little childish giggle.

I open the paper carefully, untie the twine and unwrap it like a precious prize to reveal a black velvet box with a familiar jeweler's brand in Manhattan. I screw up my face and open the box with a click. Inside there's tissue paper in layers of black, which covers the contents. I pull it back gently and slowly to reveal a fine silver chain necklace with a small puzzle piece hanging from it, nestled on a little padded cream cushion. The initials 'A&S' are carved so very daintily onto it.

Moisture instantly fills my eyes as extreme heartfelt emotion hits me in the stomach, and I get exactly what this means. Tears fall fast at how thoughtful and perfect this is, knowing exactly why he would choose it, and I stifle a sob, screwing up my face to curb the urge to cry.

"I'm your uniquely shaped puzzle piece?" I sniff again, fingering it tenderly, blown away by the depths of love he showers on me every day. I never expected this at all.

"You are. Don't ever doubt that I would walk to the ends of the earth for you because I will follow you anywhere. Even Paris." He takes the box from me, removes the jewelry carefully, and unhooks the catch, motioning for me to turn around for him. I get up on my knees and scoot around, so he can put it on me, moving my hair as he fastens it gently behind my neck, nestling perfectly at collarbone level. It's so beautiful in so many ways.

"I never got you a present, you didn't tell me we were doing this," I answer softly, through soft sniffles, fingering the pendant lovingly, turning back to him with so many intense feelings for him at this moment.

"You're my present. Anytime I see you smile and know it's because of me... That's all I need." He leans in and hits me with a peck on the lips. Swift and spot on, and I giggle when I try to catch his mouth for more and almost fall forward onto him. He catches me and puts me upright again.

"You're such a loser." I poke fun at him, wiping my tears, trying to reign the way my heart is pounding achingly in my chest. He looks so very content and happy at this moment. Smiling at how his whole expression softens and that irresistible full-on smile comes out to play.

"That's probably the most beautiful sentence that ever comes out of your mouth." He smiles, stroking my face with his thumb, bends down, and kisses me again. My lips part on touch for a little tongue action, before pulling back and pulling me into his arms so we are both kneeling on his couch, face to face and almost molded together perfectly.

"Only you would like it." I giggle at him, overcome with intense feelings that I'm lightheaded.

"It's why I'm perfect for you. No one knows you like I do, baby, and no one ever will. Guess we better start getting ready to tell our families we're going to Paris for a year, huh? New adventure.... A new chapter."

End of book two

A note from the Author

I hope you enjoyed my book; it would mean a great deal to me if you took the time to leave me a review. I regularly and actively read reviews, and I appreciate you taking the time to leave me one. x

L.T.Marshall

Find the Author online

You can find L.T. Marshall across all social media, and she regularly interacts with fans on Facebook.

Facebook Fan Group
https://www.facebook.com/groups/LTMarshallFans

Website: www.ltmarshall.com

Printed in Great Britain
by Amazon